IN YOUR HEART

MICALEA SMELTZER

- A WILLOW CREEK NOVEL -

Ashli,
Willow Creek
Forever!

It was so nice
to meet
you!

Willow Clark Forever!

Ashi!!

Sori 1x wor ok wary 20 nics.

Cover design and photography by Regina Wamba at Mae I Design

Formatted by Ready, Set, Edit

BOOKS BY MICALEA SMELTZER

Trace + Olivia Series

Finding Olivia

Chasing Olivia

Tempting Rowan

Saving Tatum

Second Chances Series

Unraveling

Undeniable

Willow Creek Series

Last to Know

Never Too Late

In Your Heart

Standalones

Beauty in the Ashes

Rae of Sunshine

"Music exists to speak the words we can't express."

—Unknown

CHAPTER ONE

I WAS GETTING married in two weeks.

I was getting married in two weeks and I was standing here watching my so-called fiancé stick his dick in a woman that wasn't me.

An inhuman shriek crawled out of my throat and I grabbed the first thing I could get my hands on which happened to be one of Braden's baseball caps—granted, it wouldn't do much damage, but at least it was something—and threw it at his bare back. He was already turning to look at me over his shoulder, his hips still thrusting against the skank beneath him, when the cap hit him.

"What the hell?" He glared at me.

At *me*, like I was the one doing something wrong.

"Excuse me?" I stormed forward. My whole body shook with barely contained rage.

Before I could reach them he stood up, wrapping the bed covers around his waist and leaving the woman in *our* bed lying there completely naked.

That was Braden for you, ever the gentlemen.

He held his hands up in a placating gesture. "Let's talk about this, Sadie."

"Yeah, let's *talk!*" I screamed, waving a hand in the direction of the woman lying on *my* sheets. "Let's talk about the fact that apparently you slipped and fell and your penis ended up in someone else's vagina! Thank God she was there to break your fall!" I yelled sarcastically.

"It's not what—"

I slapped him across the cheek. My hand left behind a red imprint on his skin. His teeth snapped together and he glared down at me.

"Don't you fucking *dare* tell me it's not what it looks like," I shouted, my hands shaking at my sides.

The woman in our bed was still lying there. Why, I didn't know. Maybe she thought I'd be kind enough to leave and let them finish.

As. Fucking. If.

"Sadie—"

He grabbed my arm and I screamed so loud that I was sure everyone in the apartment complex heard me. "Take your fucking hand off of me!!"

Braden, surprisingly, let me go. He took a step back and I swore his skin had paled a shade.

That's right asshole, be afraid. Be very afraid.

I poked a finger into his chest—a chest I had once found to be a magnificent piece of masculine perfection.

"I can't fucking believe you! After *everything* you've put me through you go and do this! Seriously?! What the fuck did I ever see in you?!" The words poured out of my mouth. I was beyond hurt and pissed off. This was the man I'd planned on spending the rest of my life with, the man I'd given up so many important things for, and here *he* was fucking another woman only weeks before our wedding.

It was comical really, the irony of it all, since he'd been convinced I was sleeping with my friend Ezra. I thought of all the ridiculous accusations Braden had lobbed my way, and I couldn't help wondering if his own indiscretions led to his insecurity.

Hell, Braden had practically forced me to end my friendship with Ezra.

Why? Why had I been so blinded? When did I become this weak, sniveling excuse for a person that I let an asshole like him walk all over me? And *why* did it take me seeing him fucking someone else, to finally snap back into reality and realize what a complete asshole he was?

Fuck.

It was like I'd been brainwashed.

I tore at my hair, my breaths coming out in little gasps.

Anger at myself, at him, and at the bitch in my bed simmered dangerously in my veins. It wouldn't take much for me to snap and lose my ever-loving mind.

"Sadie, let's talk about this—"

"Should I get dressed?" The woman in our bed spoke up.

"Yes!" I screamed.

Her eyes widened and she slipped from the bed, looking around for her clothes.

With another scream I started for the kitchen.

"Where are you going?" Braden asked, trailing behind me.

He kept stopping to untangle his feet from the too-long sheet wrapped around his waist.

I wished he would trip and die.

"Sadie," he started in again.

I opened one of the various drawers in the kitchen and pulled out a knife, waving it around like a crazy person.

He paled further.

"Sadie, put down the knife."

"No!" I screamed. "I think I should cut your dick off so you can fuck yourself with it! Would that suffice?!"

Braden's mouth fell slightly open.

He was afraid.

Good.

The asshole should be afraid for his life.

Or the life of his penis, which was really the most important thing to him.

"I'm calling 911!" I heard the woman shout from my bedroom.

"Go ahead, bitch!"

"Sadie, be reasonable," Braden started.

I thrust the knife in his direction, flailing my arms about like I'd seen jousters do on TV. "Reasonable?! You want me to be reasonable?!"

"I'm a man, I have needs—"

"Oh for fuck's sake!" I threw my hands up in the air. "Your *needs*? That's seriously the excuse you're using? Wow, you're dumber than I thought." Laughing manically, I cried, "Who am I kidding? *I'm* the dumb one for being with you."

When I met Braden he'd been...perfect. I knew that sounded cliché, but it was true. He was everything I'd always wanted and more. He treated me nicely and was always a gentleman. Once things got serious he started changing. I chalked it up to the fact that he'd recently started a new job. When things got worse after our engagement I found every excuse possible to explain his behavior. I'd been so naïve.

Everybody had tried to warn me that something wasn't right.

But I'd been blinded by...love?

No, that wasn't the right answer.

I think I'd been more blinded by my own need not to be *wrong*.

It was like I felt by giving up on my relationship with Braden it was admitting defeat—admitting that everyone else had been right about him.

Look where that got you? My conscience piped in.

"Sadie." He took a few steps forward.

"Stay away from me!" I jabbed the knife in his direction. I wasn't *really* going to hurt him, but oh how I wanted to.

"Sadie, put the fucking knife down and let's talk about this," he pleaded.

I wiped the back of my hand over my tear stained face.

Why the fuck was I crying over this loser? He didn't deserve a single tear from me.

"Talk about what?" I spread my arms wide. "The fact that I've wasted the last two years of my life with you? Or the fact that if I hadn't caught you in the act I would be your *wife* in two weeks." I shook my head, laughing under my breath. I began to slow clap. "Thanks for saving me the nightmare of divorce court, asshole."

"We can work this out—"

"Work this out!" I shrieked, charging forward. "Are you fucking crazy? I am *done* with you!"

To further prove my point I pried off my engagement ring, throwing it at his head. He tried to catch it, dropping the sheet from around his waist in the process.

"You disgust me," I spat through clenched teeth.

He hurried to grab the sheet to cover himself once more, as if I might charge forward and make good on my previous threat.

He opened his mouth to speak, but I stopped him.

"I swear to God, if you say my name *one more fucking time* I will cut off your tongue too!"

"Don't worry, babe," the slut from my bed strolled down the hall, dressed only in skimpy lingerie, "I called the police and I recorded everything she said on my phone."

I gulped, suddenly not feeling so bold.

The evil glint in her eye told me I was in trouble.

She leveled me with a smirk. "I'm a lawyer," she said the words slowly like I was too dumb to process them, "and this," she waved her phone around, "is enough to get you arrested."

Oh, fuck.

I steeled my shoulders, refusing to let the bitch know her words had gotten to me.

Braden glanced from her to me, not saying a word.

Two years together and the asshole couldn't even come to my defense and tell the bitch that I hadn't really meant anything by it. Heat of the moment and all that jazz.

Nope, he just stood there blinking like it was the only thing he was capable of doing.

My teeth gnashed together and I dropped the knife on the floor. I wanted to launch myself at the bitch with my claws out, but she'd already won.

Although, that was laughable, because apparently the prize was Braden and I could see now that he was hardly worth bragging rights.

She could have him.

And I would laugh when he cheated on her.

Because he would.

Men like him didn't change.

I turned to Braden, my shoulders slumping with exhaustion. I'd been so wound up and now the air had left my sails. I was just...done. I wasn't going to waste another breath yelling at him. Nothing I said would penetrate its way through his thick skull the way he penetrated his mistress. He definitely wasn't worth it either. I'd been crazy to ever think he was the guy for me.

Sirens sounded outside the apartment building.

"I'll go let them in." The tramp smiled.

"Shouldn't you go put some clothes on," I snapped.

She looked down. "Oh, right."

She disappeared back into the bedroom while Braden and I stood staring at each other. When she returned she was wearing *my* ripped shorts and *my* lavender tank top.

The calm defeat I'd felt a moment before instantly disappeared.

How dare she wear *my* clothes.

I screamed again, charging forward, and grabbed the bitch's hair before Braden could stop me.

That's when the cops knocked on the door.

From there, things escalated.

I scratched her.

She hit me.

I hit back.

She pulled my hair.

I bit her.

And then I got arrested.

Today was not my day.

CHAPTER TWO

I SAT ON the cold metal bench inside the holding cell, contemplating my life choices.

I wondered what shitty decision led me to this moment.

Was it when I attacked the bitch?

Or grabbed the knife?

Or when I first started dating Braden?

I was betting on the latter.

From the first moment I met him he screwed with my life and I let him, because I'd been dumb. There was no other explanation. I'd been so desperate to love someone that I'd tricked myself into thinking he was better than he was.

I kept going over and over in my head different things he'd said and done, and wondered why I'd always swept his behavior under the rug.

When did I become this girl that turned a blind eye?

I'd always spoken my mind, but with Braden I let him speak for me.

I put my head in my hands, letting out a small groan.

I wasn't going to be that girl anymore. I was going to get my fire back and conquer the world.

Well, as soon as I got out of this jail cell.

Footsteps sounded on the concrete floors and I stood up, praying that they were coming to let me out.

A moment later a figure appeared.

He was tall and thin. He kept his head ducked down and his unruly black hair hid his face.

Slowly, he lifted his head to face me. His dark eyes were hidden behind a pair of round glasses and his cheeks and chin were covered in scruff like he hadn't shaved in a week or more.

My breath caught on an embarrassing gasp.

It'd been six months since I'd seen him and he still took my breath away—not that I would ever tell him that.

Once upon a time I'd had a crush on Ezra Collins, but soon his friendship became too important to me to ever cross that line.

He tilted his head to the side, shoving his hands into the pockets of his jeans.

"I thought I'd never hear from you again." His eyes bore into me, hurt lacing his words. Chuckling, he added, "Let me tell you, I was quite surprised to answer the phone and hear your voice. Jail? Really, Sadie? What is it with you and Emma getting arrested?"

I lifted a finger. "That wasn't her fault." I reminded him. "This..." My lower lip began to tremble with the threat of tears. "This is all me."

And that was the sad truth.

"What exactly happened?" He asked.

I stepped forward, wrapping my hands around the metal bars. "Do you think you can get me out of here first and then we can chat?"

"Oh, right." He shook his head, pushing his too long hair out of his eyes. He cracked a small half smile. "They didn't want to let me back here, but I had to see this for myself."

I sighed, sitting back down on the bench with my hands splayed on my legs. "I'm glad you find this amusing, Ezra."

He shook his head, his eyes growing serious once more. "I'm sorry."

I flinched. I'd told him when I called that I caught Braden cheating on me.

"Why?" I found myself asking. "You hated him."

"But I love you." He paled, lifting his hands in surrender. "Not like that," he added. "You're my best friend, Sadie. I might've hated the asshole, but I still wanted you to be happy. This was the last thing I wanted to happen to you."

"But you knew it would," I whispered, looking away from him and staring at the cinderblock cell wall instead, "you warned me and I didn't fucking listen."

"You were in love." He defended my actions.

I turned back towards him. "Was I?" I retorted. "Because I don't know anymore."

My shoulders sagged with my words. I didn't think there had ever been a time in my life when I felt this defeated.

He frowned, his mouth twisting as he struggled with something to say. Finally he muttered, "I better go take care of this."

"Yeah, that would be great," I sighed. "I mean, this bench is nice and all, but I don't really want to sleep here."

He shook his head and walked back down the hall.

I felt bad that after six months with no communication this was what I called him for, but I knew I could count on him to bail me out.

My parent's would have too, but frankly I wasn't ready to tell them all the gory details.

Plus, my dad might kill Braden when I told him.

I knew Ezra would keep his cool, even if he probably did dream about maiming my ex-fiancé.

In fact, the last time I saw Ezra he punched Braden in the face.

Now, I wished I could go back and give Ezra a round of applause for that one.

It took a while, but eventually they released me.

Neither of us spoke as we walked out of the building. Ezra guided me through the parking lot and to his shiny black Cadillac Escalade.

As soon as we were both seated in the car I broke down in tears.

He didn't say anything, which I was thankful for.

He reached for my hand, holding mine in his and offering the smallest amount of comfort that he could.

After a few minutes I wiped my face free of tears and he started the car.

He pulled away from the police station and I watched the trees and traffic go by.

"I don't have anywhere to go," I realized.

I'd moved into Braden's place when we got engaged. At the time I'd still been living with my parents but they'd since downsized. I wouldn't have wanted to impose on them anyway.

I couldn't stay with Emma either—my best friend since we were in diapers. She and her fiancé, Maddox—the drummer for Willow Creek, the band Ezra played in—still lived in the guesthouse behind his foster parent's house. Maddox's foster parents also happened to be Ezra's real parents. They'd taken in Maddox and his twin brother Mathias when they were put into the system as teenagers. Maddox and Ezra were close, like brothers, while Mathias had always remained distant. That seemed to be changing though, according to things Emma had told me. Apparently, since Mathias rekindled with his high school love, Remy, and subsequently married her, he'd stopped distancing himself from his brother and band mates. They were also having a baby. Mathias Wade as a dad...I definitely hadn't seen that one coming.

"You'll stay with me." Ezra said simply, his eyes on the road ahead.

I shook my head. "No." My voice was firm. "I can't impose myself on you like that. I *won't*," I reiterated.

He glanced at me and then his eyes went back to the road. "You're not *imposing*. You're my friend and I'm doing you a favor."

"I don't want any favors," I ground out between my teeth, "this was enough." I added, referring to him bailing me out of jail.

"Yeah, care to explain the details to me? Seriously, what the fuck did you do to get arrested?"

I swallowed thickly and looked out the window once more. I could see my reflection in the glass. My lips were turned down in a frown and my light brown hair hung limply.

"I grabbed a knife and told him I was going to cut off his dick and then I threatened to cut off his tongue too. The bitch he was cheating on me with happened to be a lawyer. She recorded the whole thing and it was enough for them to arrest me." I shrugged, playing it off. "Can you believe that?"

I glanced at him. A muscle in his jaw twitched and I knew he was irritated. Not at me, but at the situation.

"It's like the world is conspiring against me," I muttered, picking at the tear in my ripped jeans. "No, not conspiring...it's laughing at me. At how completely fucking stupid I am." I shook my head back and forth, swallowing past the lump in my throat. Tears stung my eyes once more. "I hate myself so much right now."

"Don't," Ezra snapped, his tone harsh as he spared me a glance, "don't fucking say that."

"But I do."

"Everybody makes mistakes, Sadie," he interjected, turning down a street and heading out of town.

"I was going to *marry* him." My voice cracked. "I was going to marry an asshole that treated me like shit, who cheated on me, and who just isn't a very nice fucking person, and *why?*"

His Adam's apple bobbed as he swallowed. His lips pursed as his tongue rolled around, searching for the right words. "I don't know," he answered.

"Yeah?" I laughed, but there was no humor in the tone. "Me either." I buried my head in my hands and let out a small scream. "Why didn't I listen to you? Why didn't I listen to any of you? *Everybody* warned me against him."

"You're stubborn," he responded, his voice flat.

"Yeah," I agreed, "and look where that got me. I'm now fiancé-less and homeless. I'm such a role model."

His lips twisted. "Now's not the time for your sarcasm."

"Are you mad at me?" I asked, hating that I sounded hurt. But I was. Hurt, that is. He had every right to be mad at me though. I mean, what kind of crappy friend calls a person up because they're in jail and then doesn't even have a place to stay?

"Yes, I am mad at you," he replied, "but not for the reason you think."

He always did know me so well, like he could read my mind. We'd only become friends when our best friends fell in love four years ago. They were so enamored with each other that we both ended up being left out. We started hanging out and bonded, soon becoming best friends ourselves. The last six months without Ezra in my life had sucked, to put it bluntly, but Braden was my fiancé so I thought I was doing the right thing by cutting Ezra out of my life since that's what Braden wanted. Little did I know that was simply another way he was manipulating me.

"So, why exactly are you mad at me?" I asked.

"Because," he took a deep breath, trying to calm himself, "you're acting like this is your fault. You're not the one that cheated, Sadie."

"But I'm the one that stayed with an asshole for no good reason. I mean," I pushed my hair away from my face, "I don't feel like I ever really loved him...if I did I would feel more hurt, right?" I asked him. "Because that's not what I feel, instead—"

"Your ego is bruised," he supplied, turning down another road. Farmland stretched as far as I could see as he drove to his house.

"Exactly," I agreed, nodding.

"I think you *wanted* to believe he was the one for you," he glanced at me for a moment, his dark eyes serious, "but he wasn't."

"Maybe I'm meant to be alone for the rest of my life," I mused, "with like fifty cats."

He chuckled, shaking his head. "You're twenty-one. You have plenty of time to find the guy for you."

"I think I'm just going to become a nun." I nodded, affirming my words.

He snorted and I glared at him. "I think it's a bit late for that."

I crossed my arms over my chest, the seatbelt digging into my collarbone. "I'm glad you find amusement in my suffering."

"Don't be like that." He chuckled. "Think about all that you've accomplished. You own your own store, Sadie. That's a big deal. Be proud of yourself. Focus on that and not trying to find a guy to settle down with."

"I wanted so desperately to be in love," I confessed. "Real, soul deep, shaking in the knees, forever, kind of love."

"You'll have that one day," he assured me.

I sighed heavily. "But not now."

He shook his head and took my hand once more, giving it a reassuring squeeze before letting go. "This is a good thing. You're going to be a stronger person because of this."

"I hope so," I agreed.

I knew I was better off without Braden, and I hated that it had taken *this* to get me to see that. But it still hurt. I'd spent two years of my life with him, and there had been good memories with him. I stayed with him for stupid reasons, and I was mad at myself for that. I'd given up so much for an ideal I'd conjured up in my mind of what my life was supposed to be like. I would not let this break me. Nope.

Oh God, was I crying again?

I tentatively reached up and there were more tears.

Shit. So much for not letting this break me.

Ezra turned onto the driveway leading up to his house. Although, calling it a house was a stretch. His home was small, more like a cottage. I'd been there plenty of times before...well, *before*. It was cute and nestled between shady trees with a lake in the back. There were also no other houses close, which I knew was a big draw for Ezra. Seclusion from nosy people and the media was highly coveted among the Willow Creek boys.

He parked the SUV in the detached garage he'd had built to match the house. Both were covered in dark blue siding with white shutters beside the windows. I'm sure most people expected a rock star like Ezra to live in a mansion, but that'd never been what he wanted. I admired him, and the other guys too, for not letting fame go to their heads. Not that they didn't love their shiny toys, like their various cars.

He turned the vehicle off and sighed into the silence.

"How about I make some dinner? Fettuccine?"

I flinched. Fettuccine Alfredo was my favorite meal. Ezra knew that, but that was something Braden could never remember.

"I'm not very hungry," I muttered, reaching for the door handle.

Before I could slip out of the vehicle he grabbed my arm, halting me. "Don't let him win." His eyes bored into me, burning me with their seriousness.

"I'm not," I argued.

"That's exactly what you're doing," he snapped. "He's not worth it."

I sighed, scrubbing a hand over my face. "Ezra," I huffed, "this *just* happened. I think I'm allowed a day to wallow over the complete shit-fest that is my life."

His lips quirked into a small smile and he ducked his head. Releasing my arm, he sobered. "Yeah, you're right. I'm sorry."

"I'm sorry too," I whispered, a frown turning down my lips. He gave me a quizzical look so I quickly explained. "I'm sorry for throwing away our friendship like it meant nothing to me. I was wrong to do that."

"You felt like you had to." He sighed heavily. Shaking his head, his black curls tumbled forward to hide his gaze. "I'd be lying if I said that didn't hurt, especially since Braden is such a prick," his teeth ground together, "but it was your life and I couldn't force myself to be a part of it. So, I let you go."

"And yet, you didn't let me spend the night in jail. It's what I deserved."

He stared at me for a moment. The intensity in his dark eyes rooted me to the spot. "I'll always have your back."

I lowered my head, feeling forlorn. Ezra was much too kind to me.

"You should hate me," I breathed, my words hanging heavily in the air.

He grasped my chin, forcing me to look at him. His eyes seared into me as he spoke. "Friendship doesn't work like that. I could never hate you for making the decision that you did."

"Even if it was the wrong one?"

His fingers momentarily tightened against my chin and anger pulsed in his brown eyes. "For you, it was the right decision at the time. Life is a series of choices that we make, some of them are good, and some of them are not, but everything always works out in the end. Things will be better now, you'll see."

He released his hold on me and I looked away with a sigh. "Better," I repeated. "I hope so."

"I know so." He reiterated with a smile. "Everything happens for a reason, Sadie. Sometimes we don't understand why, but eventually we look back and can see that everything worked out."

"I think it already has," I whispered.

He nodded at my words, processing them. "Come on," he reached for the car door handle, "let's eat. I'm starving."

This time at the mention of food my stomach came to life.

I climbed out of the large SUV and followed the gravel pathway over to the front porch steps.

He pulled out his house key and swung the door open.

"After you." He waved a hand.

I stepped inside the cottage and immediately felt an overwhelming sense of comfort. The home was decorated with the coastal colors of navy and white. The floors were a dark hardwood that shined as if they'd just been cleaned. The family room sat to my left with a white couch and chair, with blue and gray throw pillows.

Across from the family room sat the kitchen. It had white cabinets with concrete countertops. The appliances were shiny stainless steel. It was a work of art, and almost looked untouched, but I knew that Ezra wasn't that kind of guy. He actually enjoyed cooking. His mom had made sure that he, Maddox, and Mathias, all knew how to cook and not just microwave frozen pizza rolls like most guys.

Beside the kitchen was a small table with four chairs, but the area wasn't large enough to be considered a dining room.

The downstairs also had a small powder room and the laundry room—the laundry room being an addition Ezra had insisted on since the home didn't have one when he moved in.

Upstairs there were two bedrooms and a shared bathroom.

Straight ahead lay a pair of French double doors that led out to a large deck overlooking the lake. I knew if I went out there he would have several rocking chairs lined up, a grill, and a fire pit. The view of the lake, and the deck, had been one of the things Ezra loved the most about this place.

He'd dragged me to various homes during his house hunt. That seemed like a lifetime ago even though it hadn't been more than three years.

"You act as if you've never seen the place before." He chuckled, noticing my lingering stare.

I lifted my shoulders in a shrug and gave him a small smile. "I missed this place."

He beamed at my words. "Yeah?"

I nodded. "This has always been one of my favorite places."

I always felt at peace here. I didn't know why. Maybe it was the fact that the home was so cozy and welcoming, or maybe it was the breathtaking view of the lake. Or maybe it was simply because this was where my best friend lived, and being near him filled me with a sense of security.

"You can stay here as long as you need," he said, moving into the kitchen. He began to rifle through cabinets, setting out pots.

I wrapped my arms around my body, as if I could hold myself together. "Thanks," I forced a smile. I hated intruding on Ezra's space, but I was truly thankful for his kindness. Especially after the last six months with no contact. Without him...I didn't know where I would stay. I couldn't afford my own place right now.

He flicked a piece of dark hair out of his eyes. "Want to help?" He asked me.

I nodded, stepping around to the other side of the counter beside him. He quickly gave me instructions and I went to work.

We laughed and joked as we cooked, slipping into our once familiar roles as best friends. God, I'd missed this. Ezra might not have been my friend for as long as Emma—who I had known since we were babies—but our bond was just as strong. Sometimes I even felt like it was stronger.

We fixed the table and sat down across from each other to eat.

"So," I started, picking up my fork, "how was the tour?"

Willow Creek had been on a tour across the United States since January. They'd only been home a few weeks.

"Good," Ezra nodded. "Tiring, but fun. It was nice to get back out there and play on stage, but I'm also ready to get back in the studio."

"So, you guys are already working on the next album?" I swirled the noodles around and then took a bite. "Oh my God," I moaned, "that's delicious."

Ezra smiled at my words. "I'm glad you like it."

"It's certainly better than a restaurant."

He'd made the sauce from one of his mom's recipes and it was as good as I remembered.

"To answer your question," he reached for a wine bottle, filling each of our glasses, "yes we're already working on it."

"Do you guys ever sleep?"

He choked on a laugh. "No, not very much."

"You all have lots of dedication," I told him.

He tipped his glass in my direction. "So do you."

Me?" I snorted. "No."

He clasped his fingers together, studying me like I was some fascinating specimen. "I don't know how you can dismiss your accomplishments so easily."

"They don't feel like accomplishments when I'm currently homeless."

He set his glass down, crossing his fingers together. "You're too hard on yourself. Why?"

It was a simple question, one I should've been able to answer, but I couldn't.

"I think," he continued when I didn't speak, "that you need to focus more on your accomplishments and less on your failures." He slowly raised the glass to his lips.

I sighed, taking another bite of fettuccine to stall for time. "I'll get right on that."

He shook his head, fighting a smile. I expected him to call me on my sarcasm like he usually did, but he didn't.

"You know," he said, "when I met you, you were..." He paused, his lips twisting as he searched for the right words. "So vibrant," he settled on, "and from the moment you got with Braden I've had to watch him strip your identity from you. You went from this carefree girl to this...shell. It's like you're a stranger."

"I was a teenager then. I grew up," I defended, his words stinging me.

He shook his head, looking at me pityingly. "No, it's more than that."

I knew he was right, but that didn't make it hurt any less to have him point it out to me. Reluctantly I mumbled, "Yeah, I know. You're right."

"We're going to change that," he stated. He tilted his head to the side, daring me to contradict him.

"How?" I asked, not even bothering to hide the challenging tone in my voice.

He tapped his lips. "I don't know yet, but I'm going to figure it out."

I believed him.

In fact, I always believed in Ezra, because he'd never let me down.

We grew quiet as we finished our dinner. I offered to wash the dishes, but he refused my help and I reluctantly settled on the couch.

Ezra joined me a little bit later, turning on the TV and settling into the chair.

The silence between us should've been awkward since we hadn't seen each other in so long, but it wasn't. In fact, it was like no time at all had passed.

I let out a heavy sigh, suddenly feeling exhausted. It wasn't even eight o' clock yet and I felt like I could pass out asleep any second.

At my sigh Ezra cast his dark eyes in my direction. "Tired?" He asked, the corners of his mouth wrinkling with concern.

I nodded. "Yeah, I think I'm going to go to bed." I stood up, as if to do that and my face crumbled with the realization that I had no clothes, no toothbrush, nothing. "I don't have any of my stuff," I sniffled.

"Sadie," Ezra's eyes darkened with worry, "we can get your stuff tomorrow. We'll make do for tonight."

"Right." I nodded, rubbing a hand over my face. I couldn't believe I didn't have *anything*. Not even my purse. I'd been so distracted by my anger, and then getting arrested that I hadn't even thought about all my shit at Braden's place. I really hoped that tramp didn't do anything with my stuff.

"Sadie," his eyes narrowed on me as he repeated my name, "are you sure you're okay?"

I wrapped my arms around myself, my eyes shifting to the stairway. "No," my lips began to tremble, "I'm not."

I *wanted* to be okay. I knew I was better off without that asshole and should've dumped him a long time ago, but it still hurt. I might not have been *in* love with him like I thought I was, but I had loved him in some way or I wouldn't have been with him.

Ezra didn't say anything. He simply stood up and wrapped his arms around me. I didn't return the embrace at first, but slowly I wrapped my arms around his lean chest. I inhaled his familiar woodsy scent as my tears stained his white t-shirt.

"This is the beginning of new and better things," he vowed.

I nodded against his chest.

Taking a step back I dried my tears with the back of my hand, silently vowing that they'd be the last tears I cried over Braden. He wasn't worth my sorrow.

Ezra stared down at me, his eyes raking over my face as he looked for any signs of another imminent breakdown.

"I'm okay," I assured him. "I just needed to cry again."

"And that's fine," he reached out, wiping away a tear I had missed, "tears aren't a sign of weakness, but of strength of the heart. They show you care and caring is never a bad thing."

"Even when it gets you hurt?" I questioned, leaning my head back to look up at him. At six-foot Ezra was much taller than me.

"Even then." He nodded at his words like he was agreeing with them. He turned for the stairs. "Come on, I'll let you borrow a shirt to sleep in. I have some extra toothbrushes too."

I followed him upstairs and stood awkwardly in the doorway of his bedroom.

He opened his dresser drawer, rifling through it and procuring a plain black t-shirt. His heavy boots clapped against the creaking hardwood floors. "Here," he held the shirt out for me.

"Thanks." I mustered a genuine smile for him as I followed him down the short hallway into the bathroom. He grabbed an unopened blue toothbrush from beneath the sink and gave me that as well.

"If you want to shower you can use my soap. I don't care."

I nodded. "A shower would be nice."

He cleared his throat and stepped out of the bathroom. "You know where the guestroom is, and I'll be downstairs for a while if you need me."

I nodded, sliding the door closed. "Thanks for everything, Ezra."

"Anytime." He nodded his head once and then bound down the steps.

I closed the bathroom door completely and laid the shirt on the shiny marble countertop. I turned on the shower, letting the water grow warm before stripping out of my clothes.

I stepped beneath the spray and the heat began to work out the tension in my coiled muscles. An audible sigh of relief passed through my lips.

I didn't bother washing my hair—not wanting to deal with the tangled nightmare it would become if I didn't use conditioner—but I used Ezra's soap to wash my body. It smelled like mahogany with hints of oranges, nothing like the coconut-scented body wash I usually used.

I turned the shower off and grabbed a clean towel, drying off my body. I returned the towel to the rack and shrugged into the t-shirt. It fell to the center of my thighs and was incredibly soft. I knew that even though it was a plain t-shirt it probably cost more than my car payment.

I had a ponytail holder on my wrist and I used it to pull my hair back while I scrubbed my face clear of makeup.

I gathered up my clothes and opened the bathroom door, promptly bumping into Ezra as he topped the stairs.

"Sorry," he grabbed my arms, righting me from my stumble, "I wanted to check on you."

"I'm fine," I assured him, edging towards the bedroom.

He stared at me for a moment, dissecting my words and trying to find the truth in them.

"Yeah, okay," he finally mumbled, starting back down the stairs. "Good night," he called.

"Night," I said back, but it was merely a whisper and I doubt he even heard it.

I stepped into the guestroom and closed the door behind me.

The room was small, but cozy. The walls were painted a pale yellow with white furniture and soft gray bedding. I'd helped Ezra decorate it. In fact, he'd asked for my opinion on lots of things when he'd been renovating the cottage. He'd fussed that he was a guy and had no idea what matched and what didn't. I'd loved helping him.

I sat down on the edge of the bed, running my fingers over the silky fabric of the bedspread. I'd missed out on a lot these past six months. Not just with Ezra, but with Emma as well. She'd gone on tour with the band and we'd hardly been able to talk. I'd become so out of the loop, and I couldn't help wondering if that was something

Braden wanted. He'd always hated it when I spent any time with someone that wasn't him.

With a groan I stood up, pulling back the bed covers and climbing beneath.

I reached for the remote, turning on the small TV and keeping the volume low for background noise in the hopes that it would help muffle my racing thoughts.

I turned on my side, facing the window that overlooked the lake. It was completely dark, no moon in sight, but out this far in the country I could still see the twinkle of stars.

I closed my eyes, wishing upon a star—wishing for happiness and most importantly wishing that I would find my true love.

CHAPTER THREE

I WOKE UP, struggling to understand my surroundings. The room wasn't familiar and there was nobody lying beside me.

It all came rushing back to me and I lowered my head in my hands.

In my dreams I'd been able to believe it wasn't real, simply a figment of my imagination, but with the sunlight streaming into the room that wasn't mine I couldn't deny the truth.

My life felt seemingly over.

Melodramatic? Yes.

But also the truth.

The life I'd had was no more. From this point forward things were going to be different. My future was now heading down a new path.

One for the better.

But I knew I would stumble and fall before this path felt like the right one.

I eased out of the bed, the TV in the room now off. I hadn't turned it off so Ezra must've checked on me before he went to bed.

I opened the bedroom door and stepped out into the hall.

It was early, around seven, but Ezra was already up.

The bathroom mirror was still slightly fogged so I knew he'd already taken a shower and from the sounds of cabinets banging downstairs he was making breakfast.

I brushed my teeth and hair, braiding it on the side so it rested against my collarbone. I had no makeup with me and my skin looked pale with purple rings beneath my eyes. I hoped I didn't scare Ezra.

I dressed in my clothes from yesterday, silently squirming at the fact that they were dirty, but I knew I'd get my stuff today.

I padded down the stairs and rounded the corner, smiling at Ezra.

"Morning," I said, feigning cheer.

Ezra glanced over his shoulder where he stood at the stove making scrambled eggs. He was already dressed for the day in a pair of jeans and a heather gray t-shirt. His black hair was still damp from the shower, one curl sticking to his forehead.

"Hey. I'm almost done with this."

"You didn't need to make me breakfast." I walked over to the refrigerator and grabbed the bottle of orange juice and then the glasses from the cabinet by the sink.

Ezra shrugged, sliding the eggs onto the plates and topping both with a sprinkle of cheddar cheese just the way I liked. Toast popped up from the toaster and he added it to the plate.

"It was no big deal."

"Don't dismiss your kindness so easily," I told him, setting our glasses down on the table. He'd already put out paper napkins and utensils.

He glanced at me out of the corner of his eye as he sat the plates down. "It's breakfast, Sadie," he chuckled, "it's not a kitten."

"Does that mean you got me a kitten?" I joked.

His lips quirked into a smile. "No kitten. Sorry."

"Darn," I tsked, reaching for the fork.

Ezra sat down and began to eat, keeping a careful eye on me like he was waiting for any signs of an imminent breakdown.

"I'm okay," I assured him, piercing a piece of egg, "I'm not going to crack."

"It would be the normal thing," he argued.

I stared across the table at him. "I'm not normal."

"No, you're not," he agreed, "but it's okay to break."

I leaned forward, lowering my voice like I was letting him in on a secret. "I might bend, but I will not break. Not because of this at least."

His dark eyes seared into me and he nodded once.

He returned to his food and I sat back once more.

"I thought we would eat and then go get your things."

I glanced at the old-fashioned cuckoo clock—a quirky gift I'd bought him as a joke. "Braden won't be up until at least ten."

He gave me a disgusted look and spat, "Do I look like I give a fuck?"

I fought a smile at his use of the word *fuck*. Ezra wasn't one to curse a lot. That was usually left to Mathias—the lead singer of the band.

I shrugged. "I just want you to be prepared to deal with his wrath."

His brown eyes narrowed on me like laser beams. "*He* should be the one prepared to deal with *me*."

"Are you going to punch him again?" I asked, recalling their last encounter.

"I'm not planning on it," he violently speared an egg like he wished it was Braden he was stabbing, "the last thing I want to do is stoop to his level again, but I might be unable to control myself."

"Well, if you do punch him make sure you punch the right side of his face."

Ezra's brow wrinkled with confusion and he flicked a stray curl from his eyes. "Why the right side?"

"Because he thinks it's his good side."

Ezra snorted and shook his head. "The guy has no good side. He's ugly through and through."

I nodded in agreement, glaring down at my food.

"Sadie," his voice was soft, "there's nothing wrong with you for not realizing how bad he was."

"I know," I replied softly.

The look he gave me clearly said he didn't think that I did know.

He finished eating and I gathered our plates to clean them.

As I ran water in the sink I felt him standing near my back but I refused to acknowledge his presence.

Eventually he spoke. "You don't have to do the dishes you know."

"I want to help," I shrugged, rinsing a plate, "I don't expect to stay here scot-free. I'll help out."

"You know I'd never ask that of you."

I spared him a glance. "And I don't want to be a charity case."

He sighed heavily, his chest expanding as he let out a breath. "I have a maid, so don't start trying to clean the floor with a toothbrush or something," he muttered, rubbing the back of his head awkwardly.

I fought a smile. "I'll stay away from the toothbrushes then."

"I mean it," he warned, pointing a finger at me, "you don't need to do anything."

I turned the water off and opened the dishwasher so I could place the dirty plates and cups on the rack.

"Ezra," I started, "this makes me feel better."

He looked like he wanted to argue with me, but he surprised me by saying, "Alright. Fine. Whatever."

I nodded my head in thanks.

I closed the dishwasher and he grabbed his keys off the kitchen island. "Are you ready to go then?"

"Yeah," I said, even though *ready* was the last thing I felt. I didn't want to face Braden. I never wanted to see him again.

I also knew that today I would have to call my parents and Emma, break the news to them that my engagement was no more and the wedding was off. I would also have to call and cancel everything to do with the wedding. I didn't want to deal with any of those things, but I couldn't ignore my responsibilities.

I followed Ezra outside, the front porch steps creaking as we stepped down. I liked that he hadn't fixed the creaky floors in the cottage. It was things like that, that gave a place character and charm.

Above us the summer sun already shined brightly, promising a day of scorching temperatures. The Virginia summers could be brutal, the humidity alone was enough to kill you, not to mention the bugs. I would never survive living somewhere further south.

Ezra opened the garage door and I tried to ignore the way he watched me—still waiting for another breakdown.

I kept my shoulders back and my chin held high.

I was fine.

I was fine.

I was fine.

Maybe if I repeated it enough I would start to believe it.

Not likely, but it was worth a shot.

While I was having my internal debate Ezra unlocked the SUV.

"Are you coming?" He asked, opening the driver's door and looking back at where I stood.

"Yeah." I shook my head free of my thoughts and joined him.

We were silent on the drive over to Braden's apartment. The radio provided background noise, but it wasn't loud enough to drown out my racing thoughts as I imagined all of the different ways this meeting with Braden could go.

None of them were good.

On the way, Ezra stopped by the office supplies store and picked up some boxes. I hadn't even thought of that.

When we arrived at the apartment Braden's truck was nowhere to be seen in the parking lot. I said a silent thanks to whatever god or deity had been on my side today.

Ezra glanced over at me. "This is it."

It was, in more ways than one.

I nodded, reaching for the handle and stepping out of the vehicle.

I trudged slowly up the steps and stopped in front of the door, letting out a string of colorful curses.

"What is it?" Ezra asked, fighting a smile as I kicked the door.

"I don't have my key." I groaned, slamming the heel of my hand against the door like I could force it open.

Ezra lightly pushed my shoulder, forcing me to step away from the door.

"I've got this." He flashed me a crooked smile.

I stood back with my arms crossed over my chest, trying to peer over his shoulder to see what he was doing, but he was careful to shield me.

The door swung open and I stared at him open mouthed. "Did you just break into my apartment?"

He suppressed a laugh. "For starters, it's not your apartment. Secondly, it was already unlocked." He winked.

"No, it wasn't," I defended.

His lips twitched. “Are you sure about that?”

I sighed. “Fine, if the cops show up again I’ll stick with the story that it was already unlocked.”

“That’s all I ask.” Pausing, he tilted his head to the side and muttered, “They better not show up.”

I shrugged and moved past him to step inside the apartment.

Twenty-four hours ago this place had been home, and now I wanted nothing more than to destroy it. I had to put a lid on my temper. It was going to get me in trouble again.

“Do you have tape?” Ezra asked, laying the flat boxes down on the small kitchen table. “I can start putting these together while you gather your stuff.”

“Yeah.” I padded into the kitchen and rifled through the junk drawer, producing a roll of packing tape. “Here you go.” I held it out to him and he took it with a small smile. He knew this was hard for me, but he also didn’t know what to say to make it better.

I left Ezra to assemble the boxes and headed back to the bedroom.

I glared at the bed, remembering what I’d walked in on yesterday. I’d left my store early hoping to surprise Braden and maybe have a nice dinner since it was Friday night. Braden had obviously had other plans.

With a violent yank I began to pull the sheets off the bed.

I would never use them. Not now anyway. But I bought them and I refused to let him have them on principle.

Tears clogged my eyes as I tossed the sheets out into the hallway. Ezra would pack them up for me.

First I grabbed my stuff from the dresser, careful to keep everything folded so I wouldn't have to do it again later.

I strode over to the closet, yanking the doors open so that they clattered harshly against the walls.

"Is everything okay in there?" Ezra called, the concern evident in his voice.

"Just dandy," I said sarcastically.

I heard his chuckle echo through the small apartment.

I took everything off on the hangers and laid them on the bed.

Soon nothing was left in the closet except for Braden's clothes and one lone garment bag.

I grasped the bag, rubbing my fingers against the material that hid my wedding dress.

Stupidly, I reached for the zipper, exposing the white princess dress.

My lower lip began to tremble as I pulled it out of the bag and clutched it to my chest.

I sunk to the floor with the white fabric billowing around me.

Tears fell from my chin onto the dress.

I was crying for so many things.

For my life that imploded in my face.

For the love I'd thought I had that was nothing more than a farce.

For hurting Ezra and pushing him away.

For pushing *everyone* away.

"Sad—oh shit," Ezra cursed, stopping in the doorway of the bedroom. He set the boxes down hastily and hurried to my side. He crouched down beside me, pulling me against his chest. I tried to push away, ashamed of my tears, but he wouldn't let me. "Shh," he cooed.

I finally stopped fighting and relinquished myself to his embrace.

He smoothed his long fingers through my hair and then kissed the top of my head.

I clung to his shoulders, trying to even my breaths and stop sniveling.

He rested his chin on top of my head and he leaned his back against the open closet door.

I fisted the tulle fabric of my dress in my hand.

"I want to burn it." I confessed to him.

He rocked me back and forth, not saying anything for a moment. "Then we'll burn it," he declared.

"Thank you."

I pressed a palm flat against his chest and pushed away.

I dried my eyes with the back of my hands.

Before he could say anything else, I said, "Let's get this stuff packed and get out of here. I don't want to see this place ever again."

Ezra nodded and stood, holding out a hand to haul me up.

I flashed him a grateful smile.

He had all the boxes assembled and we hurried to get all my stuff in them.

I left Ezra in the bedroom to finish, while I tucked an empty box under my arm and headed into the bathroom. I flicked the light on, ignoring my reflection in the mirror. All my makeup and hair things were thrown haphazardly in the drawer, but a hot pink straightener lay on the counter—a straightener that wasn't mine.

Anger overrode me and I picked it up, throwing it at the mirror. The mirror cracked and began to shatter, the pieces raining down.

"Sadie!"

Ezra came running into the bathroom and his mouth fell open at the mess.

I acted like nothing had happened. I started grabbing my things and dropping them into the box. "I hate him," I muttered under my breath, "I hate him so damn much."

Ezra lingered in the doorway. "I know."

"You don't have to watch over me," I assured him.

He still stayed. After a pause he pulled away from the wall. "I'll start loading the other boxes in the car."

He walked away, the sound of his heavy boots muffled by the carpet, and then I heard the front door close.

Once the drawer was empty I grabbed my shampoo, conditioner, and body wash from the shower.

In the kitchen I grabbed the tape and secured the flaps of the box. It felt symbolic somehow. Like I was taping up the wound Braden had left on my life.

I'd begun stacking the boxes by the door when Ezra ran inside. He rested his back against the closed door and his chest rose and fell as he gasped for breath.

What the hell did he do? Run up all three flights of stairs?

"Braden," he panted, waving a hand to point out the door, "is here. He saw me."

My eyes widened.

"Shit," I cursed.

Not only did I never want to see him again, but I also didn't want to deal with his bullish behavior. He'd be intolerable since he saw Ezra.

I squared my shoulders. "We haven't done anything wrong."

"We haven't," Ezra agreed. "But I wanted to beat him here to tell you so you were prepared."

At that moment the door began to move behind Ezra's back and he stepped away so it could swing open.

Braden's large frame took up the whole doorway as he stared angrily at me.

I kept my chin held high, refusing to cower in his presence.

Ezra stood beside me, his hand grazing my waist like he was trying to remind me that I wasn't alone.

Braden's eyes flicked down to where Ezra's hand sat, and let out a growl as he stomped forward. He raised his arms, as if he was going to physically push us away.

"I can't fucking believe this," he spat, glaring at me like I was a disgusting piece of scum stuck to the bottom of his shoe, "not even a day later and you're with him. I always knew you two were fucking."

Ezra growled, ready to barrel forward but I put a hand on his shoulder to halt him. He looked down at me and I shook my head.

This wasn't his fight.

It was mine.

"If I've told you once, I've told you a thousand times, Ezra is my *friend.* F. R. I. E. N. D. The definition being, a person attached to another by feelings of affection. Not attached by a penis and vagina, which is apparently *your* definition." I crossed my arms over my chest, glaring at him. “Don’t try and put your transgressions on my shoulders. I’ve been nothing but faithful to you. Now that I know you’re nothing but a cheat I completely understand your insecurity.”

He stared at me, baffled. His face began to turn red. “Insecure? I’m not insecure.”

“Of course you’re not.” I patted his chest in a placating manner.

He grabbed my wrist and something in me snapped. My right arm shot out, my closed fist connecting with his jaw.

“Oh motherfucker!” I cried, clutching my fist. “That hurts!” I fanned my hand around like that alone would remove the sting of pain.

Braden started towards me, whether to offer assistance or not I didn’t know, because Ezra stopped him from approaching me with a withering glare. “I’ve got her,” he spat at my ex-fiancé. “I think you’ve done enough, don’t you?”

He turned me into his arms and inspected my fist. The skin around my knuckles was red and throbbed painfully. “He has a hard head.” I defended my pathetic punch.

Ezra twisted my hand around looking at it closely. “You can wiggle your fingers?” He asked.

I did.

“It’s not broken and I don’t think it’s sprained either, so that’s good news.” Lowering his voice, he whispered,

"He's going to have one heck of a bruise on his face to try to explain."

"Really?" I brightened.

The pain in my hand would be worth it to know that my asshole ex was walking around with a black eye.

He nodded and I heard the freezer open. When I looked over my shoulder I saw that Braden was getting a bag of ice for his face. I hoped his face hurt as bad as my hand. He deserved worse than that, but I'd settle for this.

Ezra let my hand drop and took a step back. "I think we should go now."

I nodded. I was done here. There was nothing else I needed, or wanted, to say to Braden.

When I turned around fully I saw that Braden leaned against the kitchen counter, holding the ice to his cheek. He seemed resigned and I was glad that I wouldn't have to argue with him about it anymore.

Ezra grabbed two of the last three boxes and waited by the door.

I grabbed my keys off the counter where they'd been left yesterday and took off the key to Braden's apartment.

I swallowed thickly as I looked down at the key, remembering how happy I'd been when he'd asked me to move in. Now, my happiness seemed so silly.

I held the key out to him. "Here," I waved it at him.

He took it with his free hand, his fingers grazing my hand. His touch had once filled my body with a pleasant warmth and now I felt nothing.

We stared awkwardly at each other for a moment, neither of us knowing what to do or say.

Finally I shrugged and said, "Well, goodbye."

He nodded once and I knew I'd been dismissed.

Ezra stepped outside and I grabbed the last box.

The door had almost closed behind me when Braden cleared his throat and grabbed it, holding it open so he could peer outside at me.

He stared down at me from his looming height and his lips twisted. "I'm sorry," he finally said, and I reeled back in surprise at his apology.

He eased the door closed before I could react.

I turned to Ezra, gaping like a fish. He looked just as surprised as me.

"That was interesting," he muttered before starting down the stairs.

I nodded my head in agreement even though he couldn't see me.

I followed him over to his car and we put the last of the boxes into the trunk.

"Thank you," I told him yet again. Something told me I was never going to run out of reasons to thank Ezra.

He tipped his head in acknowledgement of my words.

"I'll meet you back at the house," I said, tossing a thumb over my shoulder to point at my white Jeep Wrangler.

"Oh, wait." He caught my arm to stop me from leaving. He shoved his hand into the pocket of his jeans and rummaged around. His tongue stuck out adorably from the corner of his mouth. "Ah, there it is." He held a key up.

I outstretched my palm and he placed it onto my hand.

"What's this?" I asked, closing the fist of my uninjured hand around it.

"The key to my house." He shrugged, shoving his fingers through his unkempt curls. "If you're staying with me then you need to have a key."

"Yeah, I guess so." I frowned, squinting up at him. "I really don't want to be in your way."

"You're not," he assured me, "don't worry about it."

That was easier said than done.

He leaned against his vehicle. "I have to make a couple of stops before I go home."

"I need to go by the store," I mused.

Arden was manning my store today, so it was really unnecessary for me to swing by, but I always liked to check on things. My store was my baby in many ways and I wanted to keep things running smoothly.

"I'll see you later then." He flashed me a smile before turning to get into his SUV.

I waved goodbye, even though he couldn't see me, and crossed the lot to my car.

When I started the car the radio was loud enough to give me a headache. That's normally how I loved to listen to it, but right now I craved silence so I turned it off.

I backed out of the parking space and ended up behind Ezra at the exit.

He turned right while I turned left.

My store was about fifteen minutes from the apartment; so it didn't take me long to get there.

It was located on the walking mall with an antique store to its left and a pizza shop on the right.

I didn't know what had possessed me to decide to open a clothing store. One day I just woke up and it felt right. So, after getting my degree I went for it. People thought I was crazy, but it worked.

Sew in Style was my baby, a complete labor of love.

It had been scary going out on a limb and starting a business at my age, but I'd done it. It also helped that my best friend was a rock star and had been willing to loan me the money to start up. Ezra had already been paid back months ago, and he never brought up his helping hand in my business. In his eyes I had done this on my own.

I parked on the side of the building and grabbed my purse as I headed in the back.

I set my bag on a working table and stepped out into the store.

Arden was one of my two employees, and she stood by a rack speaking with a woman about a green and white polka dotted dress. Arden spoke softly, her long red hair curling down her back. She was pretty, with fair skin and a smattering of freckles across her face. The day she'd walked in here asking about a job had been my saving grace. Even though the store wasn't hers, I knew she loved it as much as I did. She'd been working here for the last year and over that time we'd become friends.

When she saw me she lifted her hand in a small wave before returning her attention to the customer.

I busied myself straightening a few racks of clothing.

The woman decided to buy the dress and Arden rang up her purchase. Once the woman left Arden turned to me with her hands on her hips.

"What are you doing here?" She asked. "Shouldn't you be working on last minute details for your wedding."

I flinched and held up my left hand, wiggling my fingers. "I'm not getting married."

Her mouth fell open. She scurried forward and grabbed my hand like she thought the ring was going to magically reappear.

"What happened?" She took a step back, trying to look remorseful even though I knew she wasn't. She, like everyone else, hadn't hid her distaste of Braden. She'd said once that he reminded her too much of her ex-husband. She'd gotten married young, just out of high school, and then got pregnant only for her husband to bail. She'd remained strong through it all, and I admired her for that.

I turned around and began to refold some shirts on one of the tables near the front of the store.

"He cheated." I said the words fast, like ripping off a Band-Aid.

Arden followed me, her lips downturned in sympathy. "Are you okay?"

I smoothed the wrinkles out of the shirt and stood up straight. "Yeah," I held my head high, "I am."

My pride had taken a major bruising, but I really was okay with all of this. It had been eye opening.

"Well, that's good," she said, although her tone suggested she was doubtful of my sincerity.

"This is a new beginning," I stated.

She leaned her hip against the table. "We'll have to get dinner soon if I can manage to get a sitter for Mia. I think we both need some girl time."

"That would be nice," I agreed, moving through the store.

There wasn't anything else for me to fix. Arden was always on top of things.

"I guess I'll head out."

"I have everything covered," she assured me.

"Thanks." I flashed her a grateful smile.

She reached her arms out and hugged me briefly. "The best is yet to come," she whispered in my ear.

I closed my eyes, hanging onto those words and praying that she was right.

CHAPTER FOUR

IT FELT WEIRD being in Ezra's house by myself. I knew he would want me to make myself at home, but it *wasn't* my home.

I'd been here for hours and he still hadn't come back. It was late afternoon now and I'd spent the whole day making phone calls to cancel everything associated with the wedding, as well as to let my family know. My dad and brother had both offered to castrate Braden for me. I turned down their offers, as tempting as they might be. When I told my mom, she said, "Oh thank God." I would've been more hurt by her words if I hadn't come to see what an asshole he was. Emma hadn't said much when I told her. I got the impression that she was afraid, "I told you so," might pass through her lips while she was trying to be supportive.

I heard the roar of a car and rolled off the couch, hurrying to the front window.

Ezra's large SUV zoomed down the drive with Maddox's sleek sports car behind him. I saw Emma sitting in the passenger's seat and a smile spread across my face. She hadn't said anything about coming over when I talked to her earlier and I hadn't wanted to ask and sound whiny, but I really needed her right now.

I waited for them to park before opening the door and rushing outside.

Emma had barely gotten out of the car before I crashed into her arms, squeezing her tight. I'd seen her only a week ago when we got together to catch up after her being gone on tour with the guys, but it felt like so much longer.

She hugged me back just as fiercely.

"Why are you guys here?" I asked, flicking my head in the direction of Maddox and giving him a small wave.

He smiled and waved back. His brown hair fell messily over his forehead and stubble dotted his jaw. He crossed his arms and laid them on the roof of his car. "This one," he pointed at Ezra who was walking towards us, "said something about a party."

"A party?" My brows rose in interest.

"Yeah," Ezra nodded. "I'm calling it the Thank-God-That-Asshole-Is-Out-Of-Your-Life party."

Laughter burst free of my lungs and I couldn't seem to stop. "That's quite a long name for a party."

He shrugged. "It seemed appropriate."

"I hope you got alcohol."

At my words he walked over and opened the trunk of his SUV, revealing two twelve packs of beer stacked beside my belongings.

I put a hand to my forehead and pretended to swoon. "You're a life saver."

"I also got cake." He smiled proudly. "And fireworks, because what party is complete without blowing some shit up."

"Yeeeaaah!" Maddox clapped his hands together. "Beer and fire, I like this party." He held out his fist for Ezra and Ezra bumped his against it.

Boys.

Emma shook her head, a small smile turning up her lips. She eyed the boxes in Ezra's car. "Do you want me to help you unpack?"

I had told Emma on the phone that I would be staying with Ezra for the foreseeable future.

"That would be great." It would make the time go faster and we could talk.

We each grabbed a box and Ezra told me that he and Maddox would bring in the rest. I flashed both guys a grateful smile.

Emma followed me up the porch steps and into the cottage. Since Maddox and Ezra were best friends she'd been here plenty of times before.

I trudged up the steps and pushed open the door to the guestroom with a shove of my shoulder.

I set the box in my hands down on the bed and Emma did the same.

The guys were right behind us with more boxes.

Ezra lingered in the doorway, looking back at Maddox and then Emma before his eyes landed on me. "I...uh..." He scratched the back of his head, a nervous habit. "I cleared out a drawer in the bathroom for you to put your things."

"That's nice of you, but you didn't need to do that. The last thing I want to do is disrupt things for you." I felt like I kept telling him that over and over again, but I sincerely meant it. It was never my intention to swoop in and unsettle things.

"You're not disrupting anything." He assured me.

Emma watched our exchange with a careful eye.

"Well, thanks for the drawer then. If you're sure?" I questioned further.

"I am." He nodded.

He ducked out of the room then with Maddox behind him.

Emma's lips twisted as she fought a smile.

"What?" I asked, knowing exactly where this was heading but refusing to be the one to initiate the conversation.

"What's going on with you guys?" She asked, trying to hide her growing smile.

I fiddled with my keys, looking for the chain with the small pocketknife. My dad insisted I always have one with me, and he'd also stuck a can of pepper spray in my car. He took the over protective parent role very seriously.

Once I found the knife, I used it to slice open the tape on one of the boxes.

Shrugging, I began to lay the stuff on the bed. “We’re friends. We have been for years. Nothing has changed.”

She eyed me for a moment and then let out a sigh. She opened another box and started unpacking that stuff.

“You haven’t talked to him since New Year’s,” she whispered, “that hurt him.” She glanced at me out of the corner of her eye, waiting for my reaction.

I set a stack of jeans on the bed before turning to the dresser and opening a drawer.

“I did what I had to do.” I swallowed past the lump in my throat, waiting for her to ridicule me for my stupid decisions.

“I know,” she replied, shocking me. “There’s something I’ve been wondering, though,” she started.

I raised a brow for her to continue when she trailed off.

“Why did you call him when you got arrested and not me? I can see why you wouldn’t want your parent’s to know, but you and I have been best friends for longer than you and Ezra.”

I hadn’t told my parent’s about getting arrested, but I had let Emma in on that detail.

I began to place the jeans in the drawer, weighing my answer. "I guess I was afraid you'd judge me." I shifted my eyes nervously in her direction.

She reeled back, shocked by my admission. "How could you think that?"

I put the last pair of jeans away and closed the drawer.

I waved a hand at her and said, "Look at you, Emma! You have the perfect relationship with the perfect guy. You're *happy*. You didn't get with some fuck up like I did." I opened another box, my back now turned to her.

"You think my relationship is perfect?" She snorted. "I assure you, it's not. We have our ups and downs like everybody else."

"Yeah," I agreed, grabbing the stack of clothes from the box. These were on hangers so I walked over to the closet to hang them up. "But you guys are...ugh.... You're *perfect* for each other. Braden and I were not. You warned me that he was the wrong guy, so I guess I was afraid you'd say 'I told you so.'"

"You know I would never do that," she defended, "and Ezra could just as easily have said that to you. My God, he's the one that punched Braden, not me."

I finished hanging up the clothes and faced her with a frown on my face. "I didn't want to be a bother to you, okay? You're always wrapped up in Maddox and now you're planning your own wedding," I pointed to her hand where a unique purplish pink diamond glittered, "so I didn't want to be an inconvenience. I knew I could count on Ezra."

"But you can count on me too." Her voice was no more than a whisper and hurt swam in her blue eyes. Her mouth fell open and she let out a small gasp. "Are you lying to me? Is something going on between you guys and that's why you and Braden broke up?"

I snorted. We were back to square one. "No," I emphasized the word. "We're only friends and Braden is a lying, filthy, cheating scumbag." My fists tightened at my sides.

"Did you start the name calling without us?" Maddox joked as he and Ezra arrived with more boxes. "I'm hurt." He set the boxes on the floor and then swooped down to give Emma a kiss on her cheek.

Ezra smiled as he watched the gesture. We were both so used to Maddox and Emma's constant displays of affection that we were no longer grossed out.

"Do you have enough room for everything?" Ezra looked concerned as his eyes flitted about the area. He seemed to be taking stock of the furniture to see if there was enough space for all of my belongings.

"It's fine," I assured him, my hand briefly landing on his arm. I let go hastily when Emma's eyes fell to where I touched him. She was reading into nothing. "You don't need to worry about me," I told him, pretending Emma wasn't listening to and analyzing every word that left my lips, "you letting me stay here is enough."

It was kind that Ezra was going out of his way to try to make me feel comfortable but it was completely unnecessary. I couldn't help but feel safe in his presence. Was it my ideal scenario to be crashing here for a while? Definitely not. But I was okay.

He nodded and flashed a small smile. "I'll try to stop worrying then."

Expecting Ezra not to worry would be like anticipating the sky turning green. It was never going to happen.

Ezra was usually a laid-back guy, but when he cared about someone or something it worried him endlessly.

Ezra turned to leave once more but Maddox appeared in the doorway. I hadn't even realized he left.

"These are the last two," he declared, setting the new boxes on the floor beside the others.

"We'll be out back while you finish unpacking." Ezra nodded at Emma and then me.

The guys left, their shoes smacking against the wood stairs.

I went to work opening the new boxes and noticed that the one containing my wedding dress and the sheets were suspiciously absent.

Emma eyed me with a speculative look as she set about removing items from boxes. "So...you don't have any feelings for him?"

I sighed. This wasn't a new question.

"I love Ezra as a friend. Nothing more." I muttered the words as I stuffed my bras and panties into the top dresser drawer. I could refold them later.

Emma made a noise that sounded like a grunt of disagreement. "You guys have been skirting around your chemistry for years. It's only a matter of time..."

"A matter of time until what?" I asked.

"Until you fuck each other's brains out."

I laughed, the kind of laugh that came deep from your belly. Before Emma met Maddox she blushed as red as a tomato at any mention of sex. That girl was long gone.

"That's not going to happen," I declared once I'd sobered.

She quirked a brow and eyed me with indignation. "We'll see."

We finished unpacking all of my stuff and I changed into a pair of jeans and a lightweight sweater. While the summer days were scorching hot, the evenings could be downright chilly where you wanted to snuggle beneath a blanket.

Emma and I found the guys out back seated around the fire pit. A fire roared and the makings for s'mores lay on a side table.

Emma scurried over to the chair beside Maddox, but he snagged her around the waist before she could sit down, and she fell onto his lap with a giggle.

I took the chair beside Ezra, wanting to distance myself from their sickeningly sweet displays of affection. Their relationship was one for the storybooks—one I didn't think I'd ever find for myself.

Was I jealous?

I didn't think so. I was happy that Emma had found something so special, but I was also smart enough to know that it was rare and the chances of me finding it were slim to none.

"Did you get everything unpacked?" Ezra asked, stealing me from my thoughts.

"Yes," I answered, staring at the roaring fire as it soared higher. I leaned back in the Adirondack chair, making myself comfortable.

"Good," he replied.

I felt like there was a slight awkwardness between us at moments, and I guessed that was perfectly understandable since I'd ignored him for the last six months and then come barreling back into his life with a mountain of baggage.

"Oh, here," he said suddenly, reaching down. He removed the top on a longneck bottle of beer and held it out to me.

"Thanks," I smiled, taking it.

Maybe to someone else it would seem surreal to be sitting around drinking beer with the bassist and drummer for one of the most popular bands in the world, but for me it felt right. Initially, when I first met the guys I'd been starstruck. I'd been a fan of their music before I knew Emma was dating Maddox, so it was bound to happen. But you didn't have to be around them long before you realized they were like everybody else.

"It's been a long day," he commented, leaning back in the chair and stretching out his legs.

"It's been a long *two* days," I corrected.

He chuckled and the shadows of the flames danced over his handsome face.

Across from us Maddox nuzzled Emma's neck and she let out another giggle before kissing him on the lips. He grasped her hair in his fingers and murmured, "I love you."

I let out a sigh.

Ezra's head swiveled in my direction. "You'll have that one day," he declared.

"I hope so," I replied, "I really hope so."

He lifted his bottle of beer to his lips and drained what was left. He stood up, placing the empty bottle on the nearby table.

"I think it's time for us to get to the real reason for this gathering."

Emma and Maddox immediately broke apart, giving him their full attention.

My brows rose in interest and I set my beer on the ground beside my chair.

"I'll be right back." He looked at me when he said the words, warning me to stay in my seat.

I raised my hands in surrender and sat back.

He disappeared inside and I looked at Maddox across the fire. "What is he up to?" I asked, giving Maddox my best glare—daring him not to tell me the truth.

He chuckled. "You'll know soon enough."

He was right.

Ezra breezed out onto the deck with two boxes and down the steps over to where we sat around the fire.

When I saw the boxes I knew immediately what he was up to. He set them both in front of me and smiled down at me.

"You said you wanted to burn it," he kicked the box where my wedding dress overflowed from the open flaps, "and I thought you might want to burn this too." I looked at the other box and my suspicions were confirmed when I saw the sheets from the bed I had shared with Braden.

"You're the best," I told Ezra, meaning those words more than he could possibly understand.

He grinned a mega-watt smile at my words. "Ready?"

"Do you even need to ask?"

He chuckled and stepped back, giving me access to the fire.

Emma and Maddox both watched with a smile.

I grabbed the sheets first.

With a cry I launched them into the fire.

The flames licked the fabric, slowly burning away the floral material to a black crisp.

Emma let out a whoop and waved her hands in the air. Maddox said something to her that sounded a lot like, "You're so adorable."

"How do you feel?" Ezra asked, standing beside me. His arm brushed mine and my body hummed with familiarity.

"Unstoppable." I answered with the first word that came to mind.

He smiled down at me, his hands shoved into the pockets of his jeans.

The four of us watched the fire eat away the sheets until they were barely recognizable.

I headed for the dress, struggling to get the massive thing into my arms.

Ezra grasped my elbow and I stopped what I was doing.

"Are you sure?" He asked, his eyes flicking from me to the dress.

I took a deep breath. "Yeah, I am. If I get married I won't be doing it in this dress."

"When," he said.

"Excuse me?" I questioned, confused by his seemingly random response.

He smiled crookedly. *"When* you get married."

"Right," I sighed. That possibility seemed so far in the future now that I couldn't even picture it happening.

Without a second of thought I launched the dress into the fire. Smoke licked the sky as the dress went from white to black.

How symbolic.

Ezra's arm fell around my shoulders and I leaned against his body for support. His lips pressed against my forehead in a quick kiss and then the warmth of his lips was gone, replaced by his fingers as he wiped tears away from my cheeks.

"I'm okay." I assured him before he could ask. "I really am."

These tears weren't of sadness. They were cathartic, clearing away all the negativity that had been clinging to my shoulders the last few years.

I felt it all drift away like a seed carried away by the wind.

I knew in that moment that I would be okay. Everything happened for a reason, and I needed this speed bump to teach me a lesson.

"Can we have s'mores now?" Emma asked, interrupting my thoughts.

Ezra's arm dropped away from my shoulders and he grabbed the bags of stuff, passing them half.

I sat down once more and he set the items between us. I grabbed a marshmallow, sticking it on the skewer. I held it over the fire until it was a soft golden color. When I pulled it away from the fire Ezra already had a graham cracker with a block of Hershey's chocolate on it waiting for me. He was always looking out for me, no matter the situation.

I bit into my s'more and the gooey marshmallow clung to my lips.

Ezra noticed and began to laugh.

"Don't laugh at me." I leveled him with a glare.

He shook his head. "You're cute."

I rolled my eyes, wiping the sticky residue off my lips. He was still laughing at me, so with narrowed eyes I reached out and wiped the goo on his arm.

He glanced down at his arm and his mouth parted slightly with disbelief.

"I can't believe you just did that," he muttered.

I grinned, bouncing in my seat like an excited child.

"You're going to pay for that," he warned.

I prepared to spring from my chair and run away, but he was faster.

His finger had dipped into the melted chocolate of his own s'more and he reached out, swiping his finger down my nose.

A gasp emitted from my lips. "Ezra!" I shrieked.

"Payback's a bitch." He grinned.

I shook my head. "You're just mean."

He chuckled, the sound warm and husky. "We both know that isn't true."

"Right now it is." I stuck my tongue out at him.

He smiled at me, flicking a piece of hair away from his eyes.

Before I could retaliate Maddox called, "What about the fireworks?"

"Oh, right." Ezra shoved the last of his s'more into his mouth and hurried over to where he'd left the boxes of fireworks. Maddox joined him and while they got everything set up I made myself another s'more.

Emma stood from her chair and made her way over to Ezra's now vacant one. Her wild blonde hair blew around her shoulders from the evening breeze. She plopped into the chair, crossing her legs.

"Do you feel better now?" She asked.

I nodded, my eyes flitting to the fire where the remains of my wedding dress and those blasted sheets were barely distinguishable. "Much."

"I'm sorry you have to go through this, but I'm also happy that he's out of your life."

My lips lifted with a smile. "You're not the only one."

She opened her mouth to reply, but was cut off by a loud boom. We both turned to look at the same time as a small firework fizzled.

Maddox stood with his hands on his hips beside Ezra, both guys looking at the disappearing firework with a *what-the-fuck* expression.

"Well, that was anticlimactic," Maddox muttered. "Should we try another?"

Emma and I both laughed as we watched the guys fiddle with another firework. It went off, burning out quickly like the last.

"Where did you get these?" Maddox asked, picking up one of the boxes and inspecting it from all angles.

Ezra shrugged. "It was a booth beside the gas station."

Maddox huffed and threw the box on the ground. "That explains everything. The next time you decide to buy anything explosive call me, or Hayes. But not Mathias, he's not to be trusted with fire."

Emma and I both laughed again. It didn't seem possible that I should feel this *happy* only a day after finding my fiancé in bed with another woman, but I did, and it was all thanks to the fact that I had the greatest friends in the whole world.

"So these are a bust?" Ezra pointed to the unopened fireworks.

Maddox nodded. "Sorry, bud." He clapped Ezra roughly on the shoulder. "Those sparkers are doable, but rather boring."

Ezra grunted and rolled his eyes, but picked up that box and opened it. He extended it in Maddox's direction and he removed two of the sticks, one for himself and Emma. He ventured over to us and handed one to her.

Ezra grabbed two as well and gave me one. He held out a lighter and lit the tip of mine, then Emma's, before lighting his own and Maddox's.

I stood up from my chair and he eyed me, wondering what I was doing.

I waggled my brows and grinned. "Catch me."

I took off running, swirling the sparkler through the air.

Ezra's feet pounded behind me, urging me to run faster.

"Sadie!" He cried suddenly. "The lake!"

Oh, shit. I'd completely forgotten about the lake and it was dark enough that it completely blended in with the grass.

Before I could slow down my feet landed in the water, sinking into the mud.

I went down into the water, getting my whole body wet. The poor sparkler got lost in the water, extinguished by the wetness before it could meet its own fiery demise.

I came up gasping for air as his arm snaked around my waist.

Ezra pulled me against his now wet body and muttered, "You're honestly the craziest person I've ever met."

I laughed, clinging to his shoulders. "I'm not crazy, I'm *alive*."

He shook his head, hauling me out of the water like he was afraid if he didn't I wouldn't get out on my own.

"Why'd you come in after me?" I asked, shivering when the cool night air touched my wet body.

He set me on the ground and tucked a piece of hair behind my ear that clung to my forehead.

"Because that's what friends do," he replied with a small shrug of his shoulders, "you jump, I jump. Always."

My lips quirked into a smile. "I didn't jump, though. I face-planted into the water."

He laughed, hooking his thumbs into the back of his wet t-shirt and pulling it off. His lean chest was exposed with a smattering of dark hair trailing beneath his belly button. I tried not to notice how my heart pitter-pattered.

"Same difference," he claimed, shaking his head so that water droplets flew from his hair.

"What are you guys doing?" Maddox called. It sounded like he had his hands cupped around his mouth.

Ezra scrubbed a hand over his heavily stubbled jaw. "I think the party is over."

I shivered, my teeth chattering together. That water wasn't exactly the warmest. "I think so too," I agreed.

He tucked his t-shirt into the back pocket of his jeans and started back to the house.

It was easier to see going this way since the fire was in front of us.

When we approached, Emma rushed forward. "Are you okay? We heard a splash."

"Just peachy," I replied, wringing out my wet hair.

I shivered again and she said, "You need to get inside and take a hot shower. You're going to get sick."

"Yeah," Ezra agreed, "go ahead. I've got to clean up down here first."

"Are you sure?" It was his house and I felt bad for going first. He had to be as cold as I was.

He nodded. "Positive."

I didn't fight him on it, because I was freezing and a hot shower sounded like the best idea ever right now.

"Thanks for all of this," I waved my hand around, "and thank you guys for being here." I looked at Emma and Maddox then.

Maddox dipped his chin in acknowledgement.

Emma smiled sweetly. "There's nowhere else we'd rather be." She paused, biting her lip. "I'd hug you goodbye, but you're soaking."

I laughed. "We can save the hug for later."

She nodded and watched me head up the porch steps. I hadn't missed the flash of worry and speculation in her eyes. I knew she thought there was something more between Ezra and me, but she couldn't be more wrong. We were friends and that's all we ever would be.

CHAPTER FIVE

"GET UP." Ezra demanded, turning on the ceiling light in the guestroom.

I sat up in bed, the blankets pooling at my waist. "What the hell?" I blinked sleep from my eyes and looked at him dazedly.

"Get up," he repeated.

"What are you *wearing*?" My eyes widened at the sight of him. He had on a pair of khaki shorts, a white sleeveless shirt, and...was that a fisherman's hat on his head? One of those with the little dangly things? Oh my God, it was!

"We're going fishing," he stated, which explained the hat, "so get your ass out of bed, get changed, and meet me downstairs. You have ten minutes."

He slipped out of my room and closed the door.

I would've thought the whole thing was a strange dream if it wasn't for the fact that the light still blinded me.

I glanced at the clock on the bed and gasped. "It's six o' clock!" I screamed. "I'm going back to bed." I lay back down and tossed the blankets over my head.

The door creaked open and his shoes slapped against the hardwood.

The covers were yanked unceremoniously from my body.

I gasped, trying to grab the sheets from his hands.

"No," he demanded. "We're going fishing."

"It's six o' clock," I repeated, a whining tone to my voicc, "on a *Sunday*. Thc day of *rest*." I madc a grab for the covers once more, but he yanked them completely off the bed and threw them on the floor. "Ezra!" I yelled.

He ignored my outburst and headed out the door once more. "You're down to eight minutes now. Tick, tock."

I hated him.

No, I didn't.

But seriously?! Six o' clock on a Sunday?

He better have at least made breakfast or I might turn into a raging beast.

I forced my tired body out of bed and changed into a pair of jean shorts, a tank top, and sneakers. I grabbed my sunglasses from my purse and stuck them on top of my head.

When I reached the stairs Ezra was starting up them. "Coming to get me?" I asked, a brow rising in interest.

He grinned and nodded. "Yep. I thought you were flaking."

"Did you think I might try to make a break for it and climb out the window?"

He shook his head as I joined him downstairs. "I wouldn't put anything past you," he confessed. "I made biscuits and gravy if you want any."

"Is there anything you can't cook?" I asked him, heading over to the coffee maker.

Oh sweet sustenance.

He chuckled, rubbing his stubbled jaw. "Not really."

"You're going to make some girl very happy one day," I told him, standing on my tiptoes to grab a coffee cup from the top cabinet.

He grunted in response to my comment and came up behind me to grab one of the mugs for me so I didn't topple them over.

"Thanks." I took the cup from his hands and filled it with the steaming black liquid before I added a heart attack inducing amount of sugar. "What ever happened to you and that actress?"

A few months before I stopped speaking to Ezra he'd gone on a few dates with an up and coming actress. She'd been gorgeous and exactly the kind of girl you'd expect a rock star to date.

I'd asked him before why things ended and he never wanted to tell me.

Today, he shrugged and leaned his backside against the kitchen counter with his arms crossed over his chest. "She was too vain. I want someone with a little more substance. Someone who's..." He paused, staring off as he searched for the right word. "Real," he finally settled on. "I want someone I can picture myself growing old with and who doesn't throw a temper tantrum at the sight of a wrinkle."

I nearly choked on my coffee. "She did that?"

He nodded reaching up to further secure the hat on his head.

"Is that why you haven't dated since then?" I asked.

He shrugged. "No, I just haven't found anyone worth my time."

I fixed myself a plate of biscuits and gravy, taking a seat on one of the barstools.

Ezra pulled out the one beside me and sat down as well.

"So," I started, shoveling a fork full of food into my mouth, "why do you want to go fishing?"

"The better question is why *wouldn't* I want to go fishing." He smiled boyishly, fiddling with the edge of the hat. He propped his elbows on the countertop and tilted his head in my direction. "I thought it would be fun. We haven't hung out in a long time."

I raised a brow, fighting a smile. "Admit it, you only want to see me scream and run away from a worm."

He tossed his head back and his laughter echoed around the kitchen. "You caught me." He reached into his back pocket. "Here," he extended a baseball cap in my direction, "you'll need this."

I took it and removed my sunglasses from the top of my head so that I could put it on. Pouting my lips I turned to him. "How do I look?"

"Beautiful." He answered without a second of thought. He promptly cleared his throat and looked away. He jumped up from his seat like he'd been burned. "I'll be outside."

He hurried away and I watched him leave, wondering what I'd done.

I didn't dwell on it for long.

I finished my breakfast and cup of coffee, washing both the plate and mug before joining him outside.

I saw him standing on the small dock that led into the lake. His hands were on his hips and he had his head turned towards the sky. When he heard me approach he turned and smiled. The sun glowed behind him, making him look otherworldly.

I stopped in front of him, fixing my sunglasses onto my face.

"I wasn't joking about the worms. I will scream like a five year old girl if you make me touch one."

His lips twitched as he fought not to laugh. "Fine," he agreed, "I'll do your dirty work."

I grinned. "Does this mean if I decide to kill Braden you'll help me hide his body?"

This time he couldn't contain his laughter. "That's what best friends are for, right?" He reached for a fishing pole. Glancing at me over his shoulder, he whispered, "I'll even be your alibi."

"How kind of you."

Sobering, I sat down on the edge of the dock, kicking my legs back and forth over the open air. The dark lake water glimmered with the reflection of the sun and nearby trees. Above us birds chirped happily.

I closed my eyes, letting the sun warm my face. A small smile lifted my lips.

It might've been too early to be up on a weekend, but this was actually nice.

Ezra handed me a fishing pole and sat down beside me with his own.

He instructed me on what to do and soon the hook, or whatever it was called, was bobbing on the surface of the water.

We sat in silence for a while, enjoying the peaceful setting.

I was the first to break the quiet minutes later.

"I'm sorry I missed your birthday." My throat closed up. I'd spent his last few birthdays with him, well not just *me*, but all of us—Emma, Maddox, Mathias, and Hayes.

"I wanted to call you," I confessed, looking straight ahead at the water.

He swallowed audibly. "Why didn't you?"

"I was afraid if I did I wouldn't be able to stop at a phone call. I've missed you."

I'd missed him more than I'd been willing to admit to even myself. The last few years we'd been so impossibly close—and anybody that said that guys and girls couldn't be friends were liars, because in a way I was closer to Ezra than I was Emma. Girls were always quick to judge, even I was guilty of that, but guys were different.

"I can't believe I'm twenty-four," he whispered.

"You say that like it's a bad thing."

He shrugged. "I feel like I haven't accomplished much."

I snorted. "You have a Grammy, Ezra," I said, referring to their recent win, "I'd say that's pretty accomplished."

He turned to me, his dark eyes shielded by the flap of the hat he wore. "I don't mean with my career, I just mean with my life in general. I've traveled to all these places and had so many amazing opportunities, but I feel like I haven't ever really *lived.*"

I mulled over his words, seeing how that would be true. The last few years of his life had become so consumed with music, performing, and traveling, that he hadn't really had a chance to be his own person. He wasn't just Ezra Collins. He was Ezra the bassist for Willow Creek.

I rested my head on his shoulder. "We need to change that."

He chuckled. "How?"

"I don't know," I answered truthfully. "I guess by finding what makes you happy."

"Music *does* make me happy," he replied. "It's more that...it feels like something is missing from my life."

I lifted my head. "We'll have to keep searching until we find what that is."

He smiled over at me. "Even if it takes a long time?"

"You know me," I bumped his shoulder with mine, "stubborn to a fault. I won't give up until we find it."

He shook his head, a small smile playing on his lips. "That's one of the things I like most about you."

I frowned, ducking my head. "Even when it made me stay with a guy that wasn't worth my time?"

His thumb and forefinger grasped my chin, lifting my head so I was forced to look at him. "I don't believe it was stubbornness that made you stay with him."

"What was it then?" I asked, truly curious.

He stared down at me for a moment, his lips twisting. "You're one of the kindest people I know. You love with all your heart and you're extremely passionate. You choose to see the good in people even when you shouldn't. I think that's why you stayed with him." He nodded at his own words, squinting against the sun.

I swallowed thickly, my chest feeling tight. "You're too nice to me."

He shook his head. "I'm being honest."

Suddenly I felt a tug on the line and let out a small cry. "I think I caught something!"

"Reel it in," Ezra commanded, gesturing with his hand.

"Oh, right."

I began to do as he said, fighting against the pressure on the fishing line. He gave me a few pieces of advice, but mostly left me alone.

With a groan I pulled and the fish came out of the water, dangling from the end of the line.

I glared at the tiny thing. It couldn't have been bigger than five inches.

I turned to Ezra, my mouth turned down in a grimace. "Well, that was anticlimactic."

He looked from the fish to me and we both burst into laughter.

All the seriousness from our previous conversation drifted away.

"Hold it steady," he commanded. He'd already reeled his empty line in and set his fishing pole on the dock.

I tightened my hold on the pole and he got the wiggling fish free. He clasped it between his hands. “Do you want to put it back in?”

“I’m not touching that thing!” I cried, scuttling backwards like he might toss it in my lap any second.

He shook his head, laughing under his breath at my antics. He bent forward, lowering his hands into the water. He let go and the little fish swam away.

He grabbed the pole from my hands and fixed more bait onto the end before handing it back to me.

I settled myself beside him once more and we both cast our lines.

“This is pretty nice,” I admitted.

He chuckled. “Does this mean you won’t kill me for waking you up early?”

I smiled, adjusting the brim of the baseball cap I wore. “The day is young.”

“How’s your hand?” He asked me suddenly, steering the conversation in a different direction.

“A little sore,” I admitted, “but it’s worth it.”

He smiled and little wrinkles creased the corners of his eyes. “I’ll never get the image of you punching him out of my head. It was awesome.”

“Even better than when you punched him?” I questioned with a laugh.

He nodded his head eagerly. “Way better. The look on his face was priceless. He didn’t see that coming.”

"Why did he cheat on me?" I asked, looking up at Ezra. "You're a guy, so tell me, what's so repulsive about me that he had to seek it elsewhere?"

Ezra reared back, surprised by my random question. "There's nothing *repulsive* about you." He mimicked my tone. "Some guys can't be satisfied with anybody because they're not happy with who they are."

"I feel like I must have done something wrong."

He looked at me like I was crazy. "Sadie, the only thing you did wrong was loving someone that wasn't good enough for you."

I took a deep breath and let it out slowly. "I feel like I should feel more hurt, devastated even, but really I'm just confused." Panic snaked its way through my veins and I looked at him with widened eyes. "I didn't love him the way I should have. What if I don't know how to love someone in that way?"

"You do," he assured me, looking out at the shimmering water, "but you haven't found him yet."

I looked up at the sky and the birds flying above us. "I feel like I don't know who I am anymore. I spent two years with a guy that stripped me of my identity. I feel like all I have of myself is my store and the rest I'm left questioning. I tried so hard to please him, to make him happy, and in the end I made myself miserable. I was so desperate for it to work out that I overlooked how toxic our relationship was. How stupid is that?"

"You're human," he replied. "We have this inane desire to belong to something that is greater than we are on our own. That desire is so strong that we can fool ourselves into believing things that aren't true."

"So, I'm not crazy?" I cracked a smile.

"Definitely not crazy."

His smile was comforting and I reminded myself for the hundredth time that everything would be okay.

I rested my head on his shoulder and then his head rested on top of mine.

A smile touched my lips.

I'd missed this—having someone that understood me completely, even when I didn't know myself.

CHAPTER SIX

I LOCKED THE door leading into my shop, switched the sign to CLOSED, and shut the blinds.

I was exhausted, and certain that this had been the longest week of my life. It had seemed unending as I dealt with phone calls from family and endless Facebook notifications from people wanting to know why Braden and I broke up so soon before our wedding. The gestures would have been nice, if I hadn't believed that most of them were only asking because they were nosy and didn't really care that I'd been hurt. I told them all that we decided mutually that we weren't meant to be. It seemed unfair to let the scumbag off the hook so easily, but I didn't need everybody knowing all of my business and talking behind my back.

I straightened the clothes and shoes, making sure everything was in order for the next business day.

I closed out the register and turned off the lights.

I headed into my office and sat down in the chair behind my desk, letting out a hefty sigh. I glanced at all of the papers on my desk, the numbers and information blurring together. I'd planned to stay a little while longer, but I was beginning to think that wasn't the smartest idea. I'd probably end up messing something up and having to start my paperwork over again tomorrow.

I decided to leave it until tomorrow and stood, grabbing my purse.

I reached for my car keys and flicked off the light on my desk.

I'd only taken one step when I heard someone knock on the front door of the store.

Oh, shit.

I froze where I stood, holding my breath.

The knock sounded again.

I had no idea who could possibly be at the door and I certainly wasn't going to check.

My phone buzzed in my purse and I thanked God that I always kept it on vibrate. If the person outside was a murderer I didn't want to alert them to my location.

I checked the screen and read a text from Ezra.

EZRA: I'm outside.

I breathed a sigh of relief and put a hand over my racing heart, silently scolding myself for my silly thoughts.

I hurried to the front door and opened it.

He stood there in a pair of jeans and a black t-shirt. His dark curly hair tumbled over his forehead, shielding his eyes.

"You scared me," I scolded him.

"Sorry." He appeared sheepish. "Are you done?" He asked, flicking his finger towards the darkened store. "I thought we could get dinner and celebrate."

"What are we celebrating?" I asked.

"The fact that it's been a week." He shrugged, toeing the ground with his booted foot.

"A week since I've been dumped?" I raised a brow.

"Well, it sounds insensitive when you say it like that," he grumped, brushing his long fingers through his shaggy hair. "You've been strong through all of this and I think you deserve to celebrate that." He leaned against the side of the building and lowered his head as he looked at me. "Don't you?"

I tapped my lip. "Are you buying?"

He snorted. "Of course."

"Then yes, I do deserve to celebrate, and I plan on getting shit-faced." I pumped my fist in the air.

He shook his head and tried to hide a smile. "Are you ready to go?" He asked.

"Yeah," I nodded. "I just need to lock the back door first. Are we going in your car?"

"I thought we could walk." He pointed across the street to where one of my favorite local restaurants sat.

“Wait here.” I held up a finger, telling him I’d only be a second.

I quickly locked the back door and the door to my office before rejoining him outside. I stopped, locking that one as well.

Ezra shoved his hands into the pockets of his jeans as we crossed the street onto the back patio of the local pub. You seated yourself, and we managed to snag a seat on the upper deck.

Within a minute a waitress hurried over with menus and silverware.

“What can I get you guys to drink?”

“Alcohol,” I answered. “You can surprise me.”

She looked at me like I was crazy. “I’ll have the bartender make you our special...it’s kind of strong.”

“Perfect,” I grinned.

“For you?” She turned her attention to Ezra and her mouth fell open. “Oh my God!” She jumped up and down—I kid you not. “You’re Ezra, from Willow Creek! Oh my God, I can’t believe this! I mean, I knew you guys lived here, but I never thought I’d meet one of you. Wow! This is amazing! Can I get a picture and an autograph?”

Ezra flashed me an apologetic smile before smiling full watt at the waitress. “Absolutely. Anything for a fan.”

I sighed and looked around at the attention her scream had drawn our way. In no time we would be swarmed.

She pulled her cellphone out of her apron and he posed for a picture. She then gave him a pen and he signed a piece of paper on her notepad.

"Thank you so much!" She gushed. "I'll be right back with your drinks."

"You didn't get mine!" Ezra called after her.

She quickly did an about-face, her face flushed with embarrassment. "I'm so sorry about that. What can I get you?"

"Water," he replied, "and an order of nachos. They're her favorite." He pointed at me.

She glanced at me and I could tell she'd already forgotten my existence.

"I'm sorry," Ezra mouthed as a group of girls rushed our table.

I shrugged. I was used to this happening when we went out in public. Usually it happened in L.A. and not here, but it was the same thing. Besides, a bunch of squealing teenage girls were nothing I couldn't handle.

Ezra posed for picture after picture and signed autographs. Our waitress had to fight her way through the mob to give us our drinks and nachos. Then I had to yell over the screaming girls to give her my order, and Ezra's too, since he was currently occupied and couldn't order for himself.

Before the waitress left I grabbed her arm. "Would you mind getting management to break this up?" I asked.

The girls had already gotten what they came for, so I wasn't being rude, but they had overstayed their welcome.

"I'll send the manager over," she assured me.

I took a sip of whatever concoction she'd brought me. Whoa. She hadn't been lying. It was strong.

I sipped some more and the burn gradually disappeared.

The guy that was obviously the manager showed up and escorted the girls away.

"Your ticket is on me. I'm so sorry for this inconvenience," he apologized.

Ezra shrugged, sitting down once more. "It's not a big deal. I'm used to it." He smoothed his fingers through his ruffled hair—one of the girls had mused it. I hated that so many people treated the guys like they weren't even human.

"Still," the manager said, "I'd like to take care of it."

"Of course." Ezra smiled and nodded. He hated getting special treatment so I wouldn't be surprised if he ended up leaving a wad of cash on the table before we left.

The manager smiled in goodbye and I was finally alone with Ezra.

"Is anybody else joining us?" I asked. It wasn't unusual for the other guys to join us, and Emma of course, and I guess Mathias' wife now—but I'd only ever met her once and the meeting had been brief since that happened to be the time Ezra punched Braden. Braden had spent half the night bitching about that and had continued to grumble for a good month afterwards. He was such a diva.

Ezra shook his head. "Just us. Something wrong with that?" He asked, bringing the glass of water to his lips.

"Of course not."

Ezra and I went out just the two of us plenty of times in the past, not so much when I started dating Braden. He was too jealous.

"I ordered that burger you like," I told him, finishing my drink.

"Thanks," he smiled. "Was it good?" He nodded at my now empty glass.

"Fan-freaking-tastic, but it will take more than that to get me drunk."

"Why do you want to get drunk?" He asked. "You'll only regret it in the morning when you feel sick."

"Because, for the last few years I've been nothing but responsible. Tonight," I lifted my empty glass, signaling the waitress, "I want to be a normal twenty-one year old." I answered with complete honesty. "And I know you won't try to take advantage of me in my inebriated state," I added.

He laughed, hiding his smile behind his hand.

"Also," I continued as the waitress set down a new drink, "we live together. Therefore, you can haul my drunken ass home and not have to make an extra stop. It's very considerate of me, I know. No need to praise me," I joked.

"I'm happy to see you're finally regaining your sense of humor. I was beginning to worry I was stuck with this melancholy version of you for a friend and that was really beginning to suck." He winked.

I thought winking was the most ridiculous gesture ever, but Ezra made it downright sexy.

Wait...did I just call my best friend sexy?

What did they put into this magic potion to make me think such things? I proceeded to glare at my drink.

Eh, whatever.

I picked it up and drank half, wiping my mouth on the back of my hand.

So lady like.

I grabbed my fork and put some of the nachos on the plate the waitress had brought. Ezra was already devouring his own pile.

"These are so good," I moaned, stuffing one into my mouth. This wasn't a date so I could be as messy as I wanted.

He nodded his head in agreement, wiping his hands on his napkin.

"When was the last time you ate?" He asked me, noticing how I was devouring the chips.

My nose scrunched as I thought. "Uh...breakfast. I had a cereal bar for a snack."

He glared at me. "You've only eaten once today?"

"I had a cereal bar!" I defended, gesticulating wildly with my free hand.

He shook his head as his teeth ground together. "Sadie, you can't skip meals like that."

I frowned. "I know, but I forget."

"How do you forget to eat?" His hands landed roughly on the table as he leaned forward.

I shrugged, picking up another nacho chip and eating it. "I get busy and forget how much time has passed."

He wasn't pleased by my explanation and his nostrils flared.

"I'll set a reminder in my phone," I mumbled to appease him.

He still looked doubtful.

"Look, at least I'm eating now." I pointed at my plate of nachos. Lifting my drink in the air, I added, "And drinking. Oh, alcohol, how I love thee." I downed the rest of the drink. When a frown still marred his face, I said, "Eat, drink, and be merry. Your sourpuss vibe is killing my buzz and I need this right now."

He laughed, the tension easing from his shoulders.

"Okay, I'll let it go...for now." He eyed me for a moment, letting me know that this conversation was far from over.

We'd unintentionally been leaning towards each other and jerked apart when the waitress appeared with our meals.

She set the burger in front of Ezra and a small pizza in front of me.

"Would you like another drink?" She asked me.

"Yep," I nodded eagerly. "Go ahead and bring two."

"Sadie." Ezra warned with a low growl.

"Don't listen to him," I whispered conspiratorially, "someone pissed in his cheerios this morning."

She glanced at Ezra, back to me, and then to him once more.

"Just bring her the drinks," he grumbled. "Don't make me regret this." He warned me.

"However would I do that?"

"Wow, the stars look so pretty from here."

Ezra kicked the car door closed with his booted foot. "That's because I'm carrying you."

"Look at all of them. They're so sparkly. Can I have one?" I reached my hand up and tried to grab one. I frowned. "I can't reach it. Can you get it for me?"

"You're never drinking ever again," he groaned, adjusting his hold on my body as he climbed the porch steps. "Wrap your arms around my neck," he demanded. "I have to put you down so I can get the door open."

I did as he asked and my shaky feet touched the ground. I wobbled and he wrapped an arm around my torso, holding me against his chest so that I didn't fall.

The door swung open and cold air hit my face.

"Oh, that feels good." I smiled, leaning forward and trying to get closer to the deliciously cool air.

Ezra chuckled. "Come on, up you go."

My legs were whisked out from under me once more and I tightened my hold around his neck.

"Are you carrying me across the threshold?" I asked, laughter filling the words.

"No," he groaned, "I'm carrying my drunk best friend home. And could you loosen your arms? You're choking me."

"Oh, sorry," I giggled. I leaned my head back and looked up at the ceiling as he started up the steps. "Everything looks so different like this. Oh, ew, you need to clean up there." I pointed to a cobweb.

He sighed as we reached the top of the stairs and he turned down the hallway to the guestroom.

My fingers tangled in the silky strands of his black hair as he pushed the bedroom door open with a nudge of his shoulder. "Your hair is so soft," I gasped. "Like a puppy." He snorted. "I want a puppy," I told him, my words slurring. "Can you be my puppy?" I rubbed his head as he laid me down on the bed. "I'd name my puppy Oliver. Isn't that a good name for a puppy? I think it is."

He chuckled, untangling my fingers from his hair. "Sadie, you might be the most hilarious drunk person I've ever met."

"Aw, thanks." I reached for his hair again—seriously, it was the softest thing I'd ever felt—and he grabbed my hands and held them in both of his.

"Sadie, stop," he warned.

"I want to pet the puppy!" I pouted.

"My hair is not a puppy."

"Well it sure feels like one. Could've fooled me," I huffed.

He sighed heavily and released my hands. He grabbed my shoes and began removing them.

"Are you trying to get me naked?"

"No," he glared at me, "I'm trying to get your shoe off."

"I'd be fine if you wanted to get me naked."

"Sadie," he warned.

"I haven't had sex in..." I tried to count, but my brain was too muffled to form a coherent thought. "A long time.

That should've been another tip that Braden was cheating. I'm so stupid." I smacked my forehead.

He grabbed my hand. "Don't hit yourself." His voice softened.

He finished removing my shoes and they dropped to the floor with a crash.

"What's so wrong with me?" I asked him. "Am I so repulsive?"

"Sadie, repulsive is the last thing that you are. Braden is just...well, there are no words for what Braden is."

"I used to have a crush on you," I admitted. "Shit," I slapped my hand across my mouth, "I wasn't ever supposed to tell you that. I'm never drinking again."

He chuckled and shook his head. "Yeah, you won't be drinking again if I have anything to say about it. So," he grinned, "you had a crush on me?"

"Well, yeah," I shrugged. "You're hot. Who wouldn't?"

He laughed and grabbed the blankets, trying to tuck me beneath the covers. My stomach rolled and I grabbed his wrist.

"I'm going to be sick," I warned.

"Shit," he cursed. In a lightning fast move he grabbed the small trashcan and held it over for me. He held my hair back with his free hand as my body heaved.

I panted heavily, sweat breaking out across my skin. "Yep, I'm *never* drinking again," I vowed.

He set the trashcan aside and looked me over. "Are you okay?"

"I think so." I replied, my eyes growing heavy.

"Don't go to sleep yet," he warned. "I'll be right back."

He eased out of my room and flicked the light on in the hallway. I heard him fumbling in the bathroom and the sink running.

A minute later his shadow darkened the doorway and he strolled forward with two cloths in his hand. He crouched down beside me, his dark eyes full of worry.

Ever so gently he cleaned my mouth and then laid the clean cloth across my forehead.

"I'm not done yet." He warned with a pointed look.

"I'll try not to fall asleep, but no promises."

He left me again and the stairs creaked as he went back downstairs.

I rolled onto my side, forcing my heavy lids to stay open.

Sleep. I needed sleep, and maybe some duct tape for my mouth before any more truths slipped past my lips.

When Ezra returned he had a glass of water and two pills.

"Here, take this." He thrust the pills out to me.

I took them and the water. I set the glass on the table and he glared at me.

"What?"

"You need to drink all of the water."

"Ezra." His name sounded like a whine.

He crossed his arms over his lean chest and stared down at me. God, he was fucking relentless.

With a groan I picked up the glass once more and downed it.

"Happy?" I asked him, thrusting the empty glass into his outstretched hand.

"Immensely."

He turned to leave and I grabbed his wrist. His steps halted and he looked down at me, his eyes shielded by his shaggy hair.

"Stay with me," I begged. "I don't want to be alone."

Indecision warred on his face.

"Please?" My hand wrapped around his, tugging with as much force as I could muster, which admittedly wasn't much in my current state.

"Why can I never say no to you?" He mumbled, looking up at the ceiling as if it held all the answers in the world.

"Because I'm irresistible?" I supplied.

He chuckled, his shoulders shaking. "Yeah. That must be it."

He tugged his hand from my hold and started to leave. I let out a small sound of protest and he glanced back at me.

"I have to turn the hall light off." He pointed.

"Oh."

He did just that and darkness blanketed the space. I blinked my eyes, trying to get them to adjust to the now darkened room.

He left my bedroom door open and kicked off his boots before removing his shirt. Sadly, his jeans stayed on. I might've pouted. I really hoped it was too dark for him to see that.

He padded over to the other side of the bed and climbed in behind me, pulling the covers up and over us both.

I rolled over onto my other side to face him. He lay on his back and turned his head to look at me.

"Go to sleep," he warned, his voice a low gravel.

"I don't want to sleep," I sulked.

"You need to."

"You're such a buzz kill." I proceeded to poke his face.

He pushed my hand away. "And you're drunk."

"Really? I hadn't noticed."

He shook his head and put his hand over his mouth to hide his laugh. I sat up a bit, propping my body weight on my elbow.

"How come you've never made a move on me?" I asked, the words tumbling out of my mouth. "Why don't you like me as more than a friend? I admitted to having a crush on you, but you've always been indifferent."

He reached up and grasped my cheek. I startled at the gesture and my small gasp echoed through the room.

"I'm far from indifferent," he growled lowly. "Trust me, there have been plenty of times where I wanted to make a move, as you put it, but I never did because your friendship is far more important to me than a quick fuck."

I reached out with my other hand, laying it flat on his chest over his heart. "So, that's all you thought we'd be if we moved past the friend stage? A quick fuck?"

I didn't know why I felt so hurt by his words.

He put his hand over mine and swallowed thickly. "We were both young and the chances of us making it as a couple seemed slim to me. I wasn't going to throw our friendship away to test the waters, so to speak. And then you started dating Braden. But if you really must know, I am insanely attracted to you." His voice lowered to a husky whisper.

My breath came out in small little pants. I wanted desperately to lean down and kiss him, but something told me that he didn't want that, and also I'd yet to brush my teeth after vomiting so that was a kiss no one wanted.

"You are?" I asked stupidly, blinking my eyes rapidly like he was a mirage that might disappear at any second.

"I don't lie."

I continued to stare down at him, not sure what to do with this information.

Ezra made the decision for me. He pushed me down lightly and pulled me against his chest.

"Sleep, pretty girl," he commanded.

I didn't know how he could possibly expect me to sleep after he told me he was attracted to me. The man was lucky I hadn't thrown my panties across the room and mauled him with my vagina.

His fingertips brushed lightly against my neck as he pushed away my hair. My skin prickled with Goosebumps when his lips replaced his fingers in the barest of touches. My eyes fluttered closed and a happy sigh fell from my lips. Ezra was never so bold, and I wondered if he was only being this way because he believed I'd be too drunk to remember in the morning.

I would remember though. There was no way I could forget this.

CHAPTER SEVEN

DAYLIGHT SPILLED ACROSS my body and I groaned as it penetrated my closed eyelids.

"It's time to get up." A hand smacked my foot. "It's noon already."

"Go away," I groaned, burying my face in my pillow.

"No."

"You're killing my buzz."

"Your buzz wore off hours ago, now you're just hung over. Get up, we have to go."

"I'm not going anywhere." I hugged the pillow tighter to my body and slowly peeled open my eyes. I was supposed to do paperwork at the store today since I put it off last night, but there was no way I was doing that now. "Gah!" I quickly covered my eyes with a hand. "Turn the fucking ceiling light off," I spat.

"No," he said again. I really hated that word. "Get out of bed and then *maybe* I will."

"You're evil."

"Get out of bed, Sadie. Seriously, we have to go in..." He looked down at the shiny watch on his wrist. "Thirty minutes."

"Where are we going?" I whined, still not making a move to get out of bed.

"Mathias called, he and Remy are moving into their new house today and he needs me to help."

I reached out and poked his chest. "You said he needs *your* help, not mine."

He captured my hand in his. "And *I* want you to come. Everyone will be there. Come on."

I pried my hand away from his hold. "Fine, but I'm going to need more Advil."

"I can get that," he chuckled. "Anything else?"

"My sunglasses."

He grabbed them off the dresser and handed them to me. I slipped them on and sighed in relief. "Much better."

"Shower and get dressed."

"Do I stink?" I asked, lifting my arm to smell.

He laughed and paused in the doorway. "You smell like a bar."

"Lovely," I sighed.

His boots slapped against the steps as he went downstairs, leaving me alone.

It took more effort than it should have to shower and get dressed. I chose to forgo drying my hair and instead tied it back in a messy bun. Even though I felt like shit I took the time to apply my makeup. Nobody wanted to see me looking like this. It was scary. And Mathias was the kind of guy to make a rude remark. I didn't think he honestly meant to be so rude to people, he was just crass and didn't think before he spoke.

I met Ezra downstairs and he already had a glass of water waiting with Advil. I'd tell him he was a saint, but he did wake me up so he was still on my shit-list for the moment.

I took the pills and emptied the glass of water. I poured some more water into the glass while Ezra fiddled with the toaster. After a minute two browned pieces of toast popped up.

He buttered them both, sticking one in his mouth, and put the other on a plate before handing it to me.

I waved it away. My stomach was too queasy to eat.

"Come on." He set it in front of me, chewing on his. I swore the thing was gone in three bites. "It's just toast. It'll help."

"You know what else will help?" I asked, pushing my sunglasses further up my nose. "If I poke you in the eyeball with a fork."

"I don't think rendering me eyeless would be helpful in this situation." He washed his hands in the sink with his back turned to me. I was tempted to pelt the buttered toast at his back, but I refrained.

He turned back around, crossing his arms over his chest. "Eat, Sadie. You're holding up progress."

I rolled my eyes and stuck the toast in my mouth, making a very dramatic show of taking a bite. Crumbs dotted the corner of my mouth and I wiped them away.

"Happy?" I asked.

"For now."

He smacked his hand on the counter. "Eat in the car. Mathias has already texted me ten times in the last five minutes."

I followed Ezra out to the garage and paused. "When can I get my car?"

"Later," he answered vaguely.

"You're testing my patience," I muttered under my breath.

He merely chuckled at me.

I was glad that he was still acting like himself though, after the truths we shared last nights.

And those truths...well, they had me thinking.

Thinking things I should not be thinking, that is.

Like me, and Ezra, naked and rolling beneath the sheets.

Yep, my thoughts should *so* not be going there. Especially after I had *just* ended my engagement to the Douche Lord.

Damn you treacherous thoughts!

Maybe I was still drunk...yeah, that explained it.

We didn't talk on the way to Mathias' house. Frankly, my head couldn't take it. How he expected me to act like a civilized human being today was beyond me.

Ezra turned into the neighborhood, one I recognized since it was where his parent's house was.

"Mathias bought a house in your parent's neighborhood?" I asked, not bothering to hide the shock from my voice.

He nodded. "Yeah, a few streets over. He and Remy liked the fact that the houses were a nice size, but not too large, with decent sized lots. You know how Mathias is, he didn't want to be too close to neighbors."

I laughed at that. Mathias Wade might've been the lead singer of Willow Creek, but he was not a people person.

Ezra turned into a driveway, and I gaped at the pretty home. It wasn't what I was expecting. The driveway wound up a hill, where the house sat overlooking the street.

The two-story home was covered in light gray siding with white trim. It had a gorgeous wraparound porch with a swing. There was a glass double front door and the windows were large, giving it an airy appearance. The grass was so lush and green that it reminded me of a golf course, and pretty flowers were planted across the front.

A moving truck was parked on the driveway and guys unloaded furniture and boxes.

"Why do they need our help again?"

He sighed. "It's Remy and Mathias."

I didn't know much about Remy, but I did know Mathias, so that was enough of an answer for me.

Maddox's sports car was parked in the grass and a large pickup truck that I knew belonged to Hayes took up another space.

Ezra put his car in park, blocking the exit of the driveway.

Before I could ask him why he was doing that and not parking in the grass like the other guys, he said, "Mathias is going to shit a brick when he sees that those two idiots parked in the grass. Just wait."

I managed a small laugh and then winced when my head pounded. I rubbed my temples, trying to get the throbbing to go away. I really shouldn't have drunk so much. Lesson learned.

Ezra slipped out of the vehicle and I was forced to follow him.

Immediately we stepped into drama.

"I'm going to kill him!" Remy shouted—I recognized her immediately with her platinum blonde hair and signature red lipstick. "I swear to God I'm going to smother him with a fucking pillow." She stomped down the porch steps, Emma hurrying behind her. "Oh," Remy paused suddenly, her hand falling to her small baby bump, "sorry baby, mommy said a bad word. Please forgive me, but your dad is being a pain in my ass. Butt. I meant butt." She frowned at Emma, not noticing our presence yet. "Between Mathias and me our baby's first word is going to be 'fuck'. This kid is doomed."

"Hopefully 'mom' will be a close second in the word department." Emma shrugged.

"Eh," Remy shrugged, "second will probably be 'asshole' because that's what I keep shouting at Mathias. He is driving me nuts."

"Ahem," Ezra cleared his throat as we approached them.

Remy glanced away from Emma and sighed in relief. "Oh, thank God you're here. Maybe between you and Maddox you can talk some sense into my husband. He's trying to bubble wrap the fucking walls." She winced and mumbled, "Crap, I did it again." Taking a deep breath, she continued, "Anyway, he's going way overboard with this whole baby-proofing thing and it's just...a nightmare." She rolled her eyes. "And he's getting in the way of the movers, so they're getting mad."

Ezra saluted her. "I'm on it. We'll tag team him."

I watched him leave, disappearing into the house. I was left alone with Remy and Emma—and the moving guys that were wrestling with a massive dining room table.

"I'm sorry you had to walk into all of this drama," Remy sighed, her hand rubbing absentmindedly against her stomach. "Mathias has been... extremely overprotective since we found out that I was pregnant." She glanced at Emma and then me. "Do you know the other day he got mad at me for picking up my *cat*. He thinks if I pick up anything that weighs more than five pounds that the baby is going to fall out of my vagina. I've got news for him, the process of childbirth, sadly, isn't that simple."

Emma laughed and patted Remy's shoulder in a familiar gesture. "He loves you."

"He's smothering me with his love. Seriously, I'm suffocating. And he will too if he doesn't stop."

I snorted and then burst into laughter, Remy and Emma joining in too.

"Ow," I groaned when my head pounded with renewed vigor.

Note to self: Stop laughing while hung over.

"Are you okay?" Emma asked.

"Yeah," I nodded, closing my eyes behind my sunglasses as I tried to get the blinking white lights to go away, "just a little too much to drink last night."

"Why'd you have too much to drink?"

"Because I wanted to," I replied. "Anyway," I rubbed my hands together, "what can I do to help?"

"Whoa, whoa, whoa." Emma shook her head. "Who did you go out with?"

"How do you know I went out? I could've gotten shit-faced at Ezra's place and passed out in my vomit on the kitchen floor."

"Did you?" She asked doubtfully.

"Well, no." I admitted.

"Then answer my previous question."

"Ezra took me out." I squirmed, wanting to run back and hide in the safety of the SUV.

"And let you get drunk? Did you have sex?"

"No!" I screamed a little too loudly, causing the moving guys to turn and look at us. "Why are you so convinced that there's something going on with us? I *just* broke up with Braden."

Emma stared at me with a calculated look as if she was measuring the weight of her words. "I see the way you look at him." She said the words slowly, gauging my reaction to them. I gave her nothing and remained stone faced. "The way you've *always* looked at him," she reiterated. "I'm not sure if you even realize it."

"I realize that you're absolutely insane. He's my *friend.* Nothing more." I pushed the sunglasses further up my nose, hoping my cheeks hadn't reddened with the lie. Only minutes ago I'd been picturing him naked, and now I was having to steadfastly defend the fact that were only friends. It was the truth though. Ezra didn't want to take things further. He'd said as much last night.

"Who are you trying to fool?" She raised a single brow. "Me or yourself?"

"Nobody," I replied easily.

"Mhmm," she mumbled in disbelief.

"Haven't you ever heard of friends with benefits?" Remy asked, interjecting herself into the conversation.

I choked on a laugh. "Of course, but me and Ezra? No way."

"Crazier things have happened." Remy shrugged. "I mean, I married that asshole." She pointed at Mathias who stormed down the porch steps and proceeded to yell at the movers. From what I could gather they'd scratched a piece of furniture.

Behind him a large dog and cat bound out the door, down the steps, running through the yard. It didn't look like the dog was chasing the cat, but more like they were playing.

"Mathias!" Remy yelled, heading over to her husband. "You let Shiloh and Percy out again. They're going to get hit by a car."

Mathias turned his attention from the movers to Remy, his hands resting on his hips. "Your cat is a fucking demon, Rem. You have to let it out once a day so its toxicity doesn't pollute the house. It's in the *Taking Care of a Demonic Creature Handbook*. You should read it. It's also how I've learned to deal with you." He grinned.

"You are so lucky that I love you more than I hate you."
She laughed, fighting a smile.

"Back at ya." He smiled lovingly at her and grasped her waist, pulling her in for a kiss.

I quickly looked away when it became heated.

"No surprise why they have a baby on the way, right?" Emma laughed at the expression on my face.

"None at all." I shook my head.

"We'll leave them to it," she said, starting towards the moving truck.

I followed, happy to have something to do. She ventured onto the truck and grabbed a box labeled KITCHEN and handed it to me before grabbing another for herself.

Mathias and Remy were still making out in the front yard while their pets played. Maybe Mathias would be so distracted he wouldn't notice the vehicles parked in the grass.

Emma knew the layout of the house already, so I trailed behind her to the back where the kitchen sat overlooking the backyard. There was a large pool and since the lot was so high up you could practically see the whole town from here. It was spectacular.

Emma sat her box down on the island in the middle of the open kitchen, and I did the same.

"This house is gorgeous," I murmured, looking around in awe.

The floors were a dark, luxurious hardwood. The walls were all painted a neutral cream color that brightened up the space. The cabinets in the kitchen were also cream colored with a gold-brown granite countertop. The kitchen even had a built in bench with a table. Across from the kitchen was the family room that was currently in disarray. To our left was an archway where I figured the dining room was meant to be.

"Yeah, it's amazing." Emma grabbed a knife off the counter and cut into the tape. She handed me the knife before opening the flaps on the box.

I opened my box and discovered it was full of plates.

"Just pick a cabinet and start putting stuff away. They don't care where it goes, and Remy wasn't kidding about Mathias freaking out over her lifting things. He'd bust a vein in his forehead if she was in here trying to organize those." She nodded her head at the plates I now grasped in my hands.

"It seems like they'd want some say," I started.

She gave me a look. "I've been here since seven, so trust me when I say it doesn't matter."

I looked at her in disbelief. "Since seven? But you hate mornings."

"I know," she groaned. "Maddox bribed me."

"With what?" I asked, mystified.

She cracked a smile. "Sexual favors."

I laughed, shaking my head. The naïve little Emma I once knew was no more.

I carried the plates over to the counter by the sink and opened one of the upper cabinets. I carefully stacked the plates on a shelf—terrified I'd chip them. The last thing I wanted to do was break something that wasn't mine. Except Braden's nose. I'd enjoy breaking that.

Once those were put away I went to work on organizing the utensils in a drawer. Remy joined us, sitting on the floor to put away dishtowels. The guys argued by the staircase about how to install a baby gate.

"I don't know why he insists on putting that up now," Remy muttered, folding a towel. "We still have four months until the baby comes, and he won't walk for a while."

"*He?*" Emma shrieked, dropping the cup she was holding. Luckily it was plastic and didn't break.

Remy's smile was blinding. "Yeah, it's a boy. We just found out this week."

"I'm so excited." Emma bounced on the balls of her feet. "There's going to be a Willow Creek baby!"

I looked at her like she was crazy.

She frowned when she saw my expression. "Sorry," she mumbled, "I'm just a little excitable these days. I think being cooped up on tour was really bothering me. So," she turned back to Remy, "names? Spill."

Remy bit her lip and peered around the edge of the counter where the guys stood.

"We already have a name picked out, but Mathias doesn't want us to tell anyone the gender or name, in case it gets back to the media. He said this was a moment in his life he refused to share with the world until he had to." She shrugged.

"You're really not going to tell me?" Emma put her hands up in a begging motion. "Please, please, oh please tell me."

Remy sighed. "Give me one of those." She snapped her fingers and pointed to the knives I was currently organizing.

"Uh, why?" I asked, holding the knives against my chest like she might maul me for them at any second.

"Because I'm pregnant and I said so," she huffed. I reluctantly handed her one. "If I'm going to tell you guys, and go against my husband's wishes that *no one* know, then you're going to have to swear a blood oath."

Emma held her hand out.

"Are you crazy?" I asked Remy.

"No," she drew out the word, "I'm a Mama Bear protecting my cub, work with me here."

I grumbled, but held my hand out.

She nicked the meaty part of my hand, Emma's, and her own. She joined our hands together and peeked around the corner at the guys one last time.

"You both have to swear on your lives that you'll tell *no one* the name of the baby or the gender. And by no one, I mean these words better not even be muttered to your reflection in the mirror. Got it?"

"Got it." I said.

"You have to swear." Remy huffed in exasperation.

"I *swear.*" I had to resist the urge not to roll my eyes at her melodramatics.

"I swear," Emma piped in, vibrating with excitement.

Remy smiled, satisfied with our vow. "There are paper towels over there if your hand is still bleeding."

I looked at mine and saw that it had already dried since the cut was so small. Emma made no move either.

"Come on," Emma pleaded, "the suspense is killing me."

Remy laughed and rubbed her stomach. "His name is Liam Maxwell Wade."

"Awwww," Emma clapped her hands together, "I love it! It's such a strong name."

"We think so too." Remy beamed.

"It's adorable," I piped in, because I felt like I needed to say something.

"Thanks." Remy smiled in my direction. "Now get back to work," she shooed us, "Mathias will get suspicious."

Emma reluctantly returned to organizing the pots and pans while I finished with the utensils.

Several hours later all of us were tired and starving, so we took a break and ordered pizza.

We sat around on the floor of the family room, using paper towels as our plates. Emma and Maddox talked quietly together. Remy and Mathias were absorbed in their own little world as Mathias sang lovingly to her stomach in-between bites of pizza.

That left Ezra, Hayes, and me as the odd ones out.

Good times.

I sat sandwiched between the guys, eating my pizza in small dainty bites compared to the way they gobbled it.

Ezra stretched out his long legs and picked a piece of pepperoni off his pizza. He handed it to me and I gobbled it up greedily. I loved pepperoni.

"Thanks." I bumped his shoulder with mine.

"So, how have you been?" Hayes asked. "I haven't seen you since..." He scrunched up his nose, thinking. "New Year's? Whoa, has it really been that long?" He muttered the last part in disbelief.

I turned to the band's guitar player.

Josh Hayes was a good-looking guy, with angular cheekbones and sandy dirty blond hair that he kept swept away from his face. He was put together in a way that looked effortless, but you knew it actually took him quite some time to achieve it.

"Yeah, that long." I took a sip of orange soda.

He shook his head in disbelief. "What have you been up to?"

"Catching my fiancé fucking someone else."

Hayes shook his head. "Uh, yeah, Ezra told me." He awkwardly scratched the back of his head and glanced over at Ezra, as if he was worried he wasn't supposed to admit to knowing this bit of information.

"I'm pretty sure the whole town knows," I mumbled, spinning the white soda bottle cap between my fingers.

"I'm sure it's not the whole town." He cracked a grin. "I bet those old ladies that Maddox knits with don't know."

"Hey!" Maddox glared, pointing a finger at Hayes. "Those ladies are my friends, don't diss them."

Hayes raised his hands in surrender, laughing under his breath.

"They're sweet old ladies," Maddox continued, "who not only teach me how to knit *all the things*, but they also bake me pie. Do you have pie, Hayes? I think not!"

We all busted out laughing, even Maddox.

I wiped tears away from eyes and said, "If you had a super power you'd be The Knitter."

"And I'd knit my little minion creatures." He grinned.

"Oh God," Hayes laughed, "do you realize if our fans heard half the shit we talk about they'd realize what a bunch of nerds we are."

"Speak for yourselves." Mathias glared, huffing under his breath.

"Dude," Hayes waved a hand in Mathias' direction, "you wear fucking suspenders and look at those glasses you have on. You're a nerd too."

Mathias frowned and whispered something in Remy's ear. She said something back and he kissed her, a smile tugging up his lips. In all the time I'd known the guys I'd never, not once, used the word *happy* to describe Mathias, but he definitely was now.

"So," Hayes turned his attention back to me, "now that you're single we should go out." He grinned, waggling his brows.

Ezra stiffened beside me, but said nothing.

"Uh..." I started. I had no idea what to say.

"Come on," he said, when I took too long to speak, "I don't bite and I hear I'm a lot of fun."

I laughed at that. "I don't know."

"Give a guy a chance, Sadie," he pleaded, grinning at me, "don't bruise my ego. It's a gentle, easily hurt, thing. It's just dinner."

"Fine," I agreed. I wasn't ready to date, but I figured one night out with Hayes could be fun. He was a nice guy.

Ezra stood up and threw away his pizza crust, mumbling that he was going to the bathroom.

"Did I piss him off?" Hayes asked. "If y'all have something going on I don't mean to butt in."

"No, nothing's going on," I said quickly.

Hayes seemed appeased by my words and smiled broadly. "Good. I'll call you."

Across from where we sat Emma's gaze seared me to the spot. She was mad.

I turned to look at her and mouthed, "What?"

She didn't respond and instead continued to glare.

Ezra returned to the room, not making eye contact with anyone. "I have a few things I need to do." Finally his gaze dropped to me. I couldn't read anything in his brown eyes. They were flat. Emotionless. "I'll drop you off at your car."

"Uh...yeah, okay." I stood up, putting the slice of pizza back in the box that I hadn't finished yet.

Hayes stood up too, looking between Ezra and me. "I can take you to your car," he said.

I knew he was only trying to be helpful, but I really wanted to kick him in the shin right now.

Ezra smiled weakly. "Great, Hayes can take you then." He clapped his hands together and somehow it felt like a gesture that he was washing his hands of me.

Before I could respond Ezra turned sharply on his heel and stalked out of the house.

I was left there wondering what I had done to piss him off.

"I'm really sorry," Hayes apologized yet again, "I didn't mean to make things awkward for you. You said there was nothing going on with you guys, and he said he had somewhere he had to go. I was trying to be helpful," he rambled.

"I know," I assured him. "I don't know what's going on with Ezra."

While Ezra might've been one of my closest friends, there were still times where I felt like I didn't know him at all. Today, being one of those days. Sometimes he retreated into himself and there was no prying his thoughts past his lips.

Hayes parked his truck beside my car and turned the volume down on the radio. "So," he started, "it's still okay if I call you?"

"Yeah, that's fine." I laughed lightly, reaching for the door.

"You don't feel weird about it, right? I mean, I know you just broke up with Braden, so I don't want you to feel pressured."

His sincerity was endearing.

"Just dinner?" I confirmed.

"Only dinner," he nodded, "and then we go from there."

"I'm okay with that." I gave him a small smile.

He nodded. "I'll see you soon."

"Bye."

I slipped out of the vehicle and into my store. I was feeling better and determined to put a dent into finishing up my paperwork and doing inventory.

Hours passed and when I finally left it was after six in the evening.

Once again, the whole day had managed to go by without me realizing it.

Ezra wasn't at his house when I got there.

He wasn't there when I made dinner either.

He still wasn't home when I went to bed.

And I couldn't help feeling that his absence was my fault.

CHAPTER EIGHT

I SAT AT the kitchen island, eating a bowl of cereal, and flipping through a magazine when Ezra walked into his house.

I glanced over at him, noting that he was wearing different clothes.

I quickly looked back at the magazine, refusing to let him know that I'd been waiting anxiously for him to return. I'd worried something bad had happened to him, but after three unanswered texts I'd stopped bugging him—knowing that if he'd been hurt Maddox and Emma wouldn't have kept me out of the loop.

"Did you have a good night?" I asked.

He stepped into the kitchen, dropping his keys and wallet on the countertop. "Not in the way you're implying."

"I wasn't implying anything." I shoveled a mouthful of Cheerios into my mouth.

He propped his elbows on the counter and stared down at me with those intense dark eyes. "Yes, you were."

I shrugged. "You were gone all night. What you did isn't any of my business."

And it wasn't.

I didn't care either.

That was a lie. I did care, even though I shouldn't.

My feelings seemed to be swirling in a whirlpool and I couldn't make sense of them. I'd always *liked* Ezra and there'd been attraction mixed into that, but I'd never planned to act on it. This jealousy I felt at the possibility that he spent the night with a woman was ridiculous. I'd not only just ended my engagement, but I'd also agreed to go on a date with Hayes, so I shouldn't have been thinking of Ezra in that way at all.

I was also wondering if I'd agreed to go on a date with Hayes too soon after breaking up with Braden. But when was the right time to move on? Did I have to live my life on some invisible timeline that was respectable to what people found appropriate? I didn't want to spend the next six months, or year, sniveling over the end of my engagement to a man I now realized never even owned my heart. I *wanted* to move on and live my life the way I chose.

"Sadie, did you hear me?"

"Huh? What?" I snapped my head up, my gaze colliding with his.

"I stayed at my parent's house." He turned and grabbed a mug before pouring himself a cup of coffee. He leaned against the counter once more, arching his brow as he waited for a response from me.

"Did you not come home because of me?" I asked, swirling my spoon through the milk. Suddenly, I wasn't very hungry anymore. "This is your house, Ezra, and I don't want to keep you from it."

He pinched the bridge of his nose. "That had nothing to do with you and everything to do with me," he sighed.

"Is this because I told Hayes I'd go out with him?" I asked, lowering my head and staring down at the cereal like it was the most interesting thing I'd ever seen.

"Yes. No. I don't know." He mumbled, running a hand nervously through his hair. "Things are complicated." His jaw snapped together and he glared at the nearby window.

"How so?" I prompted.

"You're my best fucking friend." He slammed his palms down on the countertop. "It can't be more than that. I told you I wouldn't lose you, and I meant that." He dumped out his coffee in the sink and muttered, "I'm going to shower," before heading upstairs.

I sat dumbfounded, not knowing what to do or say.

So, I did nothing.

Several days passed, and Ezra kept his distance from me.

Boys could be so incredibly frustrating, and they thought girls were complicated creatures.

Hayes called and texted me some, but we'd yet to go on an actual date. Although, we'd made plans to go out for dinner next Friday, so it was still happening.

Now, it was the Fourth of July and everybody was headed to a party at the Wentworth's. The Wentworth's were a wealthy family in town, and Hayes happened to be related to them.

I rode with Ezra, but the entire car ride was filled with awkward silence.

I didn't know how to fix this, mostly because I didn't know what I'd done wrong in the first place.

He'd made it clear that he didn't want a relationship with me beyond friendship, and frankly I didn't feel that I was ready for more with anyone. I already regretted saying yes to a date with Hayes, but I hated to let him down now. Besides, one date wouldn't hurt anything.

We arrived at the mansion and I took a deep breath. Things had changed a lot since the last time I was here. Then, I'd been engaged and blissfully ignorant.

Ezra got out of his car and I was forced to follow, more awkward silence descending upon us.

Normally, it was a comfortable silence between us, now it felt like he was building an invisible wall between us to block me out.

I followed him to the backyard. Although, calling it a *yard* seemed an injustice. The space was expansive with a beautiful pool and the greenest grass I'd ever seen. There were several cabanas set up so that you could escape the boiling hot July sun and servers walked around with trays of food and drinks.

A gust of wind blew by and my skirt billowed around my legs.

"Hey, you guys are here!" Hayes waved from a nearby cabana. He stood up and grabbed two beers from a cooler before jogging over to join us. He only wore a pair of navy board shorts slung low on his lean hips. His chest and arms were sculpted and on the start of one arm was a half-sleeve tattoo. Dark sunglasses covered his eyes, but nothing could hide his blinding smile. I felt bad that his smile did nothing to me, but it wasn't...I refused to finish the thought.

Hayes held out a beer to Ezra and then me, the caps already popped.

"Thanks," I said, taking it. It wasn't my favorite beer, but it was the thought that counted, right? Although, the way Ezra glared at the drink in my hand I knew he believed differently.

"I'm okay," Ezra replied, waving away the beer, "maybe later."

Hayes shrugged, unfazed by Ezra's dismissal.

"I'm going to see Maddox." Ezra pointed and strode off, leaving me alone with his band's guitar player.

I forced a smile for Hayes and tried to give him my attention, but my gaze kept drifting in the direction of Ezra.

"How have you been?" He asked, lifting his beer to his lips.

"Uh...good," I replied, shielding my eyes from the sun. "Busy with the store."

"'Course," he nodded. "Fuck," he rubbed his forehead, "it's blazing hot out here. I'm getting back in the pool. You want to?" He tossed a thumb over his shoulder at the crystal blue water.

"Sure." I shrugged, not knowing what else to say.

I'd worn my bikini underneath my skirt and tank top so I followed Hayes to the cabana he'd commandeered and stripped them off. My bikini top was bright orange, flowing down in a triangle cut. The bottoms were orange and blue zig zags that tied at the sides.

Hayes' cousin, Trace, occupied one of the lounge chairs with his baby son sitting in his lap. The baby—who was probably old enough to walk now—was dressed in a pair of pale blue plaid swim trunks with oversized red sunglasses perched on his tiny nose. The baby blew bubbles, spit dripping down his lips and onto his chubby stomach. Trace chuckled and kissed the baby's cheek before looking up at me.

"Sadie, right?" He asked.

"Yeah," I nodded.

I hadn't seen Trace Wentworth since the disaster last New Year's. He had been absent from the ballroom when Ezra and Braden got into a fight, but he'd caught Braden and me in a hallway on his way back from putting his son to bed. Braden had been shouting at me, making everything out to be my fault, and I'd stood there, mute, as I took his verbal assault. Trace interrupted, cutting Braden down with quick, sharp words. Braden didn't yell at me again that night—he still bitched though.

"How have you been?" He asked. "Where's...?" He paused, waiting for me to fill in the blanks.

"Sleeping with someone else," I replied, not batting an eye. I didn't even care anymore.

Trace winced. "Sorry?"

"You said that like a question." My lips quirked into a half smile as I folded my skirt and top to tuck into my bag.

"Well," he paused, seeming to search for the right words, "he didn't seem very nice, which wouldn't be much of a loss in my book." He shrugged.

The baby made a noise and Trace started playing peek-a-boo with him.

"Yeah, I'm glad it's over." It was the first time I'd said the words aloud and I felt a stirring in my gut at the truth in them. I was better off without Braden. Bigger and better things were headed my way, and when the time was right I would fall in love again, for real this time.

Trace rubbed his finger against his son's lips so that the baby made a whirring noise. Turning to look at me, he said, "I'm happy to hear that."

"Are you ready?" Hayes asked. He'd slipped off somewhere and I hadn't even noticed he was gone.

"Yeah."

I put the untouched beer back in the cooler and followed him to the pool. I'd put on sunscreen before I left the house, so I wasn't worried about getting burnt.

It was a humid day and sweat already clung to my neck as I stepped into the cool water. It felt amazing against my heated skin.

Hayes chose to forgo the steps leading into the pool, and instead padded over to the diving board. Before he stepped up on it he rubbed his hands together and blew into them. He pointed in my direction and grinned. "Cheer for me!"

"I've got my Pom Poms at the ready." I shook my fists in a mock cheer.

He chuckled and stepped up onto the board. It wobbled with his weight.

He bounced several times before soaring into the air, doing a somersault, and diving into the water.

When he surfaced he swished his wet hair away from his eyes while I cheered. That had been impressive. I'd been expecting a belly flop.

He swam over to me and a dimple pierced his cheek when he smiled. “Some party, huh?” He asked, looking around.

“They go all out,” I commented, taking in all of the decorations and guests. I didn’t know how they knew so many people. “Are your parent’s here?” I asked.

I knew Hayes was related to the Wentworth’s, Trace being his cousin, but I’d never actually met his parents.

“Nah,” he said, pushing his wet hair away from his blue eyes.

“You’re kind of a lone wolf, aren’t you?”

He chuckled. “I am, but they’re on vacation in Hawaii. I sent them there for their anniversary.”

“That was sweet of you,” I commented, swimming over to the side of the pool and resting my arms on the concrete side. I kicked my legs out behind me as Hayes joined me, mimicking my position.

“I figure I owe them.” He smiled. “They put up with all of my teenage angst and paid for my guitar lessons.”

“I guess those definitely paid off.”

“They did.” He smiled, squinting against the sunlight. He stretched his palms out on the concrete and I noted the callouses on his hands. Ezra had similar ones. They came from all of the hours of playing the string instruments.

I’d asked Ezra if they hurt once and he said it looked worse than it felt.

"How was your tour?" I asked.

"Fun," he grinned.

I chose not to comment. I'd heard stories of what Hayes did on tour and most of them involved him getting naked with groupies.

"I wish I could've gone to a show." I'd been planning to attend their concert in D.C. at the Verizon Center, and maybe two others in Virginia, during their Coming Home tour, but after the blow up at New Year's I'd decided it was best not to go. I'd seen them in concert plenty of times, though, and the excited rush I felt never diminished.

"There's always next time." Hayes winked, his arm bumping into mine as he drew closer to me.

"Yeah—" I started to say, but the word quickly turned into a scream when someone cannonballed into the pool right behind me, drenching my upper body which had remained dry up until this point. I turned, ready to go off on the ignorant asshole, when Ezra surfaced beside me. "Ezra?" I asked. "What the hell are you doing?"

He shook his head, sending water droplets flying. "I was hot, so I'm cooling off."

I was tempted to shove him under water. I glared at him, my tongue working behind my closed mouth as I tried to form words. "You're ridiculous," I finally settled on. With an apologetic smile thrown in Hayes' direction, I said, "Excuse me."

I swam to the steps and climbed out of the pool. I rang out my hair, heading for the side of the house. I needed a moment to collect myself before I hit my best friend. His odd behavior the past few days, coupled with his obvious attempt to disrupt my conversation with Hayes, was more than enough to piss me off. And let's face it, with all the shit thrown my way lately I was already a little testy.

I'd barely rounded the house when a warm hand caught my elbow. Tiny little pinpricks zinged down my spine and I knew before I turned around who would be standing there.

"Let me go." I jerked my arm from his grasp and he did.

I glared at Ezra, letting him see the anger simmering in my eyes.

His bronzed chest glimmered in the sunlight from the reflection of the water droplets and his flowered board shorts hung dangerously low on his hips, enhancing the V shaped muscle that disappeared beneath along with the trail of dark hair.

"What do you think you're doing?" I snapped at him, my tone venomous as I crossed my arms over my chest. "Because from where I'm standing you're acting like a five year old."

He looked away from me, a muscle in his jaw ticking. He turned back, lowering his face into his hands. He let out a small groan. "I don't know what the fuck I'm doing," he admitted.

"You cannot tell me that you want nothing more than friendship from me and then get into a pissing contest. This isn't high school. This is my *life*." I stared him down, daring him to dispute me. "I've been through a lot in the last few years, especially the last few weeks, and I don't need to be worried about my best friend hating me for trying to rebuild my life."

"I know," he hung his head in shame, "I'm sorry."

"I'll call my brother tomorrow and see if I can crash on his couch. I'll be out of your way," I vowed. I felt like living with him was only serving to bother him more. The close quarters were wearing thin for both of us because they only served to intensify the attraction between us.

"No," he said adamantly, shaking his head, "that's not necessary. I'll get my shit together. I promise."

I stared at him, calculating the sincerity in his words. Finally, I nodded. "Okay, I believe you." Anytime Ezra had made me a promise in the past he'd always kept it.

He swallowed thickly and took a deep breath. His lips lifted in a slow smile of relief. "Let's pretend the last few days didn't happen."

"I can do that." I smiled and his shoulders relaxed.

He rubbed his hands together and pointed over his shoulder. "I guess we should get back over there."

I nodded and followed him. We'd no more than rounded the house until we bumped into Hayes. He gave us each a sheepish smile and rubbed the back of his head.

"I thought I should come check on you in case you guys were trying to claw each other's eyes out or something." He shrugged, letting his hand drop.

I lifted my hands and wiggled my fingers. "No claws. See?" I joked, hoping to ease the tension.

It seemed to help as both of the guys relaxed.

"I'm going to go see Emma." I nodded towards the cabanas. Before either of them could reply I ran off. I hoped if I left them alone for a bit that it would help ease the awkwardness between them that was my fault.

I found Emma and Maddox in one of the various cabanas along with Remy and Mathias.

Remy and Mathias shared one of the lounge chairs with her sitting in front of him. Mathias rubbed her shoulders and she relaxed against him.

Maddox and Emma occupied two of the other chairs, quietly talking together. They looked up when I entered and I grabbed one of the regular chairs and pulled it over to Emma's side.

Her blonde curly hair was piled on top of her head in a messy bun and she was wearing a cute pale blue floral bikini set. The top came down farther on her midriff, reminding me of a corset.

"We saw what happened." She said immediately, refusing to let me skirt over the events of a few minutes ago.

I sighed, propping my feet up on her lounger. She made no move to push them away.

I sat back, weighing my words. “You know Hayes asked me on a date,” I started, “and Ezra has been weird since then. This was the culmination of that. I think everything’s settled now, though.” I shrugged.

“Settled?” She repeated and Maddox leaned forward to peer at me around her.

He lifted his black Ray Bans to the top of his head. “I’ve never seen Ezra act like this before and I’ve known him since we were little.”

Emma turned to look at him and then back at me. “We’ve noticed things…”

“Oh my God,” I groaned dramatically, “here we go again. Ezra and I don’t like each other like that. Stop trying to make something out of nothing. It’s annoying.”

“I think you guys would make a cute couple.” Remy piped in behind me and I heard Mathias chuckle.

I ignored those two, remaining focused on Emma and Maddox.

Emma looked at me pityingly. “You don’t really believe that, do you?”

I glared out at the pool and away from my friend. When I looked back at her I let out a sigh. “It is what it is.”

I jumped when Mathias yelled behind me, “Collin, stop that!”

I looked over to see a kid of about six or seven running after people, squirting them with a water gun. I’d never met him before and I was confused as to why Mathias would be calling him out.

I swiveled around in my chair to look at the brooding lead singer. His lips were pursed in a snarl as he pointed a finger in warning at the boy.

"Who's Collin?" I asked.

Mathias hands fell to Remy's exposed baby bump. She was dressed in a white bikini with a crocheted black tank top that covered her top half. A floppy hat was perched on her head and when she turned to look at me it smacked Mathias in the face. He laughed and reached up to remove it, smoothing down her ruffled blonde hair with a stroke of his fingers. I never thought I'd see the day where Mathias was a loving and doting husband. It was weird, but a good weird.

"He's my little brother," Mathias replied, returning to massaging Remy's shoulders. "I signed up with the Big Brothers Big Sisters program a while back and they assigned Collin as my Little Brother," he explained. "His mom had to work today, so I offered to watch him so that she didn't have to pay a babysitter."

"That's...nice of you." I mumbled, shocked that those words had left my lips.

He smiled, ducking his head. "I can be nice when I want to be."

Remy reached back, rubbing his thigh. "Go get in the pool with him. He's restless."

Mathias sighed. "But what if—"

"If I need something I can get it myself." Before he could protest she leaned back with her head on his shoulder and covered his mouth with her hand. "Or ask Emma to get it for me."

"Fine," he agreed, albeit reluctantly.

He slipped out from behind her and ran after the little boy that was currently using his squirt gun to water the grass since he'd been scolded.

I turned back to Maddox and Emma and adjusted my chair so that I was sitting more angled and not blocking Remy.

"How are the wedding plans?" I asked them.

Emma hadn't peeped one word about her upcoming wedding since my engagement fell apart. I knew she thought it would make me sad hearing about her dream wedding when mine wasn't happening, but I was truly okay with everything. I wished everyone would stop treating me like glass. I wasn't going to break.

Emma was slow to smile. "Good."

"Good? That's all I get? You're getting married in September, I know you have more details than that."

She frowned, her nose crinkling. "Are you sure you want to hear about this?"

"Yes!" I threw my hands up, sighing in exasperation. "I'm your best friend, so yes, I want to know about your wedding and I want to help if you want me to! I'm *okay*," I emphasized the word, "so stop treating me like I'm not."

She looked at Maddox and back at me. “Okay,” she replied. “I’ll stop.” A smile broke out across her face as she launched into details on the wedding. I listened and inserted comments here and there, getting excited. She deserved this and so did Maddox. I was honestly kind of surprised they’d waited this long to get married. I knew it was Emma’s doings though. Maddox would’ve married her as soon as she graduated high school. I had no doubts on that.

Halfway through our wedding talk Maddox left, joining his twin, Hayes, and Ezra in the pool.

Remy ditched us too, saying that she was starving.

Emma finished gushing about her wedding plans, her cheeks flushed a pleasant pink color.

“So,” she started, reaching over to grab a drink off the table, “you’re really okay?”

“Not one-hundred percent,” I answered honestly, “but I’m getting better.” I draped my arms over my bent knees. “I realize now that my life was headed in the wrong direction. Braden and I would’ve ended up divorced within a year, I’m sure of it.” I sighed, looking off in the distance. “It sucks feeling like I’m back at the starting line while all of you are moving on to the next step. Everything happens for a reason, right?”

She nodded, setting her now empty glass aside. “It does.” She stood up, stretching her arms above her head. “I’m getting in the pool, before I die and all they can find of my body is a puddle of sweat.”

I laughed at her and pushed up from the chair. "Good idea."

Sweat clung to my arms and the back of my neck. I'd lived here my whole life and I still wasn't used to the summer humidity.

We joined the guys in the pool. They played with Collin, all of them now the proud owners of squirt guns. When Emma and I stepped into the pool all of them turned their water guns on us and squirted us in the face. Even in their twenties they all still acted like a bunch of little boys.

Emma yelped holding her hands up in defense. "Maddox! I'm going to kill you!"

"Hey!" Trace yelled and I turned to see that he and his wife were in the pool now, their son sitting in a tiny float. "Don't get my kid wet."

"Sorry," the guys chimed, lowering the guns.

"Where's Remy?" Mathias asked, his voice sounding panicked as he swam for the stairs.

"Stop getting your panties in a bunch," Remy's voice boomed as she neared us, "I'm fine. I wanted something to eat." She held a plate piled high with food in her hand. She stuffed a grape in her mouth. "You worry too much."

Mathias sighed, his shoulders sagging in relief. "You can't scare me like that." He swam over the edge of the pool and I noticed he'd gotten a new tattoo. I'd missed it before since Remy was sitting in front of him. Above his heart was one word: *Hope*.

I swallowed thickly, knowing the significance behind the tattoo.

"Aw, poor you. Would you like me to put a tracking monitor on my ankle so you know where I am all the time? I can be your prisoner. Maybe," her voice lowered, "if you don't irritate me too much, I'll even let you use your handcuffs on me."

Maddox cleared his throat and muttered, "Well, this got awkward really fast."

Remy gasped and the plate tumbled out of her hands, falling to the ground. I knew her reaction had nothing to do with what Maddox said.

In a lightning fast move Mathias leapt out of the pool and over to his wife. "What's wrong?" He asked, fear sticking to his words. He looked her over, searching for what had caused her distress.

She grasped his wrist and brought his hand to her stomach. "The baby. I felt it." Her mouth parted in wonder and tears pooled in her eyes. "It's kicking. Do you feel it?" She asked, looking up at Mathias with wide, love-filled eyes.

He held his hand to her stomach and gasped when he felt it too. "Wow," he murmured, looking at her lovingly. "That's amazing."

"I never thought I'd see the day," Maddox whispered.

When I turned to look at him he was smiling at Mathias and Remy with a look of awe. I think we'd all worried that Mathias would remain angry and brooding for the rest of his life—and he still was those things occasionally—but you couldn't deny the fact that for once he was actually *happy*. Seeing someone that had once been so miserable find a light in their life was a truly beautiful thing.

"What are you guys looking at?"

We all turned around to see a pretty redhead standing on the other side of the pool, her hand clasped tightly in the hold of the guy beside her. The guy was wearing a fedora—yes, a fedora—with his sandy colored hair peeking out of the bottom. They were both dressed in swimsuits, but the girl had a bag slung over her shoulder like she'd only just arrived at the party.

"Avery!" Olivia, Trace's wife, chimed. "I was afraid you weren't going to make it."

The woman named Avery straightened her pale blue bikini top that had white stars. I noticed that her bottoms had red and white stripes. It was the perfect bikini for the holiday. "Yeah, we spent more time at Luca's parent's house than we meant to." She shrugged. "Where should I put my stuff?"

"Our cabana's fine." Olivia pointed.

"Thanks." Avery set off in that direction and the guy, I assumed he was Luca, followed her like a puppy.

The next interruption came in the form of Trace's younger brother, Trent. He let out a war cry and bound towards the pool, executing a perfect cannonball, and drenching all of us in the process. It was a good thing we were already wet.

Trent surfaced, grinning.

Dean began to cry, not pleased that his face got wet. Trace pulled Dean out of his float and into his arms as he glared at his little brother. “Look what you did. Now my kid’s going to be terrified of the water.”

“Oh, shut up,” Trent kicked his feet swimming away, “a little water won’t hurt him.”

Trace continued to glare at his brother, but chose not to argue, and instead bounced the baby in the hopes of cheering him up.

Ezra swam over to me, his curls plastered to his forehead. He cracked a small smile and treaded water. “Enjoying the party.”

I smiled back. “It’s nice to be with my friends.”

“I’m still your favorite, right?” He joked, winking.

I mock gasped. “I don’t pick favorites.”

He chuckled and lowered his lips, blowing bubbles in the water before speaking. “But if you did I would be number one?”

“Maybe.” I splashed him.

He splashed me back and soon it was an all out war.

“You guys are children!” Maddox called, he and Emma now at the other end of the pool to avoid our splash fight.

“Coming from you that means nothing!” Ezra laughed, shoving a wall of water at me.

I didn't turn away in time and some of it went up my nose. I coughed and sputtered.

Ezra immediately ceased his attack. "Are you okay?" He asked.

I nodded. "Yeah, I'm fine."

Before I knew what was happening he had my back pinned against the pool wall with his arms on either side of me. He stared down at me, his dark eyes intense. I watched as a droplet of water fell from one of his curls and onto his nose, before rolling down his lips.

My heart thudded in my chest at his proximity and my muscles locked up. When he got this close I never knew what to do. My body had *always* reacted to Ezra, I just denied what I felt. I tried to pretend it didn't exist, because it was easier that way. He was right, we couldn't ruin our friendship even if I did daydream about the way his lips would feel against mine. Even when I was with Braden I'd still felt this intense connection to Ezra. I guessed maybe Braden had been right to be so jealous.

"So, we're good?" He asked.

"Huh?" My brows knit in confusion. I'd been too busy staring at his lips to process his words.

"Are we good?" He repeated. "After our talk earlier...we're still good, right?"

"Oh," I shook my head, "yeah."

His smile was blinding, shedding light on all the darkest parts of myself. Ezra, in many ways, was the best parts of me. There was something about him that was so pure and good that you couldn't help but be affected by that if you were around him for long. I swore he had one of the kindest and pure souls that ever existed. There weren't many people like him and I was lucky enough to call him my best friend.

"I want you to know that I really am sorry for acting like such an asshole the past few days. It was wrong of me." He took a deep breath. "I'm going to be a better friend to you." He reached up, tucking a piece of hair behind my ear.

My eyes closed and the skin on my cheek tingled where his fingers had brushed against it.

I swallowed past the lump in my throat. I hated that I was so affected by him—that I *wanted* him in a way that he refused to want me. I knew it was still too soon to want a relationship—and I didn't—but I hated that he refused to even entertain the idea of an *us* one day. My feelings were obviously stronger for him than his were for me. I'd been denying my feelings for so long, trying desperately to ignore them, but from the moment Ezra dove in the lake after me during my Thank-God-That-Asshole-Is-Out-Of-Your-Life party they'd become impossible to ignore. At least the night I got drunk he admitted to being attracted to me. If it weren't for that I'd still be convinced that my feelings were entirely one-sided.

"You already are the best friend I could ask for. You've gone above and beyond best friend duties," I joked, finally answering him.

"I'd do anything for my friends. You're my family." He waved his arms, encompassing his band mates and their girls.

The Willow Creek boys really were like family, and by extension the people they brought into their inner circle became family too.

I knew I'd become a better person by knowing them, especially by befriending Ezra. He'd become my anchor when I was lost and confused. I knew without him I would've never had the courage to pursue my dream and own a store. He believed in me when most people didn't—but as a teenager I'd given people a reason not to have faith in me. I'd spent more time chasing boys than figuring out what I wanted in life. And then once I had things figured out, I'd met Braden. He'd completely fooled me. I'd believed I'd finally found the right guy for me, but I'd never been more wrong. I didn't regret my time with Braden though. The way I saw it, being with him taught me a valuable life lesson—to appreciate the good in my life, and to stop striving for an unrealistic ideal.

Ezra snapped his fingers in front of my face. "Sadie?"

"Sorry, I zoned out," I laughed. I squared my shoulders, the water sloshing around my body as I swam away from the edge of the pool, putting more distance between us.

I hated the way my heart came to life when I was near him. The stupid, treacherous, organ didn't seem to know that he was off limits.

Ezra swam away, back to the guys.

Emma and I got out of the pool to grab some food. We ended up back in the cabana and I took over the lounger Maddox had vacated.

Emma put on her sunglasses, smiling out at the scene that played before us.

Chatter, music, and laughter filled the air and children ran around with sparklers, their happiness contagious.

Off in the distance a group of guys, Trace and Trent included, began to set off fireworks.

I smiled at the sight, then at Emma, and the guys as they got out of the pool.

Hayes ran over to us, his hair slicked back off of his forehead. He held his hand out for me. “Come on, you can’t see the fireworks from over here.”

I wanted to argue that it was still daylight, so even up close you’d barely be able to see them, but I let him lead me away.

We joined the group I’d watched earlier and they set off another round of fireworks.

“Wait until you see the ones they have for tonight.” Hayes whispered in my ear. “They’re epic.”

I believed him. The Wentworth’s were loaded, so they could pay to have the best.

“This is nice, huh?” He asked as a firework crackled, sparks flying low to the ground.

“Yeah,” I replied, but I couldn’t keep my eyes from drifting behind us to Ezra.

I’d tried many times to get over my ridiculous crush on my best friend, but it was impossible.

Even when I thought I’d moved on with Braden, a flame in my heart still burned for Ezra—reaching and hoping that maybe he felt it too.

He lifted his head, as if he felt my gaze on him, and his eyes collided with mine.

I quickly looked away, focusing back on what Hayes was saying, but that one look from Ezra had revealed so much and it only served to make the ache inside me grow stronger.

CHAPTER NINE

"MOM, I'M FINE," I assured her for the thousandth time since I'd answered my phone. I had her on speaker while I folded my clothes and put them away.

"But Sadie," she started in again, "you were supposed to get married today. I know it has to be bothering you. You're my daughter, I can sense these things."

I sighed. "Things are hitting me harder today," I confessed, "but in all honestly, I dodged a bullet. I wouldn't have been happy with Braden in the long run. You know that. You never were his biggest supporter."

"That's because he treated you like you were beneath him. You need a man who wants to stand at your side, not one that acts like you're a child."

My mom. So, wise. Too bad I tended to ignore her advice.

"I know," I agreed, putting away the last of my laundry.

"Why don't you come over today, sweetie?" She asked. "We could bake cookies like we used to."

"I just don't feel like it." I grabbed my phone off of the bed and switched it off of speaker before holding it to my ear. "I have some things I need to do today," lie, "and I really am fine. You don't need to worry so much. I'm a big girl."

Her sigh echoed over the speaker. "Sadie, you'll always be my baby to me. The sooner you realize that, the better."

"Okay, okay." I tucked the phone between my ear and shoulder as I reached for the water bottle on my nightstand and took a sip. "I have to go now, mom."

"Alright, but if you change your mind and want to come over I'll be home all day."

"Okay," I said again. "I love you."

"Love you too."

I hung up the phone and grabbed my tennis shoes, sitting on the edge of the bed as I tied them on. I hoped going on a run would help clear my head. I hadn't lied when I told my mom I was okay, but it was still a hard pill to swallow.

Downstairs I found Ezra lying on the couch, reading a book.

He laid the book on his chest when he heard me and crossed his arms behind his head. "Where are you going?" He asked.

"For a run," I replied, heading to the refrigerator for a fresh bottle of water.

He sat up, dropping the book on the coffee table. "Mind if I join you?"

I paused with the water bottle halfway to my lips. "I don't mind...but I don't think I've ever seen you run."

He laughed. "I might not be the most fit of the guys, but I *can* run." He stood up, heading for the steps.

I didn't bother to tell him that I thought his body was perfect, even though the words were on the tip of my tongue. The last thing I wanted to do was make things weird between us again. We were finally getting on normal footing again. Although, with my upcoming date with Hayes I feared things might be headed for another nosedive.

While Ezra changed I stepped out on the front porch, inhaling the morning air.

Here, on the lake, there was something magical about the mornings. Everything sparkled with dew and the animals weren't afraid of us. From where I stood I could see a deer grazing in the woods and a squirrel scuttled along the porch railing.

Smiling to myself, I sat down on the top step and stretched my legs.

Behind me I heard the screen door creak open. I peered over my shoulder at Ezra and oh my Lord I think he was trying to kill me.

"What are you wearing?!" I squeaked, hating the appalling way my voice spiked.

His dark brows furrowed together and he looked down. "Uh...shorts?"

"Where's your shirt?" I huffed, staring at his bare chest and those low slung basketball shorts that were like the worst kind of delicious torture on the planet. It seemed wrong to be checking out my best friend on the day I should've been married, but let's face it, a lot had changed in the last two weeks and I no longer gave a crap about Braden. He could move on with his bitchy lawyer and I could do whatever I wanted with my life—including drooling over Ezra.

"I'm not wearing one...obviously."

I let out an exasperated breath and jumped to my feet.

"Besides," he continued, "where's *your* shirt?"

Now it was my turn to look down. I wore a pair of running shorts and a jog bra.

"Forget I said anything," I huffed, glancing away in embarrassment and cursing myself yet again for my ridiculous feelings towards him. I wished there was some magic potion I could drink to make them go away, because now that I'd realized how strong my attraction to him was I couldn't tamp it down like I had in the past. It didn't help that he was one of my best friends, and therefore a truly decent person. He was the whole package and I hadn't lied when I told him he'd make someone very happy one day. But I knew if he had his way—which he always did—I wouldn't be that person.

His lips quirked as he fought a smile clearly amused at my dismissal of the conversation.

I started down the porch steps and looked back at him. "Are you coming?"

"Always, sweetheart." He joked, tossing in a wink for good measure.

I rolled my eyes and started to run, setting the pace. He fell into step beside me.

Since the road leading to his house was dirt and cut a windy path through the woods it was the perfect place to run.

Even though it was early in the morning it was no time until sweat clung to my body and my breath came out in small pants.

Ezra kept up with me, unfazed by my fast pace.

The sun filtered between the branches of the trees and I watched the way the shadows from the leaves danced over the dirt path.

That was the thing I loved most about running, how it allowed me to empty my mind completely and focus on the beautiful things in front of me that I normally overlooked.

We came to the end of the driveway and turned right, heading down the dirt road that led to another house several miles away. Ezra had once told me it belonged to an old guy that owned a farm and all of the surrounding land. He'd actually owned the cottage Ezra bought, but decided to sell it when it began to fall apart and he didn't have the funds to fix it.

"How are you holding up?" I asked him between breaths.

"I'm fine."

I picked up my speed, enjoying the burn in my arms and legs.

After two miles I turned around. Ezra managed to stay by my side the whole time, even though he looked like he was about to keel over dead.

When his house was in sight I veered off of the path and into the grass. I sat down and brought my knees up to my chest.

Ezra followed, his body wet with sweat. He collapsed beside me onto his back with his knees bent. His chest rose and fell with each lungful of air he pulled in.

"You're insane." He panted a few minutes later. "Completely and utterly insane."

"Then why did you come with me?" I asked, my breath under control now.

He turned his head to look at me, pushing the damp black curls away from his dark eyes. "I know what today is." His voice was barely a whisper. "I wasn't going to let you go off by yourself."

I cracked a smile. "Were you afraid I might hang myself from a tree?" I stuck my foot out and lightly kicked his leg in jest.

"No," he shook his head, "but I still didn't think you should be alone."

"Well, thanks." I smiled, truly grateful.

"Let's do something today."

"Like what?" I plucked a piece of grass from the ground and wrapped it around my finger.

He shrugged. "How about we watch a movie and just hang out? Wc havcn't had a chancc to do that in a while."

"No, we haven't," I agreed. Smiling, I nodded. "Yeah, that sounds good."

He grinned and stood up, extending a hand to me. "We better shower first."

I took his hand and couldn't stop myself from saying, "Together?"

He reared back in shock.

"I was kidding, Ezra." I bumped his shoulder with mine and started walking. I turned around backwards to face him. "First one to the house gets the shower!"

I took off running and when I reached the porch I turned around to see that he was still walking leisurely down the driveway. He lifted his hand to wave when he saw me looking.

"You lose!" I called to him.

"Really, because I feel like a winner from where I'm standing! You have a nice ass!" He yelled back.

My mouth fell open in shock and I turned abruptly to head inside without comment, but his laughter followed me.

We both showered and after a quick snack we sat down on the couch with a bowl of popcorn. Ezra had already picked out the movie and the previews began to play. Most people skipped through this part, but we never did.

"What did you pick out?" I asked, curling my legs beneath me. My damp hair tickled my shoulders and I reached for the cream colored blanket that sat on the back of the couch and wrapped it around me.

"*Benchwarmers*." He reached for the popcorn and shoved a handful in his mouth.

"A classic," I responded, wiggling around until I got comfortable.

He stretched his long legs out on the coffee table and chuckled under his breath. "Only you would consider this a classic."

I smiled. "And what would you consider a classic?" I countered, popping a piece of popcorn into my mouth.

He pursed his lips in thought. "*The Godfather*."

I shook my head. "Okay, so maybe *Benchwarmers* isn't a classic."

He chuckled, crossing his arms over his chest. "You gave in easily. That's rare."

I shrugged, grabbing another piece of popcorn. "I'm tired." And I was, for so many different reasons.

"Come here," he coaxed, moving the popcorn bowl to the coffee table.

"What?" I asked stupidly.

He put a pillow on his lap and motioned for me to lie down. After a reluctant sigh, I did. I felt weird about it, which was stupid, because I'd done this often with him in the past. But with the way my 'crush' had intensified since he let me live with him, it suddenly felt different. You know, typically when you live with someone it's hard in the beginning working around each other's quirks—Braden and I had fought a lot when I first moved in—but Ezra and I flowed naturally together.

"Comfortable?" He asked, fixing the blanket so that it covered my shoulder.

"Yeah, thanks." I said when he grabbed the remote and pressed play.

I tried to relax and watch the movie, but it was impossible.

Ezra was everywhere, invading my senses and making my brain fuzzy.

When his hand settled on my arm I nearly jumped out of my skin.

I knew he meant nothing by the touch, but I couldn't stop myself from wishing it was more.

So much more.

Crushing on my best friend really freaking sucked.

CHAPTER TEN

MY HEART POUNDED in my chest as I swiped pale pink lip-gloss over my lips. Hayes would be showing up any minute to pick me up and I felt sick to my stomach. I didn't know why I'd agreed to do this. I felt like I was cheating, even though that thought was beyond silly considering I was no longer with Braden and I certainly wasn't with Ezra either. But that knowledge didn't stop me from feeling dirty. It was all so stupid and ridiculous.

I took a deep breath and closed my eyes.

I had to get a grip.

Hayes was a nice guy and it was one date.

This wouldn't change anything.

I nodded my head in affirmation at my own thoughts and put the gloss away.

I sprayed on some perfume and turned out the bathroom light before heading downstairs. I grabbed my purse from the counter, checking my phone for any messages. There was one from Hayes saying he'd be here in ten minutes that was sent five minutes ago.

"You look nice."

"Ah!" I let out a scream and whipped around. "Jesus, Ezra, you scared the crap out of me. I thought you were still out."

"I got back early." He leaned against the back of the couch with his arms crossed over his chest. "Seriously, you look nice."

"Oh, thanks." I mumbled, still scattered. I'd dressed in a long white skirt with a loose over the shoulder beige sweater on top. I was going for nice, but casual.

Ezra shoved his hands into the pockets of his khaki cargo shorts. "So...Hayes?"

"Yeah." I nodded, tucking a piece of wavy hair behind my ear. "You're okay with that right?"

He'd been fine since the Fourth of July party, but the way he stood now with squared shoulders and a tense jaw only reiterated my feelings that I was doing something wrong.

"Of course," he scoffed. "Why would I have a problem with it?"

I shrugged. "I don't know."

My hand tightened around my phone, willing Hayes to get here faster so that I could end this awkward conversation.

"What are you going to do today?" I asked him.

He shrugged, scrubbing a hand over the heavy stubble on his cheeks. "I need to mow, so I guess I'll do that."

It always amazed me that Ezra liked to do things such as mowing his own grass. I mean, he was a rock star. He could easily pay people to mow his yard—which was far bigger than most—but he wanted to do these things himself.

"Maybe we can watch a movie later?" I suggested, wanting to get rid of the mountain that seemed to be growing between us.

"I'm not in the mood."

"Oh." I sighed, glancing towards the door. My phone buzzed in my hand and a second later the sound of a car horn could be heard outside. "I guess I better go." I pointed at the door stupidly.

He nodded, forcing a smile. It was so incredibly fake that I nearly called him out on it. "Have fun," he said, the tone lacking any enthusiasm.

"Thanks," I mumbled, for lack of anything else to say.

I headed to the door and before it closed behind me Ezra caught it. I turned back to look at him, raising a brow. "What?" I asked.

He stared down at me and then up at Hayes who was climbing out of his truck. When his eyes fixed on me all he said was, "Be careful," and the door closed in my face.

I was tempted to barge back inside and yell at him—to tell him he was being a jackass *again*—but Hayes was waiting on me so I plastered on a smile and headed over to his truck.

He stood waiting by the passenger door. "Hey, you look beautiful," he greeted me, lowering from his towering height to kiss my cheek.

I smiled up at him. "Thank you."

He opened the truck door and held onto my hand as I climbed inside. His hand was warm and calloused like Ezra's from all his hours of playing guitar.

He jogged around the front of the truck and climbed inside. The music was blaring and he reached over to turn it down.

"Where are we headed?" I asked. I'd been surprised when Hayes wanted to pick me up at one in the afternoon, but I rolled with it.

"I thought we could go to the park and have a picnic." He nodded to the backseat of the truck and I turned around to see an old-fashioned looking picnic basket.

"That'll be fun." I grinned, truly meaning it. "But won't you get mobbed?" I asked.

"Aha." He reached down between the seat and kept his eyes on the narrow driveway as dirt billowed around us. "That's what this is for." He held up a baseball cap and sunglasses. I looked at him in disbelief. "It helps, believe me." He added.

"I'll take your word for it," I laughed.

He grinned, his eyes crinkling at the corners.

I began to relax once he pulled out onto the main road. "Why a truck?" I asked.

"Huh?" He glanced in my direction.

I shrugged. "Maddox and Mathias drive sports cars, Ezra has an Escalade, and you drive a truck. Granted, this is a fancy truck, but it's a truck," I remarked.

He laughed, shaking his head. "I'm a country boy, Sadie, and country boys drive dirty, mud covered trucks." He took on an exaggerated southern drawl.

"Did you grow up around here?" I knew a lot about the other guys in the band, but Hayes had always been a mystery to me. He didn't open up easily.

He nodded. "Yeah."

"How'd you get to know the other guys?" I knew it sounded like I was prying, but this was one story I'd never been told.

He glanced at me briefly before his eyes returned to the road.

"We went to school together. I was two years ahead of them, and I'd always played guitar so when they started their band and needed a guitar player they reached out to me. They're cool and we all clicked. It was easy to become friends with them and then everything else sort of fell into place," he shrugged.

“Do you like living the rock star life?” I knew his answer—Hayes was the band member that most took advantage of his celebrity status.

“Absolutely,” he answered with an easy going grin. Sobering, he added, “But I like being home and living a normal life too. I guess I like having the best of both worlds.”

“I can understand that.”

“So...” He started, glancing in my direction with an awkward smile. “How’s Ezra with this?” He waved a finger between us. “Is he cool now?”

I shrugged. “Fine, I guess.” Based on his odd behavior this afternoon *fine* was the last thing he appeared to be, but I didn’t want to tell Hayes that. “Let’s not talk about him.” I didn’t want my thoughts to become entirely absorbed in Ezra.

“Okay, that’s off the subject table then.” He smiled over at me, tapping his fingers against the steering wheel in time with the beat of the song playing softly on the radio. “What do you want to talk about?”

I thought for a moment. “If you weren’t in Willow Creek, what would you be doing?”

He didn’t hesitate to answer. “Working in construction. My dad owns a company. It was my plan to work for him while I was in high school, get a degree in business management, and take over the company one day...but plans,” he pursed his lips in thought, “they have a funny way of changing.”

He pulled into the parking lot of the park and turned the vehicle off. He put the red baseball cap on, making sure the brim covered half of his face and added the sunglasses.

"How do I look?" He asked me, striking a playful pose.

"Like a rock star in disguise." I laughed.

He smiled crookedly. "Come on, it totally works."

"Yeah, it kind of does," I agreed.

The baseball cap kept most of his sandy hair hidden from view and the dark sunglasses obscured his blue eyes. But if someone were observant he'd still be easy to spot.

"Are you just saying that to make me feel better?" He frowned.

"No." I shook my head.

He rubbed his hands together before reaching for the door handle. "Picnic time! I'm starving!"

I rolled my eyes as I got out of the car and met him on the other side of the truck. "You guys are always hungry."

He laughed and nodded his head in agreement, reaching inside to grab a blanket and the basket. Once he had both secured in his hands we started in the direction of the grassy area. There were picnic tables, but Hayes chose a spot beneath a large tree that was shaded by the sun.

He set the basket down and shook out the blanket. We sat down and he opened the basket. He handed me a sandwich and smiled sheepishly. “I asked Emma what your favorite was. I hope that’s okay.”

My mouth fell open as I unfolded the saran wrap. “You *made* this?”

He shrugged like it was no big deal. “It’s only a sandwich.”

“Which you made...with your hands...by yourself?”

He snorted. “Is it really that surprising to you?”

“Yes,” I answered without hesitation.

He ducked his head. “You don’t know me at all.”

“You’ve never given me the chance to know you,” I countered, “over the years you’ve kept yourself pretty separate from the rest of us.”

He sighed, pulling out a bag of chips and bottles of water from the basket before closing it. “Yeah, I guess I have...I feel like I’ve always struggled to fit in with the band.”

“Why is that?” My brows furrowed in confusion. Hayes was a confident guy that wasn’t afraid to speak his mind, so I was surprised that he’d feel that way.

He unwrapped his sandwich and took a bite. Once he’d swallowed he finally answered me. “Don’t get me wrong, I consider all three of those guys as my friends...but they’ve known each other since they were kids. They’re like brothers while I’m the outsider.”

I couldn't stop myself from laughing. "I have to admit, Maddox and Ezra have one hell of a bromance going on."

Hayes laughed to. "You've got that right." He shrugged and took a sip of water. "I guess Mathias is a bit of an outsider too, but he's been changing since he married Remy and now he's having a fucking kid." He shook his head and his whole body shuddered with a sigh. "It's too weird to think about him being a dad."

"Yeah, I have to agree with that."

Mathias was the last guy in the band I ever pictured settling down so early, but people change.

I bit into my sandwich, surprised by how good it tasted. "Hey, this is delicious." I told him.

He chuckled. "It's just a sandwich."

"It's a yummy one," I countered.

"So, I did okay?" He asked, motioning to our set up and lunch.

"You did great." I smiled at him. I was actually having a really nice time with him, which surprised me completely.

"How are things with your store?" He popped a chip into his mouth.

"Good," I answered vaguely.

He raised a brow. "That's all I get."

"There's not much to tell." I shrugged. "It's just a store."

"It's what you love, though, right?"

"Yeah."

He cracked a small, half smile. "That's good to hear. Too many people these days are miserable."

"Are *you* miserable?" I asked.

I expected an immediate answer, but he surprised me by pausing and mulling over my question.

"Not miserable, per se," his lips pursed, "but sometimes I feel like something is missing from my life."

"Is that why you asked me on a date?" I questioned. "You've always...uh...gotten around." I frowned, hating to sound so blunt, but it couldn't be avoided.

He chuckled. His laugh was deep and husky sounding. "Yeah, yeah, I know." He hung his head, hiding a smile. "I love women and I'm not ashamed of that. But I guess...the meaningless hookups have gotten a little old. Is it stupid that I see Maddox and Mathias with their girls and I want that?"

"Not stupid at all." I finished my sandwich and wiped my hands on a napkin that he'd so thoughtfully packed. "But why ask me? You've never acted interested in me before. Even when I was single," I added.

He shrugged. "You're different, Sadie. You're not like the girls that throw themselves at us when we're on the road. Besides, I might not know you well, but I do know you'd never be with me because of my money and status."

He leaned towards me and I held my breath as the distance between us lessened. My heart thundered in my chest—not because I was excited by the thought of Hayes kissing me, but because I couldn't decide whether I wanted him to or not.

His fingers tangled in my hair and his breath fanned over my lips, waiting.

I closed my eyes, my thoughts and feelings a raging inferno inside me.

I was promised to no one, but my heart didn't know that.

"I'm sorry," I mumbled, turning my head away.

His hand fell and he sighed, not in disgust but resigned. I felt bad, because Hayes truly was a nice guy and I believed him when he said he wanted more than a meaningless hookup, but I couldn't see myself with him.

"Is it Ezra?" He asked. He didn't sound angry.

I winced and reluctantly raised my head to look at him. "I know it's stupid, he doesn't even like me like that," I winced, hating the fact that I sounded like I was in elementary school, "but yeah...I can't feel this way towards him and kiss you. It's wrong and I won't use you like that."

"I can respect that." He sat back, putting distance between us. He surprised me by holding out a hand to me. "Friends?"

"No," I put my hand in his, "family."

He grinned—the smile lighting up his whole face. "The Willow Creek family."

"Exactly."

"Thanks for…uh, giving me a shot, I guess." Hayes said with a laugh when he parked his truck in Ezra's driveway.

I laughed too. "Hayes, you're going to find the girl for you someday, it's just not me."

He nodded. "I know."

He leaned over and kissed my cheek before I slipped out of the truck.

He waited in the driveway until I had the door unlocked and then he turned the truck around to leave.

I stepped inside and locked the door behind me.

A small squeal left my lips when I turned around to find Ezra standing behind me.

"You have got to stop sneaking up on me like that." I put a hand over my racing heart and moved to drop my purse and keys on the kitchen counter.

"Sadie?" He swallowed thickly.

"What?" I looked at him curiously. He didn't look right, slightly sweaty and pale. His fists opened and closed at his sides.

I was about to ask him if he was sick when he threw his hands in the air in defeat, cried, "Fuck it," and stormed towards me.

I stood frozen, completely transfixed as he closed the space between us in three powerful strides.

He cupped the back of my neck and my back hit the wall beside the refrigerator as he towered above me. Before I could blink his lips were on mine.

Let's face it, I'd fantasized about kissing Ezra. He was hot, and I had an unrequited crush so it was bound to happen.

In those fantasies he'd always been sweet and tender.

But I would never use those two words to describe this kiss.

His lips were rough and demanding.

There was something feral about the way he moved—how he *consumed* me.

He growled low in his throat and my own moan captured the sound.

Holy shit, I was kissing Ezra.

Actually, he was kissing me and I was just along for the ride, but oh what a fun ride it was.

My hands began to wander up his chest and he grabbed my hands, pinning them above my head.

His hips dug into mine, and—*holy hell.*

A breathy sigh escaped me and his tongue pressed beyond my parted lips.

My knees began to quake.

I had never been kissed like this before.

No, that was a lie.

A kiss had never *felt* like this before.

Our lips moved together like they were singing the same song.

My fingers twitched in his grasp, desperate to touch him, but his hold only tightened.

I had never expected Ezra to be this rough, and aggressive, and *hot*. He was always so nice and gentle, but apparently there was a side to him I'd never experienced before and I was all for getting to know this part of him...intimately, and by the bulge pressing between my thighs he was up for that too. No pun intended.

"Finally." He breathed the word against my lips before pulling my bottom lip between his teeth and letting it go.

I moaned and my hips jerked forward.

A chuckle rumbled in his throat and then he deepened the kiss.

My brain grew fuzzy from the lack of oxygen, but the last thing I wanted to do was stop kissing him.

With one last slow stroke of his tongue he retreated and he let go of my hands. They fell onto his shoulder and my chest pressed against his with each breath I took.

He reached up, caressing his fingers lightly against my cheek. "I've wanted to do that for so long. You have no idea."

My eyes closed and I chanted in my head, *this has to be a dream.*

But when I opened my eyes Ezra still stood there and my lips were swollen from his kisses.

"Why now?" I couldn't stop myself from asking.

"Because," his teeth ground together, "seeing you with Hayes..." He looked away, fighting to gain control of his temper. "It was even worse than seeing you with Braden. At least I had a legitimate reason to hate him, but Hayes? I couldn't hate that guy if I tried, and that made it a thousand times worse."

"What do we do now?" I asked.

"It was only a kiss." He started to pull away, but I tightened my hold around his neck.

"No, don't you *dare* say that," I spat.

"Sadie—"

"Please, stop." I laid my head against his chest. "Please, don't take it back."

"I wasn't going to." I felt his fingers smooth through my hair.

"Why won't you let this—let *us* happen?"

His Adam's apple bobbed and he peered down at me. "You're my best friend," he reminded me yet again, "what if things didn't work out between us? I can't lose you."

"And I'm not worth the risk," I snapped, the words laced with venom as I reared back. I shook my head at him and stormed away, up the steps, and slammed my bedroom door like a surly teenager.

Rejected, yet again.

CHAPTER ELEVEN

IT HAD BEEN a week since our kiss.

Seven whole days.

And in those seven days I hadn't spoken one word to him.

He'd talked plenty though. He liked to tell me my behavior was 'childish' and I guess the silent treatment was childish, but I was afraid if I opened my mouth to talk to him I might scream.

I was so incredibly frustrated, and hurt, and...horny.

Yeah, that last one *really* sucked.

I'd avoided Ezra's place as much as I could—usually hanging out with Maddox and Emma. But they were annoying to be around after a while. I honestly didn't know how they were still so lovey dovey after being together for four years. Or was it five? I'd lost count. But they were still all over each other and I could only handle Maddox sticking his tongue down her throat so many times.

Now, I was sequestered in my bedroom while Ezra made dinner.

He always made enough for me too—and then I would make a point of not eating it. Even if it meant I OD'd on sour patch kids or something else equally sugar filled that I kept hidden in my room.

Tonight was different, though.

I had an idea, one I hoped he'd go for.

Although, after my silent treatment he was probably apt to kick me out and not listen to what I had to say.

I paced restlessly around the small bedroom that had become mine the past month.

This idea of mine...it was crazy.

Stupid, even.

The chances of Ezra agreeing were slim.

The chance of him laughing in my face, however, was a high percentage.

I blamed Remy for this idea.

Yep, it was all her fault.

She'd planted the seed in my brain and now I couldn't get this festering thought out of my head and I had to act on it.

I had to do something.

Because tiptoeing around this was impossible.

I pressed my ear against my bedroom door, listening intently like a nosy teenager eavesdropping on a conversation. I waited until I heard the kitchen chair scrape against the hardwood floors before darting down the stairs.

I had to do this fast before I lost the courage.

Ezra looked up when he heard me, the burger he'd grilled halfway to his mouth and another sitting on a plate in front of him waiting for me.

Before he could say anything the words tumbled out of my mouth.

"I have a proposition for you."

His brows quirked and he set the burger down without taking a bite. He motioned to the empty chair in front of him and I quickly sat.

He folded his fingers together and stared at me with that intense dark gaze that always sent me reeling.

"You haven't spoken one word to me in a week, and the first thing you say to me is that you have a proposition for me...I'm really looking forward to hearing this." He tipped the chair back so that the front two legs came off the ground.

While I tried to gather myself he continued to stare at me, his fingers stroking the heavy stubble on his face.

I laid my palms flat on the cool surface of the table and took a deep breath.

You've got this, Sadie! I tried to pep talk myself, but it wasn't working.

"I want you to fuck me." Shit. That hadn't been how I was planning to lead into this. I quickly added, "Just sex. That's it. Not a relationship. You don't want to lose our friendship, and I don't either, but we have a mutual attraction and I don't think we should fight it. I'm proposing that while I live here—which I promise to be out in the next two months or so—we should have sex."

The chair clamored back to the floor and his mouth hung open.

"Don't look at me like that," I squirmed, "I'm not crazy. This is a rational idea. We're adults. We can have sex without it complicating things."

"So..." He started, shaking his head like he couldn't believe what I'd said. "You want us to be friends...with benefits." His lips twitched with laughter.

I squared my shoulders and lifted my chin defiantly. "That's exactly what I'm saying."

"You're serious?" He sobered, his expression back to shock.

"Very serious."

He looked at me carefully, like he was searching for any sign that I might be lying.

"Sadie—"

"Don't say no yet," I pleaded, "and don't say yes either. Just...just think about it. *Please?*"

He breathed in shakily. "Okay."

I was surprised he agreed to that so readily. I expected him to slam me with a firm no and tell me there was no way he would ever sleep with me.

I wanted so much more from him than sex, but I knew he would never cross that particular line with me.

But sex, he might.

Sex did not a relationship make.

Four days passed and neither one of us peeped a word about my proposal. I was too embarrassed to bring it up, and I guessed he'd been counting on that.

I turned on the TV switching it to Hallmark and sat down to watch whatever sappy movie they were playing. I needed a good cry and a bowl of cookie dough ice cream—which reminded me Ezra had mentioned picking some up at the grocery store. Well, actually his groceries were delivered so he could avoid getting mobbed at the store, but logistics.

I didn't bother with a bowl. I grabbed the gallon carton of ice cream, a spoon, and made my way to the couch. Despite the fact that it was eighty degrees or more outside I was dressed in sweatpants, a sweatshirt, and had a blanket wrapped around me like a burrito.

I needed comfort in my time of sorrow and warmth brought me that.

Although, I was positive Ezra's warm body wrapped around mine would bring me *a lot* of comfort.

Fuck.

I had to stop thinking about him like that.

It was never going to happen and it only made me depressed thinking about it.

Especially, after that kiss.

Oh, sweet Lord, *that kiss.*

It had been everything dreams were made of.

It was downright magical.

I'd felt it all the way down to the tips of my toes.

And even now, almost two weeks later, my lips still tingled from the bruising pressure of his possessive mouth.

I shoveled a mouthful of ice cream between my lips and focused my eyes on the TV screen.

No more thoughts about Ezra.

Which should be easy, since he wasn't home. So it wasn't like he was sitting around tempting me or anything.

But I was always tempted when it came to him.

My God I wanted to lick him all over like I was currently going after this ice cream.

I had problems.

I put the ice cream away. It was making things worse.

I burrowed into the couch once more and this time I did manage to get sucked into the movie. It also made me cry, so bonus points for that.

It ended and another one came on. I lay down with my head on a pillow and tried to keep my eyes open.

As a teenager I'd been wild.

As an adult, this was as exciting as my Saturday's got.

I was pathetic.

I needed more excitement in my life than sitting around watching Hallmark movies.

I startled from my thoughts when the front door opened.

"Hey," Ezra said in greeting, his back to me as he closed the door.

"Hi." I squeaked. Yes, *squeaked* like a mouse.

He set the case he kept his bass in beside the door. The guys were already working on their new album as much as they could, but things were slow since their personal lives kept complicating things.

"What are you watching?" He came around from behind the couch and lifted my legs before sitting down and placing them in his lap.

"I have no idea," I answered honestly.

He tapped his fingers against my leg and focused on the TV.

"Are you seriously going to watch a girly movie with me?" I glanced away from the TV at him, raising a brow.

His gaze swiveled in my direction. "Sure, why not?" He shrugged. "I don't have anything else to do."

"Okaaaay, then." I drew out the word, looking at him like he'd grown another head.

"Hey, I can watch a chick movie and not shrivel up and die." He defended, scrunching up his face to appear mad.

I tried to hide my smile but it was impossible.

"Are you laughing at me?"

"I would never laugh at you," I scoffed.

"You definitely are."

Before I could respond he pounced on me. Giggles burst forth from me when he tickled my stomach.

"Stop! Stop!" I pleaded between bouts of laughter.

"You have to promise never to laugh at me ever again." He grinned, moving to my side where I was even more ticklish.

"I promise!" I cried. "Please stop tickling me!"

Miraculously his assault ceased. We were both panting and out of breath, although I had no idea why he was so breathless.

His hands moved down from my sides, over my hips, and stopped at my thighs.

My throat closed up as his thumb rubbed slow circles against my thigh.

His chocolate colored eyes darkened even more.

My heart sped up and I struggled to find my voice. “What are you doing?” I finally asked.

His tongue flicked out to moisten his lips and his eyes remained steady on mine.

“Accepting your proposition.’”

My body clenched all over and I ceased breathing. “What?” Surely I didn’t hear him right.

“I’m accepting your proposition,” he repeated.

Sweet baby Jesus. Was this real life? I had to be dreaming, right?

I pinched myself.

Yes, it was real life.

Ezra chuckled, the sound of it vibrating through my body. “Did you just *pinch* yourself?”

I nodded my head. I had no words. Every single word in the English dictionary had fled my mind.

He chuckled again, hovering above me. “You don’t believe me, do you?”

I shook my head.

“I guess I’ll have to show, not tell.”

Before I could inhale my next breath his lips were on mine and he became my oxygen. My fingers tangled in the silky soft strands of his hair and I let out a small moan as his hips ground against mine.

"Are you sure?" I asked between kisses.

"Abso-fucking-lutely."

He gathered me in his arms so that he was sitting on the couch and I was straddling him.

He cupped the back of my neck, holding me to him as he kissed me thoroughly.

A rush of emotions flooded my veins.

Excitement.

Lust.

Fear.

His hands moved lower, to the hem of my sweatshirt and he pulled it over my head, revealing my thin tank top. He cupped my breasts and let out a satisfied growl when he discovered I wasn't wearing a bra.

He kissed his way down my neck and then back up.

I leaned forward to kiss him when he stood up with me gathered in his arms. My legs automatically wound around his waist and I held on tight to his neck.

"Where are we going?" I panted the words.

"To my bed. Did you really think I was going to have sex with you on the couch?"

"We're having sex *now?*" The words came out as a screech.

He topped the stairs and stepped into his bedroom. "Only if you want to."

He set me down on his bed and took a step back, waiting for me to make up my mind.

I kept running through silly thoughts in my head. Like, did I brush my teeth? What about my hair? Oh my God, did I *shave?*

Finally I said, fuck it, and dismissed every last one of them from my mind.

I stood up and grabbed his t-shirt, pulling it over his head. He continued to stand there, not touching me. He tilted his head to the side, waiting.

I knew he wouldn't do anything until I gave him permission.

My palms pressed against his chest and slid down, stopping at the belt that held his jeans on his narrow hips.

"I'm not walking away," I breathed, "this is what I want."

"We're really going to do this?" He asked, his Adam's apple bobbing. "Once we cross this line we can't go back." He stared down at me from his looming height, as if he was hoping he could intimidate me into chickening out.

"Just shut up and kiss me."

Surprisingly, he listened.

He lowered his mouth to mine, sealing our lips together in a soul-stealing kiss.

He backed me up until the backs of my knees bumped into his mattress.

I lowered onto the bed and he followed, his body blanketing mine.

My heart beat in an out of control rhythm as his hands snaked under my tank top and he touched my bare skin.

A shiver raked my body and he smiled against my lips.

"Lift your arms," he commanded.

I did as he asked and he pulled the tank top off, throwing it into the corner of his room.

I resisted the urge to hide my body.

I'd never been shy or self conscious before, but I suddenly felt that way.

He pulled back, his eyes skimming over my body hungrily. I shivered and Goosebumps dotted my skin.

His lips pressed lightly against my neck and he murmured, "You're so beautiful."

I closed my eyes, letting his words sink in. I grasped onto them, believing them because of the depth of his conviction when he spoke them.

My breath came out in a short gasp when his lips trailed between the space between my breasts and down lower. His fingers found the waistband of my sweatpants and he yanked them off forcefully like he couldn't wait to get to what was underneath.

He grinned when he saw my underwear. "Iron Man? Really?"

"Every girl wants Tony Stark a.k.a. Robert Downey Jr. in her pants."

He snorted. "Well, *I'm* the one getting into your pants so..."

"Robert was here first." I snapped the band of my underwear.

He growled and with a sharp pull he removed them as well.

I pouted. "You better not have ripped those. They're my favorite pair."

"I'll buy you new ones," he promised, covering my body with the heat of his as he kissed me all over.

My fingers tangled in his unruly mane of hair when his mouth found my center. "Oh God," I panted in a long moan.

Lights sparkled behind my closed lids as his tongue swirled around and around. It had been far too long since I'd had sex and my body was overly sensitive to every stroke of his tongue and fingers. I felt like a rocket, ready to go off at any second once the right button was pushed.

"Ezra." I panted his name like a prayer.

I felt him smile against me and his fingers crooked inside me.

"Oh God," I moaned as my orgasm hit me. My whole body shook and he held tightly to my thighs so I couldn't get away.

He kissed his way back up my body and took my lips between his own. My heart pounded in my chest like a caged bird fighting to get free.

With shaky hands I framed his face.

"I want you inside me," I begged. I'd been waiting for this moment for what felt like years, and now that it was here I didn't want to wait a second longer.

"Eager, are we?" He chuckled, kissing the sensitive skin behind my ear.

"Very."

He kissed me again, long and deep, imbedding himself on my heart and soul. I would never be the same after this, but I couldn't stop it. I didn't want to. I needed this—I needed *him*—more than I needed my next breath.

Once my lips were tender from his kisses he pulled away from me and stood up.

I swallowed thickly and watched as he walked the two short steps over to his bedside table and grabbed a condom.

The rush of my blood roared through my ears as it raced towards my heart.

He stood in front of me, his eyes capturing mine as he reached down and undid his belt oh-so slowly. Next, his fingers went to the button and then the sound of the zipper going down on his jeans filled the silence between us.

He reached out, grazing his fingers against my bare thigh and I shivered.

Raising a brow he stepped forward and bent down so his lips brushed my ear when he spoke. "This will change everything."

"This changes nothing."

Neither one of us believed my words, but both of us were too needy to back out now.

He crawled back until he towered above me once more.

I held my breath in anticipation of what was to come.

He kicked off his jeans and removed his boxer-briefs, leaving himself bare to my viewing pleasure. I licked my lips and he chuckled.

"Like what you see, sweetheart?"

I sat up and my hands landed on his chest. His skin was heated and his heart beat as fast as mine. At least I wasn't the only one affected and we'd barely even started.

My eyes flicked down taking in the impressive length of his cock.

Gazing back up at him I said, "I like it...a lot...but don't call me sweetheart ever again."

He grinned and stuck the foil condom wrapper between his teeth, ripping it open. "Whatever you say...sweetheart." He winked.

My heart stuttered and then stopped before picking up speed once more.

"Lay down." He commanded in a soft voice.

I wasn't one to take orders, but I listened to him.

Once I was lying down he grabbed my thighs and pulled me to the edge of the bed. He'd already put the condom on, but he didn't push into me. Instead, he stared down at me and several emotions flashed in his dark eyes. I was terrified that he was going to back out and leave me naked and wanton on his bed, but he didn't.

He grabbed the base of his cock and guided it inside me.

My body tensed all over at the delicious pleasure coursing through my body.

With one hard thrust he was all the way inside me. We both gasped and then I swore he said, "It's better than I fucking imagined."

"What did you say?" I wanted to hear him repeat them so that I'd know I wasn't crazy.

"Nothing." His teeth gnashed together and a vein pulsed in his forehead.

His hands tightened around my thighs.

"Uh...Ezra?"

"Yes?" He ground out between his teeth, his head ducked so that his dark curly hair concealed his eyes.

"This is the part where you should be moving your hips. Just saying."

He let out a breathless chuckle and raised his head to look at me. "Sadie, if I move I'll blow my load like a fourteen year old kid. Bear with me for a minute."

"Well, we can't have that." I took a deep breath and let my body relax.

He shuddered and slowly pulled back before sinking back inside me.

My eyes closed and a long moan left my parted lips. My hands landed on his shoulders and when I opened my eyes he was staring at me with a look of awe, his mouth slightly parted.

"Kiss me," I pleaded. Not only was I desperate for the feel of his lips on mine and his stubble rubbing my face, but I needed him to stop looking at me like that, because that look...it showed me more than he was willing to give and I refused to get my hopes up.

He brushed his lips against mine in the lightest, most fleeting of kisses and I groaned out loud. My fingers fisted around his silky hair, holding him to me as I arched my neck to kiss him more fully. A growl vibrated in his chest and his teeth nipped my bottom lip. His hands roamed over my hips, down my sides, before he palmed my breasts. I moaned when he rubbed his thumbs over my nipples.

"Fuck," he growled, his lips sucking against my neck. "This is everything."

My hips lifted to meet his and I saw stars behind my eyes.

I'd never known sex could be like this, and if I had I think maybe I wouldn't have given up my virginity at such a young age. He was right when he said this was everything.

His hands left my breasts and he grabbed my hips, lifting them off the bed. He hit something deeper inside me and I let out a small cry.

He paused, his face tightening with the effort it took to hold back. "Are you okay?" Sweat clung to his skin and the pupils of his eyes were dilated.

"Yes," I panted, "don't stop. Please, for the love of God don't stop."

With a deep exhale he let himself go and we both became lost in the feeling of each other.

He was wild and unrestrained as he fucked me. It was a beautiful sight to see and to know that *I* made him come undone like that.

I felt myself building to another orgasm and I gasped when it hit, my back arching. Ezra watched me with a look of awe and delight. A moment later he reached his own peak. He growled lowly, a curse passing between his lips, and his fingers dug harshly into my thighs. I wouldn't be surprised if it bruised.

He collapsed against me, his head buried in the crook of my neck. Our bodies stuck together from our perspiration and he was careful to brace his weight on his arms so he didn't crush me.

After a long moment he sat up slightly and kissed me deeply.

He took my chin between his fingers and forced me to look at him. My chest rose and fell harshly with each gasping breath I took.

His tongue flicked out over his lips and he breathed, "I think this is the best idea you've ever had."

I smiled and said, "Yeah."

Even though I already knew this was the *worst* idea I'd ever had, because I was dangerously close to falling in love with my best friend and I'd only end up with my heart broken.

CHAPTER TWELVE

I SAT ON the dock, dangling my bare feet out over the water. The sun warmed my exposed skin and I reached up to adjust my sunglasses.

"You're unusually quiet today." Emma commented from beside me.

I guessed I was. I kept replaying what had happened yesterday with Ezra, then again in the shower, and then yet again this morning. We were both insatiable.

I shrugged. "I have a lot on my mind."

"Want to share?" She asked, adding another layer of sunscreen to her nose, momentarily hiding her freckles beneath the white lotion like substance.

"Not really."

"Everything's okay, though, right?" Her voice was full of concern.

"Yeah, of course." I forced a smile.

"You know..." She started and then trailed off like she wasn't sure she should continue.

"Come on, spit it out." I bumped her shoulder with mine.

She winced—not in pain, but at whatever she had to say. "It's just that...I thought after you broke up with Braden you'd return to the normal, bubbly Sadie you used to be, but you're still..."

"I'm still what?" I didn't snap at her, even though a part of me wanted to.

"Withdrawn." She settled on.

I guessed that was an accurate description of what I'd gradually become over the last two years.

"I'm working on it," I mumbled, adjusting the straps of my bikini top.

"Is there anything I can do?" She asked, her toes skimming the surface of the lake.

"Nah," I shrugged, "I have to find my way back to myself on my own."

"Hey, Em!"

We both turned to look behind us, and saw Maddox barreling straight for us.

"What is he doing?" She mumbled.

He wasn't slowing down and reached us in a matter of seconds. Somehow, without stopping, he grabbed Emma around her torso and jumped into the water with her in his arms. Water splashed everywhere, and I ended up drenched.

They surfaced a few feet in front of me and Emma smacked her fists against his muscular chest. "You asshole! That was mean!"

"Aw," he reached for her, pulling her body against his and she immediately melted into his embrace, "you know I love you."

"I think you just like dragging me into bodies of water," she mumbled, but she was smiling. She kissed him quickly and swam away.

"What are they up to?"

I jumped at the sound of Ezra's voice. I tilted my head back and—oh Lord. I swallowed thickly at the sight of him in a pair of white low hanging swim trunks and a blue baseball cap sitting backwards on his head. Pieces of his black curls curled around the edges of the baseball cap, refusing to be tamed.

"Oh, you know, the usual, being the sickeningly cute couple that they are." I hoped he didn't notice the pitch in my voice but based on the quirk of his lips he definitely saw how I was eyeing him. I felt like I was dehydrated and stranded in the middle of the desert, while Ezra was the cool glass of water just out of my reach.

While we might be having sex now, our friends didn't know that and they had to remain blind to our deal. They wouldn't understand.

Unfortunately, that meant around them we had to keep our hands to ourselves.

When Ezra said Maddox and Emma were coming over I hadn't expected that to be a problem, but even though they hadn't even been here an hour I was ready for them to leave so I could have him all to myself.

"Oh, here." Ezra mumbled and handed me a bottle of beer. I hadn't even noticed he was holding two, one for me and one for himself, since I was too busy checking him out. "You only get one, though." He joked.

"Ha, ha, ha." I rolled my eyes. "I'm an awesome drunk and you know it."

He sat down beside me and brought the beer to his lips. "You're definitely entertaining, that's for sure."

"Darling!" Maddox called in a joking voice to Ezra. "Are you going to sit there all day or join us?"

"I'm fine right here." Ezra chuckled. "*Darling*."

"You guys are so weird." I snorted, shaking my head.

Ezra shrugged. "We're practically like brothers, after a while you find you don't care what the fuck you say to each other. Besides, if you can't joke around life gets pretty boring."

"That's true."

I set my beer aside, not bothering to take a drink. The last thing I needed was a buzz right now.

"Come on! Get in! It's hot!" Emma called, floating on her back. Maddox splashed her and she retaliated with an even bigger splash.

"They're not going to leave us alone until we get in," I told Ezra.

He sighed. "You're right."

He emptied his beer and stood up, tossing his baseball cap onto the dock. He reached a hand down to me and I took it, letting him haul me up. I stumbled into his chest and he steadied me before we both toppled over.

He chuckled lowly and smoothed my hair away from my face. "Are you okay?"

I swallowed thickly. "Mhmm, yeah. Great." I definitely was not affected at all. Nope. Not even a little bit.

"We have an audience," he whispered in my ear.

I jerked away from him like I'd been electrocuted.

When I looked out at the lake Maddox wasn't paying attention to us, but Emma was. Her eyes were narrowed and I could tell she'd be asking me about this later. Fantastic.

Ezra reached for my hand again and we stepped up to the edge of the dock. I wanted to pull away since I knew Emma was watching, but I didn't.

"Ready?"

"Yeah."

Together we jumped into the water. The temperature of it was cool, but it felt like heaven against my heated skin.

We came up and Maddox hollered. "Perfect score!"

"That wasn't even a dive!" Ezra yelled back as he swam towards his friend.

Emma was already headed my way and I wished I could sink beneath the surface of the water and disappear.

When she reached me she pushed the wet strands of her blonde hair away from her eyes. "Are you still going to tell me nothing is going on with you guys?" She arched a brow.

"I think you need your eyesight checked," I quipped, "because you're seeing things."

"I'm not blind or stupid." She glared at me, the skin beneath her freckles turning red—and not from a sunburn. "You used to tell me everything, even things I didn't want to know, and now you tell me *nothing*. I feel like I don't know you anymore." She frowned, her shoulders sagging even as she moved her arms to stay afloat.

The truth was, Emma and I had been growing apart for a while. That was why Ezra and I had grown so close the last few years. Our best friends ditched us for each other, so we ended up becoming friends. While Ezra had maintained his close relationship with Maddox I hadn't done the same with Emma. It wasn't all her fault though. She'd been wrapped up in Maddox and I'd been wrapped up in Braden.

"We used to do everything together," she continued. "I miss our sleepovers and pigging out on way too much pizza while watching those stupid shows you seem to love."

I laughed and began to smile. "Yeah, that was always fun."

"Maybe we should do that again?" She suggested, her voice meek sounding.

"We're grown ups now, Emma."

"So?" She countered. "Maybe the mistake in growing up is thinking that everything you used to do was childish."

"You really want to have a sleepover?"

She nodded eagerly. I hated to let her down, because lately I'd been letting everyone down, including myself.

"Let's do it then. You provide the pizza, I'll pick the *stupid shows*." I mimed her tone with a laugh.

"Deal." She smiled back.

"We'll have to do it at your place, though," I told her, "I wouldn't feel right taking over Ezra's place with girly stuff."

"Sounds good. Tonight?"

"Sure," I said, even though I cringed

I sent up a silent prayer that at this sleepover she'd let the topic of Ezra go, but I knew that wasn't likely. Emma was too perceptive. Besides, she'd already brought it up too many times for me to believe she'd suddenly stop asking me about it.

She swam away from me, over to Maddox, no doubt to tell him about our plan for a sleepover.

Ezra swam over to me, his dark hair plastered to his forehead. “Is everything okay?” He asked. “It looked like you were having an intense conversation.”

“Everything is fine,” I assured him, “but we’re going to have a sleepover tonight. Emma wants us to...reconnect,” I said, for lack of a better word.

“Reconnect, huh?” He arched a brow.

I shrugged. “We haven’t hung out much in a long time.”

“Ezra!” Maddox called, drawing his attention away from me and over to his friend. “The girls are having a sleepover tonight, which means we are too! Are you ready for me, buddy?” Maddox raised his fists in the air. “I’m going to whoop your ass on Call of Duty.”

“You wish.” Ezra rolled his eyes.

They began bickering back and forth about different video games and Emma swam back to me.

“We’ve lost them to nerd land,” she declared, but she smiled when she said it. She glanced over at Maddox and love shone in her eyes.

I wondered if I’d ever looked at Braden like that—like he was my whole world. I doubted it.

I swam away from Emma and onto the shore. I grabbed my towel and shook it out before lying down on top. Emma joined me, doing the same with her towel. The guys continued to goof around in the lake. No surprise there.

It grew quiet between us when Emma picked up a book to read, but a little while later she voiced, "Are you happy?"

I glanced over at her, puzzled by the random question.

"I'm just wondering," she defended, "after everything that's happened the last month if you're happy now."

I looked away from her and out at the shimmering water of the lake. "No," I answered honestly. "I mean, I'm not miserable, but I'm not exactly happy either." How could I be when I felt like a shell of the person I used to be?

Emma rolled over onto her stomach and propped her body up on her elbows. "What can I do to help?"

I gave her a small smile. "No one can help me with this. This is all on me. Don't worry," I assured her, "I'll find my way back to my happy place one day."

"Good." She reached over and gave my arm a playful squeeze. "I miss the peppy Sadie."

I laughed. "Admit it, you totally want to choke me when I get hyper."

She grinned. "Okay, so I have had some fantasies of knocking you out when you get a little crazy, but I miss that you're not like that anymore. Maybe the sleepover will be step one into resurrecting you," she winked.

"Yeah, maybe so," I agreed.

I really hoped so.

"I can't believe you're abandoning me so soon after our...arrangement."

I turned around sharply at the sound of Ezra's voice.

"That's it, you need to wear your boots all the time so that I can hear you, because otherwise you sneak up on me all stealth-like. Stop trying to be a ninja, Ezra." I scolded him, taking a deep breath to calm myself.

He chuckled, leaning against the doorway. His hair was still damp from his shower and the woodsy scent of his soap filled the air. He'd changed into a white wifebeater and a pair of basketball shorts. I hated how he made such a simple ensemble look so amazing. It was completely unfair.

He strode into the room and sat on the edge of my bed. Or—er—I guess technically it was his bed, since this was his house, and—why the hell was I obsessing over this? The answer was simple, because I was trying to ignore the searing force of his dark gaze.

"Going away for a while?" He arched a brow.

"I'm a *girl*," I defended, zipping my overnight bag closed, "we need a lot of stuff."

Sobering, he bowed his head and his shoulders tightened with tension. When he looked up at me there was worry in his eyes. “You’re not leaving tonight because of me, right? Because of what we did?”

I expelled the breath I’d been holding. “No, definitely not,” I shook my head. “I...I don’t regret what we did.” My hands shook at the memories.

He cleared his throat. “Good.”

He looked so awkward sitting there that I had to feel sorry for him.

“I promise I’m not running away. And,” I grew bold and sat down in his lap, his hands landed on my hips and the tips of his fingers dug into me, “I’m really looking forward to doing it again.”

Before he could reply I kissed him.

His body instantly relaxed at the feel of my lips and a low growl rumbled in his throat. His hands fisted the fabric of my t-shirt, like he was tempted to tear it off of me but knew he shouldn’t.

The kiss quickly grew heated and desire blossomed low in my belly.

I felt him harden beneath me and within seconds he’d maneuvered us so that I was lying flat on the bed with him above me.

I wrapped my legs around his waist, our lips never breaking.

He began to ease my shirt up while I reached for the band of his shorts and that was when the doorbell rang.

Ezra tore his lips away from mine and rested his head in the crook of my neck while he tried to regain his breath. “Fucking hell. I’m going to kill Maddox. He has the worst timing ever.”

Maddox and Emma had left a little over an hour ago so that they could shower and Maddox could grab a change of clothes since he was staying the night here. Emma was supposed to ride back with him and pick me up.

“Hello!” We heard called downstairs. “Honey, I’m hoooome!”

Ezra cursed and pulled away from me, muttering under his breath. “And why the fuck did I *ever* think giving him a key to my house was a good idea?”

I laughed, biting my lip. “Uh, Ezra...you might want to hide that?” I pointed to his hard-on tenting his shorts.

He cursed again and headed for the bathroom.

“Are you seriously going to jerk-off?” I hissed under my breath.

He started to close the bathroom door, but poked his head out so he could see me sitting on my bed. “I don’t have much of a choice, do I?” He slammed the door closed and I dissolved into a fit of laughter.

“Is everything okay?” Maddox called and I heard him start up the steps.

"Yeah," I yelled back, grabbing my bag. I met Maddox at the bottom of the stairs and he took my bag from me.

"What the hell do you have in here?" He groaned against the weight.

"It's not that heavy." I smacked his side, heading for the door.

He mumbled, "Yeah, it is."

I shook my head and stepped outside. I was surprised to see Emma had brought her car, but I guessed that made sense because she hated driving Maddox's since it was a stick shift. She didn't like the SUV very much either, but that was only because she thought spending a lot of money on a vehicle was ridiculous. It was a nice car though, a pretty white Porsche Cayenne. I'd been happy when Maddox got it for her. The old Volkswagen beetle she'd been driving had definitely seen better days.

Maddox put my bag in the backseat and leaned in through the open driver's window to kiss Emma goodbye.

"I love you," he told her, grinning widely.

"I love you too." She kissed him quickly one last time as I climbed into the car.

Maddox jogged up the porch steps and disappeared inside.

"Ready for girl time?" Emma asked.

"Definitely."

"I like that color." Emma pointed to my pale blue toenails as we left the nail salon.

"Me too," I agreed.

When we left Ezra's house we ended up stopping off to get a manicure and pedicure. I'd been shocked when Emma pulled into the parking lot, because I knew this wasn't really her thing. I had to give her credit; she really was trying to cheer me up.

We walked over to the nearby pizza place to grab our order that Emma had called in a few minutes ago.

Once we had that we got back in her car and she drove us to her house. Well, it wasn't really a house since she and Maddox still lived in the guesthouse behind his parent's house. It was funny, since they could afford to live elsewhere, but they loved the guesthouse. I knew they were planning to move soon though since they were getting married in a few months.

"Have you guys found a house you like, yet?" I questioned, getting out of the car and grabbing the pizza boxes.

Emma wrinkled her nose as she fiddled with her keys, looking for the right one.

"No," she sighed, opening the door and waving me inside. "Maddox wants to buy a piece of land and build a house, but that seems like a major headache to me. I'd rather get something older and remodel. Who knows what we'll do," she shrugged, tossing her keys on the kitchen counter.

The guesthouse was actually pretty large. It was two-stories, with two bedrooms upstairs along with a bathroom. Downstairs was the kitchen and living room. The living room used to be where the guys had band practice, but they'd long ago moved most of their instruments into the recording studio they'd installed in their parent's home. The piano still remained though.

I took a seat on the couch and Emma turned the TV on before handing me the remote. The TV was huge—which I knew was Maddox's doing. Emma rarely watched TV. She preferred her books and music.

I put the TV on one of the entertainment channels and set the boxes of pizza on the coffee table.

Emma lifted the lids and grabbed a slice. "I love pizza," she moaned, taking a bite. "Pizza is life."

I laughed, grabbing a piece for myself. "Do you love pizza more than Maddox?"

She pretended to ponder my words. "It's a tie." She tucked her legs underneath her and turned towards me. "This is nice. I can't remember the last time we did something like this."

"I think we were still in high school," I mumbled around a bite of pizza. After we graduated Emma jetted off to L.A. with Maddox, and started writing songs for the band. I stayed behind and went to college. It'd been weird being without her at first, since we'd been friends since we were kids. Luckily, Ezra spent most of his time in Virginia so I'd still had him.

"Yeah," Emma nodded her head in agreement, "it probably was."

"Have you found a wedding dress?" I asked her. She was still struggling to discuss her wedding plans with me, but I really didn't care. My relationship with Braden might've fallen apart, but I wasn't angry with everyone else for being happy.

She bit her lip and set her pizza crust in the box. "I've been meaning to talk to you about that...I know it's short notice, but I was kind of hoping that maybe you'd make my dress." She held her breath while she waited for my answer.

Tears stung my eyes. "You want *me* to design your wedding dress?"

Let's face it, Maddox was loaded and Emma made plenty of money on her own writing songs, so she could definitely afford to have one of the top celebrity designers to make her dress, but she wanted me.

"Of course," she gasped. "Your designs are amazing! And I know you focus mostly on styling, but you're an amazing designer as well, Sadie."

I tackle hugged her and she laughed, wrapping her thin arms around me.

"I take it this means you'll do it?"

We sat back up and I brushed my tears away. "Absolutely. Let's brain storm tonight."

She smiled widely. "Thank you."

"No, thank you," I told her. "So, have you picked a venue yet?"

She nodded. "Yeah, we're going to get married here. We want to keep the wedding small, just our family and friends, so there's enough space for that."

"That'll be nice."

"I want to keep things simple," she grabbed another piece of pizza, "you know me. I'm low maintenance."

"It'll be beautiful." I knew whatever she had planned would be.

"I can't believe I'm getting married." Her face flushed with a pink hue. "I was never like you," she continued, "I didn't dream of falling in love and getting married, and yet here I am."

"Things change," I commented.

"They do," she agreed.

I ate another slice of pizza and drew my knees up to my chest. "What kind of dress do you think you want?" I asked, already brainstorming in my head.

"Simple," she said, and then laughed. "Can you tell that's my thing?" Sighing, she tapped a finger against her lips. "I want it to be lightweight. It's still going to be blazing hot in September, so I don't want it to be heavy. Maybe something with a thin strap," she suggested, "my boobs are too big to go strapless, I'd be afraid they might pop out."

I laughed at her, making a mental note of the things she'd said. "I'll get to work on some designs. We don't have much time."

She clapped her hands together, vibrating with giddiness. When we were younger Emma was always quiet and guarded, once she met Maddox she really came out of her shell. It was nice to see her so vibrant and living life, instead of hiding behind the pages of a book.

"You know," she sobered, draping her arm along the back of the couch, "for a while I was scared to get married. I know Maddox has wanted us to get married for a while, but I thought it might change things—put more pressure on our relationship," she shrugged. With a wistful smile she added, "But it hasn't. In fact, I think I've fallen more in love with him through this whole process and I can't wait to have him be my husband."

I smiled, reaching for her hand and giving it a squeeze. "I'm glad. You deserve all the happiness in the world." And that was the truth. Emma had been through a lot at a young age and having a drunken asshole for a father had made her untrusting of guys. But Maddox had barreled into her life, breaking down all the walls she'd built around herself.

She tilted her head, a small smile gracing her lips. "So do you."

I sighed. I should've known she'd find a way to circle back to my happiness, or lack thereof, eventually.

"I'll find my happiness again," I muttered, picking at a loose thread on the couch. "Things are just...rough right now."

The breakup with Braden had taken a lot out of me. Even though I knew in my heart I'd never really loved him, I'd still spent two years with the guy, and there'd been fondness there. Throw on top of that the stress of running my store, and then skirting around my feelings for Ezra, and I was exhausted. Maybe things would get better in the Ezra department now that we had our agreement, but it was doubtful. I just hoped it didn't make things worse.

"You know what you need?" She grinned, leaning towards me. "A vacation!"

I snorted. "I don't have time for a vacation. I can't leave the store."

She shook her head rapidly. "You had a two-week honeymoon planned, Sadie. I think you can take a week off and go on a vacation."

"By myself?" I hissed.

"No," she shook her head, "we'll all go. The guys, Remy, me and you."

"I don't know about this..." I trailed off. A vacation sounded nice, but...

"Please, oh please." She held her hands beneath her chin and pouted her bottom lip. "We can get a beach house somewhere. I'll plan the whole thing...okay, that's a lie, I can't plan very well so I'll get Maddox to do it, but you won't be bothered with any of it. I promise."

"Do you think the others will agree?"

She pointed to her face and pouted again. "No one can say no to this face."

I smiled, feeling myself grow a little excited. "Let's do it!"

"Yay!" She stood up and started dancing around. Pulling her phone out of the pocket of her shorts she pressed a button and music flooded the small space.

Laughing, I stood up too and joined her crazy dancing.

Our laughter filled the air as we tripped over our own feet.

I'd been reluctant to agree to this sleepover, but it was proving to be exactly what I had needed.

CHAPTER THIRTEEN

HIS LIPS MOLDED to my neck and my fingers tangled in his silky soft hair.

It was safe to say I had an obsession with Ezra's hair.

Actually, I had an obsession with the man himself. It was completely unfair how amazing he was. Inside and out.

His fingers skimmed down the sides of my bare torso and my body arched at the sensation.

His touch electrified me.

His hips rocked against mine and my nails raked his back.

I was so close.

He sat up suddenly, pulling me with him so that we never separated. I let out a long moan at the new sensation. I rolled my hips and he cursed.

He grasped the nape of my neck and pulled my lips to his, kissing me deeply. Our lips parted and I panted from the lack of oxygen.

I closed my eyes, tightening my hold on his shoulders. “I’m coming,” I warned.

“Fuck, I’m close too,” he breathed, his lips skimming mine when he spoke.

Our chests pressed together, adding even more friction.

I moved faster and his own thrusts sped up.

I tipped over the edge, and my cry filled the room. With a groan he came too and we fell back onto the bed in a tangle of limbs.

My chest rose sharply as I struggled to get enough air.

I didn’t think it was possible, but it got better every single time.

I didn’t know how I was ever going to give this up, but I knew eventually our arrangement would have to come to an end.

He wrapped an arm around my waist and pulled me against his body, tenderly kissing the crook of my neck.

My eyes closed as a happy sigh escaped me. The gesture had been so sweet, something a real boyfriend would do, but I had to remind myself that we weren’t really a couple.

All too soon he pulled away and rolled out of bed. He put on his boxers and stuck his hands on his narrow hips.

“We better get ready.”

I glanced at the clock on his nightstand. He was right. It was a little past noon, but the guys were playing at a local festival later this afternoon. Even though the guys were a big deal now they still made an effort to perform local gigs. I thought it was nice that they still appreciated their roots.

I sat up and began gathering my clothes strewn about his room. With them clutched in my arms I mumbled that I was going to take a shower.

He nodded, already distracted by something on his phone.

After my shower I dried and curled my hair. Instead of putting on a pair of shorts I opted to wear a dress. It was new and I hadn't had a chance to wear it yet. I wasn't dressing up for Ezra, though. Nope, definitely not.

I slipped the dress on and admired my reflection in the mirror above the dresser in my bedroom.

It was white and hugged my body. It had an open design in the middle that exposed parts of my stomach and the design continued at the bottom of the dress. The back was low cut, and my tattoo was on full display. It was a dream catcher that started between my shoulder blades with the feathers extending down my back. I got it a while ago, straight out of high school. Ezra had been with me when I got it, since I didn't want to go alone. I'd gotten it, because at the time my dreams had seemed so far out of reach and I wanted something to remind me that I could go after them and, well *catch* them.

Satisfied with the dress I put on a pair of strappy gold flats and added a flowered headband to my hair.

"You look beautiful," Ezra commented, appearing in the doorway.

"Thanks," I smiled at him.

He was dressed simply in a pair of khaki shorts and a white t-shirt.

"I thought we'd head on over now," he looked at the large watch on his wrist, "and have some time to do a few things before the show."

My brows rose. That sounded suspiciously date-like to me, but I wasn't going to say anything.

"Sounds good." I swiped some more gloss onto my lips before following him outside.

"Security is meeting us at the festival. Just to be safe," he told me, slipping inside the Escalade.

I didn't like going places where their security tagged along, but it was better than being swarmed. Most fans were pretty chill, but there were still the crazy ones. Someone gave Mathias a lock of hair one time. The look of disgust on his face would've been comical if it hadn't been downright gross. She literally ripped it out of her head and thrust it at him. She'd also said something about them being destined to be together and that she'd already picked out the names of their children. She then proceeded to rub her stomach and told him that little Leopold would be arriving in the fall. Mathias hauled ass out of the meet and greet room after that.

They were actually doing a meet and greet today after they performed. Hopefully no more scenarios like that one played out.

Ezra and I were quiet the whole drive over. He parked in a section off to the side where the people working at the event parked their cars. I immediately spotted two hulking security guards. Each of the guys had two of their own security personnel. Ezra's were named Jon and Kenny. They were massive—all of their bodyguards were—and built like linebackers.

Ezra hopped out of the car and the bodyguard's met us at the parking lot exit. They flanked us on each side as we headed into the festival.

It was already packed, and as we walked the whispers and stares started up. Soon it would be all over the festival that Ezra was here walking around.

The guards kept people from approaching, but it didn't stop them from taking pictures as we passed.

"I thought we could go see the circus." Ezra glanced down at me to see if I was in agreement. He was completely oblivious to the crowd growing around us. He was so used to it at this point that he didn't even bat an eye. "It's supposed to be one of those aerial acts. Not clowns," he winked.

"You're never going to let me live that down, are you?" One time I confessed that I was terrified of clowns and Ezra thought it was the funniest fear ever. But those things were scary. Yes, things, because I did not believe clowns were people. They were far too horrifying to be human.

"Definitely not." He smiled at me boyishly, a slight skip in his step.

He seemed to know where he was going so I followed him, while the bodyguards kept the crowd at bay.

He approached a red and white striped tent and ushered me inside. One of the guards stayed by the entrance while the other followed us.

The place was packed with people waiting for the start of the show.

Ezra continued forward and I grabbed his elbow, hissing, "I think they're sold out."

"Just trust me."

He turned to the first row and sure enough there were three empty seats. "After you." He waved his hand dramatically.

I shook my head and took the end seat. "You had this planned," I accused.

He smiled and sat down beside me with his bodyguard on his other side. "Maybe," he whispered in my ear.

A girl, no more than thirteen, sat beside the guard. She leaned forward, peering around his massive body and let out a small shriek of excitement before skirting back and hiding her red face behind her hands.

Ezra chuckled and leaned forward. “Hi, I’m Ezra.” He held out a hand to the girl who was still hiding behind her hands. Her friends sat beside her, both of their mouths hanging open in shock.

The one beside the girl bumped her with her elbow and said, “He’s talking to you!”

The girl lowered her hands. “I’m Sarah.” When she noticed that he was holding out his hand she stuck hers in it.

He gave it a quick shake before letting go.

Sarah looked like she’d just won the lottery. “You’re my favorite,” she exclaimed suddenly, finally finding her voice. “I know most people overlook the bass player, but yeah, I love you.”

Ezra chuckled, flashing a smile. “I’m happy to not be overlooked.”

“We’re going to the concert later.” The girl that elbowed Sarah piped in.

Ezra grinned, pushing strands of his dark hair away from his eyes. “Cool. Hey, Jon make sure these ladies get passes into the meet and greet.” He pointed to Sarah and her two friends.

The one that had been quiet up until now let out a shriek that had everybody in the nearby vicinity covering their ears. “You mean I get to meet Maddox?!” She gasped, fanning her suddenly flushed face. “Oh my God, I love him so much. He’s beautiful and when he plays the drums…" Her whole body shook with excitement. "He's amazing."

It was then that I noticed her shirt.

SAVE A DRUM. BANG A DRUMMER.

Oh shit. We were in for it.

I gave Ezra a look and he merely chuckled.

Maddox had no idea what was headed his way.

The lights began to dim and then everything began to glow with a purple and blue hue. Ezra sat back and the girls grew quiet, only the occasional whisper and giggle, as the show began.

Music began to play, something slow and haunting.

Dancers came out with some sort of white glow stick clasped in their hands. As they danced the lights began to blur, creating an otherworldly effect.

The music began to quicken and then stopped all together.

The tent went black.

I blinked my eyes, trying to see anything.

My heart picked up speed at the total darkness, and I was tempted to reach for Ezra's hand, but we were in public and I was afraid someone might snap a photo of us on their phone and the rumors it would cause weren't worth it.

Before my panic could escalate the lights came back on, pointed at the peak of the tent.

I gasped in awe when I saw that heavy looking lengths of fabric now dangled from the top. A female had the fabric wrapped around her arm and spun through the air. On the other fabric piece a man spun in the opposite direction.

Their faces were tortured and full of longing as they reached out for each other, always failing to reach the other one.

The music sped up again, as did their movements. They began to blur and then she let go of the fabric. He caught her easily and their bodies tangled together as he held them up with only one hand.

The lights changed to a pink hue and their expressions became filled with lust.

They were absolutely incredible.

I'd never seen anything else like it.

"This is amazing," I breathed.

When I glanced over at Ezra he was looking at me and not the show.

"You're missing it," I hissed, pointing in the direction of the aerialists.

He shook his head, his dark brows drawn together. "I'm not missing anything."

My heart stuttered and skipped a beat and I looked away from him hastily.

But still, his eyes lingered upon my face.

When the show ended we headed back out into the festival once more. The crowds had doubled in size and I worried the two guards might not be enough.

I stuck close to Ezra's side, trying to ignore the stares.

I should've been used to them by now since I was friend's with him, but I was convinced the prying eyes and nosy looks from strangers was something you just didn't get accustomed to.

"Let's go get some cotton candy." He slung an arm over my shoulder, steering me over to a cart.

The guy working it quickly handed over a cone of cotton candy. He didn't appear starstruck by Ezra, but I could tell the growing crowd was freaking the guy out. They were turning into vultures.

Ezra handed me the cotton candy and turned us away from the cart.

I dug my heels into the ground. "Aren't you getting one?"

He shook his head and grinned. "Nope. I thought we could share." He then leaned over and took a bite of the cotton candy, shoving the strands that stuck to his lips into his mouth.

He was definitely trying to kill me.

Or my ovaries.

What he did shouldn't have been so hot, but it was, and based on the swooning going on around us I wasn't the only one affected.

I continued to watch as he reached out and pried away a small handful of the blue fluffy sugar goodness. He then proceeded to stuff it in my mouth.

"What the hell, Ezra?" I chewed and swallowed.

He grinned, rocking back on his heels. "You were drooling. I was trying to clean up."

"I was not drooling," I defended, squaring my shoulders. "I was merely...appreciating the view."

"Mhmm," he smiled, biting his lip. He glanced away and pointed, "Let's go over there."

"To the games?" I questioned. "You know those things are rigged, right? They only want your money."

"I think I can afford to lose a few bucks." He winked.

"True," I agreed.

He stopped in front of a booth, one where you had to throw baseballs at different targets.

"What do I get if I win?" Ezra asked the guy manning the booth.

"A goldfish," the guy replied, pointing to where several goldfish swam in mason jars.

"Sweet," Ezra rubbed his hands together, "Sadie, why don't you think of a name for our future pet."

I raised a brow, taking another bite of cotton candy. "*Our* pet? Do you really think I could manage to keep that thing alive for more than a day?" I pointed at one of the happily swimming fish. "I can't even remember to feed myself."

He laughed, ducking his head. "Fine, I'll take care of it."

He laid some money on the counter and the guy handed over several baseballs. "You get three tries on each target and you have to knock down all three targets to win."

"Easy enough." He smiled, rolling his shoulders.

He blew out a breath and I laughed. "You're really taking this seriously, aren't you?"

"I always take my balls seriously."

I rolled my eyes and poked him in the ribs.

"Hey, you gave me the perfect opening. I had to take it."

I shook my head, smiling even though he was ridiculous. I'd missed our banter though. It felt like it had been missing the last month, but with everything that had been going on and the months we went without speaking to each other it was reasonable for us to be a little wary around one another.

But now we were back to the old Sadie and Ezra.

Only we were sleeping together.

But that wouldn't change our relationship.

Nope.

Definitely not.

I forced myself to pay attention to the silly game. He'd already knocked down one of the targets and had moved on to the second. That one fell too and he stepped over to line up with the third target. He missed, and then missed again. When he raised the final ball I couldn't stop myself from lightly kicking the back of his knee. It wasn't hard enough to hurt him, but it messed up his aim.

"Sadie," he groaned, but then began to laugh. "You really don't want me to bring that goldfish home, do you?"

I shrugged innocently. "I just thought you should work harder for Toby. You know, show him that you really want him."

"Toby?" He raised a brow.

I feigned a gasp. "You said I could pick a name."

"And you said you didn't want a pet."

"Well, I mean, I do already have a puppy." I reached up, ruffling his hair.

He laughed and ducked away.

Around us strangers took photos and videos on their phones. I did my best to ignore them.

"You want the fish or not?" He asked, already pulling his wallet out of his back pocket.

I shrugged again, fighting a smile. "Only if you think your balls have what it takes."

“You’re baiting me and it’s working.” He chuckled, smacking a twenty-dollar bill on the booth counter.

“That’s what I’m here for.”

The guy handed him his change and some more baseballs.

“You’ve got this, Ez.” I gave him a thumb’s up while making a silly face.

He batted me away and mumbled, “You’re distracting me.”

“Come on, you’ve gotta show Toby that you’re serious about this life-changing adoption. Work for it.”

“Shhhh,” he covered my mouth with his hand, “I can’t concentrate with you babbling.”

I licked his hand.

He lowered his head and muttered, “I should’ve known you’d do that.”

“I’ll be on my best behavior now.” I raised my hands and took a step back. I bumped into the solid steel wall of Kenny and stumbled. The large ogre of a man grabbed my elbow and immediately steadied me. Thank God for that, the last thing I wanted to do was fall and show the world my Britney. Granted, I was wearing underwear, but accidents happen.

Ezra successfully knocked down all the targets this time since I didn’t distract him. He gladly accepted his new pet goldfish with a boyish grin. As we left the booth a crowd of people rushed it, all of them now wanting to win one of Toby's brothers or sisters.

It was getting close to the start time for their set so we didn't have time to do anything else.

Jon and Kenny ushered us both into the talent tent.

"Dude," we heard almost immediately, "why the hell are you carrying a goldfish?" Hayes strode forward, holding a bag of chips.

"I won him," Ezra said, setting the jar down on a table.

Hayes merely shook his head. "How are you?" He asked, nodding at me.

"Uh, good." I smiled awkwardly. Hayes was a nice guy and I felt bad about how things had gone on our date, but the way he acted he didn't seem to have any hard feelings.

"Has Ezzie-poo taken you on a date yet?" He grinned, looking between the two of us with a knowing smile.

"No," I said adamantly.

Ezra changed the subject by asking where his bass was. Hayes told him and he hurried off, leaving me alone with his band mate.

"So," Hayes started, chewing on a mouthful of chips, "you two haven't banged each other's brains out yet?"

I rolled my eyes and took a seat on one of the plastic chairs dotting the tent.

“Why does everyone think there’s something going on with us?”

“Um...” Hayes looked at me like I was crazy. “Number one, we’re not blind. Two, the sexual chemistry stemming off the two of you is about to smother all of us. Just do it already so things can go back to normal.” He leaned his hip against a table covered in food, waiting for my reply.

I simply laughed. “You’re crazy.”

“Maybe,” he agreed, and tipped a finger in my direction, “but I’m not stupid.”

“Touché.”

Behind me the tent opened again and Mathias walked in. Immediately Hayes groaned, waving his hand dramatically at the lead singer.

“*Duuuude*,” he drew out the word, “you cannot wear a fucking nerdigan on stage. Plus, it’s like ninety degrees. Aren’t you dying?”

“What did you call my cardigan?” Mathias stopped in his tracks, glaring at Hayes.

“A nerdigan. It’s the proper name for it. Seriously, take it off. You look ridiculous.”

Mathias smirked. “If you wanted me naked all you had to do was ask.” His hands went to the belt on his jeans.

Hayes sputtered. “No dude, just the fucking nerdigan.”

Mathias shook his head and took it off. Hayes smiled in glee. "I'm only taking this off because it's fucking hot out there and I don't want to pass out on stage. So stop gloating."

"I'm not gloating." Hayes defended.

"You're smiling," Mathias' glare was icy, "it's the same thing."

"Where's Remy?" I asked.

Mathias turned his attention to me. His lips turned down into a deeper frown. "She doesn't like dealing with the crowds now that she's pregnant. It makes her nervous."

"Her or you?" I countered.

His lips twitched. "Mostly me."

"That's what I thought." I smiled. Mathias was crazily overprotective of Remy, but even pregnant the chick was a definite bad ass.

At that moment a woman working for the festival entered the tent, wheeling a cart with audio equipment to wire the guys.

Maddox and Emma entered right behind her.

"I need you guys back here." The woman pointed to the back of the tent.

"See you soon." Maddox leaned down and kissed Emma quickly.

He waved at me and then playfully shoved his twin before the three disappeared behind a curtain.

"Have you been here a while?" Emma asked, plopping down in one of the other plastic chairs. She wore a black crop top and pale yellow skirt that came up higher in the front and was long in the back and sides. Her favorite floppy black hat sat on her head with her wild blonde hair curling beneath it. I was slightly envious of her effortless, almost hippy, style. I knew Emma spent hardly any time picking out her clothes, and yet she still managed to look gorgeous. Although, she'd argue the fact that she looked like she'd just rolled out of bed.

"Uh, yeah. I guess." I replied. "Why?"

"You look a little sun burnt."

I turned my head to look at my shoulders and discovered that they were slightly red in color. "I forgot to wear sunscreen."

"Yours?" She nodded at the fish swimming lazily in the jar.

"Ezra's. He won it in one of those stupid games." I waved my hand to encompass the festival.

"Have you been having fun?" She asked, straightening her skirt and crossing her legs.

"Yeah," I nodded. "We saw the aerial circus act and it was amazing."

"Oh!" Emma clapped her hands together and leaned forward. "So, Maddox found a great place for us to stay in the Florida Keys. Do you think you can be ready to leave in a week?"

I nodded. "I can make it happen."

"Perfect!" She did a little dance. "This is going to be so much fun!"

I smiled in agreement. I hadn't been on board with this in the beginning, but the more I thought about it the more excited I became. I knew being around everyone for a week would make it hard for Ezra and I to get any alone time, and that sucked, but I needed this.

Maddox returned, smacking his drumsticks against his legs and jumping up and down. "Are you guys ready to rock? Because I'm ready to rock."

I glanced at Emma. "Did he drink too many Diet Pepsi's again?"

She smiled and shrugged sheepishly. "Maybe."

"Dude, chillax." Hayes appeared next, his bright blue guitar slung across his body. "You're like a fucking monkey on crack. What's with the jumping?"

"We haven't performed in a while and I'm really excited," Maddox replied gleefully, still drumming his drumsticks against his leg.

Hayes' face crinkled in thought. "We just finished a six month tour a month ago."

"I know but it feels like forever." Maddox went back to jumping.

"He's going to give me a headache," Hayes pinched the bridge of his nose, "I never thought I'd say this, but someone get that guy his knitting bag."

“It’s in the car,” Emma said, digging through her clutch for car keys.

“Hey, you.” Hayes grabbed one of the festival workers that was milling around the tent. “Go get Maddox his knitting supplies before he blacks out from excitement. He needs to calm the fuck down.”

The worker’s eyes widened. “Uh...”

“I’ll get it,” Emma stood, heading for the tent flap. “You,” she pointed at Maddox, “try not to break anything.”

Maddox grinned, now tapping his drumsticks on the concession table. “No promises.”

Emma sighed and left.

Mathias returned, fiddling with his earpiece.

He strode over to his twin and snatched the drumsticks.

“Hey!” Maddox made a grab for his stolen drumsticks, but Mathias was faster and turned away. “Give those back!” Maddox demanded, jabbing at his brother.

“Ladies and gentlemen, I present to you the Wade Brothers: forever twelve years old.” Ezra entered the room, carrying his bass.

The twins continued to scuffle, completely oblivious to Ezra.

“You want some water?” Ezra asked me, striding over to the small refrigerator in the corner.

"I would love some, darling," Maddox called, still trying to get his drumsticks back from Mathias.

"I wasn't talking to you," Ezra chuckled.

Maddox gasped, forgetting his drumsticks. "Lovebug, have you moved on? I thought what we had was real. I'm devastated."

Ezra rolled his eyes and grabbed a bottle of water, tossing it to Maddox.

"You guys have the weirdest bromance ever." Hayes shook his head.

"Aw," Maddox reached up to put his arm around Hayes' shoulders, "Ez and I are open to making this twosome and threesome." He winked.

Hayes shrugged out of Maddox's hold and his lips twitched with suppressed laughter. "Yeah, I don't want in on this particular threesome."

"Such a shame," Maddox shook his head, "Ezra and I are a lot of fun."

"I'll live." Hayes chuckled, leaning his hip against the concession table. He grabbed a handful of chips and started munching.

"Here," Emma grouched, shoving the tent flap open, "now chill out." She held out a blue duffel bag to Maddox.

"Ooh," Hayes smiled, "sounds like someone's in trouble. Will he be sleeping on the couch tonight?" He turned to Emma.

She smiled, laughing under her breath. "Possibly."

"If I knit you a sweater will I redeem myself?" Maddox asked, his eyes round and his lower lip jutting out.

"It's ninety degrees outside. Do I look like I want you to knit me a sweater?" She tried to sound serious, but laughter soon infused her tone.

"You look like you want to be wrapped in my arms."

She snorted and then laughed out right. "That's quite possibly the cheesiest thing you've ever said to me."

"Come on," Maddox held his arms out, his t-shirt stretching to fit across his broad chest, "let's hug it out. Hugs make the world a better place."

Hayes gagged. "I'm choking on the sweetness. I need to breathe normal air." He set his guitar aside and headed for the back part of the tent. Bright sunlight streamed in for a moment when he exited and then the tent was plunged into its shaded state once more.

Ezra appeared in front of me and handed me a bottle of water before sitting down in the chair. "There's never a dull moment around here," he commented.

I nodded in agreement. I sipped at my water as Maddox and Emma pulled up another set of chairs.

Mathias paced in the corner, talking on his phone. From the sounds of it he was checking in on Remy.

Maddox sat the duffel bag on the ground and began rummaging through it. Small items fell out and I eyed them before reaching out and picking one up.

It was a tiny sweater and I had no idea why he would make something so small. I fit it onto my hand and eyed him. "What did you make this for?"

He looked at me like *I* was the crazy one. "For Sonic of course. He gets cold."

"Your hedgehog?"

"Do you know any other Sonic's?"

"I guess not." I tossed the small sweater back into his duffel bag.

He began knitting and I couldn't make out what it was. "What is that?" I asked, my brows wrinkling in confusion.

He held it up. "It's baby socks. For my future niece *or* nephew, since my asshole brother won't tell me what his kid is." He raised his voice and glared at his twin. Emma tried not to smile since we both knew the gender of Mathias and Remy's child.

Mathias ended his call and stuffed the phone in his back pocket. "It's a fucking boy!" He lifted his arms at his sides. "Happy now?"

"Immensely." Maddox grinned, sitting the yellow yarn away and pulling out baby blue. "Now I can make my *nephew* a proper sock and blanket set."

Mathias closed my eyes. "How on Earth are we twins?"

"Well, you see," Maddox started, "a sperm met an egg, and said, 'Oh hello, Imma fertilize you.' So then the fertilized egg split in utero—"

"M'kay, I got it." Mathias held up a hand for Maddox to shut up.

"Does my nephew have a name?" Maddox returned to the previous conversation.

Mathias scrubbed a hand over his lightly stubbled jaw. "It's Liam."

"So...are you going to tell mom she's having a grandson named Liam, because you know she's pissed you guys haven't revealed the gender."

"I might as well now." Mathias tossed his hands in the air. "Can't keep a fucking secret in this family. Everybody has to know everything." He grumbled under his breath.

"You guys are going on in five." A guy appeared at the front of the tent, holding up five fingers and wiggling them around. "Are you going to be ready?"

"Absolutely." Maddox said, packing up his knitting supplies. "Although, we're currently missing our guitar player. He's probably getting a blowjob behind the tent. Would you mind fetching him for us? I've seen his dick one too many times."

"Maddox!" Emma hissed, smacking his arm.

He chuckled and kissed her. She made a big show of wiping her mouth off with the back of her hand.

The festival worker looked at Maddox in horror.

"He's messing with you," Ezra put the poor guy out of his misery, "don't worry, I'll get Hayes."

"Uh...okay...thanks." The guy ducked away.

"You know that guy is probably going to blab what you said and it'll end up on TMZ by tomorrow." Ezra eyed Maddox.

Maddox dismissed his words with a wave of his hand. "The media has said worse things about all of us before. This is nothing. Besides, Hayes has a sense of humor so he'll think it's funny. Unlike some people." His gaze swiveled to his twin brother.

"Two minutes!" Someone called.

Hayes reappeared at this call and the guys headed to the back of the tent and out into the open air.

Emma and I went in the opposite direction to join the spectators.

The crowd was huge, but that was really no surprise.

The stage was fairly large with a screen behind it, flashing the Willow Creek logo.

Maddox's drum kit already sat on the stage and I had to laugh. He'd had it custom painted with Sonic the Hedgehog—the video game hedgehog, not his pet.

Maddox was the first to bound onto the stage, so full of energy. He sat down behind his kit and began to tap out a beat as the other guys climbed the steps to the stage.

The girls had screamed at Maddox's appearance, but now that the rest of the band had joined him the screams became deafening.

"Oh my God, Oh my God, Oh my God," a girl beside me fanned her face, "I think I'm going to pass out."

If she did I wouldn't catch her.

Okay, that was mean of me, so I probably would help her out if she actually passed out but hopefully she could keep it together.

Emma snickered beside me.

Mathias grabbed the microphone, putting on his game face. He spoke charmingly to the crowd for a moment, hyping them up while Maddox continued to play a light beat in the background.

Mathias nodded to Hayes, giving him the cue.

Hayes began to play and the sound of his guitar blasted through us.

Mathias started to sing and Ezra joined in with the bass.

I loved watching Ezra play. He was always so in the zone, completely absorbed in the feel of the song. His foot tapped against the stage and he leaned into his bass, almost like he wished he could slip inside and become one with it. He bit his bottom lip and his eyes closed momentarily.

He was so beautiful.

And maybe that was a weird thing to think about a guy, but it was true. When he was up on stage, living his dream, and loving his music, he truly was beautiful.

Beside me Emma sang along to the song, really getting into it. She even busted out a few dance moves. Before Maddox she didn't even listen to this kind of music. I loved that she'd managed to come out of her shell.

I joined her, singing and dancing to the song.

It was humid and in no time sweat drenched my body, but I didn't care. I was having too much fun.

When I glanced back up at the stage my eyes connected with Ezra's. Somehow he'd spotted me, even from this distance. He flashed me a smile before ducking his head and focusing on playing.

Mathias grasped the microphone, belting out the song like his very soul demanded he sing the words.

Hayes jumped around on the stage like he was possessed. I didn't know how he managed to jump like that and play guitar at the same time.

Maddox's drumsticks clashed against the cymbals and his shirt stuck to his chest with sweat. His messy brown hair was just as damp.

When the guys were on stage they truly *performed*, they didn't just stand there. They made you feel and live the music with them.

When their set ended fireworks went off. I turned to Emma with surprise in my eyes.

“What did you expect?” She laughed. “It’s Willow Creek. This town pulls out the big guns for them.”

“Obviously.”

We ducked out of the crowd and headed back into the tent.

The guys joined us a few minutes later. All of them were sweaty, their faces flushed from the heat. Hayes grabbed a bottle of water, drinking at it greedily. The other guys grabbed waters as well.

Maddox stripped off his shirt, giving everyone an eyeful of his abs. One of the women working in the tent sighed happily and Emma glared at her.

“Put your shirt back on before you get mauled.” She demanded.

Maddox grinned, wiping a dribble of water off his chin. “Aw, babe, are you jealous?” He glanced in the direction of the woman who was trying to busy herself by restocking the refrigerator, but kept stealing glances at the half-naked drummer.

“Of course not.” Emma scoffed, crossing her arms over her chest.

“I think it’s hot when you get jealous,” he told her, striding over. “But the shirt is staying off for now. I’m too hot.” He fanned himself. “This heat is ridiculous. Are you sure you want us to vacation at a beach? Because right about now, escaping to some place cold sounds like a mighty fine idea, don’t you want to see my epic snowboarding skills?”

"Don't go changing plans now," she warned him, "you'll confuse everyone."

"When are we supposed to leave for this *vacation*?" Mathias asked, sinking down into a chair. He said the word vacation like it left a sour taste in his mouth. I figured after being on tour for so long he didn't want to travel, but Emma was adamant that she wanted all of us to go, and I knew all of the guys would do anything to make her happy.

"Next Friday, and we'll be gone for a week," Emma replied.

"When does the meet and greet start?" Hayes interrupted, running his fingers through his damp hair.

"Thirty minutes," Maddox said, looking at the watch on his wrist.

"Good. I'm starving, so that gives me a chance to stuff my face."

"Didn't you eat before you guys went on stage?" I asked.

He shrugged, grabbing a plate and piling food on it. "I'm already hungry."

"Hayes is always hungry." Mathias rolled his eyes. "He's a bottomless fucking pit."

"When you have a kid are you still going to use the word *fuck* in every sentence?" Maddox glared at his brother.

"Hey, I'm working on it," Mathias growled, "it's pretty fucking hard to stop using a word you've said all of your life."

Maddox sighed. "My nephew is going to have a potty mouth." He tossed his hands up, like he was already resigned to this fact. "He's going to end up calling me Uncle Fucking Maddox."

"Sounds good to me." Mathias grinned. Actually *grinned*—like his lips lifted and he showed his teeth and everything.

Maddox laughed and so did Mathias. They looked more like twins to me in that moment than they ever had. Despite being identical, it was always easy to tell them apart. Maddox had an easy smile, while Mathias' face was usually pinched with irritation.

Ezra came over to stand beside me, his fingers purposefully grazing my arm.

A small gasp escaped between my lips and I forced myself to remain still. I didn't want him to know how much his touch affected me. But based on the way his lips danced, he was *very* aware of what he was doing to me.

With the remaining free time we all ate the food provided and the guys attempted to regale their appearances so they didn't look so sweaty and dirty. I didn't think the fans would mind, though.

For the meet and greet more chairs were brought in and the guys sat down. I noticed they did that a lot and I figured it was to seem more approachable. When you had four giant rock stars staring down at you it could be intimidating.

"Are you excited for your little friends to joins us?" I joked, looking at Ezra.

He shrugged. "You betcha."

"Friends?" Maddox leaned around his twin to look at Ezra. "Honey, are you cheating on me? I thought our friendship was real."

Ezra laughed. "Yeah, sorry dude, you just don't do it for me."

"I feel like everything I've known to be true is now a lie." Maddox gasped, putting a hand over his heart. "What a cruel, cruel world we live in."

Ezra shook his head. "It's just a few fans that were at the circus and I told them they could come." He grinned suddenly, no doubt remembering the girl with a clear crush on Maddox. "I think you're really going to like them."

"Hey," Emma interrupted, snapping her fingers, "what are you up to?" She narrowed her eyes on Ezra.

"Nothing." He raised his hands innocently.

"We're going to start letting them in." One of the festival workers, who I had learned was named Hannah, stood by the tent entrance.

"Bring it on," Maddox clapped his hands together, "I'm ready for battle."

At his words Hannah opened the tent flap and she started letting people in.

The guys graciously doled out hugs and posed for pictures and signed whatever was tossed their way. I knew they had to be exhausted from their set, but they all kept smiles on their faces. Even Mathias.

I spotted the girls from the circus and the one with the drummer shirt looked like she was ready to pass out.

When she saw Maddox she lost all control and ran right at him.

Maddox was quick and caught her in a hug before they could fall to the ground.

He placed her down gently, but was obviously rattled.

"Hi," she peered up at him with wide eyes, "I'm Taylor and I'm your biggest fan ever. Like *ever*. Wow, I can't believe I'm meeting you. You're even hotter in person." She reached out to touch his jaw and he flinched away as she stared at him in awe. "Your jawline is more structured than my life."

Maddox's lips pressed together and the other guys dissolved into laughter.

The other girls—and reluctant parent's—gathered for the meet and greet watched the exchange.

"Uh...thanks?" Maddox said. I'd never seen him so unsure before. Normally you could count on Maddox to have some sort of witty comeback.

"I'm sorry," the girl put a hand to her forehead, "you probably think I'm so weird."

Maddox grinned, his charm slipping into place. "Weird is beautiful."

She giggled, her cheeks flaming red.

Beside me Emma laughed, shaking her head. We'd moved to the back corner to be out of the way. "I'm so afraid that poor girl is going to pee her pants."

"It's a possibility," I agreed.

Another hour passed while the guys conversed with the meet and greet attendees and I lost count of how many pictures they continued to pose for.

Finally everyone was cleared out of the room and we were free to go.

It was getting late now, and darkness had settled into the summer sky.

Mathias grabbed his cardigan and hauled ass out of there before any of us could tell him goodbye. I knew he was probably worried about Remy. Those two were almost as bad as Maddox and Emma.

Maddox and Emma headed out next, leaving Ezra and I alone with Hayes.

Hayes paused by the tent entrance and looked back at us. "I'm hanging out here for a while longer, y'all wanna come?"

Ezra was quick to shake his head. "No, I have to get Toby home."

"Toby?" Hayes asked, his forehead wrinkling in confusion.

"The goldfish." Ezra pointed at the lazily swimming fish.

"Oh, right." Hayes raised two fingers in a salute. "I'll see you later then."

Ezra lifted his chin in goodbye and waved.

Once he was gone Ezra admitted that he was tired.

"Me too," I agreed, and I hadn't even been the one performing.

We gathered up our stuff, including Toby, and met his bodyguards outside the tent so they could escort us back to his car.

The festival was still raging and seemed even more crowded than it had been earlier.

Luckily, most people seemed too drunk to recognize Ezra so we made it to his car without incident.

I held Toby's jar tightly in my hands, afraid that the car ride might jostle him too much. It would totally suck if Ezra and I ended up killing the goldfish before we even made it home.

Ezra backed out and started the drive home. Since he lived in the middle of nowhere it took us a while to get back to his place.

I dropped my bag on the floor as soon as we got in and set Toby on the counter.

"We need to get him a little fish tank," I told Ezra as I headed for the stairs.

"I'll take care of it," he assured me, grabbing a bag of chips and a drink before following me

I took a quick shower and changed into my pajamas.

I was starting into my room when Ezra called my name.

I padded down the short hallway and stood in the doorway. "Yeah?" I asked, as his eyes raked over my body. My pajamas consisted of a pair of shorts and a tank top. The shirt was pulled taut against my breasts and I was sure he was getting quite the show.

"Sleep in here tonight." He patted the empty space beside him. He was shirtless and the glare from the TV screen made his chest glow.

"What did you say?" I wet my lips. I couldn't possibly have heard him right.

He turned back the blankets on the other side and patted the empty space again. "Sleep in here," he repeated, "we don't have to do anything, but I..." He paused, clearing his throat. "Please?" He settled on.

I began to sway, suddenly feeling lightheaded, and I realized I'd been holding my breath.

"Okay," I squeaked like a mouse. I'd never been so unsure of myself before. I'd always been a confident girl, comfortable in my own skin, but Ezra shook up my insides to the point that I didn't recognize them.

I tiptoed into his bedroom and slipped beneath the smooth, silky sheets.

Ezra turned off his bedside light, but left the TV on.

He burrowed under the covers and I jolted when his arms wrapped around me.

He pulled me against his body and tucked one of my legs between his.

My heart raced a million miles an hour.

This…this was so much more than just sex.

This was something real couples did. He held me tightly, like he didn't want to let go.

He pressed a tender kiss to the back of my neck and then lower between my shoulder blades over my tattoo.

"Goodnight, Sadie," he whispered in the darkness.

"'Night."

This was nothing.

It meant nothing.

We were nothing.

Nothing.

Nothing.

Nothing.

So why did it feel like everything?

CHAPTER FOURTEEN

MY PENCIL DRAGGED lazily across the blank white page. I could see the dress perfectly in my head, now I just had to get it down on paper.

I'd drawn a few possible designs for Emma's dress already, but I vetoed them without even showing her. They were all lacking something. I wanted this dress to be one hundred percent Emma, and the idea I had now I knew was perfect.

The dress slowly appeared before my eyes and I began to flesh it out, adding the smaller details.

Downstairs something fell over and Ezra yelled, "I'm okay. Don't come down yet!"

"Alright!" I called back.

He'd banished me upstairs and told me he had a surprise for me. I was definitely curious to know what he was up to, but luckily I'd been distracted by my design. Without a distraction I would've forced myself past his barricade—yes, he made a barricade—just to see what he was up to.

I finished my drawing and I smiled at it. I *knew* Emma would love it and I couldn't wait to see her face when I showed her. I was already planning out the fabrics I would need to buy and how much time it would take to make the dress. It wasn't too complicated of a design, but I knew to account for the fact that I might run into a problem.

"I'm ready!" Ezra called. "You can come down now!"

I set my sketchpad aside and scurried down the stairs, nearly falling in my haste.

He'd cleared away the barricade and when I reached the bottom of thc steps I saw that he'd moved the furniture out of the way and covered the floor with a large white sheet.

On top of the sheet was a Twister mat—yeah, like the game—and on top of each colored circle was a splattering of a matching paint color.

"What is this?" I asked.

"Twister...with a twist." He chuckled, standing with his arms crossed over his chest as he admired his handy work.

"Why?" I stood beside him, staring at the mat on the ground in wonder.

He glanced down at me. "We leave for Florida tomorrow and I know it'll be nearly impossible for us to get any time alone, so I thought we would do something fun today."

"So...you want us to roll around in paint?"

His laughter vibrated through his chest and he shoved his unruly black hair out of his eyes. “Getting you dirty has a certain appeal.”

“At least you’re honest. But I’m not sure how I feel about ruining my clothes.”

“Such a girl,” he muttered, then cracked a smile, “it’s a good thing I think of everything.”

He grabbed a pair of brand new white shorts and a white t-shirt. I noticed then that he was dressed in white jeans and a white shirt. By the end of this both would be covered in a kaleidoscope of colors.

I took the clothes from him and stripped down right there. I didn’t think there was any reason to be modest at this point. I folded what I’d been wearing before and set it on the steps.

“You wanna go first?” He asked me, a challenge gleaming in his eyes.

“Sure.” I agreed, stepping over onto the sheet beside the mat.

He picked up the board and spun. “Right hand green.”

I crouched down and put my hand on one of the circles, right smack in the middle of the paint. It squished between my fingers and felt cold and gross, but I kept my face straight so that he wouldn’t make fun of me.

“Your turn,” I declared, waving my hand for the board so that I could spin for him. He held it out to me and I flicked the spinner. “Left foot yellow.”

He stuck his foot out and immediately spun for me. “Right foot red.”

“I’m not that flexible!” I groaned, stretching out to reach a red circle all the way on the opposite side of the mat while still keeping my hand on the green circle.

“I’d beg to differ,” he whispered under his breath.

I rolled my eyes and spun for him. “Left foot blue.” He moved his foot. “Ugh,” I groaned, “that’s so not fair! My muscles are screaming and you only had to move your freaking foot!”

“Don’t hate the player, babe,” he grinned, lifting his shoulders in a small shrug.

“I’ll show you a player,” I grumbled.

“Don’t be like that.” He continued to grin, definitely unconcerned with my current pissed off state. He spun and called out, “Left hand blue.”

“Motherfucker,” I cursed, trying to position myself. I ended up bumping into Ezra and my hands landed on his butt to steady myself, leaving behind streaks of paint.

He stumbled from the impact of my weight and then tripped over me.

We fell together in a tangle of limbs, paint getting all over our clothes and hair.

“Well, that didn’t go according to plan.” I muttered, laying flat across his chest.

“Really? Because getting you in my arms was my end game.” He winked.

I glared down at him as his hands tightened around my waist. I reached out, smearing my hand in a glob of paint. Before he realized what I was up to I pressed my hand to his cheek, the red paint getting all over his face and into the scruff on his cheeks.

His eyes narrowed on me. "Oh, you're in trouble now."

I squealed when he grabbed my wrists and twisted to pin me beneath him. Paint squished beneath me, coating my hair and clothes.

"Ezra!" I screamed.

I smeared my hand in paint again and wiped it in his hair.

He laughed and grabbed my breasts, leaving behind handprints on my boobs.

We continued to roll around in the paint, smiling and laughing, as we tried to get the other person dirtier than we were.

I fell onto my stomach and he landed on top of me, carefully holding his weight slightly above me so that he didn't squish me.

I tapped my hand against the mat. "I'm out, I'm out."

He laughed and rolled off of me, lying flat on his back. I raised my head slightly to look at him and laughed when I saw he was entirely covered in paint. I'm sure I looked much the same.

"We're a mess." I giggled, sitting up.

He grabbed my waist and towed me towards him. I slid easily on the slick surface. “Come here,” he growled lowly, and I swung my legs so that I was straddling him. He sat up, wrapping his arms around me. Slowly, one hand slid up the bare skin of my arm and then he grasped my chin. “I'm going to kiss you now,” he breathed, his dark eyes flicking down to my lips.

Not one to wait, my fingers delved into his hair and I pulled him closer, angling my mouth over his. He exhaled a deep moan and I swallowed it with a kiss.

I rolled my hips against his and his fingers tightened around my waist.

“Fuck,” he growled, “I need you.” His fingers skimmed underneath my top and he pulled it over my head, tossing it so that it landed on the sheet. He lay down, and my lips never parted from his. He sucked my bottom lip between his and I let out a mewling sound.

“You kill me,” he breathed in-between kisses, “you absolutely shatter me.”

I clasped his face in my hands and stared down into his warm eyes. There were so many things I wanted to say—to confess—but I refused to give life to the words. I'd been hurt enough, and I had to protect my heart at all costs, especially from someone who didn't want it.

Instead of saying anything I kissed him again.

His tongue swept past my lips and I breathed him in.

He was everywhere—his taste, his scent, his touch, it was all too much.

It didn't matter how many times he touched me, it always lit me on fire from the inside out. It was like my body was programed to come to life when he touched me.

He turned, pining me onto my back and his lips left mine to kiss a trail down my neck, between my breasts, and over my stomach.

My back arched above the mat and I fisted my fingers in his hair, tugging slightly and he growled in response.

Before I could take my next breath he ripped my shorts off—seriously, *ripped* them because he tugged them off so harshly. I couldn't complain about him ruining them since he'd bought them and they were already covered in paint. Plus, seeing him do that was pretty hot. My underwear and bra went next and both were removed with just as much vigor.

I palmed my breasts as he removed his clothes. His eyes darkened with lust as he watched me. I didn't have much going on in the boob area, but the way he looked at me made me feel good.

He undid the button on his paint covered white pants and started to tug them down, but cursed.

"What's wrong?" I asked, my voice sounding breathless.

"I don't have a condom," he hung his head, smiling sheepishly he added, "this wasn't about sex." He gestured to the twister mat and paint. "I really did want us to do something fun."

"Well, now it *is* about sex." My voice was full of want and desire. "Just forget the condom. I'm on birth control and I'm clean. I got tested after...well, after." He knew what I was talking about.

His whole body shook when he inhaled a breath. "Are you sure? I'm clean too."

"I trust you."

I trusted him completely—with my life, but not my heart.

He nodded once and removed his pants and boxer briefs.

My eyes immediately dropped to his erection. I couldn't help myself. I reached out, wrapping my hand around him and rubbing up and down. Air hissed between his teeth and he let out a curse.

"I need to be inside you," he murmured, grabbing my hands and pinning them above my head. He captured my lips with his and thrust inside.

I gasped at the intrusion and then my body began to relax. Pleasure zinged through my veins. I'd never known how potent and special sex could be until Ezra. I had thought I'd known, but I'd been oh-so wrong. Everything from my past paled in comparison, and I feared that anything after would never live up to this. But from the first time I let him touch me it had been a risk I was willing to take.

His hips rolled deliciously slow against mine and a breathy sigh escaped me.

He stared into my eyes, the feelings and moment far too intimate for two people that were only supposed to be friends with benefits.

I stared right back, unflinchingly.

I don't know what he saw in my eyes, but his darkened with heightened passion and he pulled his bottom lip between his teeth.

Letting go of my hands he skimmed his down my sides and then back up to palm my breasts.

My naked body was covered in paint, as was his, but I didn't care.

He lowered his head, sucking my bottom lip into his mouth. I moaned and his tongue swirled against mine.

My body began to shake as I soared to that place high among the sky.

When I fell his lips silenced my small cry.

I wrapped my fingers around his neck, holding him to me. I kissed him back with every ounce of desire that my small body possessed.

His thrusts quickened and he rested his forehead against mine, still looking into my eyes.

I knew I should look away, that watching him like this would only make me fall harder for him, but I couldn't let this moment leave. I wanted—no, *needed*—to see if any part of him cared for me the way I did him. Even if it was only a fleeting look, I would treasure it forever, because for that single suspended moment in time we would be one.

He groaned, his body shaking as he found his release.

I held his face in my hands, refusing to let him look away.

And then I saw it—that look, so full of love and longing.

I held onto it, tucking the moment into my heart where I could treasure it forever.

I knew I had to let him go, but I raised my head and kissed him again.

His lips were a brand against mine. His fingers fisted in my hair and he kissed me with fervor, like he needed me to survive.

He broke the kiss first and pressed a single, tender kiss to my forehead before pulling out and rolling onto his back.

We both lay there, covered in paint, unmoving except for the heavy rise and fall of our chests as we struggled to get enough air into our lungs.

So much hung unsaid in the air between us.

And it would remain that way.

CHAPTER FIFTEEN

"WOOO! WE'RE IN MIAMI, BITCHES!" Maddox yelled, grabbing up Emma and tossing her over his shoulder. He ran straight for the blue-green colored ocean water. She beat at his back, laughing wildly at his antics.

"We're not even in Miami!" Hayes hollered after him, shaking his head. "Fucking psycho."

"Do you think we could, um maybe keep the cussing to a minimum?" Arden asked, covering her daughter's ears.

I'd ended up closing down my shop for the week and after talking to the guys, Emma, and Remy to see if it was okay, I invited Arden and her daughter Mia to go on vacation with us. I knew it had been forever since she'd had a break—being a single mom was hard—and I felt bad that I'd blown her off a few times when she asked to get lunch or something.

"Oh, right. Sorry." Hayes smiled sheepishly at her. "That might be difficult between the two of us." He tossed a thumb in Mathias' direction.

Mathias rolled his eyes and finished unloading the suitcases from the trunk of one of the SUVs we'd rented for our stay.

I glanced up at the gigantic mansion we were staying in.

It had four stories—the bottom story was a massive garage, but the other three still remained a mystery. The siding was a pale blue and it had windows everywhere. It was just starting to get dark, but the house glowed from within making it obvious someone had been there earlier to get it ready for our stay.

On thc outside palm trees and an endless amount of sand surrounded it.

I breathed in the crisp, salty air.

This was exactly what I had needed.

Glancing over at Ezra as he finished unloading the car we'd rode in I couldn't help thinking about how difficult this week would be for us.

While Maddox and Emma played in the water—meaning he dropped her in the ocean on purpose and she retaliated by dunking him—the rest of us carried our bags into the house.

"Oh my God," Arden gasped.

My gasp echoed hers.

The house was stunning.

Actually, that was an understatement.

Magnificent was a more accurate description.

The walls and furniture were all white with pops of turquoise and hot pink in the form of pillows and vases. It was so simple, but beautiful.

But the view? That was to die for.

I dropped my purse by the set of stairs and walked straight ahead to gaze out the windows. The ocean glimmered in the last of the setting sun and below on the beach Emma ran away from Maddox. He caught her around the waist and spun her around. It was a picture perfect moment.

Ezra stepped up beside me, his arm brushing mine. Body heat radiated off of him and I found myself leaning closer to him. I itched to be wrapped in his arms, but I fought off that urge.

On my other side Arden stood with three-year-old Mia on her hip. "Wow," she gasped, "it's so beautiful it doesn't seem real."

I nodded in agreement.

"Thanks for inviting me." She glanced at me with a smile. "All of you." She glanced at the guys and Remy.

"Of course," Hayes huffed, setting down a heavy bag by the stairs. His face was red and he looked like he was starting to sweat. "What was in that bag?" He addressed me. "Fess up fashion Queen. It's yours right?"

"Not mine." I shook my head.

Beside me Arden's cheeks flamed red, making her freckles appear even more vividly. "Uh...it's mine," she admitted. Hayes began to laugh. "In my defense," she held up a hand, halting whatever he was about to say, "that's my only bag and it has all of mine and Mia's stuff."

Hayes' eyes sparkled with barely contained laughter. "I guess I can forgive you for that."

She smiled at him, tucking a piece of bright red hair behind her ear.

I eyed the two carefully, trying to hide my smile. I turned away and back out at the beautiful view.

"I'm starving," Mathias declared, heading over to the kitchen. He swung open the stainless steel refrigerator doors and cursed. "Motherfucker."

"Language!" Arden admonished, covering Mia's ears once more.

"Oh, right. Sorry."

Holy shit, Mathias Wade apologized. Somebody, put that down in the record books.

"The fu—idiot only has the refrigerator stocked with Diet Pepsi."

Ezra snorted. "Why am I not surprised?"

"I'm going to run to the store to get some food and I'll just pick up pizza for tonight or something." Mathias swiped the car keys off a side table.

"I'll go with you." Remy piped up.

He shook his head and kissed her tenderly. "No, stay here and rest for a bit."

She didn't put up a fight, which led me to believe she did need to rest. Remy wasn't one to listen to what she was told.

Mathias left just as Hayes returned with the last bag.

And by bag I meant cage.

Maddox and Emma brought their pet hedgehogs.

I wished I was joking.

Maddox and Emma ran up the beach and onto the deck steps.

Ezra unlocked the door to let them inside.

"You guys are soaking wet," I said unnecessarily.

"It's his fault." Emma poked Maddox in the side.

"Mathias went to get food since *someone* only stocked us with Diet Pepsi." Hayes muttered, strolling over with his arms crossed over his chest.

Maddox grinned crookedly and tossed an arm over Emma's shoulder. "What else does a man need in life, besides the love of a good woman and Diet Pepsi?"

"A hedgehog," Ezra chuckled.

"How could I forget?" Maddox mock winced.

Hayes sighed, but I knew he was secretly amused. "Why don't we figure out the sleeping arrangement?" He suggested. "That way we can put all this shi—crap—away." He pointed to the mountain of suitcases by the stairs and flashed Arden an apologetic smile.

"Sounds good." Emma clapped her hands together.

We each grabbed a bag and started up the stairs. The same color scheme was carried throughout the large home.

On the second level—or I guess technically it was the third—there were five bedrooms, all with their own bathrooms. There was even a little nook with a chaise lounge and a bookshelf.

Everyone picked a room and that left me. "I guess I'll take a room upstairs," I mumbled, heading for the second set of steps.

"Uh," Ezra interjected, "I will too. I don't want you to be alone."

Emma stopped outside a bedroom door with a hand on her hip and a calculating look in her eyes. "Or Sadie could take the extra room down here and *you* could go upstairs."

"But then *I'm* alone," he countered, "what if I get scared at night? Are you going to come hold my hand, Emma?"

Her lips pressed together as she held in laughter. "Does that mean Sadie is going to hold your hand?" She folded her arms over her chest. She was so on to us. She had been from the start.

"Of course." He grinned, trying to play everything off as a joke.

Emma finally shrugged. "Whatever."

The two of us headed up to the second level. There were only three bedrooms up here—and two bathrooms, one room had it's own and the other was Jack and Jill style. The nook up here was larger and had a baby grand piano and art easel. This place was so incredibly peaceful that I knew I wouldn't have any trouble unwinding.

The three bedrooms were similar in size, so I picked one based on the view of the beach and the fact that it had a balcony. Ezra chose the room across from me and set his bags inside before joining me in my bedroom.

I opened the French doors and stepped out onto the balcony. I leaned against the railing and he stepped up beside me with his hands shoved into the pockets of his khaki shorts.

"You realize I'll be sleeping in here, right?" He winked.

I cracked a smile. After the night where he asked me to sleep with him without sex we'd continued the tradition.

"I expected so."

"I've grown so used to the privacy we have at my house that being here with everyone is going to test the limits of my sanity." He grabbed onto the railing, the last of the blazing sun haloing his body. I itched to lean forward and kiss him, but he wasn't mine and I couldn't risk someone catching us.

"I know what you mean," I agreed.

Ever so slightly he brushed his pinky against mine, and then rested it overtop.

I closed my eyes, treasuring the brief touch.

"Hey, what are you guys doing?"

Maddox.

Ezra's finger fell away from mine and he whipped around with a smile on his face. "Admiring the view," he replied.

Maddox stepped outside with us and I noticed he'd changed his clothes to something dry, but his hair was still wet.

"Isn't this place great?" He grinned. "I couldn't believe I found it on such short notice."

I had to admit I was surprised too. Plus, it was nice that the houses on either side were off in the distance. I doubted we'd have to worry about any crazy fans in this neighborhood, homes this big could only be owned by celebrities and CEOs.

"Anyway," Maddox clapped his hand on Ezra's shoulder, "I just came to tell you guys that Mathias is back already and I thought you might be hungry."

"Sure," Ezra nodded, "we'll be right down."

"Cool." Maddox began to back away, watching us carefully. He was just as suspicious as Emma.

When he disappeared Ezra reached up and gently stroked my cheek.

I sighed happily and leaned into his touch. He placed a feather light kiss on my forehead and held his lips there when he murmured, "How can I do this for a week? How can I pretend I'm not spending every second thinking about the way your body hums when I touch you and you sigh when I kiss you?"

A week? How was I going to pretend to not be thinking about those things for the rest of my life? Our agreement was going to come to an end in a matter of months, maybe even less, and then...and then I didn't know.

I grasped his shirt in my hands and leaned forward, inhaling the scent that was uniquely Ezra.

I answered truthfully. "I don't know either."

CHAPTER SIXTEEN

"UP! UP! UP! GET UP!" Maddox drummed his fist against the door to my room.

"Go away!" I yelled back, tossing a pillow over my head. If I had to deal with Maddox's chipper personality at the crack of dawn every morning I might murder him, which would suck for Emma since she loved him and all. But, seriously.

The door to my room swung open and I sent up a silent prayer that Ezra had snuck over to his room early in the morning.

I tossed the pillow off of my head and rose up on my elbows to look at Maddox. I was sure my hair was a wild untamable mess, but for once in my life I didn't care.

"I made breakfast." He grinned, clearly pleased with this news, like he'd done me some kind of favor.

"It's too early," I groaned.

"It's eight o' clock," he tossed his hands up in exasperation, "that's not early. You're as bad as Emma. Now come on and get ready. We're all going snorkeling."

"Snorkeling?" I sat up completely, this bit of news making me a little excited despite the early time.

He nodded. "Yep...or you could stay here and sleep. Your choice." He shrugged nonchalantly.

I pointed a finger at him in warning. "Don't you dare leave without me."

"Wouldn't dream of it, Westbrook." He flashed his winning smile and closed the door.

I immediately tossed the covers off and ran over to my suitcase.

I pulled out all of my bikinis and dropped them on the floor, rifling through them. I ended up picking a solid black one. The top made my breasts appear larger than they actually were and had several overlapping straps in the back. The bottoms exposed more of my ass than I was used to, but let's face it, I was planning on driving Ezra crazy.

I put on a pair of old ripped jean shorts and a see-through blousy white top over my bikini.

I brushed my hair and it hung in soft natural waves just past my shoulders.

I didn't bother applying makeup, just a bit of gloss.

Before I left my room I grabbed my sunglasses and stuck them on top of my head.

Ezra's bedroom door was open, but I didn't see him inside so I figured he'd already joined the others downstairs.

Everyone was seated at the dining room table and a smorgasbord of breakfast food was sitting on the table. An empty seat was left between Arden and Ezra.

Ezra looked up when I entered the room, his dark eyes raking over my body. They flared with hunger and he sucked his bottom lip between his teeth. His eyes rose to meet mine and he winked.

I sat down and Arden smiled. “Morning.”

“Morning.” I reached for a biscuit and put it on the plate that was already waiting for me.

“They all made breakfast,” she hissed like it was some kind of secret, “the guys.”

“We have many talents.” Hayes quipped, having heard her. “Did you know Mathias can rap?”

Mathias rolled his eyes. “I can do a lot of wicked things with my tongue.”

Emma snorted and Remy nudged his arm with her elbow in a silent gesture to tell him to shut up. She also threw in a glare for good measure.

“Sweetie, do you want another biscuit?” Hayes asked.

At his words we all turned to look at him and saw that he was talking to three-year-old Mia. Her hair was a vibrant red like her mother’s and she looked up at Hayes with wide blue eyes.

She nodded her head and he grabbed one for her.

Arden watched the two in awe.

“She doesn’t normally like strangers,” she whispered.

“Everybody likes me,” Hayes scoffed, flashing a wide smile, “I’m irresistible.”

“I’m beginning to think so,” she agreed.

Beneath the table Ezra’s handed landed on my thigh and he gave it a soft squeeze. I closed my eyes and my lips parted on a breath. He quickly let go before anyone could notice and my body instantly ached for his touch.

Once breakfast was done we all cleaned up and then piled in the SUVs to head over to a different beach.

There, we met with a guy that went over instructions and what to do in case of an emergency—mainly if a shark happened to swim by. It wasn’t likely to happen, but they still had to warn us.

I bounced with excitement, eager to dip my toes into the blue-green water and see the creatures that lived inside.

“I’m going to stay behind with Mia,” Arden said, holding her daughter’s hand and moving back a few steps.

Hayes paused what he was doing and frowned. “Come on, Arden, you don’t want to miss out on this. I’ll stay with her.”

“No, no,” she waved him away when he started forward, “I don’t want to be a bother. We’re fine here.”

He shook his head adamantly. “Go,” he said firmly. “Mia loves me,” he grinned, bending down to the little girl’s level. “We’ll go hunt for seashells while you snorkel.”

Arden seemed to be contemplating his words. “Are you sure?”

“Absolutely.” He reached a hand out to Mia. She put her much smaller one on top and her pale pink nail polish sparkled in the sunlight. A little yellow hat was perched on her head to block the sun from her eyes and she was dressed in a cute bathing suit with little ruffles on her butt. She was such a cute kid.

“Okay.” Arden agreed, watching as Hayes swept Mia up into his arms. He tickled her stomach and she giggled happily. I’d never seen this side of Hayes before and it made me smile. He really was maturing and I was beginning to think what he told me on our date about settling down wasn’t a lie.

Arden had brought a beach bag with her and she rifled through it. She pulled out a small bucket and handed it to Hayes.

“For the seashells.” She smiled at him, tucking a piece of hair behind her ear. “Thanks for doing this.”

“It’s not a problem. Mia and I will have lots of fun. Won’t we?” He addressed the little girl. She nodded eagerly.

Arden stepped away slowly, still a little reluctant to leave her daughter behind.

I put the goggles on that covered my eyes and nose and turned to Ezra. "How do I look?" My voice sounded thick and funny since it had a nosepiece.

"Adorable." He grinned and kissed me quickly.

I froze and so did he. We both turned to see if anyone saw.

Luckily everyone was busy putting their own masks on and didn't notice.

We both let out an audible sigh of relief.

That had been a close one.

My heart still pounded in my chest and I eyed them all warily in case one of them was pretending not to have seen.

"Relax," Ezra whispered, his lips near my ear.

I didn't know how he expected me to do that with him standing so close.

We followed the others to the water's edge and I giggled when it tickled my toes. It was warm and the sand squished between my toes, which were painted a pretty pale purple.

I walked out into the water until it hit my hips. I fixed the mouthpiece between my lips and then dove slightly into the water, making sure to leave the snorkel sticking out so I could breathe.

Beside me Ezra did the same. Arden was close by with the others a little farther out.

Beneath me tiny bright colored fish swam around. They were gorgeous and seemed unafraid of us. One tickled my arm as it swam by.

I swam farther and saw a crab scuttling over a small rock.

The coral was gorgeous and in a rainbow of colors.

I'd never seen anything so beautiful before and I was flooded with inspiration for designs.

Seeing all of this beauty made me realize I'd been missing out on so much that life has to offer. I'd been stuck in my hometown for so long that I forgot that magic was all around us.

A piece of aqua colored coral—or maybe it was some kind of weird grass—swayed from the ocean current.

A finger tapped against my elbow and I jolted.

I turned to look and saw Arden. Her red hair billowed around her like a flame. She pointed to my right and I glanced that way.

It was a turtle and it swam right up to us, completely unafraid of us like the other fish had been. I itched to reach out and touch its shell, but the man we met with on the beach warned us to not touch any of the animals. After all, they were wild and this was their home.

I don't know how long we swam around, but eventually we all emerged from the water with wrinkly fingers and toes.

Instead of returning to the beach house and hanging out there, we set up on this beach.

Hayes met us with Mia—the bucket now full of seashells. Mia was grinning from ear to ear and clinging onto him. I'd say the little girl had a crush.

Arden went over to join him, smacking a loud kiss on Mia's cheek. Mia giggled merrily and reached for her mom.

I headed over to my bag and pulled out my towel, using it to dry my body before sitting down.

I grabbed my tanning oil and started rubbing it on my body.

Arden put her towel down beside mine and sat with Mia between her legs. Mia immediately toddled off of the towel and into the sand. She picked up a handful of sand and threw it at her mom's legs. Arden merely shook off the sand.

"It's unfair that you can get a nice pretty tan and I'm going to end up looking like a lobster and I'll probably gain a hundred more freckles." She nodded at my already natural olive-toned skin. She tugged her hair back into a ponytail and then began slathering herself in sunscreen before grabbing Mia and putting some on her too.

"Hey, I might get a tan but I'd kill for your hair."

"I guess we all want what we can't have," she quipped.

Hayes strolled over to us and squatted down so that he was at our level. "I thought Ms. Mia might want to dip her toes in the ocean, if that's okay?" He addressed Arden.

"Sure, if she wants to."

Hayes turned to Mia. "Want to be a mermaid?"

The little girl nodded her head enthusiastically and I wondered if she actually knew what he said. I wasn't around kids enough to know what they understood at what age.

Hayes picked up Mia and lifted her onto his shoulders. She grabbed the longer strands of hair on top of his head and tugged. "Horsie!" She cried.

Hayes winced and loosened her fingers. "Don't do that."

"Sowwy." She frowned.

Before she could get too upset he took off running, holding on tight to her, and her giggles trailed behind her.

Beside me Arden shook her head. "It's the craziest thing. Normally Mia hates strangers, so I don't know what it is about him that she likes so much."

"He's a nice guy," I supplied.

"I suppose so." She shadowed her eyes with a hand to her forehead as she watched Hayes and Mia in the ocean. He was holding her now, barely dipping her toes into the water. She giggled and her legs flailed wildly.

Mathias and Remy sat in chairs off behind us beneath an umbrella, far enough away that they had some privacy from the rest of us.

Emma and Maddox were talking to the man we'd seen earlier about something, while Ezra was walking down the beach.

I itched to join him, but I knew Emma would see and draw conclusions.

I hated keeping our arrangement a secret from her, but I had to. No one could know. It was already messy enough with only Ezra and I involved. But if the others found out, I knew they'd root for us to end up a couple, and when we didn't I feared that would lead them all to feel like they had to pick sides. If they didn't know, they couldn't form an opinion and pass judgment.

I watched Ezra pause and stoop down to pick something up out of the sand. He turned it over in his hand before tucking it into his palm. He squeezed it tight and continued on.

"I'm going to take a nap."

Arden glanced at me and arched a brow. "Didn't you go to bed early?"

"Uh...yeah. But the beach sun makes me really sleepy," I lied. I couldn't tell her the truth—that Ezra had kept me up most of the night. The possibility of getting caught had heightened every sensation in my body, and the effort to quiet my cries of pleasure had been exhausting.

“Okay,” she said doubtfully. “I’m just going to read for a little bit since Mia’s occupied. I never get to read anymore.”

I nodded and laid back. My sunglasses shielded my eyes from the sun and the warmth from the rays felt like a blanket.

I really was sleepy and in no time I drifted off.

Cold water prickled the skin of my stomach and I jolted into a seated position.

“What the hell?!” I exclaimed and looked up to find Hayes standing over me with a squirt gun. Where he found that I had no idea.

He smiled boyishly. “I didn’t think you’d want to miss this.”

“Miss what?”

He pointed to the sky.

“What the hell?” I repeated, blinking my eyes. “Is that—?”

“Yep,” he answered, grinning at the sight before us with his hands on his narrow hips.

“They’re insane!” I stood up, leaning my head back so I could see better.

Maddox and Emma were parasailing. To say they were adrenaline junkies was an understatement. They were always looking for another crazy adventure.

Ezra stood a few feet away with his phone held aloft, videoing our crazy best friends.

"One day they're going to get themselves killed," I groaned.

Zip lining, skydiving, and now parasailing. What was next? Cliff-jumping?

"Probably," Hayes answered.

"Did I say that out loud?"

He chuckled and nodded.

"Oops." I glanced away and noticed that Arden and Mia were gone. "Where did Arden go?"

"Mia was sleepy so she headed back to the car. We're leaving after these two finish." He pointed up at the sky.

"I'm posting this on YouTube," Ezra chuckled, "the whole world needs to see these fools."

"Wouldn't your manager have a heart attack if he knew Maddox was up here?"

"Hells yeah," Hayes laughed. "He'll probably shit his pants. Julian is such a fucking fun-sucker." He paused, his lips pursed in thought. "Maybe if he got laid he'd be happier." He snapped his fingers together with a sudden though. "Ez, we should hire a hooker for him."

I reached out and smacked the back of his head.

"Ow," he rubbed the spot and mockingly glared at me, "that hurt."

"Aw, poor baby." I pouted. "I think you'll live."

Hayes smiled and his eyes dipped to my breasts.

I rolled my eyes and pointed to my face. "Eyes up here Hayes."

"Sorry," he cleared his throat, "I just can't help myself. They're just right in my face."

"Dude," Ezra glared, anger flashing in his eyes as he completely forgot about the video he was currently taking, "do you *want* me to punch you in the face?"

"Oh, so are you two—?" He trailed off, waving a finger between Ezra and me.

"No," Ezra said adamantly, tucking his phone into the pocket of his board shorts, "but have some respect."

Hayes made a sound in the back of his throat that made it obvious he didn't believe Ezra. "Whatever. I'm going back to the cars. You guys can wait for them."

Ezra let out a heavy sigh and crossed his hands behind his head. He wouldn't look at me and that began to worry me. I stayed where I was, refusing to be the first one to break the silence.

"What have we done?" He asked, staring out at the sparkling ocean.

"What do you mean?"

He lowered his hands and plopped in the sand, draping his arms over his knees. "I knew this was a bad fucking idea, but I wanted you too much to say no," he continued, "but this fucking sucks, Sadie. Anytime another guy even glances in your direction I want to punch him in the face." He slowly raised his head and his dark gaze connected with mine. "I'm not allowed to have those feelings. You're not mine."

You're not mine. Those words stung like a slap to my face.

"This is just sex. It's not real."

It's not real. Another slap.

It was tearing me apart that he didn't return my feelings, but I was still all too willing to take what he would give me for however long. The pain was worth knowing what it felt like to be held in his arms.

"Right?"

His voice startled me from my thoughts. I sat down beside him, crossing my legs in the sand. I picked up a handful of sand and watched it sift through my open fingers.

"Right," I echoed, immediately hating that word. How could a word that by its very definition meant *correct* feel so undeniably *wrong*?

He reached over and took my hand in his, holding it until he was forced to let go.

I wished so desperately that we could have more than stolen moments, but wishing gets you nowhere, because wishes don't exist.

As our friends joined us once more we headed out to lunch and then back to the beach house. Both of us forced our conversation out of our minds.

We had to.

At least I did, because letting myself believe for one single second that I'd heard a note of longing in his voice when he asked me if he was right, would lead me to feel nothing but anguish later on because it would give me *hope*, and hope was suffocating.

We laid around on the beach for a while before the guys got the brilliant idea to play beach volleyball. They were forcing all of us to play too, except for Remy. Mathias glared at his brother and friends, daring them to go against his wishes and let her play.

Remy was fine with sitting out though, which I knew made Mathias feel relieved.

There was already a net set up on the beach, between our house and the next one, which was currently vacant, but we didn't have a ball. All three guys—minus Mathias who chose to stay behind with Remy—headed to the store.

While they were gone the rest of us ventured into the house to cool off. My skin felt heated to the touch, but I wasn't burned, unlike poor Arden who was starting to look a little red. She hadn't been exaggerating about the whole lobster thing.

I poured myself a glass of ice water and took a seat at one of the kitchen stools.

Emma ventured in and fixed a glass of water too. Her blonde hair was piled on top of her head in a messy bun and she wore a sheer ivory cover-up over her bikini. It had fringe on the hem, which made it very Emma-like.

She sat down beside me and I smiled. "So...do you want to see what I've sketched for your dress?" The wedding was fast approaching so I had to start the actual process of making her dress soon, so I hoped she loved what I'd come up with.

"Ooh! Yes!" Her blue eyes glimmered with excitement. "I wanna see!"

"Wait here." I instructed her before running upstairs to grab my sketchpad.

I returned with it clutched in my hands and I bounced with excitement. I was nervous too, though. There was the very real possibility that she might hate what I'd come up with.

"Lemme see!" She held out her hands in a grabbing motion.

I suddenly felt very unsure of my design. I reluctantly handed it over. I wanted to close my eyes so that I didn't have to see her reaction if she hated it, but I manned up and held my chin high. It was her dress and if she didn't like it, that was her right, but my designs were my babies.

Her mouth fell open and a small gasp emitted from her lips. "Sadie," her voice was full of awe, "this is amazing."

"Really?" A huge weight lifted off of my shoulders.

"I know I didn't give you much to go on, but this? This is perfect. It's more than I could've dreamed of." She reached out and tentatively ran her fingers over the sketch.

I'd opted to go simple for the dress, but kept within Emma's personal bohemian style. I wanted her to be comfortable in it and feel like herself. The shoulders were bare, but a lace draping went around the top of the dress adding more support and ending above her elbows. The dress was fitted against the stomach and then billowed out slightly around the hips, before ending in a short train with more lace detailing.

"I'll get your measurements when we get home and then we can look at fabric together so that you get something you like."

"Thank you." She set the sketchpad aside and reached out to hug me.

I hugged her back fiercely. She might be driving me nuts with her meddling, but she was still my best friend. We'd grown up together, shared each other's good moments and the bad ones too, and I knew I was lucky to have her on my side.

The front door opened and Emma thrust the sketchpad into my hands. "Hide this before Maddox sees," she hissed.

I hurried for the stairs and had only climbed three when I felt eyes glued to my ass.

"Where do you think you're going?" His voice poured over me like sticky honey, rooting me to the spot.

I casually looked over my shoulder, taking in his tousled black curls and searing brown-eyed gaze. He could be so intense sometimes.

"To my room," I answered, finally finding my voice.

He opened his mouth to say something, but Maddox strolled by then and asked him a question.

The spell was broken.

I ran up the rest of the stairs, and the next set as well.

I was out of breath from the climb, but my racing heart? That was all Ezra.

I quickly put my sketchpad away before joining everybody outside for volleyball.

"I think we should do guys versus girls." Hayes declared. The other guys nodded in agreement.

"That's not fair," I argued, "There are four of you and three of us since Remy's sitting out."

"I'll sit out." Mathias volunteered. His eyes already strayed to Remy where she sat a few yards away on a beach towel with her hands resting on her round stomach.

The other guys nodded at his declaration. They probably didn't want the liability of having him on their team anyway, since he'd be distracted checking on Remy every five seconds. Hopefully he'd relax once she had the baby, but somehow I doubted it.

"So, now are we good with guys versus girls?" Hayes asked me, grinning widely.

"I don't know," I shrugged, "depends on if you're ready to lose or not."

"Ooh," Hayes mock-winced, "the trash talking has begun already. Me likey."

"Shut up." Emma glowered, and stole the ball from his hands.

"Somebody woke up on the wrong side of the bed." Hayes whispered conspiratorially. "Maddox, you better do a better job of making sure your woman wakes up happy. You know, maybe a little oral in the morning."

Emma gasped and threw the ball at his head. It bounced off and Ezra caught it.

Hayes rubbed the side of his head, and mumbled something, before joining the other two guys on one side of the net.

"We better beat them." I told Emma and Arden.

"Oh, it's on," Emma agreed, still glaring at Hayes.

"I'm not very good at sports," Arden admitted, glancing over in worry at Mia.

Mia was sitting with Remy and Mathias. Remy had the little girl sitting in front of her and was braiding her hair.

I quickly went over the rules of beach volleyball with her, but she still didn't look very enthusiastic about playing.

Hopefully Emma and I would be able to pull off a win just the two of us.

We lined up with me on the front left, Arden to the right, and Emma behind in the middle.

Ezra tossed me the ball. "Y'all can serve first."

"Aw, look at you guys trying to be all gentlemanly." I laughed and threw the ball to Emma. "You're still gonna lose," I warned.

"We'll see." He grinned.

Emma served and the ball went over the net. Maddox hit it back over in Arden's direction. She screamed and started to run away, but I managed to bump it back over the net.

"Get your head in the game!" I yelled at her. Yeah, I was competitive. So what?

"Did you just quote High School Musical to me?" She laughed.

The ball came sailing back over the net and Emma ran forward to hit it back over.

"Oh my God," I groaned, "just play."

Arden joined in after that, but it was up to Emma and me to make sure we didn't lose. Poor Arden would never make it in sports. It was a good thing she worked in retail.

We ended up tied and my body pulsed with adrenaline. We were so close. We had this. I knew we did.

Hayes served it and it headed in Emma's direction, but was low to the ground. She dove into the sand and bumped it up. Arden hit it and it went a little higher, but not enough to go over the net. I ran over and spiked it over the net.

It landed in the sand before Maddox could get to it.

"Did we win?" Arden screamed in excitement. "We won, right?"

"Yeah, we won," I grinned, sticking my tongue out at the guys. Childish? Yes, but when you were friends you were allowed to do those silly things without it seeming rude.

Emma dusted sand off her body and I did the same.

"I think I have sand between my boobs," she groaned.

Maddox strolled over and kissed her cheek. "I'd be happy to help you clean them."

"Of course you would." She snorted. "I really do need a shower, though."

"Good, me too. We can shower together. You know, save the planet and conserve water. I'm very environmentally conscience like that."

"Mhmm," she hummed in agreement, "and it has nothing at all to do with getting me naked."

"None at all."

She shook her head, fighting a smile.

We all headed inside to shower and relax for a while. We were all tired from being outside all day.

I grabbed a quick snack before heading upstairs to my room to shower.

The bathroom attached to my room was just as dazzling as the rest of the house. Metallic glass tiles covered the walls and the floor was some kind of white tile that resembled wood. The shower was glass and there was a large Jacuzzi tub. I'd have to put that to use at least once before we left.

I turned the water on and let it get nice and warm before peeling off my bikini and stepping inside.

I felt my stiff muscles instantly uncoil and relax at the feel of the warm water.

I began to sing—don't judge me, everybody did it—and didn't notice when the door to the bathroom opened.

When the shower door jerked open I let out a scream. Ezra stepped inside, his hand falling on my mouth to stifle the sound. "Shh," he warned, his dark brows drawn together, "you don't want anyone to hear you."

The noise coming out of my throat cut off and he dropped his hand.

"What are you doing in here?" I hissed, glaring at him. I refused to let my eyes stray over his body and his hard cock jutting proudly from his body. Nope, I wasn't looking. Not. At. All.

He grinned. "You've been prancing around in that tiny excuse for a bikini teasing me all fucking day. Do you have any idea how difficult this has been to hide?" He pointed to his cock.

I swallowed thickly, pulling my bottom lip between my teeth.

"It's been the best and worst kind of torture imaginable." His voice dropped to a husky whisper. He stalked forward, like a panther cornering its prey. My back hit the tiled shower wall and water poured down around me. He placed his hands on either side of my head and leaned in close. "And now," he continued, "if I don't get to touch you, I think I might die."

"Dramatic much?" I quipped, trying to hide how much my body was reacting to him.

"Just the truth, baby."

Baby. I'd never liked pet names. I found them degrading and annoying, but hearing that word roll of Ezra's tongue gave it a whole new meaning.

He continued to hover there, the water pouring down around us, like he was waiting for something.

Finally, he spoke again. "I won't touch you until you give me permission."

I stood on my tiptoes, holding onto the wall for added support. My lips grazed his ear and I whispered, "Touch me. All of me."

Those words seemed to spark a fire inside him, one that burned for me and me alone.

He grasped my hips and lifted me up. I wrapped my legs around his waist and he pressed me into the wall.

He kissed me deeply, like he was trying to memorize the contours of my lips with his.

My fingers delved into his wet hair, tugging him impossibly closer. Our chests were pressed together fully and all he had to do was pull back and move his hips slightly and he'd be inside me.

Our pants filled the steaming air and I moaned into his mouth.

His hands palmed my ass and he lifted me up slightly, breaking our endless kiss.

"Hold onto my shoulders," he commanded.

I did as he asked and the moment I did he thrust inside me. We both let out embarrassingly loud moans. He'd fucked me senseless the night before, and yet somehow it felt like it'd been forever since we were joined like this.

He rested his forehead against mine, not moving his hips as we both struggled to compose ourselves.

When he looked into my eyes I hoped he couldn't see the fear there—the fear that I would never find this with anyone else.

His head moved from my forehead to the crook of my neck and his lips pressed gently against the spot where my pulse raced. Ever so slowly he pulled back slightly and then pushed inside me. He did it again and I thought I might cry. I wanted hard and fast, I didn't want this. This was too much like making love and things like this weren't allowed in our arrangement. Okay, so maybe it hadn't been defined that way, but in my mind it wasn't allowed. This felt too real.

"Harder," I begged, clinging to his wet shoulders.

"No," he growled lowly. He nipped my chin and then took my bottom lip between his teeth before letting it go.

"Please," I panted, trying a different tactic.

"No."

I really hated that word.

I tried to take matters into my own hands and began to circle my hips faster.

He grabbed my hips and held hard enough that I couldn't move them. "I said *no*."

"Ezra," I begged.

"Stop thinking," he whispered, his lips a breath away from mine, "just feel."

God, I wanted to. I wanted to let myself go and revel in the way it felt to be held and loved so gently by him, but I was scared. So, undeniably, terrified that I'd end up ripping my heart out of my chest and handing it to him in the process.

"Feel, Sadie," he said again, kissing me sweetly. "Feel how good we are together."

Didn't he know that was the problem? We felt too good together. Not just when we had sex, but at all times. He was my perfect other half.

A tear fell down my cheek, getting lost in the shower water.

I didn't know how I would ever find the strength to let this go.

I didn't want to.

But I had to.

I closed my eyes as his lips ghosted down my neck.

He clasped my hands in his and held them above my head. I gasped when he hit something deeper inside of me. "Ezra." I panted his name over an over again. "Ezra. Ezra. Ezra."

I was desperate to touch him, but he held my hands prisoner.

He angled his mouth over mine, and his tongue brushed into my mouth.

I was consumed.

Devoured.

Obliterated.

I did not exist.

Somehow I managed to let go of my thoughts and soon I was hurdling over the edge as an orgasm hit me.

I clung to him desperately, my legs shaking, and he let go of my hands to grasp my thighs.

He pushed into me a little harder, but still at an unhurried pace.

In a matter of minutes I was close to another orgasm.

I cried out, and he tried to silence me with a kiss.

"Fuck," he growled against my throat, nibbling the tender skin there. "Oh, fuck you feel so good. I'm gonna come."

When his orgasm hit he growled low in his throat and burrowed his head against my neck. His wet hair tickled me, but I was too tired to try to move away.

Still inside me, he murmured, "That was fucking amazing."

I nodded.

He gently lowered me to the ground and he slipped free of my body.

Before I knew what he was doing he had my shampoo bottle in his hand, and poured some into his open palm.

"Turn around," he commanded.

I did as he asked.

He lathered the shampoo into his hands and worked it into my hair. He rinsed it out and did the same with the conditioner.

When my hair was clean he reached for the body wash. He worked it into his hands and rubbed my shoulders and my arms, before cupping my breasts.

I leaned against him, absorbing his touch.

His hands roamed over my stomach and my body clenched with desire once more, hoping his hand would venture lower, but he didn't. Instead he rinsed me off and used my shampoo to wash his own hair. I really hoped no one noticed that we both smelled like strawberries.

He turned the shower off and we stepped out. I wrapped the waiting towel around my body and grabbed another one from underneath the sink for him.

When I stood back up he was *right there*. I let out a startled squeak and jerked backwards, knocking into the large decorative vase that had some kind of wooden sticks in it. It fell to the floor and shattered with a loud clamor.

I looked at Ezra with panic in my eyes. "Oh, shit."

He grabbed the towel from me and used it to rub his hair before tying it around his narrow waist. "No one probably heard." He swept his thumb over my bottom lip, like it pained him to not touch me.

I glanced down at the shattered vase. "Yeah, you're probably right."

"I'm always right." He chuckled.

He took my face between his large hands and kissed me long and deep, before stepping back. "I never want this to end."

He said the words so quietly that I didn't believe I heard him right, and was convinced they were merely a figment of my imagination.

He headed out of the bathroom without a backwards glance and I stood there, hating myself for letting my feelings get the best of me.

"What are you doing in Sadie's room in only a towel?"

Ice drenched my veins. Oh, we were so fucked and not in the good way. I *knew* someone had to have heard the vase break and of course it would be Emma. I had the worst luck on the planet.

"There was a spider in the shower. She screamed and I came running over to see what was wrong."

"And you got wet in this shower?"

I peeked around the edge of the bathroom doorway, but I couldn't see Emma. All I could see was Ezra standing there, wet, in nothing but a towel. Normally this would be a wonderful sight to see, but not right now.

"Well, the shower was running so yes I got wet. But I came from my bathroom, where I'd been taking a shower, which is why I'm in a towel."

Man, Ezra could lie pretty well under pressure. It was kind of scary.

"Mhmm, I'm sure that's what happened," she said doubtfully. "Is everything okay though? We heard something crash, so that's why I came up here."

"Uh, a vase might've been broken in the process of trying to kill the spider. It was huge. Mammoth sized. And fast. I'm lucky I escaped with my life intact."

"Yeah, well, I'm happy to see you're alive. Try not to hurt yourselves too much *killing spiders*." She said the words like they were code for something. Maybe they were.

I heard her steps retreat away and a second later Ezra closed the door and turned to look at me. Panic shimmered in his dark eyes.

"We are so screwed."

CHAPTER SEVENTEEN

IT WAS OUR third night at the beach house and Ezra and I hadn't had any more close calls. But that was only because we were doing our best to ignore each other.

"Where are we going again?" I asked Emma.

"I can't remember the name," she said, pulling on a pair of flowered wide leg pants. She was also wearing a white crop top. "But it has karaoke."

"Karaoke, great," I mumbled.

"Hey, it'll be fun," she said, swiping a clear gloss over her lips.

I leaned closer to the bathroom mirror, blending my eye shadow. I was going for a sultry smoky eye. I'd curled my hair and braided a few pieces before pulling it back into a bun. The dress I chose was hot pink with a dipping neckline and a short skirt. It made my already golden skin appear even darker.

Remy was already dressed in a simple long black dress, accented with a necklace. Her blonde hair was styled straight and she wore her signature red lipstick.

Arden hadn't joined us. She wasn't going out, instead she was staying home with Mia. I felt bad ditching her, but she had insisted that the rest of us not stay behind because of her.

Since my dress and eye makeup was bolder I opted to wear a nude colored lipstick with a pale pink gloss on top.

When my makeup was done I grabbed my strappy pale pink heels and put them on. Not to sound egotistical, but I knew those heels made my butt look amazing and my legs impossibly long. Even if Ezra and I were trying to avoid each other right now, so that we didn't get caught, it didn't mean I couldn't try my best to drive him mad.

We headed downstairs to meet the guys. They were all hanging around the TV, but looked up when we approached.

Ezra looked at me like a starving man seeing food for the first time, and I'd be lying if I didn't say it made me feel good.

I knew the others were speaking, but I couldn't hear a word they said.

For the moment, all that existed was Ezra and I.

His hands rubbed against his jeans and he bit his bottom lip. I wanted desperately for him to take me in his arms and kiss me, but that was impossible.

"You look beautiful," he said.

They were innocent words. Words he'd spoken to me many times in the past through our friendship. But somehow, right now, they felt different. The others didn't notice though, so maybe the difference was merely a figment of my imagination. Something I conjured up in an effort to make his feelings as strong as mine. I had to keep reminding myself that while I wanted more with him, he didn't want the same. Friends. We had to remain friends.

The others moved around us, heading to the door, and I snapped back to reality.

I hastily turned away from him, breaking the spell he'd cast over me. For the moment at least.

"Is Hayes not coming with us?" I asked, noticing that he'd disappeared.

Emma turned to give me a puzzled look. "Did you not hear him when he said he wanted to stay with Arden so she wasn't here alone?"

"Uh, must've missed it," I muttered.

"Are you okay?" She asked, genuine concern coloring her tone.

"Yeah, yeah," I rushed to assure her, "I think the sun is just getting to me." I laughed it off and then my body went ramrod straight when I felt the commanding presence of Ezra behind me. My whole body reacted to his proximity. It was entirely unfair. My only saving grace was that I was starting to believe that he wasn't as immune to me as he seemed.

"Should we go?" Ezra prompted.

“Oh, yeah.” Emma seemed to realize that Maddox, Mathias, and Remy were already outside waiting.

We all managed to pile into one SUV, so that the other was left in case Hayes and Arden needed it. When we got home, or if I got a chance to catch her alone, I’d have to ask Arden what was going on with the two of them.

Great, now I was going to act like Emma.

Scratch that, I wasn’t asking Arden anything.

I would not be the annoying, nosy friend like Emma. God, I loved the girl, but she was getting on my last nerve. She kept bringing up ‘killing spiders’ in small talk and then eyeing Ezra and me for a reaction. She’d yet to get one. We were masters of disguise. Okay, so not really, but neither one of us wanted to deal with the drama-fest of our friends finding out we had a friends-with-benefits relationship. They’d be mad, tell us we were stupid, and that we should stop immediately. While stopping would probably be the best thing to do the thought of it scared me more than anything else ever had and filled me with a pain far worse and than the crippling betrayal I’d felt when I caught Braden cheating on me. God, that seemed like a lifetime ago.

“We’re here,” Ezra said, bumping my elbow and jarring me from my thoughts.

I looked up to see that we were outside a shack looking building. It had bamboo sides and what looked like a straw roof. A neon sign decorated the front. It was pretty non-descript and I wondered how anyone ever found this place since there were no other establishments nearby.

We filed out of the vehicle and into the building.

It was pretty busy, which shocked me. I figured it would be empty.

A hostess greeted us and led us to a table, setting the menus down.

We were seated near the stage, where karaoke was well underway. The poor girl up there now was butchering a Mariah Carey song. I was pretty sure my ears started to bleed.

"Ow." Ezra winced.

At least I wasn't the only one that thought the girl was horrible.

When she finally finished the song I sent up a prayer that she wouldn't sing again.

She didn't.

I eyed the menu and ended up ordering a cheeseburger and salad. It seemed safe enough, and I could trick myself into thinking I was being healthy.

"So, are you guys going to sing?" I asked, eyeing Maddox and Mathias. Mathias was the lead singer of the band, but Maddox could sing too. Ezra, however, sounded like a dying cow when he sang. I knew this because I dared him to sing one time.

"Nah," Mathias shook his head, draping his arm over the back of Remy's chair, "I don't want the attention."

Remy automatically leaned into his body and smiled up at him. "And what makes you think anybody would be paying any attention to you?"

He cracked a half-smile. "Have you seen my face? And this voice? It's the sound of an angel. The combination is an attention grabber and a panty dropper."

She rolled her eyes at him and reached down like she was going to feel beneath her dress. "Really? Because my panties are still on."

He brushed his lips against her chin and growled, "Not for long." He kissed her then, and not an innocent kiss either. It was the kind that made you feel dirty for looking too long.

"Dude, stop," Maddox groaned, covering his eyes. "I'm too young to see this."

Mathias punched Maddox in the arm, all without breaking his kiss with Remy. That took some major skill.

Finally he pulled away and Remy was left breathless. Somehow her lipstick was still perfectly in place and none lingered on Mathias' lips.

Now that Remy was available to talk, I said, "So, ladies, does that mean we're going to sing?"

"Absolutely," Emma chimed.

Remy grimaced. "And this is when I wish I could drink. I hate the thought of doing this stone cold sober, but for you guys I will. The Willow Creek ladies have to stick together." She held out her fist for a bump. Emma and I quickly obliged.

I liked that. The Willow Creek ladies. But I couldn't help feeling like I wasn't really a part of that term. After all, Remy was married to Mathias and Emma would soon be married to Maddox. I was nothing but the friend, the outsider. I existed on the fringes, but not a part of the actual family. I knew if I voiced that aloud everybody at the table would tell me I was crazy, even Mathias, but it was how I felt.

Our food came and we all chatted while we ate.

We continued to talk after the food had been cleared away. It was nice for all of us to hang out and it reminded me of what things had been like before I started dating Braden. Remy hadn't been a part of our group then, and Mathias had kept to himself, but we all clicked.

"Alright, ladies," Mathias slid his chair back and crossed his hands behind his head, "it's now or never. Quit stalling."

Remy glared at him. "We're not stalling, we were having a conversation."

He reached over and rubbed her shoulder. "It's getting late. We need to head back soon. The baby—"

"Okay, okay," she agreed, and her face crinkled with worry, "you're right. One song and then we're out of here. Sound good?" She turned her attention to Emma and me.

"Yep." Emma stood quickly, nearly knocking her chair over. Luckily Maddox caught it before it fell. "Oops." A blush stained her cheeks.

"Have fun," Maddox told us, sliding Emma's now vacant chair into the table.

We went over and put our names on the list and picked a song. We were next, which didn't give us long for the nerves to set in. I knew I didn't have the best voice in the world, but I wasn't horrible. Emma was amazing though. Her vocals were featured on several of Willow Creek's songs and she even had a duet with Maddox.

The guy on stage finished his song and we were handed microphones.

"Ready?" Emma asked.

"Of course," I answered.

Remy took a deep breath, her face slipping into a mask of confidence. "I got this."

We all laughed and then stepped up on stage.

Maddox, Mathias, and Ezra began to clap for us before the song even began and Maddox threw in a loud whistle for extra effect.

The music began to play and the lyrics to Fifth Harmony's *Worth It* appeared on the screen.

Emma started singing the first part. Maddox hollered and pumped his fist in the air.

I came in next, feeling bold and daring I started to move my hips to the song. I shimmied and tried to be as sexy as possible.

If Ezra's darkened gaze, and the way he carefully covered his lap with closed palms, was any indication then I was doing a pretty good job.

Remy took the next part and she wasn't bad at all. Although, it wasn't that difficult to sound better than the girl who butchered Mariah Carey.

We took turns singing verses and even the other two joined in with the sexy dancing. I was shocked when Emma started swaying her hips, and running her hands through her hair sexily, but the fact of the matter was loving Maddox had made her more comfortable in her own skin.

The song ended and the room erupted into cheers—mostly from the guys, but whatever, it still counted.

We bowed and my hair brushed the stage floor.

We hopped off the stage and joined the guys. They'd already paid the bill so we headed outside to the car.

As we were about to exit the building I was jerked roughly into a darkened hallway by Ezra.

Before I could make a sound his lips crashed down on mine.

He pulled away within seconds, but I was still left breathless.

He grabbed my hand and put it over the hard-on straining against the zipper of his jeans. "Do you feel that?" He asked unnecessarily, but I nodded anyway. "That's what you do to me. I'm hard for you all the fucking time and it's killing me." He pressed his forehead against mine. "*You're* killing me...but I can't walk away. I don't want to."

With one last tender kiss to my forehead he tore away and I was left alone, but the ghost of his lips and words still lingered.

CHAPTER EIGHTEEN

I BLINKED MY EYES.

One time.

Two.

The sight before me was still there.

"What the hell are you guys doing?" I asked.

Maddox looked up at me from where he sat on the floor beside Emma. "We're having a hedgehog race."

"I need some coffee," I mumbled, striding into the kitchen. Surely once I had coffee all of this would make more sense.

When I returned to the living room they were still on the floor with dividers set up and each one held their pet hedgehog.

"We need to set some rules," Maddox declared, lifting the hedgehog up to perch on his shoulder.

Emma sighed. "What kind of rules is a hedgehog going to understand?"

"Shh," he scolded her, reaching up to cover Sonic's ears, "he'll hear you."

Emma shook her head. "I say we just let them go and whichever one gets to the end first is the winner. Stop trying to make things complicated."

I sat down on the couch, drawing my legs underneath me and sipped at my coffee as I watched them bicker.

"Fine." Maddox relented, and scooped Sonic off his shoulder.

"What's going on?" Ezra asked as he yawned. His hair stuck up wildly around his head, making him adorably rumpled, and to torture me even more he was shirtless and wearing only a pair of loose gym shorts that left my ovaries panting. Yes, panting.

"They're having a hedgehog race," I answered.

He shook his head. "I need coffee."

I raised the cup to my lips to hide my smile. I'd said the same thing.

Ezra returned and sat down beside me. The couch dipped with his added weight and I drifted towards him.

"How'd you sleep?" He asked, making small talk.

"Awful," I supplied.

"And why was that?"

I shrugged, pretending not to know. "I got cold."

He smiled. “Hmm, we’ll have to get you some extra blankets.”

“Yes, hopefully that will suffice.”

Below us, Maddox began to count. “One, two, three.”

They let the hedgehogs go.

Aquilla, Emma’s hedgehog, laid down and refused to move.

Sonic veered off to his right, knocking down the makeshift divider they’d made from cardboard.

“I don’t think they like this game,” Emma whispered conspiratorially.

“Sonic is clearly the winner, though.” Maddox argued.

“He didn’t do it right!” She countered.

“At least he moved,” Maddox reasoned.

She shook her head. “Fine, whatever, Sonic wins.”

“Thanks for seeing things my way.” Maddox grinned and leaned over to kiss her cheek.

She tried to feign that she was mad, but it didn’t last for long. Soon she was leaning into his touch and giggled when he kissed her neck.

I wanted that so bad, that sweet carefree kind of love, but the problem was I wanted it with someone that didn’t want me forever. I was nothing but a temporary pleasure and I hated that I’d reduced myself to that, but when you wanted something as bad as I wanted Ezra you’d do things you never thought you were willing to do. Maybe, I'd hoped that he would change his mind once we were together that way, but despite the things he said we were still nothing but a dirty little lie. Hiding from our friends, and even ourselves.

"Are you okay?" Ezra asked, his fingers lightly grazing my thigh before jerking away as if he'd forgotten we were in the presence of our friends.

"Yeah, why wouldn't I be?"

More lies.

Lies.

Lies.

Lies.

So many little lies, that I didn't even know what the truth was anymore.

He looked at me like he didn't believe me, but I stood up and left for the kitchen before he could say anything else.

I started pulling out the cartons of eggs, cheese, and spinach, to make omelets for everyone.

I heard footsteps entering the kitchen and my body tensed. "I said I was okay!" I snapped.

"Whoa! What did I do?"

I jerked. That wasn't Ezra.

I turned around quickly, nearly rolling my ankle in the process, and found Hayes entering the kitchen.

“I thought you were someone else,” I confessed.

“Obviously,” he muttered, musing his sandy colored hair. He passed me and opened the refrigerator so that he could grab the orange juice. “I’m assuming you thought I was Ezra.” He said the words slowly, like he was dropping a bomb and waiting to see what I would do when it blew up.

His tanned, muscled, back was to me as he poured the juice

I still hadn’t spoken when he turned around and eyed me over the rim of the glass. “You gonna answer me?”

“I wasn’t planning on it.”

“No answer, is an answer.” He smiled gleefully and took a sip of the orange juice. “What did he do?”

I narrowed my eyes. I didn’t want to have this conversation with anybody, but definitely not with Hayes. He’d been so sweet to me and I’d thrown away any possibility with him because I was so hung up on my best friend.

“Ah,” Hayes snapped his fingers together, a dimple appearing in his cheek when he smiled, “it’s what he *didn’t* do, isn’t it?”

“He’s just being a guy,” I finally replied, “besides, friend’s fight.”

Although, this wasn’t really a fight since I was mad at myself, and my stupid, illogical, feelings.

"Uh-huh," Hayes nodded, "*friends*. Sure."

"I don't know what you're implying." I played stupid as I got back to work making breakfast. Maybe if I ignored him long enough he'd go away.

He didn't.

Instead, he made himself comfortable by leaning against the counter right in my personal space. If he was trying to intimidate me into spilling the beans it wasn't going to happen. I grew up with a brother, sister, and two nosy parents whom I all loved dearly, but it taught me to keep my mouth shut on things better left unsaid.

"So, Arden," he started, and I breathed a sigh of relief over the subject change, "what's her story?"

"Why do you want to know?" I asked. I wasn't just going to hand out free information. The boy had to work for it.

He shrugged his lean shoulders and tried to appear nonchalant. "She seems cool."

"Are you interested?" I continued to pester him. Yeah, I knew I was doing to him exactly what I hadn't wanted him to do to me, but he brought this subject up so he should've known it was coming.

"Maybe." He set his glass down and propped his elbows on the counter. "Obviously there's not a guy in the picture..." He trailed off, wanting me to fill in the blanks.

"Her husband left her shortly after she got pregnant." He opened his mouth to speak, but I silenced him with a glare. "That's all I know. She's my friend, but

I haven't wanted to pry. I can tell it's a sore subject for her. I don't think he was a very nice guy."

His lips pursed in contemplation and he grew quiet.

Minutes passed and finally I stopped what I was doing and looked up at him. "She's a nice girl and she has a kid. Don't try to pursue something with her if you're not serious about it."

Hayes cracked a smile and leaned forward. "Yeah, I know. I wouldn't fuck her and bail. I'm done with being like that. Empty, meaningless, sex isn't worth it to me anymore. I want someone to share my life with, not just my bed. And Arden…I really, really like her."

I couldn't believe how honest and open Hayes was being with me. I was used to the fun, joking Hayes, not one that carried on such serious conversations. I liked that I was getting to see a different side of him.

"Don't hurt her," I warned him. "She's a good person and she doesn't deserve to have her heart broken."

"Hey," he held up his hands in surrender, "don't give me the third degree before I even fuck it up. Have some faith, Westbrook."

I shook my head at him and turned towards the stove.

A tingling sensation came over me and I knew instantly that Ezra had entered the room. Whenever he was near my body tingled. I should've known Hayes wasn't him.

"Hey," he said softly.

"I'm going down to the beach." Hayes announced suddenly. "Just yell for me when the grub's ready."

He hightailed it out of the kitchen like his ass was on fire. For all I knew maybe he did feel the simmering heat of the flame that burned between Ezra and I.

I didn't bother to turn around and acknowledge Ezra. I continued on making breakfast, like his presence didn't affect me at all.

He said nothing as I finished making one of the omelets. I grabbed a stack of plates and slid the omelet out of the skillet onto the top one. I picked up the plate and handed it to him.

"Hungry?" I asked.

I wasn't mad at him. On the contrary, I was mad at myself for expecting more. I was pathetic.

He grabbed the plate and opened a drawer to grab a fork. He speared a bite and I watched as he raised it to his mouth and chewed, waiting for his reaction.

"Not bad," he cracked a smile, "in fact, it's pretty damn good."

I smiled despite my dour feelings. I set about making the rest and I was sliding the third onto a plate when he spoke again.

"Would you be opposed to going somewhere with me today?"

I arched a brow and set the skillet aside. "Just the two of us?" I wondered.

He nodded, striding over to the sink to wash his plate. “Yeah, just you and me.”

“What do you want to do?” I questioned, crossing my arms over my chest as my suspicions rose.

He shrugged casually and stared at me from across the kitchen island. “I can’t tell you.”

I let out a sigh. Despite not knowing what he had planned, I refused to say no. “When do I need to be ready?”

“After you eat breakfast,” he mused. “And wear something stretchy.”

“Stretchy?” I repeated. What the hell did he have planned? “We better not be biking. That shit makes my vagina hurt, and don’t get me started on guys. Seriously, where does your junk go? It’s one of the many mysteries of the world.”

He snorted. “Sadie, you’re one of a kind. And no, we’re not going biking. Think outside the box a bit more.” He winked and then strode out of the kitchen, leaving me alone to wonder what he was up to.

No matter how much I racked my brain I couldn’t come up with one single idea.

“Ezra,” I whined, looking out the window as he continued to drive farther and farther away, “where are you taking me? If you wanted to kill me and feed my body to the sharks we could've done that back at the house."

He stopped singing along to the radio and chuckled. "Come on, you have to have more faith in me than that."

"My faith in you sailed away approximately five minutes ago. We've been in the car for an hour. I'm going stir crazy."

"Be patient."

"Why does my gut tell me I'm not going to like whatever it is you're up to?"

He grinned and shook his head like I was oh-so-cute. I wondered if he'd still think it was cute when my panic caused me to jump out of a moving vehicle.

Ten minutes later we turned into a parking lot in front of a plain building. I swung my head around wildly, looking for a sign or any sort of clue to the origins of the building.

"High Flyers," I read. "Please tell me you're not making me jump out of a plane. I know you did that with Maddox and Emma, but I'm not as brave as Emma," I admitted.

"No planes." He assured me and got out of the vehicle.

I hastily followed after him. "Then what is this place?"

"You'll see."

I was tempted to run back to the safety of the car, but something told me he'd only chase after me and drag me back.

He opened the glass door to the building and waved me in ahead of him.

We were standing in some sort of lobby. The floors were a beige tile and the walls were a pale yellow.

I rubbed my hands together nervously as he strode over to the counter and spoke with the lady sitting behind it.

She answered him and I saw her point to a doorway.

"This way." Ezra nodded his head.

I followed him and when I saw what was behind the door I thought I might throw up. "No, no, no, *no* fucking way am I doing this."

I darted for the door and he caught me around my waist, dragging me into his body.

"I'm going to die," I said dramatically. "I will fall to my death."

"You'll be fine," he chuckled, "there's a net."

"So, you're implying that I will fall?"

"Well, you have to get down somehow."

"I can't do this." My stomach rolled, looking up at the sight before me once more.

We were in a training facility of some sort and above us were these *things* hanging from the ceiling. People held onto the bars and jumped from one to the next. One man hung upside down on one, holding a woman's hands in his and spun her around. In another corner of the gym long pieces of fabric hung from the ceiling with a woman spinning from one, exactly like we'd seen at the circus.

"Ezra," I started, throwing in a dramatic gulp for good measure, "this was awesome when we saw it at the circus, but there's no way in hell you are ever getting me up there."

"Come on," his hand landed on my butt and he gave it a small squeeze, "it'll be fun. It's something we'll remember forever."

I wanted to argue with him that I would remember every single moment we shared together for the rest of my life, but I knew he'd just find another argument for getting me up there.

"If I die you better tell my parents that I love them...and tell my brother that I was the one that broke his BB gun when we were little. He was really mad about that and I blamed the dog."

Ezra snorted. "Anything else?"

"Not at the moment, but something might come to me before I plummet to my death."

He shook his head, trying to hold in his laughter and failing miserably. "If you're falling to your death then I hardly think you can impart any last words."

I shrugged, rearing my head back to watch as the man swung back and forth gaining momentum before throwing the woman into the air. She easily caught onto one of the metal bar things.

"Then I guess the world will never know my last words of wisdom. 'Tis a shame. Maybe we should leave before the world has to deal with the burden of such a loss?"

He crossed his arms over his chest. "Or maybe you shouldn't be such a scaredy cat."

"Scaredy cat?" I wrinkled my nose. "What are we? Five?"

He chuckled. "You're the one acting like a baby."

"Ooh," I mock winced, "that hurts, Ezra."

"Just calling it like I see it." He smiled innocently.

"You must be Ezra and Sadie." A voice sounded behind us.

I turned around hastily and had to rear my head back to see the face of the man standing there. He was so tall that he made Hayes seem short. He had to be at least six-foot-seven.

"That's us." Ezra reached out to shake his hand.

The man held his hand out to me next. I placed mine inside his open palm and watched it nearly disappear in his gigantic grasp.

"I'm Oscar. I'll be your instructor today."

I glanced over my shoulder once more and gulped.

"Don't be scared," Oscar said, drawing my attention back to him, "it's not as scary as it looks."

"I don't believe you," I muttered.

He chuckled, amused by my words. "You'll change your mind once you get up there."

"Why?" I asked, curiously.

He shrugged and a look of contemplation stole over his face. "Because," he replied, "when you're up there...it feels a lot like freedom."

I sighed and lifted my hands in the air. "Alright then, let's do this."

"Are you sure?" Ezra questioned. He might've been pushing me to do this, but he'd never make me do anything I absolutely didn't want to do.

"Yeah," I nodded, steeling my shoulders, "let's go make some memories."

Oscar went through countless instructions and made us do several exercises on the ground before letting us go up high. We weren't made to wear harnesses since there was a giant net beneath the bars to catch us. I would've felt better wearing a harness, but I didn't say anything. I'd already made enough of an embarrassment out of myself.

We climbed the ladder on opposite sides. Oscar chose to come with me. I think he was afraid I'd chicken out. But I'd committed to this. Besides, seeing how happy Ezra was and the effort he'd gone through to make this happen was pretty sweet.

I'd learned that Oscar, and all the professionals here, were a part of a circus in Orlando. This was their training center and they were on a break right now, preparing for a brand new show opening in a few weeks.

I watched as Ezra pulled one of the bars towards him. When he grabbed the bar he hung from it upside down, swaying in the air. I let out a scream like I was the one swaying like a pendulum.

"Your turn," Oscar spoke.

I shook my head. "I can't do that."

"You don't need to do it upside down. Just grab it like we practiced down below."

My feet tapped restlessly against the platform. "I can't do this," I whimpered.

"Come on, Sadie," Ezra pleaded. "For me."

I closed my eyes.

For him.

I reached out and jumped, grabbing onto the bar. I screamed as I swung back and forth, my feet dangling below me. I had no idea how far the fall was, and I hadn't wanted to ask. Instead I kept reminding myself that there was a net that would catch my fall.

My arms began to burn. "I'm going fall," I cried.

Ezra swung towards me. "Jump to me."

"No! Are you crazy?!" I shrieked, trying to hold myself up. Running clearly wasn't doing anything for my upper body strength. I was going to have to work on that.

Ezra's face was turning bright red from hanging upside down. "Do you trust me?"

I squished my eyes closed. "That's a stupid question."

"Sadie," he growled, "do you trust me?"

"Yes!"

"Then fucking jump. I've got you. I've always had you."

My throat closed up and I swung back gaining momentum.

I waited until I was in the right position and I let go, hurtling my body towards him.

I reached for his hands and he caught mine, somehow managing to hold onto me.

"See," he said, "I'll always catch you when you fall."

"Except when you drop me onto the net," I mumbled, my legs swaying.

He laughed, but it sounded more like a cough since he was upside down. "But it'll be a gentler fall."

I guess I couldn't argue with that.

"Ready?" He asked.

"Ready," I answered.

He let me go.

He was right. It was a gentle fall.

But when we inevitably ended I knew the fall would be anything but gentle. It was going to be fucking brutal and I wondered if either of us would come out unscathed.

CHAPTER NINETEEN

EZRA AND I spent the whole day together after leaving the training facility. We did random silly things, like racing go-carts and hanging out at this little diner. We laughed and joked, and for the moment at least it felt like we were the old Sadie and Ezra. We had no pressure from our friends, or ourselves.

When we returned to the house it was already getting late and the sun was setting.

"I thought you guys were never going to get back," Emma cried impatiently.

"Did you miss us that much?" I laughed, setting my bag down and kicking off my flip-flops.

Ezra walked past me, his arm grazing mine in the process and headed into the kitchen.

"We're going out," Emma declared.

"We are?" I raised a brow. "I didn't know."

"Well neither of you would answer your phones," she huffed, tapping her foot impatiently. "There's a club

Hayes wants to go to. Mathias and Remy are staying behind and watching Mia, so Arden's going too."

"What does that have to do with me?" I questioned, dropping into one of the chairs in the living room. Mathias sat on the couch and raised his chin slightly in greeting.

Emma followed and perched her butt on the coffee table in front of me. "Maddox and I are going too, and so are you and Ezra."

I raised a brow. "Maybe I don't want to go."

She shook her head. "You know, you were always the one pushing me to do things out of my comfort zone. *You* were the crazy one in this friendship that had all this experience and now you act like an old lady."

I snorted, fighting a smile. "I am old."

"I'm sorry," she said, grabbing my hand, "I'm really not trying to be bossy, and I'm sorry I keep coming across that way. I don't know what's wrong with me lately..." She paused, taking a breath. "But we only have one more day here and I wanted us to spend tonight and tomorrow together. Once we get home things will get crazy with the wedding and it'll be hard for us to have any girl time."

I frowned. I could see where she was coming from. We'd also both been far too bitchy to each other lately and I knew it was my fault. If I would just confess everything that was going on to her I knew this tension would disappear, but I just wasn't ready to talk about it. I knew she wouldn't approve of our arrangement. She wanted to see us together as a real couple, not as fuck buddies.

"I'm in...but you better let me do your hair and makeup."

She winced. "Just don't make me look like a hooker."

"And when have I ever done that?"

"Middle school. Lauren Hanagen's thirteenth birthday."

I laughed. "I think I've learned a few things since then. Have no fear, you're in good hands."

"So what are we doing?" Ezra asked, walking into the room with a bag of chips in his hands.

I glanced over at him and said, "We're going clubbing."

"That sounds like a disaster." He mumbled around a mouthful of chips.

Emma threw her arms in the air. "Y'all act like this is a death sentence."

"I'm sure it'll be fun as long as no one gets a roofied drink."

Emma threw a pillow at him and Ezra tried to duck away, but it still collided with his shoulder before falling to the ground.

Backing into the kitchen he held his phone up and waved it around. "It's getting late, so you ladies might want to get ready. I know it typically takes you five hours."

This time I was the one to throw a pillow at him and his laughter carried from the kitchen all the way into the living room, and I couldn't help but smile.

I finished styling Emma's hair in a loose fishtail braid and moved on to Arden.

I'd already done my own hair and makeup. I chose to straighten my hair since I'd been leaving it wavy so much and left it down. For my makeup I'd gone in a more dramatic direction—red lips and smoky gray eyes.

"I'm not sure I should go." Arden frowned, biting at her nails. "What if Mia needs me?"

I smacked her hand away. "Mia is already asleep. She's not even going to know that you're gone. And if for whatever reason she would wake up Mathias and Remy will be here. Plus, we all have cellphones if we need to get ahold of each other. It'll be fine."

I wanted Arden to go out and have fun, even if it was only for one night. Being a single mom didn't afford her much time to do things for herself. She deserved this.

"You're right, you're right," she chanted, like she was trying to convince herself.

I went to work curling her long red hair and then fluffed it out with my fingers.

"Thanks for letting me borrow this." She pointed to her clothes.

Arden hadn't packed any "party" clothes as she called them, so I'd lent her some to go out. Since I didn't have a spare dress, she was wearing a pair of black skinny jeans, and a gold-sequined strapless peplum top. It looked amazing next to her vivid red hair. We wore the same shoe size so I also lent her a pair of black pumps. She wobbled a bit in them, but I doubted Hayes would leave her side tonight so I wasn't worried about her falling over.

"Ladies," I said, giving them each a once over and then myself in the mirror, "I think we're ready."

Downstairs the guys were waiting for us. They were all dressed casually in jeans and t-shirts. No surprise there.

"You look beautiful," Maddox told Emma, his eyes moving from her head down to her toes and back up again. Even after being together this long his words still made her cheeks tinge pink.

She was dressed in a sparkly flapper style dress in colors that reminded me of a mermaid.

Maddox nuzzled her neck and kissed her cheek before they headed to the door. Arden and Hayes were right behind them, which left Ezra and I alone for the moment.

I hadn't looked at him when I entered the room, but now I lifted my eyes to his.

The look in his eyes could be described in one word. Hunger.

He was starved for me, and I reveled in that fact.

I loved knowing that my very presence had an affect on him. That it killed him that right now he could only look and not touch.

"That dress," he growled lowly, his eyes scanning my body slowly like he was savoring every inch.

"You like?" I did a little spin, showing it off. The dress was short and tight, but had three-quarter sleeves and covered me fully in the front. The back, however, was open to just above my butt and crisscrossed at my shoulders. The fabric was purple and shimmery, so it appeared to sparkle any time the light caught it.

"Fuck." He groaned, looking pained, and scrubbed his hands down his face.

I couldn't hide my grin. I loved being desired by him and pushing him past his breaking point. I wanted him to lose control.

I turned and headed for the door, purposely putting a little more sway in my hips than usual.

I heard him let out a string of curses behind me and I smiled like the cat that ate the canary.

I could feel things changing between us and I was scared as to where it was headed, but for tonight all I wanted was to feel his hands on my skin.

Music poured out of the speakers so loud that I wanted to cover my ears, but then I'd just look like an idiot. I couldn't believe that as a teenager I'd liked this sort of thing. While my teen years technically hadn't been that long ago, it felt like a lifetime. I'd changed and matured so much in the last few years. Okay...matured, not so much.

Inside the club was far nicer than the ones I'd snuck into when I was in high school.

The ceiling had these unique triangle dropdowns that glowed with different colors and the floor was shiny and clean—not covered in a layer of sticky grossness like most were.

The bar was lined with every drink imaginable and backlit in varying colors like the triangle tiles on the ceiling.

"Boys," I patted Ezra on the shoulder, "why don't you go grab a table and some drinks."

Ezra eyed me, his hands shoved into the pockets of his jeans. "And what are you ladies going to do?"

I grabbed Emma and Arden's hands. "Dance of course."

Before either of them could protest, like I knew they would, I dragged them onto the dance floor.

It was a fast paced song that immediately had my heart racing.

"I can't dance," Emma whined.

"I *shouldn't* dance," Arden interjected. "At least not like this. I'm a mom." She glared at the people around us with disdain in her amber colored eyes.

"First off, you can dance." I pointed a finger at Emma. "Secondly," I narrowed my eyes on Arden, "just because you're a mom doesn't mean you lose all sex appeal. Own it, girl."

When neither of them moved I started to dance. I reached out and grabbed Emma's hips, getting her to sway in time to the music. Once she had it I set my sights on Arden, but I was pleasantly surprised to see that she was already loosening up. She was clearly still nervous, and rather awkward, but I knew in a matter of minutes she'd let the rest of her reservations go.

Since both girls seemed to be fine on their own now I closed my eyes and let myself enjoy the moment.

All that existed was me, the music, and how it made me feel.

I swayed my hips, lifting my hair off of my shoulders when my skin began to dampen with sweat. There were a lot of people packed in here and the air was stifling, but it was all a part of the experience.

Three songs later I finally opened my eyes and saw that Emma and Arden had disappeared.

I searched the crowded dance floor for them and came up empty.

Feeling irritated I started towards the tables.

I finally found them sitting at a large booth with the guys.

I stuck my hands on my hips and gave them both the most withering glare I could muster. "You bitches ditched me."

Emma giggled. "We were thirsty." She pointed to her drink.

I shook my head. "What are you even drinking?" I asked, sliding into the booth beside Arden.

Emma lifted her brightly colored drink. "I have no idea, but it's delicious. We got you one too." She pointed at a drink in the center of the table.

I took it and cringed. It was too sweet for me, but it packed quite the punch. For someone like Emma, who didn't drink much, she'd be wasted in thirty minutes...maybe less.

"Are you drinking?" I asked Arden.

She shook her head. "No."

I couldn't blame her. She had a kid and dealing with a hangover and a three-year-old in the morning would be killer.

"Hey, hey, hey," Hayes chanted, lifting his drink in the air. "We should toast."

"To what?" Ezra asked.

Hayes' lips twisted in thought. "To the Willow Creek family and all the adventures that are headed our way."

"Hell yeah I'll toast to that." Maddox lifted his drink—which I'd bet was diet Pepsi, since he was tonight's DD, and tapped it against Hayes', before we all followed suit.

I downed my drink, and upon seeing the empty cup Ezra signaled someone over to our table.

Without me even getting a chance to open my mouth, Ezra ordered me a new drink—something completely different than the one I'd had. I'd bet money Emma had ordered the first drink for me, and of course Ezra had noticed that I detested it. But hey, it was doing its job of getting me buzzed, so it was still a winner in my book.

"Thanks," I mouthed to him, where he sat across from me.

He waved his hand in dismissal.

Emma finished her drink and bumped Ezra to move so that she and Maddox could slide out of the booth.

"Outta my way!" She cried. "I want to dance with my man!"

Maddox snorted, fighting a grin. "I think someone's buzzed already."

"Absolutely not." She pouted, standing with her hands on her hips.

Maddox leaned down and took her lips between his, kissing her long and deep. She melted into his touch and then they disappeared onto the dance floor.

Beside me Arden let out a dreamy sigh. “Is it just me or are they the cutest couple ever?”

“They are,” I agreed.

“I’ve seen cuter,” Hayes piped in.

Arden and I swung our gaze in his direction. “Like who?” I questioned, as a fresh drink was set down for me.

“One time I saw these two puppies that were clearly in love. Their little tongues kept hanging out and their tails were wagging. It was the epitome of cuteness.” He grinned easily, stretching his arm out along the back of the booth.

“Aww, that sounds precious,” Arden cried, clasping her hands together.

At the same time, I said, “You’re so full of shit.”

Arden narrowed her eyes on me. “That was an adorable story.”

“And you’re drunk.”

She wrinkled her nose in confusion. “I’m not even drinking.”

“Exactly.”

I finished my drink and stood. “See you losers later. I’m going to get my dance on.”

Before anyone could protest I stepped back and allowed my body to be carried away by the crowd.

The room was pulsing with energy and you couldn't help but respond to it.

I let the music flow through my veins as I swung my hips to the beat of the song. My arms swayed above my head and I truly let myself go for the first time on this trip.

I closed my eyes and the glowing lights glittered behind my eyelids.

One song blended into many and my body grew damp with sweat as my heart beat like a drum.

A smile touched my lips when I felt arms wind around me from behind.

I'd recognize the feel of that body anywhere.

"Do you have any idea how long I've been watching you?" He growled lowly in my ear, his teeth grazing my lobe. "You're so fucking sexy it was killing me that I could only look and not touch. It was like having my favorite candy dangled in front of me and saying one bite would kill me."

"And yet," I panted, leaning my back against his front as I opened my eyes, "you're here touching me."

"I decided it was worth the risk."

"They might see us," I warned.

I waited for him to say he didn't care, that he wanted me and it didn't matter anymore—that this arrangement was futile and he wanted me forever, as his future and not just his temporary pleasure.

But he didn't say that.

Instead he whispered, "Then we'll just have to make sure they don't see us."

I squished my eyes closed once more, silently reminding myself that I was being silly. He was sticking to our agreement and I couldn't fault him for that. But my heart was breaking a little more every day and the sex—as amazing as it was—wasn't enough to keep me whole. I couldn't keep doing this to myself, and I vowed in that moment that once we got home I'd find my own place. This needed to end before I broke completely, but for now I would let myself enjoy the feel of his body wrapped around mine for just a little bit longer. Selfish? Maybe so. But if I was going to be forced to go the rest of my life without him then I wanted to make the most of every second we had left.

"Sadie." He prompted when I'd been silent too long.

"Just dance with me."

He obliged.

I never knew Ezra was such a good dancer, but the way he moved his body against mine should've been a crime. It was one of the most erotic things I'd ever experienced, and he wasn't even being sexual about it. Not at all, actually. He felt the music and it pulsed through him and into me. It was like the beat of the song made us one.

His hands roamed down my hips to my thighs, and back up again. His fingers edged underneath the bottom of my dress and I hissed between my teeth as my core clenched. But he didn't move his hands up any further. He kept them right where they were, every once in a while his fingers would lightly stroke my skin and I would clench again.

I wound my arms behind me and around his neck. He burrowed his head against mine, nipping at the spot where my neck met my shoulders, and then smoothed the spot with a slow flick of his tongue before pressing his lips to the spot.

I let out a long moan.

Jesus Christ, the way the man could affect me was entirely unfair. He knew how to stroke and play all the right strings on my body.

"Sadie." The way he breathed my name made me shiver.

"Please," I begged. I didn't even know what I was begging him for.

To say my name again.

To touch me.

To love me.

I felt his fingers flex against my thighs, the pressure increasing as he pulled me more fully against him.

I rolled my hips and smiled in satisfaction when he hissed between his teeth.

"Fuck, Sadie."

"Yes," I purred, "fuck Sadie, please."

I didn't care that we were in the middle of a dance floor surrounded by people. I needed him to touch me in all the ways I needed to be felt.

"We can't." He breathed, sounding like those two words pained him.

"Ezra," I panted his name and I felt him growl in approval at the sound, "I need you. Here. The bathroom. The wall. The fucking car. I don't care. Take me, I'm yours."

His fingers tightened against my skin even more and I wouldn't be surprised if I found bruises in the morning, but I didn't mind. I wanted him to brand me physically the way he was already branded on my heart and soul.

I turned around so that we were now facing each other and let him see the desperate want in my eyes.

"Sadie, you've been drinking..." He trailed off.

My palms landed on his hard chest and slid up around his neck, where I curled my fingers into the silky strands of his hair. Despite our conversation we both kept moving to the beat of the song.

"You know two drinks will hardly get me drunk," I argued.

"Fucking hell." He muttered, and kissed me right there on the dance floor.

For the moment, at least, he didn't seem concerned about getting caught.

He nipped my bottom lip and I moaned into his mouth.

He tasted like cool lemonade on a warm summer's day.

"Touch me," I begged, "I need you to touch me."

I needed to get my fill of him before I was forced to say goodbye, but something told me I'd never feel satisfied.

His hands roamed up my sides, the pads of his thumbs grazing the undersides of my breasts concealed by my dress.

"More," I pleaded.

"Fuck being good," he growled, taking my hand and pulling me through the crowd. He barreled past people, making sure they didn't ram into me.

I didn't look around to see if our friends saw. My head was too clouded with lust to care.

He found a hallway and dragged me down it.

I had no idea where we were going, but Ezra seemed to be navigating the space with no problem.

He reached out and pushed a door open and we stepped into a back alley. It was littered with trash and there was a dumpster nearby.

He led me away from the mess and before I could blink he had my back pinned to the brick wall and his lips devoured mine. His kiss was nothing like the one inside. This was rough, and tinged with desperation, like he too felt that time was running out for us and wanted to make the most of it.

I started pulling at his shirt, but he grabbed my hands and pinned them above my head.

"No." He glared at me.

"But—" I protested.

"No," he said again, "I want you. God, believe me I do," he ground his hips into mine so that I could feel how much, "but not here. This, right now, is about your pleasure. Not mine."

I opened my mouth to argue that his pleasure was mine, but he silenced me with a breath-stealing kiss.

He broke the kiss when my brain grew foggy from lack of oxygen and his lips trailed down my neck and over my collarbone before he sunk to his knees in front of me.

He glanced up at me and his dark eyes were hooded with lust.

"Do you trust me?" He asked.

"I think I proved that today," I panted.

He let out a husky chuckle. "That you did."

His hands skimmed up my calves and thighs, disappearing beneath the dress. He grabbed the sides of my underwear and pulled it down roughly until it stopped at my ankles.

"Step out of them," he commanded.

I did as he asked and watched as he stuffed my underwear into his pocket.

He looked up at me again and licked his lips in anticipation. "Hold on."

"Huh?"

I let out a small squeal of fright when he grabbed my legs and placed them on his shoulders. He pushed the bottom of my dress out of his way and looked at me one more time. "Ride my face like you mean it, sweetheart."

And then his mouth was on me and I lost all trace of coherent thought.

Pleasure hummed in my veins and my limbs grew weak. He seemed to sense this and grabbed my ass to hold me steady.

"Ezra." I panted his name over and over again in the darkened alleyway.

I leaned my head back against the wall, looking at all the stars that shimmered above us. They were the only witness to the sublime pleasure Ezra was giving me. The stars saw everything. Oh, the secrets they could tell.

I felt my body begin to tighten and my legs shook. "I'm going to come," I warned, my back arching against the wall. "Oh God," I moaned. "Ezra!" I cried out his name loud enough that people nearby probably heard.

His tongue swiped against me one last time and he lowered my legs to the ground. He kept ahold of me as he stood, and brushed the dirt and gravel off of his pants with his free hand.

"Fuck you taste amazing," he growled, turning me on all over again. He swiped his thumb over his bottom lip and sucked it into his mouth. Damn him. My body was coiled tight with the need to sink myself down onto him, but I knew he wouldn't allow that.

I leaned up and kissed him, the taste of me lingering on his lips. "I think that's the hottest thing anyone has ever done to me."

"Go down on you in an alley?" He questioned, raising one dark brow.

"When you put it that way it sounds gross, but it was...incredible." I grabbed onto his shirt, my body leaning heavily against his. He wrapped an arm around me and started leading me towards the door we'd come through.

"I'm glad you thought so...it was equally as pleasurable for me."

"But you didn't get off," I whispered, like it was some sort of secret.

He grinned down at me. "Giving pleasure can be as good as receiving, and that," he nodded behind us at the alley, "was fucking amazing."

I bit my lip, wishing desperately that we were anywhere but here right now so that I could make love to him the way I wanted.

Whoa, *no*.

Not make love.

We didn't do that.

We fucked.

Because we were friends with benefits.

And that was it.

Ezra held my hand through the darkened hallway, but once we reached the main room he let go.

We found the table and all our friends, who looked grumpy and irritable.

"Where have you been?" Emma asked, her eyes were filled with worry, but her words were laced with anger. "We've been looking for you guys for forever."

"We were dancing," Ezra replied. I didn't know how he appeared so at ease after what we did. My body was still shaking with after shocks.

"We checked the dance floor five times," she argued.

"Must have missed us." Ezra shrugged indifferently. "Are you guys ready to go?"

"Dude, what the fuck is on your jeans?" Maddox sputtered, eyeing all the dirt and gravel still stuck to Ezra's jeans.

Ezra looked down and shrugged again. "Huh? That's curious."

"Curious," Emma shook her head, "y'all think we're so dumb." She muttered something to herself and then glared at us both. "Why don't you both do us all a favor and admit you're madly in love and fucking like rabbits behind our backs? Okay?"

Before either of us could protest she was out of the booth and hurrying towards the exit.

Maddox smiled apologetically and hurried after her.

Ezra let out a hefty sigh and mused his hair. “Well, I guess that’s our cue to leave.”

Hayes and Arden slid from the booth and we all headed towards the exit.

The ride home was completely silent and I knew Emma was beyond irritated. I hated having my best friend mad at me, especially when I knew it was my fault because I wasn’t being honest with her. But I couldn’t tell her, not yet at least. She’d get her hopes up that things would work out with Ezra and I, and we’d ride off into the sunset on the back of a white horse.

Or worse...

She’d tell me I was crazy and that I’d ruined everything. That by doing this I was not only going to break my own heart, but lose Ezra in the process.

Not just as a lover.

But as my best friend too.

CHAPTER TWENTY

"I DIDN'T EVEN drink that much and I've already thrown up three times this morning." Emma groaned beside me, a book propped on her knees. For now at least, she seemed to have forgotten her irritation with me. "I think this is my first official hangover, though. Does that make me an adult now?" She laughed.

I rolled over onto my stomach so that the sun could tan my back. "You barely had enough to drink to have a real hangover, so no you have not been inducted into adulthood. Secondly, if you're so hung over how are you reading?"

She sighed, turning the page. "It doesn't make me as nauseous as looking at the ocean does." She lowered her book and eyed the ocean, as if testing herself. She gagged and mumbled, "No," before returning to her book.

I pillowed my head on my arms and closed my eyes. It was our last day at the beach. Tomorrow morning we were flying home, and I knew everything was going to change once we got there. So to say I felt a little melancholy at the thought of leaving was the understatement of the century. I was downright sick and it had nothing to do with the two drinks I had last night.

"Hey, I brought you some water," Maddox said, sinking down into the sand beside Emma.

"I love you." She took the bottle of water from him and gulped it greedily.

"Here's one for you too."

I lifted my head to see that he was leaning around Emma and offering me a bottle.

"Oh, thanks." I took it. The cool water soothed my dry throat.

Instead of lying back down I stayed sitting, watching Hayes and Ezra fight over a soccer ball down on the beach.

I couldn't help smiling at the way they bickered over the ball, pushing each other out of the way—but all the while laughing.

I stood up and slipped my flip-flops on.

"Where are you going?" Emma asked.

"To play."

I grinned and ran towards the guys. They didn't see me coming and I jumped on Ezra's back. He grunted from the surprise attack, but quickly held the back of my knees so I didn't fall.

I knew Emma would probably try to make something out of this, but I'd been doing things like this with Ezra long before we started having sex, because he was one of my best friends. I'd lost sight of that fact the last few weeks. I knew when our arrangement came to an end it might also destroy our friendship, so selfishly—even if it was only for right now—I wanted to forget all about the sex and remember why it was that we were friends to begin with.

"How do you expect me to play with you hanging off my back?" He jested, glancing over his shoulder with a half smile.

"I don't. I wanted Hayes to beat you."

Hayes grinned and pointed a finger at me, while kicking the ball back and forth. "That's my girl!"

Ezra let out a growl and I poked him in the ribs so he would stop.

"Actually," I dropped off Ezra's back, "I wanted to join you."

"Sure," Hayes nodded. "As long as you're okay with losing."

I grinned widely. "I never lose."

Before he could blink I stole the ball from him and started running up the beach, kicking the ball as I went.

"Get her!" I heard Hayes bellow, which only made me laugh harder.

I made it a few more feet when an arm collided with my middle and I was jerked against a chest.

I kicked my legs wildly as Hayes dragged me into the ocean.

“Let me go!” I laughed, fighting against his hold.

On the beach Ezra laughed hysterically.

“Nope. Cheaters have to get punished.”

I had a three second warning before he plunged me into the water. Luckily none got up my nose, but he was going to pay for that.

Hayes was a hell of a lot taller than me, but I grabbed onto his arm and pulled, dragging him deeper into the water.

“Westbrook, you’re like a fucking piranha.” He laughed, letting me drag him. I say letting, because we all knew he was strong enough to escape my hold.

“I do have sharp teeth.” I flashed him a menacing smile. Well, as menacing as I could muster.

“I’m terrified.” He pretended to shake.

I let him go and started to swim back to shore. “By the way,” I called to him, “I’m not a piranha, I’m a siren, and you’ve just been led to your death.” I began to cackle as evilly as I could, but I knew it sounded pathetic. I didn’t care though, because this was the most fun I’d had in a long time.

Hayes swam towards me, sweeping the longer strands of his sandy hair away from his eyes.

“Apparently your siren buddies didn’t like me too much. I was too handsome to kill.” He joked as we stepped onto the beach once more.

Ezra stood with his arms crossed over his bare chest. His skin had grown tan while we were here and with his dark curly hair and eyes he reminded me of a Greek god of some sort.

"Does this mean I won?" He smiled crookedly, one foot resting on top of the soccer ball.

"Only losers have to ask if they've won." I winked at him as I adjusted my bikini top. When I looked up his eyes were zeroed in on my boobs. If Hayes noticed he said nothing.

Clearing his throat, Ezra said, "I think I'm going to go make a sandwich. Are you guys hungry?"

I nodded.

"Starving." Hayes rubbed his stomach.

"Cool, I'll go...uh...yeah...sandwiches." He was still staring at my chest and apparently my boobs had magical mind jumbling powers.

"I'll help." I clapped my hand on his shoulder and the gesture seemed to snap him out of his thoughts.

Hayes headed on down the beach to where Arden and Mia were building a sandcastle with Mathias and Remy's help. Maddox and Emma were where I left them. Emma was laughing at something he said, and with as crazy as Maddox could be there was no telling what came out of his mouth.

I walked up to them, and Ezra paused behind me.

"Hey, we're going to make sandwiches for everybody. Do you guys want some?"

"Yeah," Maddox nodded, "and bring some diet Pepsi." He waved an empty bottle around.

"You got it," I nodded. I looked at Emma and arched a brow. "Do you want something to eat?"

She turned a bit green at the mention of food. "No. I'm good. Just more water, please."

I nodded. I hoped she wasn't getting sick. I honestly didn't think she'd drunk enough last night to feel so ill, but then again she rarely drank so maybe it just hit her hard.

Ezra and I walked up the deck steps and into the back of the house.

The air-conditioned space felt like heaven. I hadn't realized I'd gotten so warm outside.

I followed Ezra into the kitchen and he got out the meat and cheese from the refrigerator while I grabbed plates. We worked in silence as we made the sandwiches, but it wasn't an awkward silence. The air was charged with the energy between us and I think we were both afraid that if we spoke sparks might ignite.

It was getting harder every second to pretend there was nothing between us. At least for me. It was impossible to know what was going through his mind sometimes. Ezra could be extremely difficult to read since he internalized things. He was the person that stood in the background, carefully reading and interpreting a situation, instead of jumping right in. He liked to know all the facts and predict all the outcomes before moving forward. And maybe that's why he refused to give into what I knew already—that we were perfect for each other—because he was scared, since he couldn't see where it would lead.

He was afraid of losing me forever.

I was afraid of never getting to experience what it truly meant to be *us*.

The rest of the day passed in a blur and as night fell we all gathered outside.

I was dressed in shorts and a lightweight sweater, with a blanket wrapped around me.

The fire pit was lit and we all sat around, roasting marshmallows, and telling silly stories. Mia was asleep, so luckily we didn't have to worry about filtering ourselves.

When my marshmallow was toasted to perfection I layered it between a graham cracker and a piece of chocolate. I took a bite and moaned. S'mores were one of my favorite things ever.

Ezra chuckled beside me and reached out, brushing his thumb against my bottom lip. "You've got some marshmallow stuck."

He swept it away and started to put his thumb in his mouth, but instead wiped it on his jeans when he realized what he was doing.

Across from us on the opposite side of the fire pit Emma cleared her throat and stood up so that we could all see her better.

Eyeing the two of us, she said, "I think we should all play a game of truth or dare."

My body stiffened. Something told me this wasn't going to bode well for me.

"I don't know…" I mumbled.

"It'll be fun," she protested. "Besides, it's our last night here and we might never be able to go on a trip with all of us ever again. Things are changing." She looked around at all of us with a sad look. "We're growing up and starting our own lives." Her gaze settled on Mathias and Remy before moving on to Maddox.

She did have a point there.

"Okay, fine," I agreed.

"Yay!" She clapped her hands together and sat back down, this time propped on her knees.

My stomach coiled with tension.

"Can I go first?" Hayes raised his hand like we were in elementary school.

"Sure," Emma shrugged.

"Cool." He grinned, rubbing his hands together. "Who shall be my first victim?" He looked around at everyone before his eyes settled on me. "I dare you to kiss..." He paused and I expected him to say Ezra, but instead he surprised me. "Arden."

"Me?" She squeaked, pointing a finger at her own chest. "Why me?"

"A little girl-on-girl action never hurt anybody." He grinned widely.

I laughed and shook my head. "Aren't I supposed to get to pick truth *or* dare?"

His smile grew even more. "Not the way I play. There's dare or dare."

"Ooh, that makes it even better," Emma chimed in.

"So..."Hayes sat back, "get to it."

I shook my head and stood up, walking over to where Arden sat.

"Just a quick peck, right?" She questioned.

I shook my head. "Where's the fun in that?"

Her eyes widened and before she could freak out even more I took her face tenderly between my hands and sealed my lips over hers. It wasn't a quick peck like she wanted. Instead I kissed her like I would any guy. I was never one to back down from a challenge. I swiped my tongue past her parted lips and she gasped. She surprised me when she kissed me back and behind us I heard Hayes mutter, "Fuck, that's hot." I threw in a little hair pulling to make it even hotter.

When I turned around I smiled smugly at him. "Was that good enough for you?"

"Yes." His voice sounded like that of a prepubescent teen boy. I noticed he conveniently covered his crotch with one of the outdoor throw pillows.

I sat back down beside Ezra and glanced at Arden. "You taste good," I told her. Hayes made some kind of noise of distress.

Her cheeks reddened. "It's strawberry lip gloss."

"Does this mean I get to dare you now?" I eyed Hayes.

"Uh...sure...I guess." He seemed extremely uncomfortable now.

I tapped my lips, trying to think of something good. "I dare you to shave your legs."

"What?" He gasped. "Come on!" He extended one leg out and pretended to pet it. "Do you have any idea how many years it took me to get a nice fur coat?"

I snorted and everyone else laughed. "Well, I mean I could've asked you to make out with Mathias...so..."

"I'll shave my fucking legs," he grumbled. "Give me the stuff."

I hurried inside and grabbed a razor, shaving gel, and a bucket of water.

I set the bucket of water down in front of him and held the other items out to him.

“Both legs too,” I eyed him, “don’t get skimpy on me.”

He dunked one leg in the water and then slathered it in shaving gel. “Oh, fuck, now not only am I going to be hairless but I’m going to smell like a girl too. I think I would’ve rather kissed Mathias.”

Mathias glared at him, his dark brows knitted together. “Try it and I’ll bite your tongue off.”

“Sounds kinky,” Hayes jested. Taking a deep breath he made the first swipe over his leg. Seeing the bare patch of skin he let out a small fake cry. “I’m so sorry,” he muttered to his leg, cracking all of us up.

Once he finished he let out a roar and flexed his arms. “Who’s my next victim?” His eyes landed on Maddox. “I dare you to do a handstand for one minute.”

Maddox snorted. “That’s easy.”

“We’ll see if you still think that in twenty seconds,” Hayes challenged.

Maddox shook his head and stood up. “Start a timer.”

I grabbed my phone and set it. “Are you ready?” I asked him.

He nodded.

My finger hovered over the start button. “Go!”

Maddox got into the handstand position and at fifteen seconds cried out, “How much longer?”

“Ha!” Hayes clapped his hands together. “Told you!”

Suffice to say, Maddox only made it until thirty seconds and he wasn't very happy about this fact.

The dares began to escalate. I knew it was only a matter of time before it circled back to me.

Emma eyed me smiling like the cat that ate the canary. "I dare you to give Ezra a lap dance."

I closed my eyes. It wasn't the worst thing she could've come up with, but it was bad enough. I wanted to protest, but I knew that would only highlight the fact that something was indeed going on. In the past I wouldn't have hesitated, because we were friends and it didn't mean anything. It was just a game.

I stood and Ezra grabbed my arm. "Sadie," he started, and when I looked into his eyes I saw what he wanted to say—that I didn't need to do this.

But I did.

I gave Emma a look and said, "Challenge accepted."

I was slightly pissed off, because I knew this dare had an ulterior motive for her.

"If I'm going to do this right, I need some music."

A moment later Mathias' phone lit up and music pumped around us.

Tipping my head at Emma, I began to dance.

Ezra cleared his throat behind me and when I turned to face him I saw that he was looking away.

That only served to spurn me on.

Our friends might've surrounded us but I was still going to make sure he enjoyed this.

I grabbed his chin and forced him to look at me, still swaying my hips to the beat of the song. "Don't think."

He swallowed thickly and his eyes dilated.

I turned back around and lowered my body, rolling my hips against his groin. His hands that had been lying flat on his knees curled into fists. I smiled in satisfaction.

I moved against him as sensually as I could and my hands skimmed underneath my shirt, exposing my stomach.

"Sadie," he growled, grabbing my hips and pulling me more fully against his growing erection.

I removed his hands and turned around to scold him. "Nuh-uh," I wagged a finger in front of his face, "you can look, but you can't touch."

He swallowed thickly and pulled his bottom lip between his teeth.

I laid my hands on his thighs and bent forward so my chest was right in his line of sight—thank God for push up bras—and then moved my hands up his legs, over his stomach, and settled on his chest. His heart thundered madly beneath my palm, like it was racing to escape the confines of his chest. I leaned in and skimmed my lips down his neck and he gasped.

"I thought you said no touching."

"I said *you* couldn't touch. I never said anything about me."

He looked tortured.

I turned back around and practically sat in his lap. I lifted my arms behind me and wrapped them around his neck. All the while I kept moving my body along to the fast pace of the song. I could feel how turned on he was and it made it all worth it. Hell, even I was getting turned on. Bless the poor souls watching us.

The chemistry between us burned brighter than the hottest star.

"That's enough." Emma said and the music cut off.

I moved my hips for a few more seconds before standing and moving back to my chair. I crossed my legs, trying to relieve some of the ache in my center, but unfortunately it wasn't going anywhere.

"Satisfied?" I asked Emma, tilting my head to the side.

She stood with her hands on her hips. "I'll be satisfied when you two finally admit that you're more than friends. I know you think it's not obvious, but it most definitely is," she fumed.

I shrugged innocently. "It was just a lap dance."

She groaned and sat down, muttering, "You're driving me nuts."

Something about her words made me snap. I stood up this time and leered across the burning fire at her. I probably looked menacing but I didn't care.

"Forget a fucking dare," I seethed, spitting the words between my teeth, "I want the truth...why are you so obsessed with my love life? The last time I checked it was none of your business!" The last words were pretty much a lie, yeah my love life wasn't her business but in the past I'd never kept those things a secret from her.

Her face crumbled and I instantly felt like a piece of shit. "I just want you to be *happy*," she cried. Legit *cried.* I made my best friend cry and I felt ashamed of the tear that rolled down her cheek. "That's all I've ever wanted for you. To be happy. Is that such a bad thing?" She sniffled. She wiped at her face and groaned. "I don't know why I'm crying. I'm sorry." She dashed into the house, running away from me as fast as she could.

Upon her exit I was met with silence.

"I'm sorry," I whispered, even though she wasn't there to hear it.

Ezra stood and wrapped an arm around me. He was always there to comfort me when I made a mess of things. I loved him for that.

Maddox stood too and cleared his throat. "She's been really emotional lately...I think it's the wedding. I'm going to go check on her. 'Night."

Without a backwards glance he was gone and I felt even worse.

"I feel awful," I whispered. "I didn't mean to yell at her."

"It's okay." Ezra kissed my forehead.

The others sat watching us. "No, it's not." I pushed myself away from him. I glanced at all of them before my eyes landed on Ezra.

I kept pushing away the people I cared about the most, and what for?

Fear.

I pushed Ezra away, because I was scared of what Braden thought.

Look at how that turned out.

And now I was pushing Emma away because I was scared of what she'd think if she found out the truth.

Fear was a crippling emotion and I hated it. I hated what it was doing to me. I was becoming a monster. I kept hurting the people I cared about the most and that wasn't okay.

"Sadie," Ezra pleaded, reaching for me.

I startled at the worry in his eyes and realized that now I was crying.

I wiped my tears away on the back of my hands and held my chin high. "I'm going to bed."

No one protested when I left.

I couldn't blame them. I wouldn't have stopped me either.

I headed upstairs to my room and took a quick shower. I put on my pajamas and set out my clothes for tomorrow—packing up everything else.

I climbed into bed and willed myself to go to sleep, but not even the soothing lull of the ocean could put me to sleep tonight.

I heard my bedroom door creak open and my body stiffened when a sliver of light poured across the bed before disappearing.

"Go away." I said the words with as much venom as I could muster.

The bed dipped and his warm body slid in behind me. His strong arms wrapped around me and I was too weak to fight him.

"No," he growled angrily in response to what I'd said, "you can yell, and cry, and try to push me away, but I'm not going anywhere. I'm here for you, always. You're my best friend, Sadie, and when your heart hurts so does mine."

I rolled over so that I was facing him and curled my body into his. My fingers fisted his shirt and I burrowed my head into the crook of his neck.

"You're too good to me." I cried into his chest.

He smoothed his fingers through my hair. "No I'm not." He brushed his lips against my forehead. "A good friend wouldn't have used you the way I have."

"You didn't take anything I wasn't willing to give."

"Exactly. That makes me even more of an asshole."

"Do you think we can just forget both of our assholish ways for tonight?"

He chuckled, his laughter rumbling against my ear. "We can do that."

A minute passed. "And Ezra?"

"Yeah?"

"Please, don't let go of me," I begged, my hold on his shirt tightening.

"Never, sweetheart."

I woke up a little after five in the morning.

Ezra was still wrapped around me, his dark hair tousled over his forehead, and his lips parted with sleep.

I sat up, my hair sweeping over my shoulder. I smiled at the sight of him sleeping so peacefully in my bed.

I couldn't seem to stop myself as I reached out and traced my finger over the contours of his mouth. He was entirely too perfect.

I was too restless to stay in bed so I slipped out of his arms and padded out of the room.

The house was silent and I knew it would be hours before the others began stirring since our flight didn't leave until eleven—and since we'd flown in on the record company's private jet that was reserved for Willow Creek's use, we didn't have to worry about being at the airport crazy early to get through security.

I opened the refrigerator and blinked rapidly at the sudden brightness. Once my eyes had adjusted I reached inside and grabbed a bottle of water.

I sat down at the kitchen table and looked out the window at the darkened ocean as I sipped at my water.

I tried my best to silence my mind and it must've worked, because I didn't notice when Ezra came into the room.

"Are you okay?"

I jumped at the sound of his voice and looked over my shoulder to see him standing there adorably rumpled in his pajamas with his round Harry Potter looking glasses perched on his nose.

"Yeah," I nodded, "I'm fine."

"Do you mind if I sit?" He motioned to the chair.

"I don't care."

I expected him to sit in one of the empty chairs, but instead he picked me up and took mine, before depositing me in his lap.

I settled against his chest as my body automatically curled into his. We felt so right together.

"You know more about me than anybody." I whispered into the darkened kitchen and tilted my head back so I could see his reaction.

His dark brows furrowed together and he gave me a peculiar look. "I'm your best friend. I'm supposed to know."

"Yeah...but don't you think it's more than that? Like maybe..." I trailed off, brushing my fingers against this collarbone.

"Maybe what?" He asked, his eyes drifting away from me as he looked out the window. It seemed like he didn't really want to hear what I'd been going to say.

"Never mind," I sighed.

While I felt that my connection with Ezra was deeper than friendship, he clearly didn't feel the same way. I'd thrown away our friendship once, and I refused to do it again by trying to pursue a feeling he didn't even return, although I was afraid I was going to end up losing our friendship anyway. It would be too hard being close to him and not being able to have him. I used to pride myself on being a strong girl, but even the strongest people eventually reach their breaking point. This was mine.

I sighed and leaned my head on his chest, wrapping my arms around his neck.

"I love you," he whispered, kissing the side of my forehead, "you know that, right?"

"Yeah." And I did know it. I also knew he didn't love me in the way I wanted him to.

"Good." He took my chin and tilted my head up so that he could kiss me.

"Ohhh shit."

I jumped away from Ezra, falling onto the floor and bruising my butt in the process.

Hayes stood in the kitchen with a hand slapped over his eyes.

"I saw nothing. I know nothing. I am nothing."

I snorted.

"I am a mist. I do not exist," he chanted, backing out of the kitchen with his eyes still covered. His hand fell suddenly and he grinned. "Oh, hey, look at me rhyming. Maybe I could be a rapper."

"Don't quit your day job," Ezra laughed.

"Yeah, you're right." He grumbled and started to leave.

"Didn't you come down here for something?" Ezra asked him and reached down to help me up.

"Oh, right. I wanted water." Hayes grabbed his water and started his chant all over again. "I saw nothing. I know nothing. I am nothing. I am a mist. I do not exist."

We could hear him still continuing on with his mantra through the living room and up the steps.

Ezra and I both dissolved into a fit of laughter.

"Thank God it was Hayes," he chortled, "and not someone else."

I nodded my head in agreement. That could've easily been a disaster.

"Are you ready to go back to bed?" He asked.

"I think so."

He took my hand and led me up the stairs.

We cuddled into my bed once more and Ezra fell right to sleep. When he'd been asleep for a while, and I knew there was no chance of him hearing, I whispered into the darkness, "I'm in love with you."

CHAPTER TWENTY-ONE

WE'D BEEN HOME from the beach for two weeks and in that time frame I'd been slowly distancing myself from Ezra. I knew he noticed the change, but he didn't say anything. I could tell from the way his brows seemed to be permanently furrowed together that he was worried about me. I was fine though. Really, I was.

"So, what do you think?" The guy showing me the apartment asked.

This was the fifth one I'd seen in a week, and I felt I'd finally found the one. It was small, the kitchen, living room, and bedroom were all a part of one space. The bathroom was the only thing that was closed off. But I loved the charm. It had brick walls, an open ceiling, and touches that harkened to the era in which the building was built.

"I'll take it."

"I'll get the paperwork drawn up." He strolled from the room, leaving me alone in the open space. There was no furniture so I'd have to go shopping, but that was okay with me.

I crossed my arms over my chest and strolled over to one of the long windows that overlooked the street below. The apartment was only blocks from my store and if the weather was nice I could walk there. This was going to be good for me. I needed to distance myself from Ezra and the things that could not be.

I tapped my finger against the window and watched outside as a bird swooped down, landing on the edge of the window. It stared at me intently and tilted its head at me before flying away once more.

Behind me the door opened and the landlord stepped back inside. "I'd really like to get a renter in here as soon as possible, so there's no contingency on the move in date. The place is ready for you when you want to move in...as you can see my last renter hauled ass out of here as fast as possible," he griped. "I do require you to pay the first three months up front to lock in the place. Is that okay?"

"It's not a problem." I set my purse down on the counter and listened as he went over the paperwork. It was pretty basic and when he was done I signed my name on the bottom and handed him a check.

Once he had his money he seemed to be in a better mood. He led me outside and told me to have a good day. I waved goodbye and slid into my car, heading over to my store.

I was meeting Emma in thirty minutes for her second dress fitting. As soon as we got back from the beach I'd went to work on making it since time was not on our side. Plus, it was a valid excuse to avoid Ezra. We hadn't had sex since we got back from the beach. I hadn't slept in his bed either, even though he'd asked. A part of me wanted to jump his bones every second of the day while I still had the chance, but it hurt too much. That's why I was moving out. I couldn't shove my feelings to the side anymore and he didn't have any for me, so I wasn't going to fight this.

I pulled into the parking lot behind my store and headed inside.

Arden was working today and she greeted me with a cheery smile. "Hey, I ordered you a sandwich when I got my lunch. I figured you probably forgot to eat. It's on your desk."

"You're a life saver," I told her honestly. I didn't know what I'd do without her.

I headed into my office and set my bag down before tearing into the sandwich. I hadn't realized how hungry I was until she mentioned food.

By the time I finished and washed my hands Emma was breezing into the store. She greeted Arden before heading towards me. I motioned her into my office and closed the door.

"I feel like crap." She declared, sitting down in the chair across from my desk. "I swear I've been fighting a bug for weeks."

"You need to go to the doctor," I scolded her, grabbing her dress from where I'd stashed it.

She waved away my concern. "I don't have time."

I put my hands on my hips. "Emma Rayne you do so have time to go to the doctor."

She rolled her eyes and kicked off her combat boots. "You sound like my mother...only she'd be shoving some kind of herbal tea at me."

"That's because your momma is a smart lady. Now strip down."

She laughed. "Just try not to poke me with seven hundred pins this time."

I glared at her with my hands on my hips. "Then don't wiggle so much."

Once she was down to her bra and panties I went to work helping her into the dress. It'd been a week since she last tried it on and now it looked like a real dress. She couldn't see herself yet and I hoped she loved the dress as much as I did. It fit her perfectly and the design was so her. To say I was pleased with my handiwork was the understatement of the century. It still needed some tweaks, but it was pretty close to perfect.

I covered Emma's eyes and led her over to the floor length mirror.

"One, two, three." I counted and dropped my hands.

Her gasp of delight was exactly what I wanted to hear. "Sadie," tears welled in her eyes, "this...this...is amazing." She twirled around, examining it from every angle. "I love it. I really do."

I grinned. "I'm glad."

I was stunned when she tackle hugged me.

"Whoa," I held her, trying to keep us upright.

"Thank you so much," she cried against my shoulder, "I know I've been such a bitch to you lately, and I'm sorry. Please forgive me."

I rubbed her back. "There's nothing to forgive."

"I don't know what I'd do without you." She stepped back, wiping her face.

"I think you'd be just fine." I laughed and pointed towards the stool. "Stand up there. I need to fix a few things."

She did as I asked and I grabbed my pins and tape measure.

I turned on some music while I worked and we talked for a bit as I marked things and scribbled notes down.

"Sadie," she said suddenly.

"Yeah?" I didn't look up from my notebook.

"I don't feel so good."

I looked up just in time to see her start swaying. "Emma!"

She fainted and fell off the stool. By some miracle I managed to catch her in my arms but I sagged under her dead weight.

"Arden!" I yelled. "Arden! Hurry, please!"

The door to my office crashed open and when she saw me holding Emma her hands flew up to her mouth. "Oh my God! Is she okay?"

"I don't know!" I cried, my body shaking with worry. "Help me lay her down and then call 911."

Arden nodded and rushed forward, helping me lay Emma down on the floor before dashing away for her phone. I grabbed a bundle of fabric from another project I was working on and bunched it under her head. I felt panicked and I kept trying to run through a checklist of things to do when someone fainted, but my mind was empty.

I sat down on the floor beside her and smoothed her hair away from her forehead.

"Emma," a tear coursed down my cheek, "wake up. Please."

"An ambulance is on the way." Arden burst back into the room and knelt on Emma's other side. "I thought this might help." She laid a dampened paper towel over Emma's forehead.

"Do you think she'll be okay?" I asked Arden.

Before she could answer Emma's eyes started to open. When she went to sit up I forced her back down with a hand to her shoulder.

"Just relax. The ambulance is coming."

"Ambulance?" She asked, blinking her eyes wider. She seemed confused.

I nodded. "You fainted."

"I've never fainted before." Her voice was nothing but a whisper.

"I know. That's why the ambulance is coming. I think you need to be looked over."

She nodded slightly, surprisingly not fighting me on this. Her eyes closed once more, but she wasn't asleep. Her hand felt around blindly and I reached out to hold hers.

The ambulance arrived and everything from there happened in a blur.

I followed the ambulance in my car since the assholes wouldn't let me ride in it and then had to park a mile away.

By the time I made it into the hospital and found her room she'd already had blood drawn and was lying in a bed looking incredibly weak. How had I not noticed how thin and pale she'd become? Or the purple rings beneath her eyes? Had I become so absorbed in what was going on in my personal life that I'd stopped paying attention to the things around me?

"Can you..." Her voice was barely above a whisper and she pointed to a cup of water on a tray beside her bed. Some idiot had put it far enough away that she couldn't reach it.

I grabbed it and held it for her while she took a few slow sips.

When she spoke this time her voice sounded a tiny bit stronger. “Can you call Maddox?”

“Oh! Of course!”

In all the madness I’d forgotten to call him.

“I’ll be right back,” I told her.

I stepped outside of her hospital room and searched my purse for my phone. The stupid thing was buried all the way at the bottom. I pulled it out and rang Maddox’s number.

I never called him and when he answered he seemed to sense that something was wrong. “Sadie?” He questioned, confused as to why I’d be calling him. “Is everything okay?”

I swallowed thickly. “No, it’s not.” I pressed the heel of my free hand against my forehead.

“What’s wrong?” His voice grew high with fear. “Is it Emma? Is she okay? Are you okay?”

“It’s Emma. We’re at the hospital—”

The line went dead.

I really hoped he didn’t get himself killed trying to get here.

Before I could step back into Emma’s room my phone was lighting up. Only the caller wasn’t Maddox.

“Sadie,” Ezra’s voice was panicked when I answered, “are you okay?”

"I'm fine," I assured him. "Emma was at my store and we were doing a fitting for her dress and she passed out. She hasn't been feeling well so I made her go to the hospital...although, she didn't protest, so I think she realized it was past time to see a doctor."

"We'll be there in twenty minutes. I've got to go catch Maddox before he leaves. I don't think he should be driving right now."

"That's probably a good idea."

"Bye." He hung up the phone, but not before I heard him yell, "Get out of the fucking car, Maddox!"

I stuck my phone into my pocket and stepped back into Emma's room.

She slowly rolled her head towards me. "You look like shit." I tried to laugh, but it was forced.

"I feel like shit." She tried to push herself up so that she was sitting, but it wasn't working. I rushed over to help her, trying to get her more comfortable. I hated seeing someone I loved so miserable. I hoped it was nothing bad. "I should've gone to the doctor a while ago," she mumbled, "but I've been so focused on the wedding that I just assumed it was stress."

"This," I pointed at her, "is way more than stress."

"Yeah, I can see that now." She nodded at the stark hospital room. "God I hate hospitals. They smile like death and bleach."

I pulled up one of the chairs closer to her bed and sat down. "Do you want some more water?"

She nodded and was able to drink a little more this time. "Did you get Maddox?"

"Oh, yeah." I nodded. "He's on his way...or actually I think Ezra was about to forcibly remove him from his car so that he could drive him. He was afraid Maddox might crash his car or something."

Emma laughed, but it wasn't her normal one. Instead it was more rough and tired sounding. "Maddox freaks out if I get a splinter. I can't imagine his reaction to this kind of phone call."

"He loves you." I defended his actions.

"I know." She smiled. It was a small one, but still managed to glimmer in her eyes.

I sat back and we grew quiet. I knew Emma was tired and I hoped maybe she could drift off to sleep for a little while, but a doctor ended up coming into the room.

"Ms. Burke," the doctor said, stopping at the end of the bed. "We have your results back from the blood test." The doctor was pretty, maybe in her early forties, with black hair and unique blue eyes that popped against her dark skin.

"That was fast," Emma commented.

The doctor nodded. "I had your tests fast-tracked."

That wasn't a surprise to me. Everyone in this town—unless they lived under a rock—knew who Emma was because of her association with Maddox and the whole band. All of them were practically royalty in this town.

The doctor's eyes shifted to me. "Would you mind stepping outside for a moment?"

Emma's eyes widened in fear and she grabbed onto my arm with a surprising amount of strength. "No, I want her to stay. Please. She's my best friend and I don't want to be alone."

"If it's okay with you..." The doctor paused, waiting for Emma to confirm.

"It is." Emma nodded, resolute.

I sat back down once more, hoping this was nothing bad. I wasn't sure I would be the best person to console Emma if the doctor had bad news.

Please let everything be okay, I silently chanted.

"Well," the doctor started, "the good news is nothing is majorly wrong with you."

"Majorly?" She repeated. "So something is wrong?"

"Not wrong per se," the doctor hedged.

Emma paled even further and I feared she might pass out again.

"I'm hoping this will be good news." The doctor glanced down at the chart. "According to your blood work you're about seven weeks pregnant."

Oh.

My.

God.

"What?" Emma shook her head and her eyes bugged out. "Can you repeat that? I don't think I heard you right."

The doctor smiled. "You're seven weeks pregnant."

Emma's hand went to her stomach. "I'm having a baby?" Tears filled her eyes and I really hoped they were tears of happiness.

"Yes," the doctor nodded. "We'll do a sonogram soon. We're just waiting on the technician."

"Wow." Emma wiped at her tears. "This is insane." She looked up at me with wonder and awe in her eyes. "I'm going to be a mom, Sadie. How crazy is that?"

"Pretty crazy. But you're going to be an amazing mom." I knew between her and Maddox this baby would be the luckiest kid on the planet.

"I need a tissue," she said, reaching out and failing to find one.

The doctor grabbed one for her and handed it over. "It seems that it's a combination of things that led to your extreme fatigue, the baby being one of those causes. You need to eat more balanced meals and drink a lot of water. I'll be back soon and we'll go over a few things," she said, before leaving.

Emma nodded as she left and continued to dab at her eyes. "I can't believe I'm getting married *and* having a baby."

"Life is changing," I agreed.

My phone buzzed and I stood up. "I'll be just outside the door."

"Is it Maddox?" She asked.

I shook my head. "Ezra."

"Oh. Okay."

I stepped into the hallway and closed the door behind me.

Before the phone could stop ringing I answered. "Hello?"

"Hey, I wanted to let you know I just let Maddox out at the front and I'm parking the car. I thought you should be warned though because he's on a rampage."

"Noted," I said, just as I heard a commotion around the corner. "I have to go."

I hurried in the direction of all the sound and stopped when I saw a cart had fallen over on the floor and Maddox was pushing people out of his way.

"Move! Get out of my way!" He yelled as he shoved people. "My woman needs me!"

I couldn't help but snort at that last part. Emma would throw one of his drumsticks at him if she heard him refer to her as his "woman".

Maddox saw me and ran forward. "Sadie!" He cried. "Where is she?"

"This way." I led him down the hall and pointed to her room.

He didn't pause as he threw the door open and hurried inside. "Emma." His whole body sagged as he collapsed beside her bed, taking her hand in his. His body shook and I realized he was crying. She consoled him, saying something softly under her breath, and running her fingers through his hair. I took a step back, feeling like I was invading on an intimate moment between the two. After all, Maddox was about to find out that he was going to be a dad.

I eased the door closed and slid down against the wall until my butt hit the floor.

I heard the telltale sound of boots slapping against the linoleum floors and looked up to find Ezra hurrying down the hall. Mathias and Hayes were right behind him.

"You all came," I whispered in surprise.

"Of course we did," Hayes replied. "We were worried."

"Is everything okay?" Ezra asked.

"Yeah," I nodded. "It's fine." I wasn't going to tell them about the baby. That was Maddox and Emma's good news to share.

Suddenly I felt incredibly tired. I rose shakily to my feet and Ezra grabbed my arm to steady me.

"I'm *fine*." I jerked out of his hold.

I hated being so angry in a moment like this, but Maddox and Emma's happiness was my pain. She was getting her happily ever after and riding off into the sunset with her Prince Charming, while mine refused to see that I stood right in front of him open and willing to love him. I couldn't do it anymore. I couldn't keep this up.

I started off down the hallway and Ezra hurried after me. "Sadie, where are you going?"

He grabbed my shoulder and I skirted away from his touch like I'd been burned. I whipped around in anger. "I can't keep doing this!" I cried, not caring who heard me. I was done. I wouldn't put myself through this anymore. I couldn't make him love me anymore than I could will the ocean to turn pink. Some things just weren't going to happen ever. I could see now that we were one of those things. "I can't keep tiptoeing around my feelings like they don't exist! I can't fuck you and pretend that it doesn't mean more to me than some quick satisfaction! I love you! I. Love. You. And I thought maybe you loved me too, but it's pretty obvious to me that I was wrong." I wiped at my tear-streaked face. Mathias and Hayes stood a few feet away watching our exchange in shock. "I can see that you're never going to let me into your heart." I stabbed a finger at his chest and he flinched, but I knew it wasn't from the pressure. "I'm leaving," I said the words steadily. "I found a place of my own. So I'll be out of your place today."

Moving out today would be inconvenient, but it had to be done. I'd suck it up and crash at my parent's house for a few days while I bought furniture and had it delivered to my apartment.

Ezra stood shell-shocked. His mouth opened and closed as he searched for words. "You don't need to do this."

I flinched. He wasn't stopping me. He wasn't saying he loved me.

"Yeah," I nodded, "I have to." I waved a hand at him. "You saying that is exactly why I have to leave. My feelings for you...they're far more than what you feel for me and I can't allow myself to get hurt any more than I already have. I know our deal wasn't your idea. I take full responsibility; so don't feel bad, please. I'm a big girl and I knew what I was doing, but I stupidly thought it would help me get over my ridiculous crush on you. I thought if we had sex then you wouldn't live up to my fantasy, or it would get dull after a while...but it didn't. It got better and you...well, I think I fell in love with you long before we slept together. If I'm honest with myself I think maybe I loved you even before I met Braden, but I knew you'd never go for someone like me. And I was right." I took a deep breath. "But I can't turn my feelings off, so I'm leaving."

"Sadie—" He reached for me.

I took three steps away from him. "No," I said firmly. "Don't touch me. Don't try to stop me. Don't say anything. I don't need you to feel sorry for me."

He swallowed thickly and he looked like he was in pain. "I never meant to hurt you."

"I know." I nodded. "You're a good guy, Ezra. Really, you are. This isn't your fault."

I turned to go and he whispered, “I don’t want you to go.”

I closed my eyes and paused for one short second. “I have to.”

I walked away as fast as my legs would carry me and behind me I heard the guys berating Ezra. I even heard Maddox step out of the room and say, “Dude, if you love her make her yours.”

But he didn’t love me, because if he did he would’ve never let me walk away.

CHAPTER TWENTY-TWO

I WAS NUMB.

That was the only excuse I could come up with as to why I wasn't currently bawling my eyes out. Especially considering all the tears I shed over Braden and I hadn't loved him the way I loved Ezra.

God, my life was a fucking mess.

I stuffed all of my clothes and toiletries into my suitcase. It didn't take long until there wasn't a single trace of me left in his house. Selfishly, I hoped a small part of him would miss me. It was stupid, but I wanted him to hurt in some way. Although, his hurt would never compare to the pain I felt when walking out of the hospital and leaving behind my mangled heart crushed in his hands.

I hurried down the steps, my heavy suitcase clomping behind me.

I paused in the kitchen and removed his key from my key ring. I tossed it haphazardly on the counter and it clanked against the goldfish bowl. Toby swam into his lime green castle to hide away from the sound.

"Sorry Toby," I muttered.

A part of me wanted to take the fish with me, but I didn't know the rules when it came to fish-parent custody and I didn't want him to use that as an excuse to come after me.

Although, I guessed if he was going to come after me he would've followed me here, which he hadn't.

"Fuck you, Ezra Collins," I muttered angrily to myself as I threw open the door, "fuck you and everything you make me feel."

Outside I shoved my suitcase into my car.

When I drove away I didn't look back.

I pulled into the driveway of my parent's home and knocked on the door. I had a key, but I didn't want to intrude.

My mom opened the door after only a few seconds.

"Sadie, is everything okay?" She was surprised to see me.

"No." I began to wilt as she pushed open the screen door and pulled me inside. "Everything is a big puddle of suck. Why are boys so stupid?"

"Aw, Sadie." She wrapped her arms around me and hugged me fiercely. "Boys never grow up. That's their problem."

"Is it okay if I stay here for a few days?"

She held me back by my shoulders and nodded. "You can stay here as long as you need to, sweetie. You know that." She took my hand and led me into the kitchen. "Your dad's out back starting the grill, but I made brownies this afternoon. Do you want some?"

I perked up slightly. "Do you have whipped cream?"

"Of course," she said, heading to the refrigerator.

She fixed me a piece of brownie on a plate with whipped cream and chocolate syrup. It was delicious, but it did nothing to fill the gaping hole in my heart.

The back door slid open and my dad stepped inside. "Hey, Princess." He greeted me with a kiss on the top of my head.

My dad was a tall, large, bear of a man. Some people found him scary and intimidating, but he was really a big softy. Especially when it came to my little sister and me.

He pulled out a chair and sat down beside me. "Have you been crying?" His eyes zeroed in on my face. I was sure my mascara was smudged and my eyes were probably red. When I didn't answer he huffed, "Okay, who do I need to punch in the face? If it's that prick you were going to marry I might just run him over with my car."

I laughed. Leave it to my dad to make me laugh even when I felt like curling in a ball to die.

"No, it's not him."

"Richard," my mom said lightly, "why don't you take the burgers out and put them on the grill."

"But—" He protested.

"Now, please."

"Fine." He grumbled. He stood and pointed a finger at me. "She might be dismissing me, but I *will* find out who hurt my baby girl."

He grabbed the plate from her and headed out the back door once more, grumbling the whole way.

"Why don't we go to the living room?" She suggested. "We'll be more comfortable in there."

"Sure...and do you think I could have another brownie?"

She laughed and took the plate from me. "You might as well eat them now. Once your dad starts in on them they'll be gone in minutes."

She fixed me another brownie and I followed her into the living room. The couch was a large black leather sectional that they'd had since my siblings and I were kids. There was still a long streak on the back of it from a silver sharpie.

I sat down and the cushions molded around me.

"Now, tell me what happened." My mom sat down beside me and patted my knee gently.

While devouring my brownie I told her everything. I told her how Ezra had always been there for me, and how great he'd been when I needed a place to say. I even told her about our deal. I explained how I'd always felt around him and how in the past two months I'd discovered that I was in love with him, but that he didn't feel the same way about me.

"Honey," she looked at me sadly, "how would you know he doesn't love you. Did you ever really give him a chance?"

I wiped a streak of whipped cream off of my lip. "He had plenty of chances."

"Well..." She paused. "He's a guy, Sadie. You know how boys are with their feelings."

"I told him I loved him and he just stood there." I looked down at the now empty plate.

"Maybe he was shocked," she defended.

"Hey," I pointed my fork at her, "whose side are you on here?"

She smiled. "Yours. Always. You know that. But I've also seen Ezra enough to know that he's the quiet, guarded type. You're..." She paused, searching for the right words. "You're like a tornado. You blaze through town with this wild energy, not caring what kind of disruption you cause." I pouted and she laughed. "That's not a bad thing, Sadie. I'm just saying he's different. He's the quiet moody poet in the corner while you're the one spinning through the room making a spectacle of yourself. All I'm trying to tell you is not everyone deals with things the same way."

I leaned my head back on the couch. "It doesn't matter."

"Doesn't it?"

I shook my head. "I just want to move past this."

She grew quiet and stared at me for a moment. "I think you should talk to him."

I grunted in response. "I don't think so. I did plenty of talking today."

"It sounds to me like you didn't really give him a chance to respond."

"No, I didn't," I agreed. "But I couldn't stand there in the middle of a hospital and let his friends hear him shoot me down. I know he would've told me that he only ever wanted to be friends and that he was sorry he couldn't return my feelings."

"But how do you know he would've said that?" She argued.

"I just know." I grumbled. "Look," I stood up, "I don't want to talk about this anymore."

"Okay." She sat calmly with her hands in her laps. "The conversation is forgotten then."

"Good," I nodded. Wringing my hands together, I smiled sheepishly. "Are you sure it's okay if I stay here? I found a place of my own, but I need to get furniture and everything."

"You know you don't need to ask."

"Thanks, mom." I lowered and kissed her cheek.

"Are you still hungry after all of those brownies?" She asked, standing up and heading towards the back door. "I'm sure your dad's finished with the burgers by now."

"Nah," I shook my head. "Maybe later. I think I'm going to get my stuff and lay down for a bit."

"Okay." She hugged me, the kind of hug that made me feel like I was going to suffocate, but secretly loved. "Everything's going to be okay." She took my face in her hands. "You'll see."

"I hope so," I replied. My mom had never been wrong before, but there was a first time for everything.

I was sitting at the table eating breakfast when the doorbell rang.

"I'll get it!" My dad called from his den.

My body had completely frozen over.

Could it be?

"Emma!" I heard my dad boom and my shoulders sagged. It wasn't him. Of course it wasn't, but I'd dared to hope.

Footsteps sounded towards the kitchen and then Emma and my dad appeared in the doorway.

"You look a lot better." And she did. Her skin was back to its normal color and there was some pink in her cheeks. She didn't look as tired either.

"I feel better." She pulled out a chair and sat down.

My dad quietly left the room.

"So..." She tapped her fingers restlessly against the tabletop. "I was right about you and Ezra?"

I rolled my eyes. "I'm sure he told you everything."

"He didn't say too much," she shrugged, "but it was impossible not to hear you yelling in the hallway."

"Oh, right." I winced.

She gave me a sympathetic look.

"I really made a fool of myself, didn't I?"

She shook her head. "I don't think so. I think it's about time you stood up for your feelings instead of burying them."

I stared up at the ceiling, my bowl of cereal forgotten. "I tried so hard not to fall in love with him," I whispered.

"We can't control who we love. We just do."

"It just sucks when the person you love doesn't love you back."

Her lips pressed into a thin line, but she said nothing.

"Anyway," I stood up, emptying my uneaten cereal into the sink, "I'm going shopping today for my place. Do you want to come with me? I could always use your opinion."

When I turned back around Emma was smiling. "I'd love to help. And maybe while we're shopping you could tell me all about what's been going on this summer that you tried so hard to hide." She stood and bumped her shoulder against mine.

"We were pretty obvious, huh?"

"You think?" She laughed. "I've always been rooting for you guys though. I just...I guess I always thought *you'd* be the stubborn one about a relationship, not him. It's always been clear to me how he feels about you."

"What do you mean?" I asked, padding down the hall to the tiny guestroom. It had a futon instead of a bed, and my back was aching today from how uncomfortable it had been.

"He loves you. I think he's scared, though."

"He doesn't love me," I protested, shaking my head as I searched through my suitcase for something to wear.

Emma sighed and sat down on the edge of the bed. When I looked over my shoulder at her she seemed torn about something.

"What is it?" I asked.

"Nothing," she responded quickly, too quickly.

I arched a brow.

"It's nothing," she repeated.

"Whatever." I wasn't in the mood to argue with her. We'd done far too much of that the last few months. It was time to put everything in the past.

I dressed in a pair of shorts and a loose top. I pulled my hair back into a ponytail and grabbed my purse.

"I'm ready."

We drove around to the various furniture stores in town and I was able to find everything I needed.

From there we headed to Target so I could get things for the kitchen and bathroom. I had nothing of my own to take to my place, so it was fun to be able to pick out new things. It gave me something to smile about when it felt like my life had gone to shit around me.

All while we shopped I explained to Emma about my arrangement with Ezra, and why I hadn't wanted to tell her. She seemed to see where I was coming from and gave me much needed support.

"I feel like such an idiot," I confessed to her, when we sat down at a little café to get a bite to eat.

She stayed mysteriously quiet, perusing the menu like it was the most fascinating thing she'd ever seen.

"Come on, Emma. You have to have some sort of opinion on my idiocy."

She shook her head and finally lowered the menu. "I think you're both idiots."

"What?" I laughed.

"He's a dumb boy that was too stupid to realize his feelings until it was too late, and you're stupid to have walked away without giving him a chance to explain where he was coming from." She sat back and crossed her arms over her chest, leveling me with a glare.

"What do you mean about that first part?" I asked hesitantly.

She waved away my words. "I said I wouldn't say anything. And Ezra's my friend too, so my lips are sealed." She mimed zipping her lips. "You need to talk to him though."

I shook my head and picked up my glass of water the waiter had left. "I'm not ready. I need some space to clear my head."

She narrowed her eyes. "Y'all better not mess up my wedding. You do remember that he's supposed to escort you down the aisle?"

"Unfortunately, I hadn't forgotten that tidbit of information."

"No fighting at my wedding. I mean it," she warned. "I'll kick you both. Don't doubt me."

I managed to laugh. "I'll be on my best behavior."

Ezra might get the silent treatment, but I'd never do anything to jeopardize Emma's special day.

"Promise me you'll talk to him."

"I promise," I whispered, but we both knew those words were a lie.

CHAPTER TWENTY-THREE

WE NEED TO TALK.

The four words glared up at me from the screen of my phone.

Please Sadie.

Don't ignore me.

I stuffed my phone in my back pocket. I didn't have time for this. I didn't need him to tell me to my face how he was sorry for everything, and that he'd never meant for any of this to happen, that everything was supposed to be simple until I had to go and ruin it.

I set the shopping bags down on the kitchen counter in my new place. All the furniture had been delivered and Emma had come by to help me unpack. Not that there was really anything to unpack. I think she just didn't want me to be alone.

I rifled through the bags until I found the one with the plates. Once I located it I sat it on the dining room table and took a seat to start peeling off the price stickers.

"This place is nice," Emma commented, looking out one of the tall windows.

"Thanks. I really like it."

She took a seat and grabbed half of the plates.

My phone buzzed in my pocket and her brows rose in interest. "Is that him?"

"Possibly."

She slapped her palms against the table. "I'm getting married in a *week*. Fix this," she hissed.

I rolled my eyes. "I promise that my love life will not interfere with your wedding."

She groaned. "Forget messing up my wedding, think of this as a gift instead. You two working out your problems would be the best wedding gift you could give me."

I eyed her. "Better than your dress?"

"Yep, that would be even better than my dress."

"I don't even know what to say to him." I dropped my head in my hands, the plates lying forgotten on the table.

"Then don't say anything to him. Let him do all the talking."

I nearly rolled my eyes out of my head. "Ezra? Talking?"

"It's true that he's a man of few words, but when he does have something to say it's usually important and you should listen."

"When did you become my therapist?" I jested.

She tucked a piece of unruly blonde hair behind her ear. "When you started being so blind."

I grumbled under my breath. I wasn't blind. I saw what was right in front of me and it was blatantly obvious that he didn't love me. Or, he did, but not in the way I wanted him to.

I finished peeling off the stickers and set the plates in the sink to wash them later.

"Can you do these?" I asked Emma, handing her the bag with the cups.

"Sure."

"Oh, and here's this." I grabbed a spare key off the counter. "I wanted you to have this just in case."

She smiled and tucked the key into her pocket.

While she was helping me with the cups I made my bed since it'd been lying bare.

The place was starting to look better. Even still, I missed Ezra's cozy little cottage on the lake. It felt like home. This still didn't feel quite right, and I was reminded of a quote I'd once seen that said it's the people that make the place, not the things.

After another hour of unpacking shopping bags and putting things away, Emma and I walked the two blocks over to my store for her final fitting.

Remy and Arden were already waiting, because they needed to try on their bridesmaid dresses.

I put Emma in her dress and stood back to admire my handiwork. I might have to add custom wedding dresses as something I offered in my store. It had been hard, but worth it.

Emma spun around, admiring her reflection. "This dress is so beautiful, Sadie. I can't thank you enough." She hugged me fiercely. Into my ear she whispered, "You're going to get your happily ever after too. You'll see."

I wanted to believe her, I really did, but at some point you have to grow up and stop believing in fairytales.

She patted my cheek in a gesture similar to something my mother would do.

"Chin up, buttercup."

I giggled and she smiled at having had her intended effect.

I helped her out of her dress and put it away in its garment bag.

"Alright ladies, you next." I motioned Arden and Remy over.

Originally Hayes wasn't going to escort anyone down the aisle since Emma didn't have another bridesmaid in mind, but after our vacation she'd asked Arden to be in the wedding. Arden had been surprised at first, but quickly agreed. Arden fit into our group seamlessly.

"Don't forget you have to try on your dress too!" Emma warned.

"I burned my dress." I said it as straight-faced as I could.

Her mouth fell open. "Sadie! You better not have!"

I began to laugh and she eased. "You know I would never do that."

"You scared me there for a second. I think my heart stopped." She put a hand to her chest.

"You're feeling okay, right?" I asked, suddenly worried as I pulled the dresses out of the closet in my office.

"Yeah, I'm fine. I've been a lot better since I was in the hospital."

"I'm so excited that our kids will be the same age," Remy beamed, taking the dress from my hands.

"Me too," Emma agreed. "I hope they'll be really close."

"Best friends," Remy agreed.

It was a happy moment, but my heart sagged. I'd once dreamed of having that same conversation with Emma. Only we'd been older and both married. Now she was moving on and starting a whole new chapter of her life without me.

I handed Arden her dress and grabbed mine. We didn't bother with modesty as we all stripped down and slipped into our dresses.

Emma clapped her hands giddily. "You all look beautiful!"

"I feel fat," Remy grumbled, putting a hand over her swollen stomach.

"How far along are you now?" I asked her.

She fanned herself with a spare piece of paper. "Almost eight months."

"You're getting close then," I commented.

"Not close enough," she sighed. "I'm ready to get this baby out. He's killing my back."

"If you're trying to scare me," Emma gulped, "it's working."

Remy laughed. "It's not that bad…sometimes."

Emma took a deep breath. "No more baby talk. I have enough anxiety at the moment."

I looked over Remy and Arden's dresses and everything seemed fine. I hadn't made these, but I had done the tailoring.

I stood so the three of us were lined up in front of Emma. "Do they get the bride's approval?"

She clapped her hands giddily. "They're perfect!" Standing, she threw her arms around us in a group hug. "Guys! I'm getting married in three days! This is it!"

"I still think you should have a bachelorette party," Remy said, grinning widely. "We could go to the bar where I used to work. I'm sure I could bribe Tanner into doing a striptease." She cackled.

Emma wrinkled her nose. "I never wanted a party, and definitely not any stripping."

"You suck." Remy stuck out her tongue and then reached for the zipper on the back of the dress. When her arms didn't reach Arden slid it down for her.

"Maddox and I wanted to keep everything low key." Emma reminded us. "You know us. We don't like to cause a fuss."

"That's okay," I piped in, trying to be positive, "when I get married I'll have the strippers."

Emma rolled her eyes. "Then I'm not coming."

"More strippers for me then." I laughed heartily. I hadn't laughed this much, or this genuinely, since everything blew up with Ezra.

"Amen to that."

I glanced over at Arden in surprise. "What?" She batted her eyes innocently. "Just because I have a kid doesn't mean I'm dead."

We all laughed at that and I couldn't wipe the smile off of my face if I wanted to. Everybody needed girl time now and then.

CHAPTER TWENTY-FOUR

CHAOS.

That was the only way to describe the mess surrounding me.

For a "small" wedding there sure were a lot of people running around.

I sat in a chair, trying not to wiggle so much as the makeup artist expertly applied my makeup. Across the room someone was doing Emma's hair. Beyond this room people ran through the Wade's house trying to get everything set up in time. The wedding was being held in the backyard, but they were decorating the interior for the event as well.

"I'm so nervous," Emma confessed, her fingers dancing along the arm of the chair. "What if they tell me to say 'I do' and I say 'I don't' by accident?"

I wanted to laugh, but the makeup artist was applying false lashes and I really didn't want to incur her wrath.

"That's not going to happen, Emmie." Her mom breezed into the room already dressed with her hair and makeup done.

"Looking good." I told her mom.

"Thanks, Sadie." She smiled in my direction.

"I'm sweating so bad right now," Emma continued, "I'm going to look like a hot mess, literally, when I walk down the aisle. Oh my God, what was I thinking telling that boy I'd marry him?" She rattled. "We would've been fine without all of this." She waved her hands wildly and the hair stylist scolded her.

Emma's mom pulled out a chair across from her. "Honey," she took Emma's hand, "he loves you and you love him. Stop worrying so much about everything else and focus on that fact, okay?"

Emma nodded. "I think I can do that."

"Alright," she stood, "I'm going to go find Karen and see what I can help with." She turned towards me. "Keep her calm."

"I can do that," I assured her.

The woman doing my makeup finished and went on to Remy.

I'd already done my own hair and the other girl's in a simple fishtail braid.

I slipped into my dress and went to sit beside Emma. Her hair was being styled back in a simple bun with a few strands framing her face.

"Have you talked to Ezra yet?"

I glared at her. "Today is your wedding, Ezra and I should be the last thing on your mind."

"I'm worried about you guys," she confessed with a frown.

"Don't be. Seriously, don't waste your time worrying about us."

"I'll try," she mumbled, but I doubted she'd be able to let it go.

"Think about that cute little baby you're going to have soon." I pointed to her still flat stomach. "And just so you know, I'm going to spoil that kid silly."

She laughed and began to relax. "Yeah, this will be one spoiled baby." She stroked her fingers over her stomach. "You know, this wasn't expected, and I would've liked to have waited a few more years, but...I'm really excited."

"You should be," I assured her. "You and Maddox will be the best parent's ever. And hey," I grinned, "think of all the cute baby clothes Maddox can knit."

She snorted. "He was already going crazy making things for baby Liam," she pointed towards Remy, "he's going to be even worse now."

"I guess this means you guys will be moving out of the guesthouse?" I raised a brow.

She wrinkled her nose and groaned. "Don't remind me. Normally Maddox and I are on the same page, but not when it comes to what kind of house we want. It seems like neither of us will get our way now. With the baby coming, we don't have time to build a house or remodel."

"I'm sure you guys will figure it out."

"Thirty minutes ladies," Karen, Maddox's foster mom, poked her head through the doorway.

"I'm going to be sick." Emma paled.

"You can do this," I assured her.

She took a deep breath. "I feel like my heart is going to beat right out of my chest."

"That's normal." I assured her.

The woman finished her hair, accenting it with a few small white flowers pinned into her hair.

Before Emma could freak out too much I managed to get her in her dress and then gave her a pep talk before it was show time.

We lined up at the French doors in the kitchen that led out into the backyard. All of the windows were lined with lavender tulle and string lights, thick enough that we couldn't see out and no one could see in.

I was acutely aware of Ezra standing in the corner. Even though I told myself not to look every few seconds my eyes flicked in his direction anyway. He was always looking at me too.

He looked amazing in the black tuxedo with his hair tamed away from his forehead. He'd shaved, so he wasn't as scruffy as normal, but there was still a little bit of stubble dotting his cheeks and chin.

Somebody yelled for us to get lined up and he started towards me.

I swallowed past the lump in my throat, hating how my heart sped up the closer he got to me. We were to walk out last since I was Emma's Maid of Honor and he was Maddox's Best Man. You would've thought Mathias might have been pissed that his twin didn't choose him as his Best Man, but he didn't care. He was still too busy flying high about his epic love with Remy to care about anything else.

Ezra crooked his elbow and I slid my hand inside the space.

Someone handed me my bouquet and went over a few more instructions, but I couldn't hear a word they said, because Ezra chose that moment to lower his head and brush his lips against my ear. "We need to talk. You can't avoid me forever."

"I'm not avoiding you." I was surprised by how evenly I was able to say the words.

He made a noise in the back of his throat. "Bullshit. You need to give me a chance to explain. After the ceremony, please talk to me."

"No," I said firmly, "there's nothing to say. Besides, I won't ruin Maddox and Emma's wedding by arguing with you."

"Dammit, Sadie," he growled, anger lacing his words. I'd never heard him sound so pissed and hurt in all the time I'd known him. Ezra was always even-tempered. "You *will* talk to me."

I shook my head as the French doors opened.

Hayes and Arden walked out first, and then Mathias and Remy, leaving Ezra and I to take our places.

He straightened then and we both plastered on fake smiles.

I counted the steps in my head, trying not to think about how tense Ezra's arm felt against my hand or the words he'd spoken.

As soon as I could let go of him, I did, and took my place beside the altar.

The backyard had been transformed into a magical wonderland. Small fairy lights glimmered everywhere and fake walls decorated in green foliage and flowers hid the guesthouse and surrounding homes. The pool was decorated with glowing orbs that floated on the water. I knew when the sun went down it would be even more beautiful.

I giggled when I saw what came out behind us.

Sonic, Maddox's hedgehog, scampered down the aisle in a bow tie with the rings tied around his body.

"Come here." Maddox crouched down when Sonic veered off the path. At the sound of his voice Sonic righted himself and scurried into Maddox's empty hands.

Maddox untied the rings and handed them to Ezra to hold.

He sat the hedgehog on his shoulder and then turned towards the doors.

I felt, rather than heard, Maddox's intake of breath when he saw Emma. It was like with that one single inhale he stole all of the air around us.

I glanced over at him and saw tears shimmering in his eyes, but he was trying to play it cool. Ezra clapped him on his shoulder and said something under his breath.

It must've done the trick, because Maddox let go, letting the tears flow freely.

Since Emma's dad wasn't in the picture her mom was the one that walked her down the aisle.

She placed Emma's hand in Maddox's and kissed each of their cheeks. "I love you," she whispered to the two of them before taking her seat.

Emma handed me her bouquet and flashed a smile as she turned to face Maddox.

The preacher began to speak and I tried to focus on what he was saying, but it was impossible when I could feel the weight of Ezra's eyes on me.

I heard the preacher say it was time to kiss the bride, and Maddox grabbed Emma's face between his hands and gave her a very dramatic kiss before the two of them headed back down the aisle.

"Take these." I shoved the two bouquets I held at Remy and took off away from the ceremony.

I hurried behind the fake walls and ran over to the guesthouse where I grabbed the spare key from underneath the mat and let myself inside.

I knew I couldn't run away from my problems forever, but tonight I had to. I was afraid if I spoke to Ezra I'd either scream at him or throw myself at him. Neither of which was an appropriate option at the moment.

I sat down on the couch and put my head in my hands, trying to compose myself.

I hadn't seen him since that day I walked away in the hospital and I stupidly thought that the time apart would have desensitized me to his affect. Wrong. So, very wrong. If anything it had made things worse.

The door to the guesthouse opened and I immediately jumped into a standing position, turning around sharply. I was braced for a fight, but it wasn't Ezra.

Instead Arden stared back at me with wide eyes. "Are you okay?" She asked, stepping forward hesitantly like I was a wounded animal that might snap and bite her hand off. "You ran away so fast...I was worried."

"I'm fine."

She raised her brows, urging me to be honest.

"Okay, I'm not fine," my shoulders sagged, "but I don't want to talk about it."

"Fair enough." She gave me a sympathetic smile. "I know you really want to hide in here, but they need you for pictures."

I closed my eyes and my teeth snapped together.

"Come on," Arden urged, stepping around the couch to take my hand, "it won't be that bad."

"You have no idea."

If this wedding hadn't been planned for months in advance, I'd be convinced Emma was doing everything she could to torture me.

While we were taking an endless amount of photos the wedding organizers were busy setting up tables and chairs in the backyard.

I found my name written elegantly on a piece of parchment and looked beside my plate to see Ezra's name written down.

Fuck my life.

I sat down just as Ezra appeared. He'd ditched his tux jacket and if anything he looked even more lickable. The sleeves of his white dress shirt were rolled up to his elbows and his slick black tie lay flat.

I quickly turned my head away when he saw me looking.

The chair to my left slid out and he sat down.

"You keep running from me," he drawled, "and yet we keep ending up together. Think there's something to that?" He propped his elbows on the table and tipped his head in my direction, a dark curl tumbled forward across his forehead refusing to be tamed.

"Yes," I agreed and he smirked, "the world hates me."

His smile fell. He leaned forward, his eyes flicking all across my body before he ever so slightly drew his bottom lip in between his teeth. Fuck me. He wasn't playing fair.

His lashes lowered, fanning across his cheekbones, and his breath tickled the skin of my neck. "I'll leave you alone...tonight. But soon I'm going to talk and you *will* listen."

I swallowed thickly, hoping he couldn't see the way my pulse fluttered in my throat.

"Is that a threat?"

His lips quirked up into a crooked smile and he leaned impossibly closer. "No, sweetheart, that's a promise."

I suddenly felt light-headed. Even when he sat back, out of my personal space, I still couldn't seem to get enough oxygen into my lungs.

Our food was served to us, but I merely picked at mine. My appetite was completely gone. I wished I could bow out, but since I was the Maid of Honor I was stuck here.

The tables were cleared away to make room for a stage and room to dance.

Emma and Maddox had their customary dance together before Hayes and Maddox took the stage.

"Emma," Maddox spoke into the microphone, "you haven't heard this song yet and I've been hiding it for a while. This is for you. Only you."

She smiled up at him from the edge of the stage.

He sat down on a stool beside Hayes. He tipped his head in Hayes' direction and the soft sounds of the acoustic guitar filled the air.

With a small smile Maddox began to sing. His voice was similar to Mathias', but softer.

Emma swayed to the song, looking up at her new husband with love shining in her eyes.

I was so happy for her, but that happiness didn't fill the ache in my heart.

"Dance with me."

I turned and looked up at Ezra. I said nothing as I quickly looked away.

He moved to stand in front of me and held out his hand. Other couples were already filling the dance floor.

I saw Hayes dragging a giggling Arden out onto the dance floor.

"Take my hand, Sadie." His eyes pleaded with me. "If you don't you'll regret it."

I wanted to be mean and tell him that I already regretted everything between us and that I could handle one more, but the words would be a lie, and I was done with all of the lying. It was exhausting.

He crooked his fingers, beckoning me to trust him for the moment and to put my hand in his.

Exhaling a deep breath, I somehow found the courage to give him my hand.

He smiled triumphantly and pulled me onto the dance floor.

I couldn't help the blush that colored my cheeks when I thought about what happened the last time we danced together.

He held my one hand and his other settled on my waist, above the curve of my butt, and I stiffened. "Relax," he coaxed. "I'm not going to hurt you."

"You already have." I whispered the words so softly that I thought he might not hear them, but he did.

He pressed a kiss to my forehead and I closed my eyes. "I'm going to make this up to you," he vowed, "you'll see."

I wasn't going to hold my breath.

CHAPTER TWENTY-FIVE

I CLOSED THE door to my shop and locked it behind me.

The night sky glittered above me with a thousand shining stars and a brief smile touched my lips. It had been three days since the wedding, and I was feeling surprisingly good. It was one of the first days where I'd actually felt like my normal self.

I adjusted my purse strap on my shoulder and walked in the direction of my apartment. The weather had been perfect today, so I'd wanted to walk. Walking helped me to clear my head. It was helping me to gain a new perspective, and maybe the next time I saw Ezra I wouldn't feel quite so angry. After all, none of this was his fault.

I crooked my head back, enjoying the evening breeze tickling the bare skin of my neck. Fall was in the air and I couldn't wait to wear fuzzy pajamas, and drink pumpkin spice lattes every chance I got.

My building came into view, the old brick glowing with a golden hue from the old fashioned streetlights.

My strides quickened and I hurried up the steps, passing one of my neighbors. “Hey, Frankie.” I waved at him before grabbing my key and unlocking the door to my place.

I stepped inside and immediately knew something wasn’t right.

The floor lamp beside the couch was turned on and I knew it had been off when I left.

I turned slowly, circling the room with my eyes, and stopped when I reached my bed.

My breath was sucked out of me and my whole body shook at the sight of the boy perched on the end of my bed.

“What are you doing here?” I gasped, my purse and keys falling from my hands onto the floor. “*How* are you here?”

He shoved his dark unruly hair away from his eyes and stood with a gentle grace as he untangled his long legs.

He held up a key. “Maddox and Emma let me borrow this.”

“They’re on their honeymoon,” I said stupidly.

“I know.” He took a step forward, his boots crunching something. “I’ve been planning this for a little while.”

“Planning what?”

“This?” He spread his arms to encompass the space.

I finally allowed my eyes to leave his face and I looked around me in awe. Everywhere I looked pieces of paper littered the floor.

I bent down, picking up the piece of paper nearest my shoe.

I gasped, my hand flying up to cover my mouth. “Ezra.” It was only one word, but I knew he could hear the surprise and overwhelming love behind the word.

On the piece of paper was a drawing of the first time we met. He’d sketched every little detail, and while he wasn’t the best artist it was flawless in my eyes.

I clutched the piece of paper to my heart, hugging it against me, wishing that I could squeeze it tight enough to melt inside of me.

A tear brushed against my cheek and I reached up to wipe it away. In the process, my eyes met his.

“You wouldn’t let me explain.” His voice was soft, hesitant, almost scared. “So I thought I could show you.”

“Show me what?” My voice was thick with the threat of tears.

“That I’ve loved you from the beginning.” He pointed to the drawing I held so protectively against me. “There’s not been one single moment that I’ve known you where I haven’t loved you. And somewhere along the way, that love became something bigger, something so undeniable that the force of it scared me more than anything else ever has.” He took a measured step towards me. “Somewhere along the way I fell in love with you. I think

I fell in love with you a long time ago and I was too fucking stupid to admit it, because the thought of loving you and *losing* you was too painful to contemplate. I would rather have you as a friend than not at all." Another step. "But I realized something when you walked away from me in the hospital. No matter what, I was still going to lose you, because being your friend isn't enough anymore, Sadie. I know now that falling in love with you isn't wrong. It's the best thing I've ever done. And I'm so, so sorry that it took me so long to see that." He took yet another step towards me and now no more than three feet separated us. "I've made a mess of things. Please, tell me it's not too late to fix this. I love you. I'm *in* love with you. And I will spend the rest of my life making this up to you if that's what it takes. Forgive me, please."

His Adam's apple bobbed and he suddenly seemed unsure. He clasped his hands in front of his body and rocked back on his heels, waiting for my response.

"How long?" I questioned.

"How long what?"

"How long have you been planning this?" I waved my hand around to encompass all the drawings. There had to be at least a hundred of them, if not more. Some appeared to be larger and more detailed while some were smaller. From where I stood I could see one with Toby drawn on it in his goldfish bowl.

"Since the moment you walked away from me and I realized how in love I am with you. I would've told you then, but you were gone so fast, and I also knew that it was going to take a lot more than pretty words to make you believe me." He shrugged, his hair tumbling forward across his forehead. I itched to run my fingers through its softness, but so much still needed to be said.

"You hurt me." I whispered the words, handing them to him like they were a grenade. "I told you that I was in love with you and you just *stood* there."

"I know," he said sadly, nodding his head, "and I'm sorry for that. I'm sorry for a lot of things. But even if you tell me to walk out that door right now," he pointed behind me, "and tell me you never want to see me again, I'll never apologize for every moment I spent with you." He motioned to the drawings around us. "Not just this summer, but every single time I smiled or laughed with you. I'll cherish all of it forever." He closed his hand into a fist and placed it over his heart.

"I don't want you to walk out that door," I confessed, wiping away more tears.

Damn that boy for making me cry.

A slow smile crept onto his face. "You don't?"

I shook my head. "I want you to stay." I pointed to my heart and I hoped he got my meaning.

"In your heart?"

I nodded. "I couldn't get you out of there if I wanted to. You're too much of a part of me."

He crept closer to me and touched his heart. "You're in mine too, sweetheart. You're in me so deep that I don't know what to do when you're gone. I feel like half of a person."

I took a deep breath and finally I made that final step, the one that closed the distance between us. I leaned my head back to look up at him.

"So what does this mean for us?"

He tilted his head to the side. "I hope it means that you're my girlfriend..." He paused. "Although, I really hate that word, because I feel like it diminishes how much you mean to me."

I reached up and wrapped my arms around his neck and we both sighed at the contact. "No more hiding?" I questioned. "This is real?"

"It was always real, sweetheart." He cupped my cheek. "We were only trying to pretend that it wasn't."

A question glimmered in his eyes and he must have found the answer in mine, because he lowered his head, slanting his lips over mine.

I moaned into his mouth, my body relaxing at the contact. I stood on my tiptoes and my fingers tangled in the curls of his hair as I tried to get closer.

His hands pressed into my waist, moving lower, and I startled when he grabbed my legs to lift me up.

He carried me over to my bed and laid me down. Paper crinkled beneath my back and I pulled away enough to breathe, "Don't mess up the drawings. I want to look at all of them later."

"Later?" He chuckled, brushing his lips so lightly against mine it couldn't even be called a kiss. "How about now?"

I leaned up, finding his ear. "I was kind of hoping my boyfriend would fuck me first."

He framed my face with his hands and shook his head. Before I had a chance to be upset he said, "I'm not going to fuck you, Sadie. Not right now, at least." His voice lowered to a husky whisper and his lips ghosted against my neck over the spot where my pulse raced. "I'm going to make love to you the way I've always wanted to."

I shivered at his words. "I like the sound of that."

He grinned and kissed me again, deeply, with a hunger that could never be filled. I kissed him back just as urgently and with no less passion. As hot as all our other encounters had been we'd both been holding back on the emotion part, and now it was here in full force and couldn't be denied anymore.

He slanted my head back with one hand and his tongue pressed against mine. I gasped into his mouth and the sound was drowned out by his groan. His other hand slid down the side of my waist and over my thigh. He grabbed my knee, lifting my leg so that he could fit himself more firmly against my center. His hips ground into mine and I gasped again, my hands sliding down his chest until I found the bottom of his shirt.

I tore it off of him and he chuckled at my enthusiasm. His shirt fell to the floor somewhere and I relished in the feel of his smooth, tanned skin beneath the palms of my hands.

"I love you." The words came out as a breathless gasp and I reveled in the feel of being able to say them with no restraints.

"Fuck, I love you too." He ran his thumb over my bottom lip. "So much. Don't ever doubt that."

With all the drawings of our best moments lying around us, there was only one answer. "I won't." I couldn't doubt his love for me anymore, not when he'd gone to this much trouble to literally illustrate how much I meant to him.

He kissed me again. The kind of kiss that stole your breath and maybe your soul too.

He took his time peeling off of my clothes, like he was unwrapping the most precious gift he'd ever received.

He kissed every inch of my skin that he uncovered and my heart raced impossibly faster. Surely, eventually, it would stop beating all together. At least I would die happy and knowing what it felt like to have Ezra love me.

His lips skimmed between my breasts, over my stomach, and stopped when he reached my underwear. His hands slid up my thighs and hooked into the sides. All the while his eyes stayed on mine. He pulled them down and tossed them behind him and he finally let his eyes drop to feast on my bare skin.

"You're so beautiful." The words were a whispered rasp that covered my body in Goosebumps. He said the words with such conviction that I could never doubt them. Even as his eyes fluttered over my body I didn't feel a desire to cover myself. I wanted him to see me, all of me, and the love I had to give.

He sucked his bottom lip between his teeth and his eyes finally met mine once more. “I love you,” he said, ducking his head to kiss the space where my neck met my shoulder. “I love you.” A kiss to my collarbone. “I love you.” He kissed my chest, over my heart. “I love everything about you.”

“Everything?” I questioned with a giggle when he kissed my side, his stubble brushing against a ticklish spot.

“Everything,” he repeated.

He removed the rest of his clothes and grabbed my hips, easing inside of me. We both sighed in relief at the feeling.

My hands roamed down his back, grabbing his ass. “Harder,” I pleaded desperately.

He grabbed my hands, entwining our fingers together. We fit together seamlessly, another reminder of why we were so perfect for each other.

“I never want you to walk away from me ever again,” he confessed.

“Then don’t give me a reason.” I breathed against his lips.

“I won’t,” he vowed.

With the amount of love and truth swimming in his gaze I had to believe him.

His thrusts sped up and my fingernails dug into his back.

My body tightened all over and I gasped, “I’m close.”

“Me too.” His hold on my hips tightened and his forehead creased.

We came together, both confessing our love for the entire world to hear.

When he fell asleep I crept out of the bed, wrapping my robe around me, as I padded around the apartment, collecting every single drawing. I sat down on the bed once more, beside his sleeping body. He was lying on his stomach, with his arms hugging the pillow. His dark hair was wild and unruly and perfectly him.

I giggled at the first drawing.

Paint twister. That had been fun.

Next was a drawing of the two of us getting milkshakes at this cute little diner in town. I remember the day well. It was before we really knew each other that well, and my crush had been raging in full force that day. I’d spent a good two hours picking out my outfit, only to spill milkshake on myself. I’d been upset at first, but then Ezra took his glass, spilled his own milkshake on his jeans, and shrugged, saying, “Now we match.” Laughing, I’d scolded him for wasting a perfectly good milkshake. He told me it was worth it to see me laugh and ordered two more.

I set that drawing aside as well and looked down at the next one. I couldn’t figure out what it was at first, but then realized it was a picture of me sleeping peacefully in his bed. Scrawled in the corner he'd written, *You belong here.*

I laughed at that, but my laugh didn't sound right. It was more like a choked sob and I realized I'd started crying again. But these were happy tears and I was thankful for them. Just like I was thankful for the drawings and the boy sleeping in my bed.

I thought I'd never have this.

This soul-stirring, intense, all-consuming, once in a lifetime kind of love.

But I got it.

With my best friend.

And you didn't get any luckier than that.

EPILOGUE

—TWO MONTHS LATER

"I CAN'T BELIEVE I let you talk me into this," I mumbled, carrying the second to last box inside the house. Ezra was behind me, carrying the final box—the one that marked the fact that this was my home now too, not just his. I was here to stay. "You know my lease wasn't up yet."

He set the final box down on the floor along with the others.

He cracked a smile and leaned his hip against the kitchen counter. "This is your home. This is where you belong."

"With you?" I smiled widely.

"Yes." He framed my face, kissing me deeply. "And Toby of course." He nodded towards the fishbowl. "Toby has really missed you. He cries every night. I have to rock him to sleep."

I busted out in laughter. "Oh I'm sure, seeing as how rocking a fish would kill him."

He mock winced. "Yeah, that's why that's Toby 2.0."

I gasped. "What? You killed our baby!"

He laughed so hard that he was bent over at the stomach. "You should've seen your face!" Straightening, he sobered. "That's the original Toby, I assure you."

"It better be," I muttered, fighting a smile.

I stepped forward, wrapping my arms around him. His lips brushed against the top of my head.

"So, what do you say Westbrook, are you ready to try out this love thing with me forever?"

"I don't know," I hedged, clucking my tongue, "forever is an awfully long time."

"I'm good company, I promise." He grinned down at me. The kind of smile that made him seem boyish and young.

"Hmm, sounds tempting."

"Do I need to do more convincing?" He asked, his fingers gliding beneath my sweater.

"*A lot more.*" I whispered breathily in his ear. "Preferably naked."

"I can do that." A mischievous glint sparkled in his eyes.

I squealed when he grabbed me, tossing me over his shoulder as he ran up the steps.

Instead of stripping me naked and making love to me for the rest of the day and night we ended up jumping on the bed like two little kids.

Because that was us.

Our relationship was intense, passionate, and full of fun.

And I wouldn't have it any other way.

BONUS CONTENT

Interviewer: Good afternoon, Ezra. Sadie. Thanks for sitting down with us.

Ezra: Thanks for having us.

Interviewer: Of course I have to ask you if Willow Creek is working on any new music? Can we expect a new release any time soon?

Ezra: I'm not really allowed to say, but we're working on it.

Interviewer: Good, good. So it's recently come out that you two are indeed a couple now. <points at both Ezra and Sadie> I don't think I'm speaking too broadly when I say everyone was expecting this. You've been photographed together numerous times and there's been several headlines hinting at a possible relationship, but nothing concrete. So, is this relatively new, or have you been able to hide your romantic relationship well?

Ezra: <glances at Sadie> Our romantic relationship is new, yes, but we've been best friends for a while now. But yes, I think everyone seemed to sense there was a connection between us...I just didn't want to see it. I didn't want to ruin a good thing. You know?

Interviewer: Mhmm. Sadie, do you have anything to say? You're awfully quiet.

Sadie: I read magazines. I know how you guys twist things, so no I'm not talking to you.

Ezra: <chuckles and leans in to kiss her> I love you so much.

Interviewer: <straightens clothes> I'm sorry you feel that way. Ezra, seeing as you two have known each other for a while, can we expect an engagement any time soon? Especially considering two of your band mates are now married?

Ezra: <glances at Sadie with a smile> I love this girl with my whole heart, and yes I'm going to marry her someday, but I don't know when. Besides, that kind of thing is private and none of the media's business.

Interviewer: Ah, yes. We all know how you and your band members feel about your privacy.

Ezra: <laughs> We might be famous, but we still deserve to keep certain parts of ourselves private.

Interviewer: Yes, well, I suppose...

Ezra: Do you have any more questions?

Interviewer: <looks for notes> Uh...

Ezra: <reaches for Sadie's hand> Bye. <they run down the hall laughing>

Interviewer: <watches them leave and pushes glasses up nose> And that's why Maddox is my favorite. At least he'll actually talk and not ditch an interview. <grumbles and packs up stuff> I better not get fired for this.

TAKE A CHANCE

Coming August 2015

- A WILLOW CREEK NOVEL -

ACKNOWLEDGEMENTS

Here we are yet again and I feel at a loss as to what to say.

I guess the best place to start would be to thank YOU. The fans. The response to this series has been overwhelming and greater than I ever dreamed. Thank you for your constant messages, support, and love of this series (and all of my books). It's because of you guys that I can keep writing and I'm forever thankful for that. I wish I could hug each and every one of you and tell you in person just how special you are to me. Since I can't, I'll settle for this really long and rambling paragraph.

Thank you to all of my author friends who supported me and cheered me on while writing this book. You guys know who you are and I love you!

Thank you to my beta readers Haley, Becca, Stefanie, and Kendall. You guys read my books in their rawest form and you never call me crazy, so thanks for that. I don't know what I'd do without you guys!

Regina Wamba, no acknowledgements is complete without thanking you for your phenomenal cover design and photography skills. You've managed to turn my insane babbling into the perfect representation for my books. You rock!

Michael and Rachel, I have to thank you both for bringing my characters to life! I can't imagine anyone else fitting these characters better.

Last (but certainly not least) I have to thank my family. All of you. I couldn't ask for a better support system. I know you all probably thought I'd lost my mind when I said I didn't want to go to college and I wanted to see if I could make my writing career work, but you never said that. You all supported me and believed in me when at times I didn't believe in myself. It makes my heart happy to see how proud I've made you. I hope I keep making you proud—not just as writer, but as a person.

22755226R00284

Made in the USA
Middletown, DE
07 August 2015